MW01698127

DAYBREAK

Last Days of Light

LISA HEATON

Published by:
Faith Forward Press, Lisa Heaton Books
Mt. Juliet, TN

ISBN: 978-1-7340182-7-1

Arrow

Day 0, 5:59 p.m.

No matter how many times Paige read the opening paragraph of her travel blog, a portrait never seemed to fully emerge. Words that should have evoked vibrant imagery of a popular Savannah tourist destination were lackluster at best.

Paige wished she could include the story of her first visit to the stately mansion when she had fallen into the water while walking the narrow ledge of a massive fountain like a tightrope. Her mom had just stood gawking at her while her dad had bent at the waist and laughed. The remainder of the tour, dripping wet and shoes sloshing along the path, she had strolled among the brilliant colors of immaculate gardens and lush green lawns.

Unusual peace pulsed through her at such a rare childhood memory. A slight chuckle came when Paige considered the stuffy magazine editor's reaction if she were to include something so light and whimsical in her article.

Her phone rang, the same number she didn't recognize, so she sent it to voicemail again. No more had she returned her attention to her screen when her phone sounded a third time. This was exactly why she couldn't focus on her work.

"Hello!" she said, ready to hang up on the proposal to extend her car's warranty.

"Paige, this is Dad. I don't have time to explain. I have someone coming for you. Go with him."

For a split second Paige couldn't speak, rather, she closed her eyes and conjured up his still-laughing image as he had pulled her from the water. Finally, she had the presence of mind to say, "Coming for me? Why would I –"

"When he knocks, look through the peephole. Sandy hair. Beard. Ask for the password."

"Password? What password?" Paige stood and walked toward the front door. "I've hardly heard from you this past year. You can't call and tell me to go with some stranger and expect me to just do it. I'm not getting involved in your delusional conspiracy theories."

She jumped at the sudden pounding on her front door.

"Paige, just do what I say. I'm not delusional. You're in danger. Wyatt will keep you safe until I can sort this out."

"Sort what out?"

Pops sounded on the other end of the line before it went dead.

"Dad? Daddy!"

The pounding sounded again, but all she could do was look at her phone. Was that gunfire?

With her hand on the deadbolt, Paige hesitated and stood on tiptoes to look out the peephole. "What's the password?"

The look on the man's face was impatient. "Lemonade!"

That single word brought with it a flashback of sipping on a glass of too-sweet lemonade across from her dad at a metal table in a sunny kitchen.

She blinked hard and with a trembling hand unlocked the door.

The door was barely open when Wyatt pushed his way inside. "You have two minutes to gather what you need." He held up two fingers. "Two."

Paige stood staring, her mind trying to form logical questions. Finally, she said, "Tell me what's going on. I may have heard gunfire on the phone with my dad."

"A minute and three quarters." His eyes were trained on hers. "After that I take you to the van, ready or not."

"How long will we be –"

"A minute and a half." His expression never changed.

Paige scrambled to her bedroom closet and began pulling at shirts, leaving hangers rocking and some falling onto the floor. Her next stop was for jeans and underclothes. She hesitated, momentarily distracted by the photo of her parents on the dresser taken only months before her mom had died. To see her mom's thick blond hair and green smiling eyes was like looking into a mirror.

A pit formed in her stomach when she looked at her dad and how he smiled down at his wife. The sound of gunfire on the other end of the line erupted in her head. When she had seen him last, she had been intentionally hurtful. What if she never got the chance to say she was sorry?

Seconds ticked away until her father's voice said in her mind, *Go now.* She reached for the photo and wrapped it in her stack of shirts. With her pile tossed on the mattress, she grabbed a duffle bag from beneath the bed and began stuffing it full.

Back in the living room, Paige reached for her laptop. "Grab my go bag from the hall closet," she said as she powered down her laptop and phone. With them both tucked into her duffle bag, she moved to stand before Wyatt.

"Impressive," he said with a semi-smile and reached for the bag.

"Is all this really necessary?"

"Better safe than sorry." He reached for the door handle. "Time's up."

She swung her backpack over her shoulder and picked up her wallet and keys on her way out the door.

Wyatt said to someone other than her, "Paper secured."

The van smelled like tacos and reminded Paige she had skipped lunch. Her stomach growled but was queasy at the same time. She didn't even consider reaching for the outdated protein bar as she dug her hoodie out from her go bag. Another glance at her jam-packed bag only reminded her of her overly cautious father.

"Sorry." Wyatt said and turned down the A/C, then resumed looking through binoculars, watching her little green bungalow from a few blocks away.

She couldn't be sure if the cool air or the situation caused her to shiver. Either way she added another layer. Seven minutes had passed since Wyatt's two-minute warning and nothing had happened yet.

Now that her heart was settling, her conversation with her dad forced its way into her mind. "I'm sure there was gunfire when I talked to my dad."

Wyatt only glanced at her. "Don't assume the worst."

"Can you call him and check in?"

The popping noise sounded in her head again and caused stomach acid to rise up into her throat. An open pack of peanut-butter crackers sat on the console, so she reached for it.

"They're probably stale," he said while still looking through binoculars.

"I haven't eaten since breakfast. I'll take what I can get." The first stale bite didn't hinder her at all, so she crammed the rest of the cracker into her mouth and took out another. "You didn't answer," she said with crumbs tumbling from her lips. "Can you call and check in with my dad?"

"Someone is trying to get in touch with him. For now, my job is to keep you out of sight and observe."

A third cracker later, Paige had eaten all she could handle. At least the burning in her gut was subsiding.

"A real go bag has food," Wyatt said with only a quick look at her.

"That real go bag has been packed for nearly three years."

"You're supposed to –"

"I know I'm supposed to rotate the food and water. I just didn't think I would ever need it."

Wyatt's fleeting smile made her ask, "What?"

"I'm just not surprised that Evan Donovan's kid has a go bag in the first place."

"I can't remember life without one. He's always insisted." She had to wonder now if the bag had really been in case of a storm and she needed to leave last minute for shelter. Likely not.

"So what happens if nothing happens?" Paige said with skepticism. "Do I just go back home?"

"Something will happen sooner than later."

"How do you know?"

"Your dad said it would. He wouldn't have sent me in unless they were coming."

"Who's coming?"

He didn't answer. Instead, he said once again to someone other than her, "I've got 'em inbound."

Seconds later, a caravan of dark SUVs with blacked out windows came screeching to a halt in front of Paige's house.

Wyatt pulled the gearshift into drive. "Apex was right. They look like Agency guys. If not, they know the playbook."

"Who are they? Who's Apex?" Paige watched as the first to reach her door didn't knock. He kicked his way through, and suited man after suited man entered her house.

Paige swallowed hard and steadied her hands by clasping them together as she watched her home being invaded, knowing she could have been there alone and helpless when it happened. The stale crackers had done little to settle her stomach. It lurched and griped as the van bounced along the roadway down her street.

"Head down!" Wyatt said when two guys exited her doorway at just that moment.

Paige didn't hesitate before ducking her head between her knees.

"What in the world is going on?" she said from her bent position. "And who are those guys?"

"People who'll do almost anything to get what they want."

"What do they want?"

"Your father. They want to use you to draw him out." He reached for her arm and pulled her to sit up when they were out of sight of her house.

Her heart pounded. "Is he even alive?"

"Yes."

"How do you know that? The gunfire..."

"Because I know him; he always has an exfil plan."

"Exfil from what?"

"You know all you need to for now."

Her voice grew louder. "I know almost nothing! You show up and drag me out of my house, then say 'they' want my dad. That's almost nothing!"

Wyatt sped along, his driving reckless as he failed to comply at several stop signs. Horns honked and gestures were made.

"He has something, proof of a crime against a man who can afford a militia like the one who just breached your house."

"So they're really after me now?"

He seemed to force a smile, though clearly concerned. "You'll be okay. Just sit back and relax. I've got this."

Her voice was a little louder than intended. "Did you just politely tell me to sit back and shut up?"

With a soft chuckle, he said, "I didn't mean that at all. I just mean you can trust me. You're my job. I don't fail."

His confidence hardly reassured her.

"Arrow inbound," he said without looking at her.

Paige studied his words. "What does that mean?"

"That wasn't for you."

The fact that there was someone else monitoring their progress gave her more cause for alarm than comfort. With eyes closed Paige whispered to herself, "This is real."

Refuge

Day 0, 6:32 p.m.

The route was familiar as they headed east on Washington and then barely slowed to take a right on Habersham. Paige did what most calmed her mind and took in the historic architecture of the homes that lined the Savannah streets, her fingers tapping her legs as if they were a keyboard while the van zoomed through the Victorian district.

The towering robin's-egg blue Victorian with ornate white trim will take you back to an era gone by. A stately salmon gem located on the corner boasts thick, lacey moldings and –

"You're quiet," Wyatt said. "I really wasn't telling you to shut up."

"I'm writing in my head," she said, still tapping.

He pointed toward the row of homes. "For your travel blog?"

Her head snapped around to look at him. "You know about that?"

"I've read it. I like the way you present Savannah and its history. I've gone to several sites because of how you described them."

Paige glanced ahead as he made his next turn, noting they had taken the long way around and were now heading toward Garden City.

"How did you know about my blog?"

"Your dad talks about it. He's proud of you, of your connection to the city."

Though they threatened to come, Paige wouldn't allow tears to form. "I'm surprised he's read it."

Wyatt's expression changed but not in a way that would convey his thoughts. "He follows everything you do: your work with the historical society like your mom, your blog, and the contract work you do for city tourism."

Her cheeks flushed at knowing her dad appreciated her work, but she wouldn't allow herself a sense of gratification that her now-absentee father still cared.

She looked back out the window, her fingers tapping again. *Like a lemon-yellow ray of sunshine...* Tears now stung her eyes and clouded her vision. It took a burst of blinking and a shift of focus to chase them away.

"How do you know my father?" she said.

"I served under him."

"At Hunter?"

"Yes."

"He's been retired from there for years. So you're still friends?"

"Yes."

His to-the-point answers left her wondering. They rode a minute more before she said, "Do I have to keep asking the right questions, or will you elaborate and tell me more?"

"There's not a lot I can tell you."

They pulled into the parking lot of a gleaming-white, modern warehouse. There was a small scattering of cars in the front of the enormous building, nowhere near a parking lot full. Wyatt drove around to the back of the building and to a bay door just as it opened to allow for their entrance.

Safely inside, he shifted into park and reached for her backpack on the floor between them. "Let's get you settled in and something to eat."

"This is where we're staying?"

"Yes, your refuge for now. Until the dust settles, we have to keep you out of sight."

"How long will that be?"

"As long as it takes." Wyatt reached for the door handle and exited the van. Paige sat for a second looking at the hundreds of thousands of square feet of space ahead of her. Nearly a dozen vehicles ranging in sizes and colors were parked in rows. Crates and storage lockers and cages filled with military gear were to the right of that. What kind of place was this? Clearly not a screen-printing company as the sign in front of the building suggested.

The side door of the van opened behind her, and Wyatt grabbed her duffle bag. He then opened her door.

"Look," he said, "I know this is all a lot to take in. It happened so fast that it'll take some time to wrap your mind around it. For now, all you can do is trust us."

"Who's us?"

Wyatt just started walking.

Paige slid out of the passenger seat and followed him across the warehouse to a steel door where he leaned in next to a sensor on the wall and allowed his eye to be scanned. Such advanced technology assured her this was a serious operation; Wyatt wasn't some random vet her dad had sent.

"Are you coming?" He held the door for her.

With a nod and a reemerging queasy stomach, Paige moved through the doorway into a small box of a room with another steel door. This time Wyatt scanned his eye and hand at the same time for entry into what turned out to be an elevator.

The racket of the door unlocking and opening made her jump, but she did her best to hide her unease as she entered.

When she stepped off the elevator, Paige barely heard the door close behind her. All that lay before her was such a shock to her senses that she could only stand scanning the loft space. It was breathtaking with soaring ceilings high above and stained and swirled gray concrete beneath her feet. The massive room was divided into partition-less sections. Still, the space was so enormous each area was like its own distinct room.

Nearest her was an open kitchen, a sight that set her fingers to tapping against her legs. *Distressed-painted brick and open shelving offer a modern space with vintage fixtures.*

Nearby was a living area so sizeable that it contained three dark stone-gray sofas in a u-shaped pattern facing a bank of four large TVs. *A football watcher's dream,* her fingertips said to her jeans.

"I'll take your bags to your room," Wyatt said. "See what you can find in the fridge. If you want, I can send out for something."

Paige wasn't shy about poking around for food, not with her stomach now growling out loud. A pizza box held half a pepperoni pizza and some garlic bread. When she closed the door and turned, a man stood there–not Wyatt.

"Hey," she said more in alarm than for conversation's sake.

With a lean build, unkempt dark hair, and a Hulk t-shirt, it was almost too easy to peg him as a tech guy. He must have come from what seemed to be a tech zone over in the far-right corner.

"Hey," he cocked one eyebrow, "I suppose you think you're eating my pizza?"

"I, um –"

"That's not your pizza," Wyatt said with a good-humored smile when he walked in. "It's mine, and Paige can have it." He reached for a glass from a shelf and filled it with ice. "Paige, this pizza thief is Echo. You have to watch him with your food at all times. He's a bottomless pit. All leftovers are open game for him."

"Nice to meet you, Echo."

His nod and shy grin were endearing. "Nice to finally meet you," he said as he ducked his head into the refrigerator.

Paige looked around and found the microwave was a drawer in a lower cabinet rather than a door to open. She took the plate Wyatt offered and loaded all but one piece of pizza onto it. With the pizza warming, she slid the box along the counter. "I can spare a piece."

"I'll remember this kindness," Echo said as he reached for the cold pizza and took a bite. He turned and left without saying anything more.

Wyatt pointed to the bar seat on the other side of the island. "Sit. I'll get it for you." He moved about the kitchen with ease. After placing her plate before her, he poured her a sparkling water and set a stack of take-out napkins nearby. "Need parm for your pizza?" he said.

"No, this is perfect." She folded the warm, cheese-oozing slice and took a bite, the hot cheese scorching her tongue not slowing her down a bit.

Wyatt came to sit next to her, so she slid the plate between them. "You're welcome to a slice of your pizza."

"No, I'm good. You eat."

After her first slice, the pounding in her head began to subside. With all that had happened, she wasn't sure how she was able to eat at all.

"How long have you known my dad?" she said with her mouth half full.

"Ten years, since I was twenty-three."

That put Paige at sixteen. "You were under his command when he retired?"

"Yeah."

"So how did you reconnect after all this time? I mean, why did he send you for me?"

Wyatt seemed to choose his words carefully when he said, "He knows he can trust me with you."

When he didn't answer the first question, she said, "So have you stayed in touch?"

"You could say that." He stood, went into the kitchen, and began making a sandwich.

Her tone rose at having to pull information from him. "Which means?"

"After I served out my time, he recruited me to work for him."

"Private security," Paige said and nodded. "Makes sense."

The sophisticated tech equipment just beyond the hallway where Wyatt had disappeared with her bags indicated this was a command center.

Her words were slow and deliberate as the realization dawned on her. "Does my dad work here now, at this location?"

"This is one of many locations where we operate."

Heart plummeting, she said, "But he's been here in Savannah?"

"He has." Wyatt took a bite of his sandwich and didn't make eye contact.

"Recently?"

"Not often in the past few months."

"But he does come?"

Wyatt rested his sandwich on a paper towel on the counter. "He's in and out of town depending on the job."

She pushed her plate away, food only half eaten. "I think maybe I'll go to my room if you'll show me where that is."

With an understanding nod, Wyatt led the way to a short hallway with another blue door. "Lean in close," he said to her. When Paige did so, he said, "Echo!"

She tried to move back, but Wyatt placed his hands on her shoulders and held her in position. "Stand still. Let him get a read."

A red light scanned her retina, and the door unlatched, leading them into a stark white corridor.

"Now you'll have access to all doors on this level."

Paige followed Wyatt down the hallway of several closed doors until he stopped and opened the last door on the left-hand side. He pointed. "I'm just down the hall if you need anything."

Her things were on the bed, but her laptop was noticeably missing from her open duffle bag. "Where's my laptop?"

"Echo has your laptop and phone. He'll make sure you're untraceable. I'll have it back to you soon."

Paige stepped inside the room and no more had the door closed when tears fell onto her cheeks. She tossed her bags on the floor and flopped onto the bed. It was no wonder her dad didn't want to be around her.

With her face covered by her pillow, she did her best to smother the memory of her last words to him when they had met for dinner at the riverfront the last time he was in town.

Paige's voice was low so that no one would overhear. "This end-times stuff, you realize you sound delusional, right?"

His eyes conveyed how her words had wounded him, but he didn't back down. "It's not a delusion. It's in the Bible."

"I know it's in the Bible." She grimaced and looked around again. "People have thought 'the end'," she used exaggerated air quotes to further stress her skepticism, "was coming since the words were written."

"This is different," he said. "I used to see it as the last days. Now all I can say is that we're in the final hours. It's not just coming anymore–it's here."

"Dad, why do we have to do this? I hardly hear from you. I've seen you, what, once this past year? Why do you have to mess it up with this craziness?"

"Because something dangerous is on the horizon for all of us." He sat looking at her, then shook his head. "Paige, life isn't what you think it is."

"Dad, I think you need some help." She stood and scooped her phone from the table. "I need to go. Maybe when I get my one visit next year–if you find the time–we can talk about something besides all this doom and gloom."

That could be it, the last she ever saw of her dad. His final words to her were actually his warning that she may someday need this refuge.

What if he never came back? What if she never got the chance to tell him she loved him?

Target

Day 1, 7:40 a.m.

With no windows to give her perspective, Paige wasn't sure what time it was or how long she had slept. A light tap on the door sounded once, then again, so she sat up.

"Come in."

"Hey," Wyatt said as he stepped inside.

She rubbed her eyes and sat up, squinting at him. "What time is it?"

"Nearly eight a.m." He sat on the chair near her bed. "I've been up all night praying about it. You have a right to know more than I've told you so far."

"Ya think?" She swung her feet over the side of the bed and scanned the sparse, nearly all white room.

"My objective is to keep you from getting hurt," he said. "I saw how wounded you were last night when you found out your dad has been here in Savannah. If my silence is hurting you, then I believe I'm at liberty to tell what you need to know." His tone was gentle. "He doesn't want you hurt, Paige. What do you want to know?"

"About my dad. He hasn't been involved in my life since my mom died. I've hardly seen him."

"I know, but that wasn't by choice."

"How is that not by choice?"

"He wanted to protect you."

"From what?"

He hesitated a second. "People like the ones who showed up at your house."

The blood rushed to her cheeks and she clenched her fists. "He doesn't have to do what he does. He could come home and live a normal life."

"No, he can't. That's not who he is, a man who would walk away from his call."

"A private security company isn't a calling; it's just a job."

Images of her dad after her mother's death came to mind, all the hours he had spent locked away in his office at home with notes and photos taped to the walls. He wouldn't eat and appeared to get little to no sleep. Phone calls and raised voices behind closed doors made him inaccessible to a daughter who grieved on the other side of those doors. Finally, he just up and disappeared.

She had arrived with lunch for him one day to find her family home up for sale. The place was empty. After all her dad's craziness, it had been the final straw.

"After my mom died..." She glanced away and shook her head. "I tried to get through to him, but he was never the same."

Wyatt's words were soft. "I'm not sure any man could be."

"Spouses die," she said with a sharper tone than she intended, "but most men don't do what he did. He raved about conspiracy theories and how my mom's death wasn't what they said it was." Paige stood and began to pace. "She got sick–people get sick. But my dad went off the deep end and blamed ghosts and shadows. Then he just took off."

"If only they were ghosts and shadows," Wyatt said.

Paige sat again and looked at him. Even before she said it, her heart beat a little faster. "My mom died of some respiratory thing, something in her lungs."

"It was the coronavirus."

"You mean Covid? My mom died more than a year before it came to the States."

"The virus was around long before you or the public heard about it. When it did reach the States, your dad knew without question that it was a bioweapon, even though the government was denying it. Many scientists were out there all along, warning that the natural virus had been weaponized. Did you ever hear anything about that?"

"No."

"And if you had?"

"I would've thought they were crazy," she paused, her words much softer this time, "like my dad."

"Your news sources hid that from you. Big Tech determined what you could and couldn't see. They censored those who claimed it was anything other than a naturally occurring virus, even the experts. Yet here we are, the truth now out in the open that the virus was manipulated, even when you don't hear an outright admission by government officials. Too many truth-seekers kept digging.

"Paige, whether you've seen the coverage or not, there are those who believe our government was actually involved in developing this virus with the lab in Wuhan. There are emails that tie our own officials to it. Some even suggest a DARPA connection, the government agency who develops technology for the military." His eyes grew wider. "You won't hear that spread around much, but I wouldn't doubt it at all."

He blinked long before saying, "Your mom was targeted."

Paige's palms became sweaty, and her heart beat a little faster. A list of her mom's symptoms began to tick through her mind, not at all for the first time since the pandemic had started.

"If it was Covid," she said, "why didn't anyone else catch it from her?"

"That's a question your dad pondered once the virus was activated globally. He could never be certain, but he assumed it was targeted to your mom's DNA specifically."

"You hear how ridiculous that sounds, right?"

"I really do when I say it out loud. Your dad felt the same way when he tried to convince people."

"Let's say I believe it was Covid. What did that have to do with my dad?"

"Your dad was part of a task force back then and began sounding the alarm that the Chinese Communist Party was developing a weapon to use against us. Of course, he didn't suspect at the time that the U.S. may have had a connection to the research." Wyatt paused. "His guy at the Wuhan lab warned that something biological was in the testing phase. That man and his family were found shot to death."

"My mom was killed because of my dad's work? Why kill her and not him?"

"To send a message, maybe to more people than just your dad. We didn't know it at the time, but some high-up U.S. officials were involved with the CCP. We eventually concluded that it was a warning to them to stop the team from pursuing the bioweapon angle. But," he paused, "knowing what we know now, we can't be sure it was the CCP who sent the message."

"You mean you think someone in our government killed my mom?"

"No way to be certain. I honestly don't trust anyone outside of this team anymore."

A look of discomfort in Wyatt's eyes said there was more. "What aren't you telling me?"

"It should be your dad telling you these things. Not me."

"Whatever it is, tell me!"

Wyatt seemed to deliberate until he finally blinked a few times and drew in a deep breath. "Your mom had connections from her former life and used them to help your dad when she could. Evidently she asked questions of the wrong people."

"Connections to what? My mom worked at the Chamber of Commerce and was on the board of the Historical Society."

"Paige, your mom did a whole lot more than that before you were born."

Even as the words came out of her mouth, Paige suspected she didn't want to know. "Like what?"

"Your mom worked for the CIA."

She sputtered her next words. "Like as a spy?"

"More as an analyst, but she also did some field work."

Her parents were much older when Paige had come along, but still, it was hard to imagine her mom living some secret life during those early years. "That's ridiculous. I would've known."

"When you were born, she took an early retirement. By then the Agency was so compromised at the highest levels that your mom no longer knew whom she could trust." His voice was low. "You can't imagine the ranks this collusion reaches."

"So, she was either killed to send my dad a message or killed for helping him. Either way he feels to blame."

"I'm afraid so."

She whispered, "He's carried that all this time." Tears formed and fell before she could stop them.

When she turned and wiped them away, Wyatt said, "It's okay to cry. Nothing I tell you in the days to come will be easy."

She sat still, trying to process his words and reel in her emotions. Her mom's soft voice echoed in her mind, *You were such a delightful surprise to us, Paigie, like a sweet and welcomed turning of the page in our decades-long love story.*

Another tear fell. "What if the last thing I ever said to my dad was that he was delusional?" She bowed her head. "I was angry at him because he wasn't around. I lost both parents when my mom died." When she looked back at Wyatt, she said, "What if he's gone too?"

"I don't believe he is. I know him; he always has a plan."

"I know you said that, but the gunshots..."

"We have people on it."

"People?"

"Yes. Echo is doing his best to locate your dad. We have some guys on the ground near where your dad went missing."

"What about you? Aren't you going to look for him?"

"I have my orders."

"What's more important than finding my dad?"

"You are. My orders are to keep my eyes on you. I'll do that–nothing else." At that he stood. "Paige, life isn't what you think it is. There's more that you're not ready for, not just yet." He shook his head. "You're shaken enough by this. For now, you need to trust us to do our jobs."

She sat looking at the closed door after Wyatt left. More? What could shake her more than discovering her mom had been a spy and was murdered? Or that maybe her dad wasn't delusional after all?

Wyatt's words had been the exact same as her dad's that night at dinner, that life isn't what she thinks it is. What did that mean beyond her parents' double lives?

Shaken wasn't the word to describe what she was feeling; it didn't seem strong enough. She had never been a timid or fragile woman. She wasn't raised to be, not with a Lieutenant Colonel for a father. What she was experiencing now left her dazed, unable to find her footing.

Challenges in life rarely overwhelmed her, but this was different. Any mention of her parents now seemed to elicit such an emotional reaction that she found it nearly impossible to contain. Maybe that was part of the problem: She had spent all that time suppressing her grief, and now it seemed to be erupting in a way she couldn't control.

With a deliberate shake of her head, she reached for her go bag and began emptying its contents onto the bed she had never unmade the night before. She hadn't brushed her teeth or showered. Those things now would recharge her and give her energy to face whatever Wyatt might throw at her next.

It was when she wrapped her fingers around the familiar old leather Bible and drew it out of the bag that her mind engaged, and the words came. Her father's voice was firm. *This book of the law shall not depart from your mouth, but you shall meditate on it day and night.*

There it was again; her eyes were leaking.

"I'm sorry, God, for the things I said to him. I'm sorry I don't talk to You as much anymore." Tears streamed down her face. "Please keep my daddy safe."

Something like the turning of a knife penetrated her chest and forced a loud exhale. How could she pray to a God she had distanced intentionally to spite her father? What if He took her dad to punish her for deserting Him?

At that her soft cries turned to wracking sobs she tried to muffle with her hands. The current of emotion carried with it years of pent-up anguish. Then, for the first time in a long time, only the good memories surfaced, memories of the attentive father he had been. Stationed close by at Hunter Army Airfield, he was present in a way many military dads weren't. All those early years, his devotion to their family–to her–had set her on a firm foundation in life. He adored her, and even more painful to admit, she had adored him.

Emotionally, since her mother's death, it had been easier to live in outrage over his peculiar new behavior and intentional distance. Anger had been a safer ally than affection. So she had done what she thought her dad had done and distanced her heart from his, even when his presence was what she had most needed. They had landed in a cycle of his rare visits accompanied by her often angry outbursts when he did come to town.

More damaging in the long run, Paige had done the same with Jesus, chosen anger toward Him as a safer ally than affection. The worn black Bible there on the white comforter, a possession once so prized that she couldn't conceive of a hurried exit without it, offered the way out of the barren land where she now lived if only she would open its cover.

Red letter words came to mind: "If anyone is thirsty, let him come to Me and drink."

Paige turned to the Book of John and read the seventh chapter. Just after Jesus' invitation to the thirsty, John tells that a division occurred in the crowd because of Him.

That had been her, divided and not-so-rightly so. Not divided because of Jesus, but because of her dad.

"Help me out of this wilderness, Lord," she whispered aloud. Her eyes weren't leaking this time when she said, "Please save my dad."

Newfound resolve settled within; whatever it took, she had to find him, even if that made her a moving target.

Players

Day 1, 8:35 a.m.

By the time Paige showered and went out to the common area, Wyatt was already in the kitchen making breakfast.

"I'm sorry," he said as he poured her a cup of coffee. "I shouldn't have hit you with that about your mom first thing this morning."

Her hand shook when she tried to take a drink, so she placed the cup back on the counter. "I wish I could say it's never crossed my mind," Paige blinked long before saying, "but she had all the symptoms of Covid back then.

"I had it back in the fall," she said. "It was fairly mild, but the symptoms were like the beginning of my mom's illness."

When he placed buttered toast before her, his eyes held concern. "I'll show you something after we eat. For now, just try to eat some breakfast. You hardly ate last night. I had that on my mind too."

While he went about cracking eggs and whisking, Paige watched him. He was tall and muscular with the distinctive look of an Army Ranger, clean cut except for the beard. Nearly exactly like her father's, Wyatt's Ranger tattoo with parachute and wings on his forearm gave him away. Also like her father's, the image was swathed by the stars and stripes that trailed up his arm and beneath his shirt sleeve.

She glanced at Echo in the far corner, head bent over his keyboard and headphones on. While unmistakably a coms guy and not a conventional soldier, it was evident he was just as much a skilled and lethal Ranger. That same borderless flag trailed up his arm.

Technically, she had to remind herself, this fine-looking guy and Echo might both be as delusional as her dad. That thought held little conviction when the sight of those men invading her home came to mind. Her heart beat a little faster. She was definitely a target–a target like her mom.

Her hands trembled again as she lifted the piece of toast to her mouth. Unsure if the shakes were from hunger or fear, what she did now know was that her father hadn't been delusional all that time. Since her prayer before, that's the one thing that had settled inside her heart.

Wyatt placed a plate of bacon and eggs before her and poured them each a glass of juice. Then he dragged over a basket filled with bottles and began taking out a series of pills and placing them into two piles.

"What's this?"

"Supplements. C, D, Zinc –"

"I take a multi most days." She slid her pile toward him.

He slid the pile back. "You need more than that."

She slid her pile toward him. "You sound like my dad."

He slid the pile back. "Thanks." With little humor in his expression, he said, "Take them, Paige. Your immune system is your best defense against what may come next."

When she took the pills, he said, "I'm glad to see you were able to eat your toast. You need to eat your eggs too. Vitamin D needs fat for absorption."

"You're really into this natural thing, huh?"

"Lack of D is one major factor in how people respond to and recover from Covid. Most people are low in D and don't know it. Now that you've had Covid, you have natural immunity against contracting it again. But still, after having a bioweapon in your body, it's wise to work on building your immune system to ward off any potential long-term effects."

"Great," she said, "potential long-term effects of a bioweapon in my system, that really gives me an appetite."

He sat and took a bite of eggs, then turned and flashed a quick smile, his bloodshot eyes confirming his sleepless night. "Nothing affects my appetite. I can always eat."

"You really didn't sleep all night, did you?"

"Not a wink. I had too much on my mind."

"I'm just the opposite. When I'm stressed or overwhelmed, I tap out. Been doing it all my life." Her heart grew warm at the thought. "My parents called it stress sleep."

"Do you know what a gift that is?"

"I've never really thought about it as a gift."

"Rest is good." He shrugged. "A good night's sleep gives you clearer perspective the next morning."

"'His mercies are new every morning,'" she said less to Wyatt and more to remind God that His Word still rambled around in her heart when she would allow it.

Wyatt's smile at her statement seemed to be masking pain. "You sound just like your dad."

"Funny, I've thought the same about you. You've said several things that remind me of him."

"I've paid attention all these years, learned a lot from him."

"You said you started working for him when you left the Army. How long ago was that?"

"Seven years."

Paige sat looking at her plate, a forkful of eggs hovering near her mouth. That meant Wyatt had worked for the task force when her mom had died. She rested her fork on her plate without taking the bite.

"So he still leads the task force? You made it sound like that was in the past. What you do now is not private security?"

"We do private security on the side, but mostly the other. It's not the same these days; we're not under government mandate."

"Can you explain the other? And whose mandate?"

"The other is us keeping our eyes open to the world and how things are unfolding. We watch the major players. We do what we can to wake up believers, so I guess you could say we're under God's mandate." With a quick glance between bites, he said, "And I don't mean the Q kind of awake."

"What is 'the Q kind of awake'?"

"Q is a group of people, millions of people..." He shook his head. "That's for another time. I would rather tell you what I know that's Biblically grounded."

Paige's heart quickened at him mentioning the Bible. Rapid-fire verses sprang to mind and started cluttering her current thoughts. She wasn't ready for more yet and did her best to tune them out.

"So what is happening in the world?" she said to sidetrack her thoughts. When he didn't answer right away, she said, "My dad once said the exact same thing you said this morning, that life isn't what I think it is." She heard the slight quiver in her voice when she said, "What do y'all mean by that?"

"What you think you see and experience isn't at all what's real and happening." His eyes took on a thoughtful expression. "I don't know how to explain all that's ahead of us without it crushing you."

Wyatt turned on his stool to face her without eating the last of his bacon. "Last night, I did what your dad has taught me to do when confusion comes. I prayed until an answer came. The Lord has been clear in how He's led me for many years now, but I'm not sure He's ever been as direct and specific as in the early hours of this morning." Wyatt's expression was soft and sympathetic when he said, "I'm to tell you anything you want to know," he held up one hand, "but it can't all come at once. I'll tell you how life isn't what you think it is, but you'll have to let me unfurl it a little at a time."

"After what you said about my mom and dad, I'm not sure I can handle it all at once anyway. I've got enough to process as it is." She hesitated. "But I do want to know this: Was the release of the virus intentional?"

"Officials won't say so, but I believe it was. Your dad believes it. What we can't prove is who is behind its release. There are too many players on the field to know for sure," he gave a little shake of his head, "but I have my suspicions."

"Who are the players?" she said.

"For one, the Chinese Communist Party has been systematically invading our nation for decades, buying up land and purchasing businesses under shell corporations. They have invested in our universities to influence their teachings and alter the way our nation of young people thinks and sees capitalism. Now that the CCP has bought interests in American media and Hollywood, their infiltration is nearly absolute since the ones who control the message control the masses. And sadly," he said with anger flashing in his eyes, "they've bought and bullied and swayed more of our politicians than you could ever imagine. Top officials see it, but the ones still unsoiled, those bold enough to try and sound the alarm, are ignored or threatened or bought off. People have no clue how far-reaching this all is.

"Right now, the CCP has a strong presence in the Caribbean under the guise of a humanitarian effort, providing masks and test kits for a virus they helped to weaponize. They're giving aid for hurricane relief, garnering goodwill with locals, hoping to eventually build a naval base there. Paige, that's a hundred miles off our coast!"

He looked at her and shrugged. "Even with all that, even with the lengths I know they would go to, I wouldn't swear they released it on purpose."

Paige said, "Maybe it really was an accidental leak from the Wuhan lab."

"Because of the timing of it, no one will convince me of that. I believe it's way more sinister than the CCP making a move against the U.S. I would have to guess there was someone in the Wuhan lab paid off or threatened." He paused. "This was a global move, one way too coincidental in timing to ignore."

She drew in a deep breath. "So, this is the kind of stuff you monitor, my father monitors?"

"Yes. We continually keep our eyes open for the next threat." He blinked long and shook his head. "Don't get me started on Russia and cyberwarfare. I'm sometimes more concerned over their intentions than the CCP. There are sleeper agents all across the U.S., but I don't think they're behind this either, at least not on their own."

Paige sat looking at this handsome lunatic. He was so much like her dad, not just the craziness he was spewing but also his mannerisms and passion.

"I see the way you're looking at me," Wyatt said. "Thing is, what I'm going to show you and tell you, it's only going to get crazier. The virus is only one of many means intended to cripple the U.S., our economy, and eventually our military. We call it a plan-demic rather than a pandemic. This is a move to get the U.S. out of the way of a larger global agenda."

"If it's not China or Russia, then who?"

"There's a greater threat out there, a group of elites with a plan to dominate the economy, not just here in America but worldwide. I think they were behind the release of the virus. They created the problem then proposed the solution."

He paused a beat. "I know it sounds like some ominous movie plot, but honestly, it's way more diabolical than man's mind could possibly conceive–evil at its core. Many of the players on the field are acting individually, but ultimately, Satan himself is the driving force behind each, even though they don't know they are working for a common cause.

"That reminds us that we aren't actually fighting against flesh and blood. Even when we see that it's people who further the agenda, it's ultimately the devil pulling the strings."

Paige sat looking at him. The entire thing absolutely sounded crazy, yet something stirred within, prompting her to actually listen and not dismiss his theories.

"The people who serve the darkness," he said, "don't care who they hurt or kill since depopulation has long been their goal. A lesser population is easier to control.

"The scary thing is they already control so much behind the scenes that we have no way of knowing what organizations they've infiltrated. Billionaires who are part of this group have influence over our media and social media in a way that is even more detrimental than the CCP."

Wyatt shook his head. "What better way to advance their agenda than to use a health crisis and hype it up in the media? People are terrified and willing to do whatever governments and scientists say, even when officials aren't actually following the science."

"People are dying," Paige said. "Of course they're terrified." Her elderly neighbor came to mind, how she had hardly left her house since the pandemic had begun, even after she had been vaccinated. She would only talk to Paige through the screen door, even that with an often fear-filled expression.

"The virus is real," Wyatt said with a gentler tone. "Of all people you know that." Anger flashed in his eyes when he said, "Countless people have died needlessly. They could've been saved. We will show you some data to support that. I'm not lying to you. They are."

Paige sat looking at Wyatt, believing he believed what he was saying, but she still wasn't convinced.

"Besides senseless death," he said, "the way data has been presented is intentionally misleading in order to maximize fear and ensure submission. They use phrases like 'died with Covid' rather than 'died of Covid' to bolster the numbers. No matter what a person died of, the actual illness or disease that killed like a heart attack or stroke or cancer, if they had the virus in their system, they were added to the list of virus deaths. That's manipulation and calculated scare tactics to drive fear. Did you notice that no one seemed to die of old age or natural causes in all of twenty-twenty?"

Paige hadn't noticed that. Now, looking back, she hadn't noticed a whole lot beyond her own life and heartbreak.

He stood. "Let's get you started. You have the real world and its players to investigate."

Investigation

Day 1, 9:12 a.m.

Paige followed behind Wyatt as they went toward the bank of monitors in the far corner of the loft.

He said as they walked, "For healthy people the virus has a survival rate of well over ninety-nine percent. With early treatment, those numbers are most often a hundred percent. Those aren't statistics a government shuts down an entire nation over unless it has other motives."

"You mean controlling the economy?" she said.

"Many reasons depending on who you are and your agenda: exploit people, line your pocket, crash an economy, defraud an election." He came to stop behind where Echo sat. "Those are the not-so-surprising motives of some politicians, but this goes way beyond what power-grabbing legislators understand. They're simply pawns in a last-days scenario."

Her heart was now beating in such a wild rhythm, she wondered if maybe she needed to sit. "Way to unfurl things slowly."

"You have to have a frame of reference of the larger global scheme before I can give you the evidence substantiating it." He rolled a chair over for her to sit. "Let's get started."

Echo began to type, and Paige looked at the darkened bank of monitors in front of him, expecting to see an image. When he stopped typing, he pointed to Paige's right, at a massive screen mounted on the nearby brick wall.

Event 201 was displayed on the screen. Paige scanned the words promoting a pandemic exercise held in October of 2019.

"Paige," Wyatt said, "it would take me days, maybe even weeks, to get you up to speed on all this. We've been watching for years and have an overall understanding of the major players."

His look of intention faded into one of concern. "We will try and go at a pace that's right for you, but if this ever gets to be too much, you let me know."

Echo handed her laptop to her and said, "You're totally secure to surf no matter where you are. You'll never need WiFi since you are your own hotspot. And you can log onto any site and remain untraceable."

Paige opened her laptop and scanned the screen. The only change was a new folder titled, "Research for Paige."

"With the encryption I've added," Echo said, "you'll be un-hackable. No one will get in without your password and fingerprint. You'll have to use both from now on. I'll be able to access remotely if you ever need me." He chuckled. "Like this."

Echo's face popped up on her screen. "Hi, Paige!"

His smile and wave lessened what had been the intensity of the moment. Then Echo's face disappeared.

It was Wednesday, a day before Paige's travel blog was due. "So I can email my office and submit my blog?"

"You can," Echo said, "and anyone else you may need to notify that you'll be away for a few days." He tossed her a phone. "And here's your new phone. I've moved all your apps and contacts over. Just remember, for now, anyone you contact may be under surveillance. All calls you make will link you with a cell tower, so don't ever assume it's safe."

With her phone in hand, all that kept running through her mind was: Is this really happening?

"Remember, what we'll be giving you is a lot to take in," Wyatt said. He sat backwards in a rolling chair and moved close by. "Take your laptop and do some investigating. All that's loaded for now are the links we've just shown you on Event 201 and some supporting documents on the virus that I've asked Echo to include. When you're done, we'll discuss your questions and move on to the next topic."

Paige nodded and stood, her legs a little wobbly as she tried to take a step. The room looked exactly as it had before, but somehow she was seeing it differently. What she thought had been a refuge from danger no longer seemed to be that at all. The words *training ground* came to mind. Not came to mind exactly, more like they dropped into her spirit from above. It wasn't at all comforting.

The guys began to talk, so Paige left with her laptop in hand. Even as she allowed her eye to be scanned and walked through the security door, she heard the word *awake*. It came like the others, as a word fallen from above.

Paige read the information on Event 201. Sure, it seemed more than coincidental that a large-scale simulation was done in New York City just two months prior to the outbreak in China. It was an exercise that used a coronavirus as its subject and mapped out the responses of the medical community, media, and government agencies to a global pandemic.

In addition to the Event 201 simulation, other items were included in her research folder. Reports on mask efficacy were outlined in such a scientific manner that Paige only scanned a few of them. One common consensus that she did notice was that coronavirus particles were so microscopic that you could stack tens of millions of them through one hole in the fabric weave of a cloth mask.

She stopped reading and reached for her wallet to pull out the fabric mask she had tucked inside. With it held up to the lamp, she could see light filtering through the cloth. Of course viral particles so small would escape with normal breathing.

It had been miserable trapped behind a mask when out in public. If not effective, why then would officials insist they be worn? Paige already knew what Wyatt's answer to that would be, yet another conspiracy theory that it was to control the people.

The next link took her to a report from a prominent virologist who claimed that Covid testing for the masses was highly inaccurate, and how millions of false positives had driven fear worldwide. In many cases the false positives were the result of a flu virus being detected and not a coronavirus at all.

Paige only scanned the next set of reports on six-foot distancing and herd immunity.

Why would the CDC lie? And why would the government want to keep people quarantined and apart if not to contain the spread of a deadly virus?

Wyatt and Echo's information often reeked of conspiracy theories. Everything she had looked at and researched so far could be slanted either way depending on the source or the reader.

What she knew, though, was that all the mainstream media said the same things: that masks were effective, the virus was an accident, and people would need a vaccine and boosters for life to ever get back to normal. Why would she doubt that? Why would they lie?

Paige rubbed her temples, all this technical jargon giving her a headache. Tempted to close out of the folder, she forced herself to continue on. Whatever the truth, she wanted to know.

The pages that followed were articles about the underreported effectiveness of immune system support, substantiating what Wyatt had said about the best defense being overall health, especially vitamins D, C, and Zinc.

Another set of reports and videos addressed withheld medications, one in particular familiar to Paige from a newscast she had watched.

She followed a link onto an unfamiliar site called Rumble, a video platform similar to YouTube. This particular doctor suggested that early effective treatments were intentionally withheld and dismissed through skewed medical studies, ones influenced by the trillion-dollar big pharmaceutical industry's interest in developing a vaccine.

That was only one in a long list of videos with the same message based on their titles. She decided to save them to investigate later.

Her heart beat a little faster. If what these doctors said was true, Paige closed her eyes and shook her head at the thought, then that meant...

Her eyes flew open. That wasn't possible. People weren't that wicked, even over money. She tried to ignore the question that resonated in her head: Were they?

Implausible

Day 1, 12:22 p.m.

Paige entered the living space to find Wyatt dozing on one of the sofas, reclined with his head on the headrest and his feet on an ottoman in front of him. When she drew closer, his head snapped around to look at her, and he moved to sit up.

She sat on the opposite sofa and said, "I'll admit, the 201 thing seems like quite a coincidence, but maybe it was just timely. Maybe God was watching over the world and led people to act in advance and prepare for what was to come."

"That's for sure the kind of God we serve," Wyatt said. "In this case I'm going to have to disagree with your theory. The people involved at the highest levels are anything but God-led."

Wyatt moved to the edge of his seat and sat looking at her for a few seconds. He rubbed his face as if to chase away fatigue and finally said, "Honestly, Paige, what I'm going to tell you, I really do hear how crazy it sounds when I say it out loud." After a slight pause, his face took on an unreadable expression, then he gave a shake of his head and continued. "I remember a point when I thought your dad was crazy. He isn't crazy. I'm not crazy. The fact is, Paige," he hesitated as if unsure of continuing on, and his eyes conveyed great tenderness when he did say, "you're deceived. You've been lied to for so long that the truth sounds implausible."

She sat looking at him, a pit forming in her stomach. What if he was right?

He said, "Think these questions through with me: What are the chances that a simulation for a mock global pandemic on a coronavirus was performed in October, and an outbreak of the same virus was reported in Wuhan in December?"

Before she could answer, he said, "Wait, let me add some key elements: One of the sponsors of Event 201 is a group you'll be learning about next, the

World Economic Forum. They openly say they plan to use the pandemic as an opportunity to move forward with something they've had in the works for many years, what they call the Great Reset. It's a means of changing our entire world system and eventually bringing all the world together economically."

She blinked once and then again. "That's the group of elites you said are players on the field?"

Wyatt nodded. "'All the world.' Does that scenario sound a little familiar?"

Paige swallowed hard, knowing he was talking about the one-world order.

He said, "Did you notice any other sponsors of the simulation?"

Mouth now suddenly dry, she said, "The Bill and Melinda Gates Foundation." The name had caught Paige's attention. At the time it had only served to lend credibility to the event since she knew him to be a celebrated philanthropist.

"That's right. Bill Gates just happens to be a part of the World Economic Forum as well and is working toward the same goal of a Great Reset. Besides that, he's been a major proponent of mass vaccination projects over the years, some with disastrous results. We don't hear about that since it's never covered in the mainstream media. Does anything about that seem concerning with the current push toward," his voice rose, "all people in all the world being vaccinated?"

He grew quiet for a second. "We won't get into what they call a vaccine for now, but what about the vaccine passports that some states and businesses are requiring? Those who choose not to receive the shot are losing jobs and won't be able to conduct business. Once again, does anything about that sound familiar when people eventually won't be able to 'buy or sell'?

"Next," he said, "some of the media and social media's response to the pandemic was strikingly similar to the simulation, almost as if rehearsed. Do you think that's plausible, considering the simulation was only in October before Covid reached the States in late January?"

Paige knew his questions didn't require answers. They compelled her to question her beliefs and further investigate what he called the real world she lived in.

"As individual elements," Wyatt said, "none of these are a smoking gun, but when you start compiling the evidence, what you've read today and the other things we will share, you can't help but see that we are all being methodically and systematically controlled and corralled toward a one-world system."

A full breath wouldn't come. His mention of not being able to buy or sell was what would happen to people left behind in the tribulation. This, the topic of the end, was what had always scared her the most–not scared her, terrified her.

Her look must have given her away as his eyes were now filled with concern. "Paige..." his words were soft, "should we stop?"

With heart racing and her legs just itching to run, she sat looking at Wyatt with a firm answer in mind: Yes, they should stop. Yes, this was too much. Yes, she wanted to run to her bed, cover her head, and stress sleep until her dad came back and made things better.

Thoughts of her dad helped her answer instead, "I'm okay to continue."

Wyatt nodded and moved to sit back. "What did you investigate about the masks, and did you come to a conclusion?"

"How could I with all the conflicting information? Everyone disagrees."

"You're right; they do," His slight smirk gave the impression he knew he had her trapped. "Speaking of conflicting, what were we told when the virus first began to spread, by our government's top official?"

"Not to wear them, that masks wouldn't protect against viruses."

"And then?"

"That everyone had to wear a mask."

"That's right. Everyone had to wear a mask to go into stores, businesses, and work.

"Masks have never protected against viruses because of the size of viral particles. That's why the masses have never been told to wear them during flu season." His eyes narrowed in suspicion. "Don't you think those very doctors who now recommend masks would have done the same with their high-risk patients all the years before if they actually stopped viral spread?"

"That would make sense."

"Have you ever seen thousands of people over the years wearing masks to protect from flu and colds?"

"No."

"This has never been about safety. It was about control and fear. Call me any kind of crazy you want to. It's still about fear. Social pressure grew to such a frenzy that people were bullying each other for not wearing something that doesn't even protect against viruses. Do you see the escalation of influence a lie has had on the masses?" With a shake of his head, he said, "I've seen people walking outside all alone with a mask on–outside! That's what's crazy. Or driving alone with a mask. That's the fear the lie has instilled in an unsuspecting people.

"Yes," Wyatt said, "I thought your dad was crazy, too, when he first started telling me what Revelation says about the end, how close we were. And that was years before all this: before being forced to wear masks we don't need, before they withheld life-saving treatments, before they insisted all people get these shots and tried to strip us of our rights to make our own health decisions, before they began making us stay six feet apart."

Echo passed by on his way to the kitchen, then backtracked when he heard their conversation. "It's no coincidence that people can't get together and share ideas and suspicions when socially distanced. And they can't track us or distinguish between us as individuals using our cell phones when we're clustered together." He began moving again. "They need to keep us apart to keep us in the dark."

Paige turned back to look at Wyatt. "My dad taught Echo too?"

"He did. He led a small Bible study when we were under his command. That study set my life on a new course. It was just an informal thing, but when that group would get together, I would make it a point to be there. I had very little experience with church or God. But your dad," he paused and shook his head, "he had a way of making the pages of the Bible come to life. He explained it and made it real and applicable."

Paige knew that full well, remembering a childhood of stories recited and verses explained by a dad whose love of the Word had caught her own hungry heart ablaze.

"At first," Wyatt said, "he taught me the basics, since I was new to my faith. He would meet with me alone and answer questions. I can't express to you who your dad has been to me over the years." His soft smile formed dimples just above his beard line. "He's helped me grow in my faith in ways I didn't know were possible. When he eventually started talking about the rapture and tribulation, I didn't know what to think."

With a shake of his head, he said, "It all sounded outrageous until he began showing me examples of how the setup for the end has been playing out in Europe for decades, longer even."

Wyatt's eyes narrowed, "He said something; I'll never forget its impact on how I view God's Word. 'God was literal in Genesis. He's literal in Revelation. He's the same yesterday, today, and forever.' Right now, today, you can't read the books of Daniel or Revelation and fail to see it nearly as a pop-up book as prophecies are coming to fulfillment, or at least the stage is being set for their ultimate fulfillment.

"Your dad taught me, and I listened and believed because I trusted him." His smile was understanding. "I realize you don't know me and have no reason to believe me. All I can do is give you the small pieces of a large puzzle and let you determine what picture it's portraying. I'll challenge you to revisit the narrative you've been given and then allow you to investigate and decide for yourself."

"That's fair enough." Paige tried to ignore his tender expression and how his eyes seemed to penetrate her own as if to peer within. Her pulse accelerated. "My dad used to try and teach me about this when I was younger, but it scared me too much to hear him out."

"Of course it did. You were young. When I first started seeing the scope of it, I was shaken too. Nothing shakes me, Paige. This did."

Her voice was barely a whisper. "I want him to be wrong."

"He isn't wrong." Wyatt grimaced and cocked one eyebrow. "You'll have to dig deep and go beyond what's on the surface. It's a choice we make to wake up and see. Or it's a choice we make to keep hitting the snooze button. Jesus said we are to worship Him in spirit and in truth. Seeking truth requires action. Accepting truth requires open eyes. Living truth is a product of finding it.

"Paige, if what we show you rings true, will you commit to do those things?"

His words were so gentle and pleading, they seemed to settle onto her heart with the softness of a feather. "If what you show me is true, I'll live it."

"That's all I ask of you." He smiled and nodded. "Let's take five and meet back. I've got a call to make."

"Is it about my dad?"

"No, but I promise to let you know anything I find out." Wyatt stood. "For the record, it'll be a little longer than five minutes."

She smiled. "I didn't take that literally."

Wyatt disappeared around the corner from where Echo's tech zone was, leaving Paige there waiting. She had considered going to her room for a break but knew better. With all she had heard so far, she knew her temptation would be to crawl into that scarcely comfortable bed and escape. That's not what she would do. If her dad so believed in this cause that he would train up these soldiers to live it, then she owed it to him to at least listen with an open mind, no matter how implausible it seemed to her.

Narrative

Day 1, 1:18 p.m.

Wyatt reappeared and went to the kitchen first, then handed her a bottled water when he reached the sofas. He sat again in his original seat across from her.

His words were firm. "We see so much momentum building, it's clear we don't have a lot of time. Event 201 and the other topics we've covered are only a few of the pieces of the puzzle that fashion the larger whole. When snapped into place alongside all the other pieces out there, what you get is the most disturbing image mankind can envision.

"Echo will cover a few more topics with you." His lips curved into an easy smile. "Remember, this is only day one. You don't have to hear it all. No way you can anyway. I just want you to have a better understanding of what we believe, what we risk our lives to expose." He paused and looked at her with a trace of embarrassment. "You're a bright woman and can likely poke holes in every argument we give you. Trust me, I've tried to tell people these things over the years, and I see how they look at me." With a soft sigh and tender smile, he said, "Paige, I would never lie to you. All I want is to help you gain insight and live truth."

"I don't mean to be argumentative," she said, "but truthfully, much of it really does sound nonsensical to me. This is a global pandemic. Even when they didn't get it right every time, government agencies and concerned organizations were clearly doing their best to protect people in the midst of a bad situation."

"Yeah," he said with an amused chuckle, "we can already agree to disagree on that one." He stood and led her over near Echo's desk. "I'll let Echo give you some nonsensical truth about a few concerned organizations."

After Wyatt walked away, Paige turned to Echo. "I can't help but see all this as crazy." She wasn't sure how much she meant those words. What was actually crazy was how much of what Wyatt had said was becoming plausible.

Echo's brown eyes grew wide, and he gave a definite nod of his head. "Absolutely crazy."

Paige's heart only now steadied after her intense discussion with Wyatt.

"Crazy and unbelievable are the best tactics to do the devil's work right out in the open." Echo's eyes suggested irritation. "He doesn't even have to hide it anymore since people like you would rather sleep through the chaos and ignore what's really going on than to see the writing on the wall."

When she didn't respond right away, he said, "Paige, I don't have the directive Wyatt does. We don't have time to get you up to speed delicately or over the course of weeks or months. These next few days, I'll hit you with both barrels." He broke into a grin at her expression.

With his keyboard now in his lap, he turned in his chair to face the jumbo monitor and spun Paige in her chair to face it with him. "I've got a truckload of crazy for you."

Categorized and labeled photos began to pop up on the screen in rapid-fire succession: social media CEOs and tech developers, politicians and royalty, financial giants and billionaire industrialists.

"These," Echo said, "are the faces of the conspirators. Some write the narrative, some enforce the narrative, and some make sure no one questions the narrative. Most, if not all, have one thing in common, one association."

She knew what he was going to say, and it already had her stomach in knots. "The World Economic Forum?"

"Exactly," he said. "Whatever the narrative, the collective members do their part to maintain it. For example, popular search engines filter your search results to make sure you get the desired message and social media censors what we see and how we communicate. It's way more menacing than you realize and goes far beyond canceling political figures to keep them from getting out their messages.

"You would be shocked at the level of censorship and how facts are being removed so the public doesn't hear." His eyes grew wider. "The truth is being withheld from you," he pointed at her, "from everyone who has a right to read differing opinions and form their own conclusions. Instead, anyone who speaks against masks or what they call a vaccine has their posts or videos removed, no matter if the statement is true or not. Like search engines, social media has algorithms in place to find keywords that go against the narrative. People who share their experience about post-injection medical issues or those who question the safety of it are shut down. Entire groups, some tens of thousands of people strong, have been totally deleted from Facebook.

"Outspoken medical doctors and world-renowned virologists have been deleted from YouTube for warning people of the potential long-term dangers of these unproven injections. We have a medical right to informed consent. We can't get that if all we hear is what the mainstream media is telling us. Or a medical community who's influenced and often bought off by Big Pharma.

"Pastors who are warning of where we are on the kingdom calendar are having their videos removed for speaking truth. They're warning against vaccine passports and how they might potentially be used in the tribulation."

Paige sat looking at the screen as Echo spoke. The many familiar faces looking back at her all seemed harmless enough. Would they willingly shut down truth?

"Would you agree with me," Echo said, "that the truth welcomes the light and welcomes questions?"

"I do agree."

"Lies don't want to be questioned. That's the real issue here. Since when did we in America stop valuing discussion and debate? Why can't people question the mask mandates or shutdowns or shots?"

She said, "The videos you gave me to watch were all on Rumble. That's because they were removed from YouTube?"

"That's right."

"I'm guessing," she said with growing irritation, "that most people don't even know that. I didn't."

"You know now, Paige. It's up to you to decide what to do with it." His warm brown eyes took on their first appearance of coolness. "I'm not sure anything frustrates me more than believers who do see yet pretend they don't. They won't buck the system or take a stand. They simply go along and never say anything or do anything about the injustice right in front of them. This is injustice. This is the enemy."

His expression softened. "I hope that's not you. I'm almost positive it's not." He smiled. "Paige, I hate to tell you this, but what we've covered so far is a mere drop in the bucket. Don't even get me started on the science insanity like nanotech, AI, and transhumanism. That should terrify all of us when man begins to alter what God created in His image. China is actually creating biologically enhanced snipers who can see twice as far as other humans.

"It's all so far-reaching and sinister," Echo said with a sigh, "I wouldn't know where to begin. There are the Illuminati and Luciferians," he blinked hard and shook his head. "With so much to filter through, it becomes easier to just not. There's a term to define my earliest reactions, all of our earliest reactions, when we're introduced to this: cognitive dissonance.

"That's the discomfort we feel when what we've always believed clashes with new information being given to us. Our mind can't reconcile the inconsistencies, so it finds a way to explain the contradictions, like calling them conspiracy theories. Often, for most people, the response is to ignore the new information altogether. Otherwise, they are forced to change their beliefs. We don't like doing that, do we?"

Paige gave a little shake of her head, her words to her dad–those exact words: conspiracy theories–ringing in her head.

"If we so choose," he said, "we can live in an entirely manipulated world and never see the evidence that's there before our eyes." His words were firm. "That's what I did until a few years ago. That's what you're doing now, Paige." He sat back in his seat and allowed her time to process.

Arguments flooded Paige's mind: intelligent, well-reasoned ways to dispute what both Wyatt and Echo were wanting her to believe. The well-known faces on the mega screen above her, all cast in a negative, conspiratorial light, only gave her more reason to disregard what they were suggesting. These were people who did good in the world and used their vast resources to help the underprivileged.

Every thought she had just had was exactly in line with what Echo had explained cognitive dissonance to be.

She didn't say a word. For months she had known something wasn't right. Everything inside had been telling her to dig deeper, to think more critically. Rather than going with her gut, or more accurately the Spirit's quiet leading, she had done exactly what Echo said and had rejected without questioning all the posts she had seen on social media from believing friends who were raising concerns about people being locked down and separated from one another and about churches being closed without most pastors' protests.

What if the shutdowns weren't necessary? What if...

"Paige," Echo said as he moved his keyboard to his desk, "people are so entrenched in the here and now that they refuse to see what's before their very eyes. That includes millions of believers. They're blinded but not blind. Blind means you can't see. Blinded indicates something is preventing you from seeing. Masses of people are blinded by lies and misinformation. We're trying to help you see beyond what you're being told.

"The media controls the message to control the masses." He paused. "You've been played. Now it's time you get to know the players."

Paige's heart skipped a slight beat at Echo's words about the media controlling the masses, ones so similar to Wyatt's just that morning.

He spun around and began to type. "I'm dropping a file into your research folder. First, go look at the site for the World Economic Forum, the head of the snake, or at least the precursor to the serpent. I want you to read their plans in their own words. You have to investigate and dig deeper than what they're saying. Look for what they actually mean."

She stood and turned to go but then stopped and turned back. "Did you change the search engine on my computer? I noticed this morning that it looks different."

"I did; the other search engine buries what goes against 'the narrative.' Most people don't dig any deeper than what they're spoon fed in the top few results."

She didn't dig–ever.

"I've loaded an engine that will allow you to find factual arguments that you'd never find on the other one without clicking through hundreds of pages of results."

"You know you sound like a nut, right?"

"I know and proudly own it. But I'm right. There was a Washington Post article–yet another machine supporting 'the narrative'–about the rabbit hole and how people can get drawn in too deep when searching. The article actually suggested we should accept the first five searches on Google. In essence, they're saying, 'You're not smart enough. Trust us.'"

He nodded at her. "You need to begin questioning everything, Paige, absolutely everything. Nothing in this world is what you think it is."

There it was again, that ominous phrase.

Watcher

Day 1, 1:59 p.m.

With her laptop on the kitchen island, Paige sat looking at the folder on her desktop screen, assuming Echo's "both barrels" were contained in there. Wyatt was nowhere in sight when she had left Echo, leaving her to wonder if maybe he was getting some rest after his sleepless night.

She typed in World Economic Forum in her new search engine but never hit enter. Already she had so much swirling around in her head to process, she wasn't sure she wanted to read anymore, at least not now. The same tightness in her chest emerged like when she was a teenager and her dad would start quoting end-time verses.

"Hey," Wyatt said when he entered the kitchen. "Are you hungry yet?"

"I couldn't eat a bite."

"That's understandable, but you need a little something." He handed her a banana.

While peeling his own, he said, "How did it go with Echo?"

"Like you've said, it's a lot to take in." She blinked long and gave a quick shake of her head. "I just don't know what to think."

He moved to sit next to her on a stool. "I want to talk to you about something different," he motioned toward the wall of windows behind them, "not about all that's looming out there."

"Okay."

"I told you your dad was concerned for you."

She nodded but said nothing.

"Your expression says you doubt that."

"If he was so concerned about me that he would stay away, shouldn't he at least have told me about the danger? Wouldn't bad guys still come after me just because of who I am? Would us being estranged prevent that?"

"He's wanted you to live as normal of a life as possible for as long as possible."

"Normal life?" She tossed her banana peel on the counter. "Nothing about life is normal anymore."

"Not normal as it stands now. He's known it was time to talk to you, to help you see."

"Why didn't he?"

"Your reaction, for one. He knew how you would take it."

That stung her heart, considering how she had reacted the times he even hinted at a conspiracy or that what was happening in the world was leading to the end.

"Plus," Wyatt said, "he's been gone more this past year than home."

His words were like a gut punch. "You mean my dad actually lives in Savannah?"

Wyatt nodded. "Yes, to be close to you, to watch over you."

Paige stood and walked toward the sofas. She couldn't handle a thought like that, that her dad had been near but rarely made contact. With tears burning her eyes and without turning to look at Wyatt, she said, "Did he stay away because he's angry with me?"

"No, absolutely not." Wyatt came closer. "I promise that wasn't the case at all. His only intention was to keep his business," he paused, "the darkness of what we deal with, as far away from you as possible."

"I've been alone all this time." She turned to look at him. "I've been without both parents."

"I know it felt that way, Paige. But now you know that's not true."

"You said he's been gone most of the year, so it is true." Her words weren't bitter, simply filled with loneliness and heartbreak.

"Even this past year you haven't been as alone as you think."

Paige moved to sit. "Explain that to me."

"I'm not sure which will make you more uncomfortable, some of the end-times stuff or what I'm about to tell you."

She gripped the arm of the sofa to brace herself.

Wyatt sat and for a few seconds seemed hesitant to speak. Finally, he said, "When your dad isn't here, I watch over you."

With head cocked and eyes wide, she said, "What do you mean you 'watch over me'?"

"When your dad travels, I keep an eye on you. I make sure you're safe."

Paige pondered his words. "How exactly do you keep an eye on me?"

His elbows were resting on his knees, and he fanned his hands out before her. "Now before I say this next part, you've got to agree to give me a chance to get it all out."

In a higher-pitched voice, Paige said, "Go on."

"We have audio and video in your house."

She jumped to her feet. "You what?!"

Wyatt stood too. "You said you would let me finish."

They both sat again, but whatever he had to say next couldn't possibly justify such an invasion of her privacy.

"We do not, hear me, we do not activate the internal cameras–ever–audio or video. We only would in an actual emergency. And we only watch the external video if someone approaches your home and triggers the feed."

"Triggers?"

"Sensors in your driveway and on sidewalks and porches."

Her rapid pulse decelerated only a little. "And they only come on when someone arrives?"

"Yes, and only externally."

"So, you don't watch me inside my house?"

"No way. Remember, this is all your dad's idea. He uses Overwatch, this location here, as an ops center to direct all our field operations. He chose this place because it's eighteen minutes away from your house, far enough that he wouldn't accidentally run into you, yet close enough to get there if anything were to happen.

"We're only here in case you were to need us. I promise you that." He paused and seemed noticeably uncomfortable. "We aren't here to interfere with your life."

"Be honest with me," she said. "Do you think my dad is alive?"

"I have every reason to believe he is."

"Just because he always has a plan? That's not a concrete enough reason to hope, not after me hearing gunshots before the line went dead and then nothing since."

"It's more than just that. I told you he has something on Groves, the man he has been working for under the guise of security these past months. He had intel and inserted himself to get the evidence he needed to take the guy down."

"Who is Groves?"

"Malcolm Groves, a prime example of just how twisted this world has become. No one would ever suspect him, not with his standing in the medical community. He founded one of the most advanced research labs on the East Coast and is considered one of the most brilliant minds in the industry, always on the cutting edge of modern medicine."

"So what is he doing wrong?"

Wyatt looked at her long, then blinked a few times. "I'll be right back."

Paige watched him go to the bedroom corridor door and stand before the retina scanner. It washed over her afresh, the insanity of what was going on. Less than twenty-four hours before, she was sitting at the little desk in her comfy little home struggling to put words on a page. Now, here she was with a group of... She tried to come up with the proper word. Were they mercenaries? Did that mean what she thought it meant, a private army?

What she did know was that they, Wyatt and Echo, believed in her dad and believed what her dad believed. Until she had a reason to do otherwise, she would hear them out and try to make sense of this capsize of her life.

Wyatt returned and sat on the sofa next to her. From the moment he reappeared, she had looked at nothing but the Bible in his hand. A sting of, not conviction, but of longing roused her far-from-God heart.

He said, "People like Groves bring these words from Ephesians five to mind. 'For it is disgraceful even to speak of the things which are done by them in secret. But all things become visible when they are exposed by the light, for everything that becomes visible is light.'" He glanced up and then back down. "That's verses twelve and thirteen, but back up in eleven it says, 'Do not participate in the unfruitful deeds of darkness, but instead even expose them.' That's what we do, Paige, expose the darkness we can. Groves is the worst kind of dark, a man who does unspeakable things to young girls."

When she didn't say anything, he said, "Nothing would have stopped your dad from going in and doing his best to expose this man and stop him." He paused. "Nothing would stop him from trying to protect kids."

"He has the proof he needs?"

"He must. That's why I believe he's still alive." After a slight pause and pained expression, he said, "Or if not, your dad has hidden the proof out there somewhere."

Wyatt reached for the remote on the rectangular ottoman and clicked. Images of Paige's home were on the TVs. The inside was ransacked, most all she owned broken and lying in pieces on the floor. Her furniture was torn apart and stuffing was strewn over the floor.

"They must think your dad has given you whatever it is he has on Groves. Either way, you're not safe out there. If they have your dad, then they will use you to make him talk. Or," he glanced away and back, "if your dad didn't make it out, then they will do horrendous things to find whatever evidence he got out of the Groves compound."

The damage to her home she was viewing on the feed caused her stomach to lurch. If they would do that to a house, what might they do to a body?

"I know how upsetting this must be," he said.

"I don't know what I am: scared for sure, like I'm in a fog or a dream, but mostly I'm angry. I'm furious that anyone would harm young girls, that they would do that to my home just to hide their wickedness, and that they would try to take my dad from me." She closed her eyes tight, then looked back at her watcher. "We have to find him."

"I agree. I promise we have our best guys on it."

"Who? Who's on it? Tell me about your team."

Alias

Day 1, 2:47 p.m.

"Welcome back," Echo said.

"Thanks. This has been quite a day." She didn't sound at all enthusiastic as she had intended to try and fake.

"I wish I could say the news gets better. It doesn't."

Faces began to emerge on the screens above Echo's workstation. Only now was she realizing the labels beneath the individual monitors were likely names, aliases of team members. The screens in the first two positions labeled Apex and Arrow were darkened still. As the men appeared, they would say various greetings to Wyatt and Echo. All were in differing locations. One called Wyatt boss, which left Paige to assume Wyatt was in charge with her father gone.

Echo said, "The little guy in box number three is Barricade, Cade for short. When in trouble, your best bet is to put Barricade between yourself and whatever's coming after you."

She supposed this giant of a man was Samoan or some Polynesian descent.

His warm smile came easily. "Nice to meet you, Paper."

"That's you, Paige," Echo said with a stifled laugh. "I didn't know we would ever have to call you that in person."

"That's my alias? Very imaginative of you, Echo." She looked back at the screen. "Nice to meet you, too, Cade. If I'm ever in trouble, you're my guy."

Cade's smile faded. "I really am, Paige. I'm here when you need me."

"Me too," said a man so stocky he filled the next screen like Cade. "I'm Sebastian Cray. My friends and you, Paige, call me Bash."

From his rascally tone, this Brit fashioned himself a ladies' man. "Hi, Bash. You're on my list to call as well."

"Grab a pen, luv, and take my number."

The whole group laughed except Wyatt. "Moving on," he said with arms crossed over his chest and a stony expression.

Echo pointed at one monitor to the dark-haired, suit-clad man wearing a headset and pacing behind his desk. The skyline in the background marked his Manhattan location. "That's Dollar, Dylan Reeves to the masses, youngest and brightest on Wall Street. He makes this sweet lifestyle of ours possible with brilliant investments and a little Robin Hoodery here and there."

Dollar touched his Bluetooth earpiece and turned to the camera. "It's a pleasure, Paige. I look forward to having you come to New York when the dust settles. I'll take you out on the town."

"Maybe I'll make it there someday," Paige said.

But Dollar was already talking to someone else and pacing his office again.

The monitor above the alias Fortress only now came to life when a silver-haired man appeared. "Paige," he said with a sorrowful expression, "I'm doing all I can to locate your dad." He gave a little shake of his head. "We go way back. I'm not giving up on him."

Unexpected emotion welled up at the man's mention of her father, and for a moment Paige couldn't find her voice.

Wyatt stepped in closer to Paige. "This is Hank Patterson. He's in the field with Bash and Cade. There's no better crew to have in your corner."

The others all nodded in agreement.

"Hi, Paige," Intel said with quiet regard. "I'm Landon Wells. I would know you anywhere, the spittin' image of your mama. I was blessed to have known her and worked alongside her for many years. She always said there was something special tucked away in that heart of yours. I don't doubt that. Glad to have you on board."

Paige's smile was genuine. Any mention of her mother brought distinct and rare gladness to her heart. "Thank you, sir. I'm glad to meet any colleague of hers. Maybe you can tell me more about her someday."

"I'd be honored to, darlin'."

His mention of her being on board was curious. Paige looked up at Wyatt, but rather than looking at her, he nodded ahead at the next monitor and said, "That shady-looking Brazilian there is Gunny, our munitions expert and acquisitions specialist."

"Carlos Alves," the man said with a pronounced Portuguese accent. "You are a rather lovely addition to Daybreak. Welcome."

The final screen remained blank, but Paige was more curious about some of the previous comments than the missing members.

Echo said, "Halo is in the air as we speak, following up on a lead about your dad."

Paige addressed the band of men, "Thank you for caring enough for my father to keep up the pursuit. I have no doubt he would do the same for you."

The men again nodded their agreement. Soon, faces began to disappear until all that was left was Fortress. He said, "I'll find him, Paige, or die trying." His monitor went black.

For a moment Paige just kept staring at the screens where those faces, those loyal-to-her-father men, had committed to finding him. She looked at the blank screen labeled Apex. The danger he was in felt all the more real. A normal reaction would have been fear or tears or both. Instead, something stirred within, a sense of resolve she didn't recognize as familiar. As Fortress had said, Paige was determined to find her dad or die trying.

Her new sense of determination only escalated and led Paige to turn and go for her laptop. Whatever this group all believed in enough to risk their lives for, Paige wanted to know more about it. They clearly weren't a band of conspiracy nuts locked in their moms' basements sipping on energy drinks. It was evident they were highly trained and lethally skilled men in their respective fields.

Wyatt came to stand next to her as she opened her computer. "If you want a little peace and quiet to read, I'll show you to your room."

She arched an eyebrow. "I know how to find my room. I just prefer it here where it's not quite so," she hesitated, "drab."

"That's a spare room." He cocked his hat back on his head. "I'll show you to your room."

Already Wyatt had turned to go, so Paige jumped off the stool, grabbed her laptop, and fell in behind him. Once through the security door, he moved to the second door on the right and pointed. "Your room, Paper." He turned and left.

Paige stood watching him walk away, considering her alias and how she had been a part of this team's efforts long before she knew it. Something told her this may be exactly where she belonged.

She reached for the knob and swung open the door, then stood there staring. It looked just like her old bedroom from back when she lived at home with her parents. When she had moved out with roommates, her mom had insisted on buying her a new bedroom set to get her started. More than a fresh start, her mom had wanted her to always have a home to come home to.

Her dad hadn't gotten rid of everything as Paige had presumed. In addition to her furniture, some things of her mom's were there: the small writing desk that her mom had used in the living room, a tray of vintage perfume bottles Paige had often gotten into as a little girl, and her mother's jewelry box which now sat on the dresser.

It was all too much of a reminder of the love-filled life she had once lived. Her eyes didn't leak this time, but her heart seemed to. A familiar ache arose in her chest where her heart was trickling tears. That's what she had done over the past years: quietly wept within.

Paige went and curled up on the bed. With a pillow snuggled to her chest, she just lay there allowing her heart time to weep and mourn.

Sentinel

Day 1, 6:01 p.m.

Paige woke to a light tap on the door. She sat up and ran her fingers through her hair. "I'm up."

"Come eat some dinner," Wyatt said through the closed door.

"I'll be right there."

A trip to the bathroom later, Paige was leaving her room with a glance at her computer sitting on her mother's desk. She didn't even slow down. The last thing she could handle was opening that laptop and facing Echo's both barrels.

A plate of spaghetti sat on the counter waiting for her. "Echo has already eaten, but I've waited for you."

"I fell asleep."

"I figured as much. If you can stress sleep, today's sure the day to do it."

"I've never had as much reason."

Wyatt sat next to her with his heaping plate of pasta. "This is too much for anyone to handle." He bowed his head to pray, then dug in. With a mouthful, he said, "Honestly, I'm worried about you. Do you normally eat so little?"

"Not at all."

With a shy grin, he said, "Okay, I have to admit I know that."

"You know that how?"

"You go for fast food a lot; DQ seems to be your favorite."

"You know that because I trigger the video feed?"

"Yep." He slurped a noodle that tapped his cheek, leaving a dot of sauce behind.

"Do you have a tracker on my car?"

"Uh huh," he said and nodded while he chewed.

"And you don't think that's weird, perfect strangers tracking my comings and goings?"

He wiped his face. "It's the epitome of weird."

Paige only picked at her food. The highly seasoned sauce wasn't settling well on her stomach.

"Isn't it good? Do you want something else?"

"Any other day it would be great. Today..." she said and pushed her plate away.

"Will a Blizzard help?"

"Are you serious? You'll go get one for me?"

"It's dark enough out. I'll take you there. We have another stop to make anyway."

"I've changed my mind. This," Wyatt said and looked ahead of him at the stately mansion, "is the epitome of weird." He took a bite of his Blizzard.

When they had arrived at her neighborhood of Ardsley Park and turned onto a road just one block from Paige's, she had assumed they would park and watch her house. Instead, they pulled into an oak-lined driveway. Trees dripping with Spanish moss formed a spooky tunnel. Parked now, Wyatt sat and ate his ice cream while she nibbled on a fry.

"Whose place is this?" she said.

"Before I tell you, I've got to say, you were right. Mixing the cappuccino flavor with Heath is a game changer. Glad I tried it."

"Are you kidding me right now? We're talking about ice cream flavors while sitting outside some haunted house?"

"It's not just any old haunted house; it's your dad's haunted house." He blinked long and looked back at her. "I can't think of any better way to describe it than that."

"What, haunted?"

"Yeah, by you and your mom. He never let you go, Paige. He was always close by when he could be." With a nod toward the creamy-vanilla painted brick home, he said, "We call it Sentinel."

"You guys and your aliases."

"We try to keep identities and locations secure since we're spread out across the country and mostly talk on phones or online." He shoveled in his last bite and drained the liquid from the cup, tapping the bottom to loosen the lingering candy.

Paige took another few bites of her ice cream and set her half-full cup in the holder.

When she got out, Wyatt did the same, following her up the sidewalk and to the door. "Here," he moved in front of her and unlocked the door.

Just as her room at Overwatch had taken her back to when her family was intact, so did the sight before her. Everything from her childhood was there: All the furniture was positioned the same, and family photos hung on walls and were set on tables much like her mom once had them arranged. The dining table she had grown up eating at was there covered in a thin layer of dust. A little sigh escaped her at the feeling of home.

"My dad has lived here since he sold the house?" she said.

"He has. He works at Overwatch during the day and comes here only after dark when we're not running hot."

She only wondered what running hot meant for a second or two before stepping through the open door and roaming from room to room. The layout was so similar to her home growing up that Paige had to remind herself several times this was just a replica.

Upstairs, in her parents'–her father's–bedroom, Paige stood looking at the unmade bed, a sight that made her smile, thinking of the fit her mother would throw if only she could see it. For the first time in so long, she felt her parents' presence. Even more, she now saw proof: Her dad hadn't left her after all.

"Will you give me a minute?" Paige said and reached to close the door.

Wyatt held the door. "Before I do, I need to give you one more bite of weirdness to chew on." When she just stood looking at him, he said, "I have a room here. I stay here when your dad is gone."

"You watch me from here too?"

"I do. When he's gone, I know where you are twenty-four hours a day."

What had been her intention to be alone and cry gave way to curiosity. "So he pays you to watch me when he's out of town, even at night?"

He stood there, shifting from foot to foot in what was evident discomfort. Finally, he said, "He doesn't pay me, Paige. He doesn't have to." With that he turned and left her alone.

Only a moment passed in reflection before Paige went back downstairs to find Wyatt. He sat in the living room, perched at the edge of the sofa as if waiting for her.

She stood wringing her hands, then tucked them into her pockets. "This is all real, isn't it?"

With eyes filled with compassion, he nodded. "I wish I could say it wasn't."

"You said it all shook you at first."

"Oh, I was shook alright. I had a future planned. I saw things going entirely differently."

"But what you've witnessed happening in the world has changed all that?"

"It has. I thought I'd have the dream: a wife and kids and a couple of dogs. No way I could do that now, not with what I know and see coming." His look shifted from regret-filled to one of clear intention. "I had to take time to grieve what seemed like loss then. You'll need to do that too."

Paige sat at the opposite end of the sofa from him. "Do you think we will be here for the worst that's to come?"

His answer wasn't immediate, rather, he seemed to ponder her question. "I think we will see more than we want. Persecution will occur in the U.S. like so many other countries currently experience. We can't be too surprised by that."

With a soft flutter in her heart, she said the word that had been trying to invade her mind all day. "The tribulation, is that what's here?"

"No, Paige. That would be outside the order of things."

"Right now," she said with a voice so faint she barely heard herself, "I don't even know the order of things."

His words were kind. "Your entire world has shifted beneath your feet. You lost your mom and then contact with your dad. The quarantine came, and now this. It's understandable that you feel disoriented." He scooted over one cushion closer. "I'll help you get reoriented in the Word."

"I guess that's what I need. This is one area I've never studied."

"I know I said you have a lot to learn about all that's going on, but I've got an idea: Before you look at what's coming, why don't we look at who's leaving. Otherwise, I can't imagine you'll find peace at all." He broke into a soft smile. "No better place to tell you about the rescue than here at Sentinel."

Rescue

Day 1, 6:33 p.m.

When Wyatt came back down from his bedroom, he held a Bible, a worn one with peeling edges similar to hers from high school that Paige had brought in her go bag.

He set it on the seat between them. "This is the Bible I used when I first began meeting with your dad all those years ago."

If Wyatt's hand hadn't been resting on it, Paige would have placed hers there. "In my head I often hear my dad speaking verses over me."

Wyatt was looking at the Book rather than at her when he said, "I hear that too." His eyes held evident emotion when he said, "'Only be strong and very courageous, Wyatt,' he would say. 'Be careful to do according to all the law which Moses My servant commanded you; do not turn from it to the right or to the left; so that you may have success where you go.'"

"He quoted Joshua to you too?"

"All the time."

Paige wasn't sure if it made her happy or sad to know that her dad had spoken the same verses to Wyatt as he had to her. Finally, she said, "I'm glad he was there for you while you learned."

His voice was soft. "My dad was in and out of the picture when I was a kid. Your dad has been the only consistent role model in my life. I guess you could say he's trained me up in the way I should go, like a spiritual dad. Honestly, Paige, he's family to me."

She sat back on the sofa feeling almost at ease. Wyatt's words from before, that her dad didn't have to pay him to watch over her, made more sense now. If Wyatt loved her dad so much as to consider him family, then she had every reason to listen to him and learn from him.

"I'm open to listen and not argue," she said. "I know you won't lie to me. I've known something wasn't right, that something was going on that I couldn't quite grasp. I think that's why I've stayed so isolated. My world had already changed so much that it was easier to hide from what was happening in the actual world. I couldn't stand to see partial faces behind masks. Something stirred within, some mixture of anger and sorrow. It's like people became so afraid of dying that they stopped living altogether."

"Exactly. What gets me most," he said, "is that even believers are living in fear rather than watching for our glorious hope."

"You mean the rapture?"

"I do." His words were firm but kind. "For the believer, the fear of dying and fear of the rapture are merely symptoms of a foundational issue. Those who fear don't know who God is. And they certainly don't know who they are to God.

"It's vital that we stand on the right foundation. The one who knows who God is without knowing who they are to Him will only feel smaller and farther away when their world is shaken. But the one who knows who they are to God can walk in step with Him and trust their Dad no matter the decisions He makes on their behalf. Death or even removal from this planet through the rapture can be looked forward to by the child prepared to see their Father face to face."

Paige considered his words with regard to her own beliefs. There had been a time when she didn't question either who God was or who she was to Him. That she had turned from Him and had for a long time feared the rapture now called those beliefs into question.

"If you'll allow me," he said, "I'll show you in Scripture what I believe."

"I know what the rapture is," she said with a quick nod, "some people being taken and some being left behind. But I don't know when it's supposed to happen."

"It could happen anytime. There are no signs that have to be fulfilled first, just us being gone in the twinkling of an eye. It could be this year or years from now. I just know it has to happen, and I would say sooner rather than later with such a push toward a one-world order.

"What you'll learn going forward is that the infrastructure that will be used in the tribulation to carry out the Antichrist's agenda is already well underway. We see the formation and plan, but the execution of it will be after the tribulation begins." He paused and shook his head. "I hate that I used that word."

Paige swallowed hard, wishing he hadn't used the word execution either. Finally, she said, "That's what I'm about to read next, I think. But I haven't been able to hit enter to search for it yet."

"There's time for that. What you need to know right now is that the rapture isn't something for us to fear. It's our rescue, the Groom coming for the Bride, His church. That's you, Paige." Wyatt reached out and wrapped his hand around hers. "He's coming for you."

"I should know more about this. It shouldn't scare me so much."

"Many don't know. And those who do know feel just like you. It's hard to blame you, though, when so many preachers won't talk about the rapture or the tribulation. Because it scares people, pastors stay silent. That's not right. They'll give an account for that someday. Silent shepherds are starving the sheep."

The imagery of that caused a knot to form in her stomach. "That's a powerful statement."

"A true statement. They're feeding this year's flock on outdated grain, content with feel-good messages about how to be a better Christian or live a better life. That's food that tastes good going down, but it won't nourish or strengthen the believer to walk in this year's field. There's no urgency in those pastors' messages and no urgency in the believers' hearts."

He cracked open his Bible. "Can I give you some of the basics?"

She nodded as a small sigh escaped her.

"I'll start with Jesus' last promise to come for us. Read here," he said and pointed to Revelation 3:10.

Paige pulled his Bible closer. "Because you have kept the word of My perseverance, I also will keep you from the hour of testing, that hour which is about to come upon the whole world, to test those who dwell on the earth."

He said, "Jesus is talking about the coming tribulation, when His wrath will be poured out on the wickedness of this world. But He's clear, right, that us, the church, will be kept from the hour of testing?"

She nodded.

"And here." He pointed to chapter four. "From the time John is told to 'come up here,' meaning to heaven, you won't see any more references to the church here on earth."

"You think John being caught up to heaven is a symbol of the rapture?"

"It is," Wyatt said. "All that happens in Revelation six and beyond, we aren't here for. You only see believers who are called the tribulation saints from then on, people saved after we are gone."

"So we can't get the mark that Revelation talks about?"

"Not possible. That's why understanding the timeline brings peace to a believer. But let's hold off on that for another time. Just so you know, though, the tribulation can't begin before we leave. We're told in Second Thessalonians that the Antichrist can't arrive on the scene until the Restrainer is removed. That's the Holy Spirit within us, the believers. The

Spirit will be here when we're gone or else those left behind couldn't be saved. But the salt and light will be gone. You will be gone when the Antichrist comes. Think of it this way: The Antichrist is called the beast. There can be no mark of the beast with no beast, right? So, there's no way you can take the mark. That has to be of some comfort to you."

"It is." In comments she had seen on social media, even some non-Christians were talking about end times and the vaccines being related to the mark of the beast.

Wyatt's voice was insistent. "This is why understanding the rapture is fundamental for the believer. You absolutely have to be standing on solid ground as this world begins to shift beneath your feet or you'll live constantly shaken." His smile was warm, and his eyes were tender. "Can I blast you with some Bible geek terms?"

"Blast away."

He tilted his hat back and fired. "The term *harpazo* in the Greek," he flipped to First Thessalonians four, "is what Paul uses to describe believers who are alive at Jesus' appearing being caught up in the air to meet Him." He used one hand to demonstrate picking up and a rapid lifting of something into the air. "It's a term that means a violent snatching away." Wyatt shook his head. "Not violent as in hurtful, more like snatching someone from an oncoming train." He paused. "See what I mean? He will snatch us up and out of the way of the terror that's coming. That's His promise.

"The Latin translation for that word is *rapturo,* where we get the word rapture. So even though the word rapture isn't in the Bible, the doctrine is repeatedly. I say that because it's a source of contention among some Christians. The word Bible isn't actually in Scripture. Even the word Trinity, though its doctrine is clear and present throughout the Bible, isn't either.

Some say the doctrine of the rapture is heresy and gives people a false hope. Yet," he placed the Bible in her lap, "look at what Paul says at the end of the passage, that we are to comfort one another with words about being caught up. If we as believers are to face the wrath of God, if it's not our hope of escape, then there's no spin you can put on Paul's words to make them comforting. See what I mean?"

"I do see."

"There are differing positions on when the rapture will occur. Some say pre-tribulation. That's what I believe without question. There's just too much evidence in the Word to support it. Some think it'll happen in the middle and some at the end of the tribulation, which," he paused and shook his head, "what's the point of waiting until the middle or the end if it's supposed to be a rescue?"

With a slight pause and a hint of a smile, he said, "I knew people were coming for you, to harm you, so I came before they arrived. That was a rescue. Anything else would have likely been a recovery."

The memory of him holding up his fingers and saying "two minutes" came to mind, and how, at the time, she had no idea she needed to be rescued. That's how she had been living out her physical and spiritual lives, not understanding her need of God's rescue.

His words grew in intensity. "Believers aren't appointed to wrath, Paige. God says that. The tribulation is His wrath on the unbelieving world and His reaching out to His people, the Jews. Neither of those are us, the believing church.

"It's hard for us to understand as Christians, but the whole plan is about God fulfilling His promise to His covenant people Israel. They will finally see Him as their awaited Messiah at the midpoint of the tribulation. Many don't realize that all prophecy actually centers around Israel. We can watch Israel to see God's calendar."

Her heart was pounding strong, excitement growing over the Word of God in a way that hadn't happened in so long. Something was beginning to ignite within her, the rekindling of a fire her lukewarm heart had attempted to extinguish. "I love how passionate you are about this."

"This is more my lane, the prophecy stuff. At times, it's all I can see. I look around at how others think this is about economics and politics, when really it's all prophecy coming into view." He shrugged. "I'm no scholar, but it sure sets me ablaze to see the Word coming to life and prophecy being fulfilled."

Him using the word ablaze only stoked the fire rekindling within her own spirit. They were kindred spirits in the Word; she knew that now.

Wyatt said, "There are places in Scripture where Jesus says He told his disciples certain things so that when they happened, they would believe. It's the same with prophecy." He held up his Bible. "Did you know nearly a third of the Bible is prophetic? The opening of the book of Revelation has a promise of a blessing to those who read and hear and heed the book." He held it open for her to see in chapter one. "Yet most pastors won't teach it and believers won't read it.

"When leaving out prophecy, believers are missing out on much of what God wants them to know. It's there throughout the Word, His way of telling us how things will end even from the beginning of the Book. Love does that, Paige, prepares a way and shines a light. We are told we can't know the day or hour, but we are also told we will know the season. This is the season and yet believers are looking to governments and drug companies to help them get their lives back to normal. Nothing–hear me when I say this–nothing will ever be normal again!"

She held up her hand. "Can we wait and discuss more later?"

With an embarrassed grin, he said, "I'm sorry. I get so excited when I start talking about this that I tend to go overboard." He chuckled. "Sometimes I see it, people's eyes either glazing over in disbelief or widening with being overwhelmed."

"No, it's neither of those things," she said. "I need my Bible. I want to take notes with it open before me."

Wyatt's words were soft. "Yeah, I understand. I'll give you a list of rapture-related verses to look up. I do it too, write notes in the margins with dates as a reminder of what I've learned. Your dad taught me that."

Paige nodded, the memory of all those years of her dad's teaching warming her heart and pricking her conscience at the same time. It could have been him teaching her this rather than Wyatt if only she would have been brave enough to listen.

"What?" he said. "You look upset."

She stood and walked to the recliner, the one item in the room she had tried to avoid looking at. "Why didn't I let him tell me?"

"There's no time for regrets. Until recently, your dad believed you weren't ready, not for the extent of what's happening. He's not here to make the decision, but I genuinely believe you are. I think you have a role in what we're doing."

She plopped into her dad's chair and rubbed the tweed fabric of the arms. "What could I possibly contribute?"

"Your name is no mistake. A page is where the written word settles. That's you, Paige, a carrier and a vessel of the Word. Your dad says that about you.

"In the parable of the talents, Jesus said each was given according to his own ability. You're not a soldier who fights out in the field. You fight with words, fingers tapping on a keyboard. Tell the people what they need to know."

She gripped the arms of the chair where her daddy's hands had rested over the years. "He said I'm a vessel of the Word?"

"Yeah, years ago, back when I first began to study with him. He said he had never seen anyone with your grasp of the Word of God, how you could read and spiritually discern concepts well beyond your years without him ever explaining them to you."

Her heart thumped painfully against her ribs. "What do I need to tell people? About the rapture?"

"As you learn more, yes."

"I wish I could see things as you do. The idea of a rapture still scares me more than comforts me."

"Maybe because you've lost touch with the Groom coming to take you home."

Her cheeks burned at that. "I hardly go to church anymore, but I guess you know that as the creepy guy who's been watching me."

His smile came easily. "I do know that."

"After my dad took off, I couldn't stand being at the church where he wasn't. I tried several others and finally landed at a megachurch where I just kind of blended in. When churches closed for all those months, it hit me one Sunday: I didn't miss church, and church didn't miss me.

"I hadn't truly connected with anyone even though I tried. I attended a small group where people hardly acknowledged my presence. They weren't bad people, just people already settled into groups who cared for one another. They didn't need me and didn't see that I needed them. So I'm a solo pew-sitter when I do go."

"Then you understand," he said, "exactly what people need, to know they're cared for. They need to know how much God loves them and that He's providing a way of rescue from what's to come."

Paige sat looking at Wyatt. Everything inside of her kept screaming for her to run. The idea of telling people about something so foreign, so outrageous, was infinitely more unsettling than anything he had told her so far.

Her prayer from earlier that morning came to mind, for the Lord to help her out of the wilderness. Her dad's voice spoke the words of Joshua over her now just as when she was a young girl. *Be strong and courageous, for you shall give this people possession of the land which I swore to their fathers to give them.*

"My dad said he wants me to do that, to be a part of what you do?"

"He did. It's been his vision for you since we started Daybreak."

"Gunny said that word before. What is Daybreak?"

Wyatt's smile was warm. "How about we save more for tomorrow." He glanced at his watch. "It's getting late. We should get back to Overwatch."

Daybreak

Day 2, 6:52 a.m.

The soft sound of Wyatt's snoring near her ear woke her. Paige turned to find his face on her pillow, his warm breath on her neck. A smile came, not just on her face but in her heart, one that lasted even when her lips stopped.

With one eye peeked open, she glanced at her left hand resting on the covers, at the thin gold band circling her finger. "Thank You, Lord," she whispered aloud and closed her eyes again.

This time when Paige awoke, her cold feet searched beneath the covers for Wyatt's. That was his least favorite way to wake in the morning. Her foot felt only emptiness, and she rolled over to find him gone.

Wait! Something didn't feel right. This wasn't her life. Paige bolted upright and scanned her look-alike bedroom at Overwatch. Her eyes traveled to gaze at her ringless finger. It had only been a dream.

For a few seconds she sat paralyzed, her breath coming in quick bursts. Never, not once in her life, had she had a dream seem so real or be so vivid. Even the feel of his warm breath had... She shook her head and jumped from the bed trying to chase away the goosebumps on her skin.

Paige showered and dressed but then hesitated there in her room, almost too embarrassed to go and face Wyatt. A quick glance at the bed, however, urged her to the door and a fast getaway.

"Morning," Wyatt said when Paige entered the kitchen and poured herself a cup of coffee.

"Morning," Paige forced herself to say as casually as she could. She dropped some bread in the toaster.

"Want me to make breakfast?" Wyatt went to the refrigerator and looked inside. "We have –"

"Toast is fine." Paige waited for him to clear the way before she went for the butter and jelly. The last thing she wanted was to be close to him.

He set the carton of eggs on the counter and stood looking at her. "After yesterday, did you have any trouble sleeping?"

"Not at all. When I got to my room, I fell asleep before brushing my teeth. I finally did that just after midnight."

He chuckled. "I wish I could check out that way. I'm not sure I've gotten a full night's sleep in the past few years."

Paige knew she was being silly by not making eye contact. It was only a dream, something she couldn't control. Finally, she turned to look at him. "I can't even imagine what's been on your shoulders."

The look he gave her was odd, one she couldn't read, so she said, "I don't see how you do it, keep a straight course when the world is tilted sideways."

"That's not all that keeps me awake. My mind just gets going and never shuts down."

"Well, I'll sleep an extra hour tonight for you."

"I'm not sure if that offer was nice of you or kind of mean."

Paige grinned as she spread butter on her toast. "Okay, so Daybreak, tell me more."

He reached around her to get the bread, his arm touching hers, then he proceeded to crack eggs. "Sure you don't want some French toast?"

Now that she wasn't feeling so squirrelly over the dream, she could eat. "Maybe a piece." With a quick smile, she said, "Or two."

"You've got a pretty good gig going on here, if you ask me."

Wyatt's teasing words were actually calming. Since meeting him, she had found him to be kind and patient with her. Maybe his feelings for her dad gave him family-like concern for her.

"Look," she said, "I was just minding my own business when you showed up. This isn't exactly a voluntary gig."

"True enough. Like cinnamon?"

"Sure. And tons of syrup."

Her dream made a fleeting appearance in her mind, only a splash of a thought, but this time Paige didn't let it embarrass her. Maybe knowing he had been watching over her was what had triggered her mind to conjure up his image. Whatever it was, it didn't bother her. If anything, in some peculiar way, it made her feel even more comfortable in his presence, as if she knew this near-perfect stranger.

Her last words lingered in her mind for more than a few seconds, on just how perfect this stranger seemed to be.

"Man, I love French toast," Wyatt said as syrup dribbled from his lip onto his plate. He wiped his mouth.

Paige hadn't talked much. Hardly eating for two days had caught up with her. So far, she had her toast and jelly, the first round of French toast while Wyatt was still cooking his, and now a bowl of cereal. "I think I love everything today."

"I'm glad to see you eating." His expression was sweet as he nudged his plate toward her. "Want the rest of this?"

"No, I think I'm finally full." She paused and sat considering the sweetness of his offer. "But thank you."

He kept eating, so Paige studied him as she could, casting her eyes to peek at him when he wasn't looking. For the first time since Echo had said it, she wondered. "What is your directive with me?"

"What do you mean?"

"Echo said he doesn't have your same directive."

His words seemed measured and his look intentional. "I'm to watch over you at all costs."

"And what does that mean exactly, 'at all costs'?"

"Seems pretty clear cut to me." He stood and took his plate to the sink to run water.

"At the cost of your food? At the cost of your sleep when you're worried about me? At the cost of your life?"

He didn't look at her. "Why are you making this a thing? I'm just supposed to watch over you."

When he did turn, Wyatt's expression, the way his cheeks flushed gave her reason to believe there was more he wasn't saying. But something stopped her from questioning him. "I won't make it a thing."

"Good, let's talk about Daybreak."

"I think I'd rather talk about the rapture and getting rescued out of this place," she said.

He chuckled. "Ain't that the truth? But in the meantime, until our exfil to heaven, let's talk about light and darkness."

Wyatt led her to the sofas and reached for his Bible still resting on the ottoman from yesterday. "Same verses in Ephesians as yesterday."

"Hold up," she said. "I'll run get my Bible."

When she was back and sitting intentionally not close to him, she said, "Chapter five?"

"Yes. Start in verse six."

Paige read, "Let no one deceive you with empty words, for because of these things the wrath of God comes upon the sons of disobedience. Therefore do not be partakers with them."

Wyatt held up his hand for her to stop after verse seven. "It's a terrifying thought, but God's wrath is coming in the tribulation. We know, though, because we are His, we aren't considered the sons of disobedience, and we're not partakers with them when that wrath happens.

"But if you look at verse eight, it says we are Light in the Lord and that we're to walk as children of Light. Then on down in eleven it says we aren't to participate in the deeds of darkness but, instead, to expose them." Wyatt looked at her with great intention. "While we are still here, while daybreak still comes each morning, we absolutely have to do what we can to shed light on the darkness that's rising. This," he said with evident frustration, "is what pastors need to be teaching believers more than dishing out sermons about being better people."

He let out a soft sigh and shook his head. "There will come a time when daybreak ends, and the world will suffer seven years of nightfall. I'm so stricken inside by that thought at times that it steals sleep from me."

A burning sensation stirred in her stomach at the thought of people she knew and cared for being left behind. What if–she tried to push the thought away but couldn't–she was one of those people left behind? What if her recent distance from God had somehow disqualified her?

His expression shifted to one of tenderness. "Talk to me. Tell me what you're thinking."

Paige sat for a few seconds looking at him, lines of dialogue and accusations now flooding her fear-filled mind.

"Do you ever fear being left behind?" she said.

"I don't fear that–ever." He paused. "Look, I've heard too much from your dad to question your salvation, but I'll ask anyway just to give you something to hang on to. Do you belong to Jesus through faith alone?"

"I do."

His eyes were now trained on hers with even greater intensity. "You haven't earned it, right?"

"No. I can't earn salvation, only what Jesus did on the cross can do that." A familiar verse came to mind, that those who call upon the name of the Lord will be saved, its promise reminding her of the day she had made that call.

"I asked Him to forgive me of my sins. I asked Him to be the Lord of my life." Her words grew quieter. "It's that last part that keeps coming to mind,

Him not being my Lord. I haven't exactly walked closely with Him since my dad left. I didn't run away exactly; I just haven't run to Him like I used to."

"We've all had those seasons. I have. But once we're His, we're His."

Reassurance came as she whispered, "Jesus said no one will snatch us out of His hand."

"That's exactly right," Wyatt said. "The rescue is for all who have called upon His name for salvation. If you don't settle this one thing, Paige, you'll know nothing but anxiety and fear in the time to come."

With an unconvincing tone she said, "I'm good. You can continue."

He sat and seemed to study her for a few seconds as if he wanted to say more. Instead, he looked back at the open Book. "Twelve is what we read yesterday about those things too disgraceful to speak of, so we won't cover that."

He glanced up at her. "Thirteen says, 'But all things become visible when they are exposed by the light, for everything that becomes visible is light.'

"I'm sure you've guessed it by now," he said. "Daybreak is here to expose the darkness to light. That's not exactly how we started, but that's what it's become."

"Since my mom died?"

"Yeah. When she was gone, and once your dad put all the pieces of her death together, he tried to get others to see it, people higher up the chain of command."

"Government people?"

"Yes. But they didn't see the threat as credible, that it was the beginning of what would ultimately be used as biological warfare."

Wyatt paused and scratched his newly close-cropped beard, then notable anger flashed in his eyes. "We know now that wasn't the case. When your dad presented his suspicions about China, the Senate committee that oversaw our operations made quick work of dismantling the team. Honestly," he paused, glanced away, and then back at her, "he did sound pretty unhinged. As you know, he went a little off the rails after your mom's death."

She nodded. "But you think they knew better?"

"Yeah. One of the senators was later linked to a corporation owned by the CCP. When that was exposed to the light," Wyatt grinned, "he was removed from the committee and eventually forced to give up his Senate seat."

"That's when you branched out and became a private entity?"

"Unintentionally so, yes. Your dad discovered that one of the daughters of the lab worker wasn't home when the family was killed. A family friend got her out of Wuhan the day after the attack. Our first Daybreak mission was to get her out of China."

"That's where my dad went when he disappeared, to save her?"

"Yes. He ran the op from Manila."

"And she's safe now?"

"She is, living here in the States. It was a victory your dad needed, but he still carries the weight of what happened to your mom and to the girl's family."

"Were all of you," she pointed toward the tech zone with the named monitors, "part of the original task force?"

"All but Dollar. After the senator was exposed, your dad was asked to resume the task force. But by then, he didn't know who in the upper ranks he could trust. When I returned from Asia, he told me he wanted to take things in a new direction. While under the command of an oversight committee, we had limitations. Now, we pursue what we deem to be a reasonable threat and help the people who really need it.

"We only really understood the extent of it after the fact, but much of what the committee had authorized us to do only served to further their personal agendas."

"You said when you returned from Asia. Did you help the girl?"

"I did."

"Did you go in alone?"

"Yes."

Paige studied him for a few seconds. Once again, unless she asked the right questions, he had no intention of elaborating. His jaw muscles were tight, and he seemed uncomfortable talking about himself.

He finally smiled. "This is the good part for you, Paige. When your dad decided to redefine our mission, he said he picked the name Daybreak because of something your mom once said. Missions were tough and the opposition was getting only more sinister. All he could see at the time was evil rising, the dark overtaking the light. Your mom reminded him that no matter how bleak things may look or how defeating a day might seem, daybreak will come again, that next rising of the sun to scatter the shadows."

"That just made me sigh inside." Paige touched her hand to her chest. "She had the most beautiful way with words."

"So do you." He glanced down and then when he looked back up, he never actually looked her in the eye. "Your words move people. You must get that from her."

"I'm not so sure about that."

"Maybe you don't see in yourself what others do. I'm praying that'll change for you."

"One thing may be changing," Paige said. "I looked up one of the verses you gave me last night. I see what you meant in your notes about Matthew twenty-four, why people disagree over it. The passage is certainly addressing the final judgment and second coming. But I can also see how some would view the part about Noah entering the ark as being a picture of the rapture."

Wyatt said, "I've had friends who don't see eye to eye with me on this–and that's okay. It isn't something believers should argue over. Where some see the entire latter portion of the chapter as only in direct response to the disciples' questions about the end of the age, I see the verses about the days of Noah as something of an insertion, a whisper of a reminder that God will rescue His church before the tribulation as He did with Noah before the flood."

"That's what I see," Paige said. "To me it seems like the focus shifted and was referring to the rapture, the righteous being removed." She paused in thought. "It's a familiar passage, but this time I noticed something I never have. It's the word 'before'; it says before the flood came people were eating and drinking, marrying and giving in marriage, clearly ignoring the warnings that Noah was giving."

Wyatt nodded.

Her heart quickened. "If this passage is indeed a whisper of the rapture, then life is more normal when He comes for the church. That part can't possibly be talking about the actual second coming at the very end of the tribulation. Life will be anything but normal; it will be hell on earth after all that Revelation says will happen."

"Exactly," he said. "There are two separate comings of the Lord: the appearing to get His Bride and the actual arrival for the battle of Armageddon when we come back with Him. I believe this particular part is about the appearing.

"Like you said, they were living life as they normally would, ignoring the warnings of Noah that judgement was coming. We won't go into it now, but there are other implications in that comparison of the days of Noah: the level of wickedness of the people and the intermingling of genetics."

"This is another reassurance, isn't it?"

"It is to me." With a broadening smile, he said, "Yeah, the Word clearly settles onto the Paige."

It wasn't easy to ignore his dimples, and understandably after her dream of him, the marrying and giving in marriage verse dusted her cheeks with a pink glow. "What's that supposed to mean?"

"Your grasp of the Word, like your dad said, the way you see things without someone having to explain them to you. Honestly, I didn't pick up on that detail on my own, about life being normal before the flood. There's no telling how many times I had read the verse but never made the connection. It was finally explained in something I read or else I may have never noticed it."

Wyatt stood. "Echo is waiting. He'll spend a little time with you looking up more of what you call nonsensical."

Paige jumped to her feet. "I don't think it's nonsensical. I think it's more that..." She blinked and blinked again. "I don't know. It's just so much to take in."

"That's okay. Everyone at Daybreak has been where you are."

Puzzle Pieces

Day 2, 7:40 a.m.

"Good morning," Echo said, then sipped on his coffee. "I hear you're planning on joining the caravan going up?"

She sat in the seat next to him and thought for a second. "You mean the rapture?"

"I do." His eyes grew wider. "If not for that hope, I'm not so sure I could get up some days."

A pit formed again in her stomach, or maybe it was the weight of three breakfasts trying to digest.

When she didn't respond, Echo said, "I know it's scary, Paige. One day you're minding your own business and living life, then Arrow shows up and brings you here." With a hint of sadness, he said, "Life will never be the same. Once you know, you can never unknow."

"Truth is, I don't think I want to know all you know."

"You don't," he said. "I can promise you that. I dig deeper and deeper and find there's no end to the putrid corruption and absolute evil I'm seeing. Some days my mind feels clouded, and I question if I'm going a little crazy. Then I look again at the evidence and follow even the smallest trail, and it reaffirms what I know."

He rolled his chair a little closer. "My mind tries to protect me by shutting down and going on auto pilot. I have to give it a little shake from time to time.

"For you," he said with a soft tone, "you don't have to know it all. From an aerial view it's still pretty easy to see the image that's emerging. It's jarring enough to wake even the soundest sleeper."

"Like you said, I don't want to sleep through this."

For the first time since arriving, Paige was more curious than frightened. She had always been a critical thinker, one who could take a series of facts and form a logical conclusion. If what Wyatt and Echo said was true, and she had been denied basic facts by a media who fed her lies, then she would keep digging until she found the facts. The idea of being duped gave irritation a primary place over fear. These men who were guiding her, men her dad trusted with her life, were voices she could trust to tell as much truth as they possessed.

While Echo typed, Paige stared at the blank screen with the alias: Apex. "When's the last time you heard from him, the last time you saw his face on that screen?"

Echo followed her eyes to the monitor. "Tuesday afternoon. When he called Wyatt to go get you."

"And you've found nothing?"

"A few dead ends."

Paige steadied her voice when she said, "I heard shots."

"I know. Wyatt told me."

"He could be..." She looked up at the screen and prayed.

"I'm not giving up," Echo said. "I know him well enough to believe he's found a place to lay low. His only concern was getting you to safety. Because he knows Wyatt will take care of you, he can stay in hiding until he finds a way to safely contact us."

"You really believe that?"

His eyes held resolve. "I really do. He's the Apex for a reason."

"Did you name him that?"

"I did. He's the tip of the spear."

"I can see him being that." She glanced up at the monitors. "And Arrow is Wyatt."

"He is, straight as an arrow."

Paige could see that too. "So, you've given them names based on personality traits and their roles on the team?"

"All but Wyatt's name. Your dad began calling him that long before Daybreak dawned." He smiled. "I've never said it that way, but I like it."

"Yeah, I like it too."

A stirring came again, the acknowledgement that her dad had such a deep and close relationship with Wyatt. This time, rather than a sense of semi-jealousy, it was a sensation of what felt like loss, in that her dad had kept someone so important to him a secret.

"Paper," he said with a quick smile, "anything and everything Wyatt tells you is true to the best of his knowledge. A word that your dad once used to describe him is incorruptible. I can't think of a better term. He won't lie for any reason, even undercover. He's the most devoted and loyal-to-the-cause-of-Christ man I've ever known–your dad included. Your dad says that of Wyatt too."

With a flash of her morning dream in mind, her cheeks flushed. She hoped to wrangle her drifting thoughts by asking, "When you said you don't have Wyatt's same directive, you meant to watch over me in part, but in context that didn't fully make sense."

His expression shifted, and like she had seen of Wyatt, Echo appeared to be choosing his words with care. "Watching over you is multi-faceted. Where any other man would consider your physical safety the only objective, Wyatt is different. He's concerned with your emotional well-being."

"You're not?" Her lips tugged into a quick grin. "That's why you're willing to hit me with both barrels?"

"I was willing to hit you with all I've got, but now my directive has changed."

"How's that?"

"I've been told to give you only what you need for now."

"I tried to read something last night," she said. "Did you remove the documents on the World Economic Forum from my folder?"

"I did."

"And my WiFi was down. Was that to keep me from digging around?"

"Just until we could talk this morning."

"That irks me more than a little." Her eyes darted to the living area where Wyatt sat scouring over a stack of documents. "I'm not delicate. I may be a little off balance with all that's happened the past couple of days, but I'm Evan Donovan's daughter. I'm resilient."

"I don't doubt that at all. But I follow orders."

She started to stand until Echo reached out a hand. "It's not that he doubts your ability to understand or process it. I just know he has a plan to roll this all out differently now. Trust him, Paige."

From across the vast space, she studied the back of Wyatt's bent head, choosing to trust him because her dad trusted him.

She looked back at Echo. "Wyatt says this is like a puzzle that forms one massive image. Give me the pieces you think I'm ready for today."

"Using that metaphor then," he said, "this is like a ten-thousand-piece puzzle. Each quarter of the puzzle is its own image made up of thousands of pieces. Those, when snapped together with the others, make up the aerial view. What if, today, we just catch a glimpse of the four corners?"

"Agreed."

Echo typed as Paige watched the big screen. A colorful timeline appeared. "This is what you need to know first, the progression of things as best we can determine from prophecy." His face lit up. "It's crazy cool that we have a prophetic map to follow. I live for stuff like this."

Crazy cool? Paige couldn't express how opposite she felt about it at the moment. None of this was even remotely cool to her.

"First the rapture," he said, "as you see by the purple arrow pointing up. Imagine what the world will look like when hundreds of millions of believers vanish: police and military personnel gone, pilots in mid-flight, and drivers no longer at the wheel. Those things alone will cause world-wide mass catastrophes."

"Like the Left Behind book."

"Very likely. I've read a pretty credible poll that would suggest in the U.S. alone there's over a hundred million true, born-again Christians. That's nearly a third of our population just gone in an instant." He shook his head. "Beyond the damage and carnage, think of the people who'll realize what's happened, that they've been left behind. How many have sat in pews on Sundays and played church? Many have had family and friends to warn them. Still, they've put off the decision to follow Christ. I can't even conceive of the fear they'll feel and regret they'll suffer when salt and light are removed."

Already Paige's heart was beating erratically, her claim to resilience now in question. She couldn't help but ask, "What will they do?"

"That's a point I'll make another time, if that's okay?"

She nodded and tried her best to swallow the lump in her throat.

"I believe," Echo said, "that the total chaos that ensues is what will eventually usher in the Antichrist. It's what will lead people to follow this man. They will be looking for answers, and he'll have them. Know this: The truth of what happens to us will be hidden from the masses." He seemed to try to hide a grin. "I have some pretty crazy theories of the lies he'll use, but that's something I'll save for another time too."

Echo wiggled his cursor over the next event on the timeline. "The next seven years is the tribulation, also called the Time of Jacob's Trouble. When the Antichrist comes onto the scene and confirms a peace treaty with Israel, that one act will be the official beginning of the tribulation. That's when all hell will break loose.

"There are two reasons we believe the rapture has to happen soon: One is that the nation of Israel has been regathered, creating what I believe to be a bit of a timestamp. That's one quarter of the puzzle. Many prophecies of the last days didn't make sense up until 1948, when Israel was reborn as a nation. They were scattered as a people for over two thousand years. Never has a nation been so decimated and dispersed then reunited as happened to Israel.

That in itself is proof of God's divine hand on His people. The story is fascinating. For our purpose today, though, I'll just say it's a mega-sign of the end. When we have time to take a detour someday, I'll tell you about the parable of the fig tree and some differing interpretations. More crazy coolness."

With a clear grimace, he said, "The second reason I believe the rapture has to be close is that the stage is already set for the key events the Bible says will happen during the tribulation. Those are our other three quarters of the larger image we'll discuss today. All the foundational elements for those three things are already in place. What we see forming right now is what will be the intensifying evil of the tribulation."

Paige whispered to herself, "We won't be here for that part."

Echo paused and looked at her. "Right, we won't." He sat for a few seconds. "Paige, you absolutely have to settle that. I know you're a believer." He leaned in and rested his elbows on his knees. "I see this a lot, though. Because people don't know much about the rapture, it seems too outlandish to be a thing. It's a thing. It's our hope, our rescue, our way out."

She nodded and then sat looking at Echo, trying to allow the puzzle pieces she had so far to fall into place. Finally, she said, "Will you give me a minute?"

"Sure."

Paige went to her room and sat with her Bible in her lap. She flipped to John, needing reassurance that what Wyatt and Echo said was true.

"Do not let your heart be troubled; believe in God, believe also in Me. In My Father's house are many dwelling places; if it were not so, I would have told you; for I go to prepare a place for you. If I go and prepare a place for you, I will come again and receive you to Myself, that where I am, there you may be also." (John 14:1-3)

Great Reset

Day 2, 8:30 a.m.

With Bible in hand, Paige entered the tech zone to find Echo on the phone. He became quiet when she entered. Eventually, he said, "Call when you hear something."

"Ready for more?" he said.

"Was that about my dad?"

"Just Cade checking in. Nothing new."

Paige gripped her Bible tighter. "I'm not sure how ready I am, but I've come a little better prepared."

"Good for you," he said and reached out to tap her Bible. "What we'll cover next is all right here.

"Our struggle in doing that is, as it's said of the devil himself, the current-day darkness often masquerades itself as light. God isn't the only one to have people in place for such a time as this. The devil has raised up people all around the globe. He wants to be like God. He tries to mimic His actions and ways.

"Those people present themselves as do-gooders and philanthropists and appear to want good for the world when nothing is further from the truth. Some are motivated by greed and power, while others are genuinely Luciferians, driven by a desire to usher in the Antichrist."

Already, the term Luciferian had Paige ready to bolt, but she sat waiting, instead, pretending she was more prepared than she really was.

He reached for his keyboard and pointed to the large screen, then typed until the site appeared with the name World Economic Forum. "Tell me what you know about this group so far."

Paige said, "They were one of the sponsors of Event 201. They plan to use the pandemic as a way to do something called the Reset to bring the world together economically."

"Great Reset," Echo said.

She nodded. "They are a group of wealthy elites. Many of the world's leading CEOs, billionaires, and prominent politicians are part of it."

"And?"

It took a few seconds for her next words to form: "They are setting the stage for the Antichrist and are the ones who are writing the narrative everyone else is following."

"That's a good start. They are doing their part on the economic side, along with the U.N.'s Agenda 2030. We're told in Scripture that a one-world government, religion, and economy will form. That's all happening as we speak." Echo reached for his tablet. "Turn to Revelation thirteen."

When Paige began to flip pages, he said, "Have you studied this at all?"

"Almost none. I know some of the terminology from sermons and what's described in the Gospels, but I've been..."

"Scared of the book of Revelation?"

"Yeah."

"That's okay. Someday soon, we will cover the letters to the churches and the other early chapters, but for today let's take a look at chapter thirteen, verse two. It says the dragon, meaning Satan himself, will give the beast, who is the Antichrist, his power and throne and great authority. So that tells us the Antichrist will rule a vast global empire. That's the one-world government.

"Verse three says 'the whole earth was amazed and followed after the beast'." He looked up at her. "That's after something that seems to be miraculous happens. Most scholars assume this fatal wound and healing is what appears to be the death and being raised back to life of the Antichrist." He paused. "Remember, he wants to do what Jesus did and be worshiped as a messiah."

Paige looked back down and studied the words before her. "In verse four, it says they, the people of earth, will worship the dragon, Satan, because he gives his authority to the Antichrist. And they will worship the beast." She looked up at him. "This is the one-world religion?"

"That's right." He hesitated, then said, "It's already beginning. I'll show you more on that in a minute." His eyes grew wider with his next statement. "I won't get us off track, but look up something called The Giant. There will be twenty-one giant statues placed around the globe, artificial intelligence that can take on a person's image and talk and move." He shuddered. "I've seen a lot of creepy stuff, but that level of AI makes my skin crawl."

"That's what the people will be forced to worship?"

"I can't say so for sure, but it sure sounds like King Neb's statue that Shadrach, Meshach, and Abednego refused to bow to and worship."

Paige said, “You know this scares me to death, right?”

“Anyone who says they feel otherwise when looking at this fast-moving train is lying.”

Echo’s words reminded her of Wyatt’s assurance, that the rapture was like a snatching away from an oncoming train.

For a moment Echo sat looking at her. “Listen to me, Paige. What I’m about to pour out here is like a waterfall of bad news. It’s more than anyone can take in all at once. I’ll give you the highlights, but even skimming the surface of evil is mind-bending.” His words were reassuring. “Just hang with me. We can stop and revisit anything you need repeated. Agreed?”

When she nodded, he looked back at his tablet. “Verse seven says that he, the Antichrist, has authority over every tribe and people and tongue and nation. Something has to happen to bring all the nations together, some worldwide catastrophic event or series of events.”

“Like the virus or the rapture?”

“Maybe both,” he said, “since the virus is what they’re currently using to condition everyday people to accept a global society as necessary. It’s a commonly embraced ideal in political and economic circles already. If they are allowed to proceed unhindered and the world economy does come together, when the Antichrist rises to power, the mechanism for controlling the people and their money will already be in place, especially with the advancement of the proof-of-jab passports. The Antichrist steps in, plug and play.”

With a wave of his tablet, he said, “Here, in these early verses, we see both the one-world government and a hint of the one-world religion components, even though those terms are never actually used.

“Still in chapter thirteen, John tells about the rising of another beast, the false prophet. That’s when the people are forced to worship the beast, some kind of image.”

She blew out a long breath. “Maybe that big AI giant.”

“It has my vote. Since the Antichrist knows he only has seven years, whatever he plans to use then has to be in place before he steps in. That means now. Everything is in place already.”

“Then people will be forced to take the mark?” she said.

“That’s right, at the midpoint. They will take a mark on their right hand or forehead.” Echo held up his right hand. “The last time I went to the dentist, they asked me to hold out my wrist to take my temp. That’s conditioning, getting people accustomed to holding out their hand to be scanned.”

Her heart plummeted. "When I go get a haircut, they check my temp on my forehead before I can go in."

"Both are conditioning," Echo said. "It's subtle, like it's for everyone's safety."

All she could do was stare at him, her mind filled with questions she didn't want answered. Finally, she said, "It's making more and more sense all the time. The mark really will be tied to the virus with the pretext of keeping people safe."

"From all I'm seeing right now, it's very likely." He flipped over to chapter eighteen. "This is a little outside of what I wanted to cover, but in verse twenty-three, it says 'all the nations were deceived by your sorcery'. That word sorcery is the Greek word *pharmakeia*, the word where we get pharmacy. So in essence it's saying the nations will be deceived by pharmaceuticals or medicine."

Paige actually struggled to swallow the lump in her throat.

As if reading her thoughts, he said, "And..."

She said in what came out as a little-girl's voice, "And we won't be here for that."

He leaned in closer. "Exactly. We will be celebrating a wedding."

Paige's heart beat a little faster. "The wedding supper of the Lamb."

"That's right." He paused and grinned. "I'm glad you know about that. We need something to steel our hearts, a promise for our future, when we are viewing all the bad that's to come." A look settled on his face, a mixture of sadness and pain. "Isn't it tragic for those left behind, though, that we will be at a massive party in heaven while they are down here suffering?"

Tears stung her eyes when she nodded.

Echo hesitated a moment as if in quiet reflection then began again. He navigated to many of the WEF's site locations, and Paige could see what he was talking about: It was openly presented that they were using the global pandemic as an opportunity to bring the world together under what it called "a new form of capitalism".

Echo said, "See here: As if they've read the Book, they intend to create exactly what's prophesied: a one-world economy managed by these benevolent billionaires and bureaucrats. This is an example of Satan presenting himself as an angel of light. The Forum uses as its foundational ideals the social issues much of the world is concerned about today: the economy, the environment, health, hunger, equality, and social justice. All these are valid concerns, ones that will tug at the heartstrings of the masses and get them on board. What the globalists portray as the solution to these issues is presented as what we know as socialism, when in reality it's an even more terrifying prospect than communism. Their intention is to take absolute control over every area of our lives, far beyond anything we've seen in world history, including Hitler and Stalin.

"This will position the world for the select few to make all the rules and everyone else to carry out their orders. That's not how man was designed. We were made in God's image to be creative and ingenious and inventive.

"Our freedom in this nation stands in the way of their plan. Notice this," Echo wiggled his cursor over a phrase, "*Build Back Better*. Does that ring a bell?"

Her eyes widened.

"Yeah," he said, "it became the campaign slogan for our new administration; no big surprise since our new president is a globalist agenda supporter."

Paige read the caption on their website aloud: "To build back better, we must reinvent capitalism."

Echo nodded at the screen. "That phrase 'reinvent capitalism' is a major red flag. During the previous years, these globalists had no hope of drawing the U.S. into a one-world economy since we were still holding onto a nationalist form of capitalism. That's all changing rapidly now. With an administration totally willing to sell us out, we could be a part of their socialist agenda in no time."

A video began to play titled: *You Will Own Nothing and Be Happy.* Sponsored by the World Economic Forum, it predicted a utopian-like society by 2030 where people will literally own nothing and rent everything, the U.S. won't be a superpower, and a handful of countries will dominate.

When Echo stopped the video midway through, Paige shook her head. "That's flat out creepy. This is all out there for anyone to see?"

"It is. Most of it's on their website. I think this video has been removed from their site, but you can find it online. You saw it. I just did a search and all that info came up."

"If we don't own anything, who will we rent from?" Paige said.

"That's a good question." He typed, and a group of familiar faces splashed across the screen, all smiling and looking honorable. "Each year this fine collection of men and women, those global elites we looked at earlier, meet in Davos, Switzerland, with a clear agenda. Under the Forum's vision, the Davos attendees will own what you'll be renting.

"Paige, do you really think this is a philanthropic agenda, that they're doing all this to help people? No! They will all make more money than they currently do and take control of the lives of the people under the guise of equality.

"At least one World Economic Forum member is buying up mass amounts of American farmland." The next image to appear on the screen was a photo of Bill Gates and a caption that listed him as the biggest owner of private farmland in the U.S.

Echo scratched his chin and narrowed his eyes. "Is that a coincidence? Could this buying up of farmland have anything to do with controlling food availability when a famine strikes the world? Or maybe leasing lands to those who will," he used air quotes, "'own nothing and be happy'?"

She sat staring at the screen. "He was one of the sponsors of Event 201."

"That's right." His words were firm. "I'm warning you; people aren't who you think they are.

"We could stay here on this one topic for hours, but I'll jump next to this one." Echo typed again. "Here's a big supporter in the drive toward the global socialist agenda." He paused and turned to her. "The implications of this are staggering."

Paige shifted in her seat and didn't look at the screen; she was pretty sure she couldn't take staggering if it was worse than what she had just seen. "I think I need a break." She grabbed her Bible and stood. "I'll be back in a little while."

Echo nodded and rolled his chair in front of her to stop her from leaving just yet. "I understand," he said, his tone gentle. "Go pray. Ask God to give you His heart on the matter. Your heart and my heart can't withstand it. We have to have His heart and live this out from His perspective."

Her words were soft. "They really are planning on taking control of the world, aren't they?"

He nodded.

She whispered, "And people like me have no idea."

"That's right, Paige. Yet they're doing it all, moving toward this Great Reset, right out in the open."

Unsure if her wobbly legs would even support her, Paige took a step to move around him.

Echo reached for her arm and said, "Remember, this isn't ultimately about people and their move toward socialism. They are merely pawns, evidence that prophecy, God's warning, is coming to pass. The true battle is good versus evil, God versus the devil. God offers salvation for the people. The enemy plans destruction for those same people."

Paige nodded. "How much will we see of this?"

"I don't know, but I do know the One who never fails or forsakes His own."

At the thought of seeing even the early shifts in the world, she actually felt herself sway on unsteady legs. "I'll come back," Paige said. "I just need some time."

With the way she was shaking, when Paige reached the security door, she could hardly stand still enough for her eye to be scanned and had to try a second and third time to gain access. Finally, when she walked through the door and heard it close behind her, she burst into tears and ran for her room.

Not Okay

Day 2, 9:22 a.m.

Rather than climbing into bed, since that would only lead to stress sleep, Paige did the only thing she could do: She dropped to her knees on the shaggy grey rug next to her bed.

Vivid images and narrative words swirled through her mind: wrists and foreheads and scanners, dollar signs and faces of greedy leaders, terms like "beasts" and "Antichrist" and "false prophet".

"My heart can't take it, Lord. My mind can't take it. I don't want this to be real." She repeated those last words several times until Echo's advice came to mind and became her plea: "Give me Your heart, or I'll never bear up under the weight of it."

Paige reached for her Bible before her on the bed and turned to Revelation. She flipped the pages past the letters to the churches and past the broken seals that would bring war and famine and death and martyrs. When she reached chapter thirteen, she scanned the passages Echo had read about the rise of the one who would rule the one-world order that was now forming. It was all right there; God really was warning them in advance.

She straightened and blinked a few times, trying to remember the things Wyatt had said about prophecy the night before at her dad's house. He had said that Jesus told his disciples certain things so that when events happened, they would believe. He said the Bible was nearly one third prophetic.

The thought came again: God was warning them, yet people like herself had done their best to ignore the signs and seasons. She had ignored it all on purpose due to fear.

Wyatt's words now echoed in her head: There was a blessing for those who read and heard and heeded the words in Revelation.

Paige flipped to the first chapter where that was promised. This hardly felt like a blessing, this tightening in her chest and trembling she was experiencing all over. Her first instinct was to try to block it out, to stress sleep in a spiritual sense.

Was that even possible now?

Individuals and major world leaders, whom the people trusted, would line their pockets and grow their power at the expense of the people's lives and freedoms. Whether they knew it or were truly pawns, those globalists were paving the way and setting the stage for the Antichrist to rise and eventually kill millions–billions–of people.

At that, Paige wept. Tears poured down her cheeks. Life as she knew it was truly over. With their plans so far underway and with this much momentum, the global agenda she was seeing wasn't something that could be stopped.

A tap at her door sounded, but Paige ignored it and dropped her head onto her bed to pray. It sounded again; this time Wyatt cracked the door open. His voice was soft. "Paige?"

She said nothing, so he stepped into the room and came to kneel beside her.

After several minutes she raised her head but didn't look at him. "I don't think I can talk about it yet."

"You don't have to. I just wanted to make sure you're not alone and that you're okay."

"Can I ever be again?"

"Not likely, not the okay you once were."

"I haven't been okay in years."

"Then you'll have to learn to live out this new not-okay life. We've all had to do that, including your dad."

Paige moved to sit and lean against her bed. "I won't hide from it anymore, all this ugliness coming our way. My dad wanted me to know."

Wyatt moved from his kneeling position to sit beside her. "I won't let you hide from it. But I'll do my best to keep it from crushing you."

"That's what it feels like already, a crushing weight."

"It takes time." He sighed and shook his head. "Echo told you too much."

"No, it was just a shock to my senses." She blinked and held her eyes closed for a few seconds. "I'll go back and hear what he has to say."

"I don't think that's a good idea."

"I'm shaken," she said, "but I need to know the high-level stuff. If I don't, then how can I prepare?"

"It's not like you really can prepare, not for what's coming. We have no way of knowing how much we'll see. All we can do is live out today."

Paige moved to stand. "That's very cliché, but I suppose you're right." With hand extended she said, "All I know about today is that my dad is missing, those men are evil, and most people are sleeping through what's coming."

Wyatt took her hand and stood when she tugged. "I'll hang with you this time while Echo shows you more."

Paige and Wyatt each sat on a rolling chair and listened while Echo spoke on the phone.

When he hung up, Echo said, "That was Hank." He looked at Paige. "That's Fortress." Then he turned his attention to Wyatt. "Bash is on the inside working for Groves. There's no sign of Evan, but he says security is so tight at the compound, it's not likely he would see him if he was there. Bash will try to do some recon when it gets dark."

"So maybe he's alive," Paige said and looked up at the black screen labeled Apex. "He last checked in on Tuesday, so he's only been missing one full day."

"Right," Wyatt said. "We have every reason to believe he's still out there, either at the compound or on the run."

"If he's at the compound..." Paige didn't want to think what might be happening to him in that case.

"We'll know something tonight. Bash will get a better look."

She only nodded, and with the hope of clearing the horrific images that were beginning to form of her dad being tortured, she said, "I've only gotten one barrel so far. Give me the second."

The look Wyatt gave Echo wasn't lost on Paige. His expression warned Echo to go easy on her.

"Just tell me," she said. "Whatever pieces of the puzzle form the bigger image, I want to know."

"This," Echo said, "is how the one-world religion is well under way." He typed and pointed to the screen.

The caption of the article said: "Pope Francis refers to the flood of Noah as a 'mythical tale' and says God will send judgment on earth not for sin but because of climate change."

Paige read the caption a second time as a burning sensation flared in her belly. "For one," she said, "that's heretical, saying the Biblical account of the flood isn't true." She pondered the statement more, then said, "God judges people for sins against Him not sins against the earth."

Echo smiled and nodded. "But wait! There's more," he said in an infomercial voice. "Pope Francis, Muslim Imams, and even protestant leaders here in the U.S. are calling for religions to unite under the name of Chrislam. There's been a strong movement toward interfaith unity since the '80s, but now it's all coming together."

An image filled the screen, the release of the Vatican's New Age-style cross encircled with the crescent moon of Islam.

"This is the official logo for Chrislam," he said. "The pope declares that a one-world unified religion is willed by God."

Paige couldn't help but let out a little gasp at that while Echo nodded and continued on.

"There are buildings already being built for interreligious worship: The House of One will be built in Berlin and the Abrahamic Family House in Abu Dhabi."

Paige read one article's title aloud: "'Pope Francis is stating his desire to unite the world's religions and create a global religion that will combine elements from Christianity, Islam, Buddhism, and Judaism.'" She blinked and went on. "'He states that 'we are all children of God' no matter what our faiths or religious beliefs might be.'"

Wyatt said, "Is that what the Bible teaches?"

"No, not at all. Only those born again through faith in Jesus are children of God."

Echo said, "Would this fit the bill for a one-world religion?"

Paige tucked her trembling hands beneath her. "Without question."

"So this," Echo said, "combined with what you saw earlier is both the one-world economy and one-world religion taking shape. Clearly, the one-world government will emerge either from those frameworks or alongside them as the Antichrist steps in to govern the world." He sat for a few seconds. "Is this enough for you to see what's beginning to form?"

"How can I not see it?"

"Here's what people aren't connecting," Echo said. "Because they don't understand this global agenda, they're missing the open way in which these globalists are using the coronavirus to navigate them right where they want them. Few are asking questions. Few will believe the answers when you do tell them." For a second, he just sat. "It's all right there. You don't even need to dive deep to see it. What used to be a hidden agenda a couple of decades ago is now their public, applauded plan."

Echo glanced at Wyatt and raised his eyebrows, then looked back at Paige. "I'll save the information about already-existing technology for the mark of the beast that Revelation predicts for later. I just wanted to give you enough to help you begin to put the pieces together for yourself. Until you see the overall agenda underway, it's hard to feel the urgency we feel."

"I see it. It's all right there," she said, "where anyone can see it."

"Still..." Echo shrugged. "I've tried to tell family and friends. They won't look because they don't want to see."

Her voice was quiet. "I've been like that."

"We all have," Wyatt said. "Now, this week, like the rest of the team, you've been thrust to the front lines of the fight."

For a woman who wasn't often fearful, Paige was experiencing a level of trepidation like she had never known. It wasn't necessarily fear for herself, instead, it was more a matter of a cluttered mind, one still filled with frightening images and words. Now, along with those already cumbersome disruptions, questions came: If she was now really on the front lines of the fight, what could she do with what she knew? How and what could she tell? Who would listen to such craziness?

"Remember," Wyatt said with a gentle tone, "the part where the Antichrist steps in all begins after we're gone."

Paige nodded, that assurance doing little to ease her now-tangled thoughts.

Echo said, "But it's becoming clearer to me that we may see the actual formation of the one-world order. As I said before, the devil knows he only has seven years, so the Antichrist will need everything in place when he steps in. I'm not sure what that'll mean for us as believers, but it'll have to lead to persecution when we won't comply."

Paige's wide-eyed expression prompted Wyatt to say, "We don't know that. We could be taken out of here at any time." He rolled a little closer to Paige. "We have to keep looking for the rescue. That's our glorious hope."

Paige nodded and tried to hold herself together, but *persecution, persecution, persecution* kept beating like a drum in her head, reminding her she would likely never be okay again.

"When the Antichrist steps onto the scene," Echo said, "the Bible uses the imagery of him rising up out of the sea. Some say that means he will likely rise up out of obscurity. Some say that means he will rise up out of the nations. The point is: we will leave, and he will rise.

"It's my guess that he's already here, but there's only one way to know that for sure and that's to be here when he rises. I don't plan to be here for that." He chuckled. "I heard a pastor say, 'If you've figured out who the Antichrist is, then you've been left behind.'"

Paige squirmed at his statement. While Echo's words were intended to be amusing, they weren't. If anything, they caused such a burning in her belly that she wondered if she might lose one or all three of her breakfasts.

"I need another break." She stood and walked away without waiting for a response.

Lemonade

Day 2, 1:01 p.m.

Paige's eyes fluttered open, and she looked at the clock after sleeping for nearly two hours. She hadn't intended to go to sleep, but after talking with Echo and Wyatt, her mind had been so utterly filled with chaos, all she could do was fall onto her bed and cover her head with her blanket.

Only now, with the fog of sleep clearing, an image reemerged of her sitting with her father at that metal table in her hazy dream just before waking. Seconds later she jumped from the bed, her feet still tangled in her blanket, and stumbled the first few steps toward the closet. With her footing regained, she opened the door, reached for her go bag, and ran to the bathroom.

Under two minutes later–that thought did actually make her smile–she was bolting through her door and down the hallway leading to the main loft area.

"It makes perfect sense now," Paige said to Wyatt as she dropped her backpack onto the sofa across from where he sat with his laptop.

"What makes sense?"

"The images from my house. They think I have the evidence. Maybe I do."

Wyatt glanced at her go bag and back at her. "You do?"

"Not yet, but I bet I know where to find it." She sat on the sofa nearest him. "I just had a dream about being with my dad at my Aunt Bertie's house. That's where he gave me the password. I couldn't have been more than five or six. My mom was out gardening with Aunt Bertie while my dad and I sat at the kitchen table. He said if anyone other than him or my mom ever tried to pick me up from school, they had to know the password: lemonade." She paused, her mind whirling. "Maybe my dad wanted me to go to her house."

"You think it's connected? It could have just been for you to know I was someone you could trust."

"Until just now, it hadn't even crossed my mind. The dream I just had was different than the day I remember from back then. My dad and I were both young at first, then I blinked once, and we were both this age. Right before I woke, he tapped his temple and said, 'You know what I'm saying.'"

"Where is your aunt's house and why do you have a bag packed?"

"Landry, a little speck on the map of a town a couple of hours south of here." Her eyes grew wider. "And because I'm going there."

"It's too dangerous for you. I'll send someone," Wyatt said. "I can have a team there by tonight."

"You're totally missing the point of what I'm saying," Paige said as she stood. "I'm inviting you along, not asking for permission." With two fingers held up, she said, "You have two minutes."

"I won't let you do this."

She wasn't smiling as she reached for her bag and slung it over her shoulder. "One and three quarters."

Wyatt actually sprinted toward the door leading to the bedrooms. He only hesitated a second, looked back, and pointed. "Don't you walk out that door without me."

Less than a minute later, Wyatt emerged with his own go bag. He stopped in the kitchen and began to rummage through the cabinets, tossing protein bars and bags of chips onto the counter. "I don't want to stop any more than we have to. Come here."

When Paige approached, he stuffed the top of her bag with the snacks, then grabbed a case of water.

With a quick glance at the clock, Paige said, "Time's up."

In the elevator on the way down, Wyatt shook his head. "They will likely be watching your family's house in case you show up."

"That's a risk I'm willing to take."

"Paige –"

"She was my mom's aunt by marriage. Her husband died and she remarried, so their names aren't the same. No one will ever make the connection."

"If you're wrong?"

"We'll pray I'm not."

When they stepped into the warehouse, Paige followed Wyatt past the van and to the row of vehicles.

"Well," he said, "this is your op. What's your pleasure?"

"That's easy." Paige walked to the Range Rover. Like all the rest of the vehicles, the windows were blacked out.

When they both walked toward the driver's side, Wyatt said, "It's your op, but I'm still driving. If you have to duck down like the other day, I don't want us to end up in the ER."

"Fair enough."

Wyatt sat in the driver's seat with the car running. "I need to know what we might be walking into. Have you called her from your phone? They will be watching anyone you've been in contact with."

"I've called her a few times." She blinked and thought about it. "But she was at her son's after her knee replacement." Her mind scrolled through their phone calls. "The last time I talked to her, she was back at her son's taking care of him and his wife while they had the virus. They live an hour away, and I always called his home phone."

Wyatt nodded and sped through the warehouse space, then toward an opening garage door. "Good girl. You always need to ask those questions. Never assume anything or let little details get by you."

Paige nodded, feeling a little queasy still after her time with Echo, Wyatt's erratic driving not helping. What was clear from her morning was: She needed to learn to take in everything around her, no matter how disturbing it was, and never make assumptions again. When they reached the front of the building, she said, "Who is using this part of the building? Is that a real company or a front?"

"They're real. We rent the space to account for our vehicles coming and going. And our deliveries are addressed there." Dimples accompanied his smile. "You're getting good at the cloak and dagger lingo."

"I'm thinking that might be hereditary."

"I suppose you're right."

Paige wanted to pretend this was an adventure, being on a mission out of her house after such a long time of solitude. That was hardly possible. Images of mass chaos and carnage still filled her mind. Billions, she thought to herself, would be left behind. People she loved couldn't see what was coming.

"Talk to me," Wyatt said. "I know you're struggling to make sense of all this."

"Of course I am. I can't. How is all this happening and no one knows it?"

What she didn't dare to mention was the one raging question that brought with it horrific images: Was her dad being tortured?

"Technically," Wyatt said, "it's been coming for thousands of years. The devil has had all that time to study mankind and know how best to keep us occupied while he goes about the business of putting all the pieces into place. He knows every subtle move to make to draw us in, and we never suspect it."

He drove a minute while Paige studied his words. Eve came to mind, how the enemy had known the exact question to ask to draw her in. Did God really say...? It was his way of making her question God and His goodness.

Not so long ago, Paige had read that perspective in her new devotional. After sidestepping a quiet time for way too long and going to church just enough to feel like she was doing her Christian duty, Paige had come to consider herself a starving sheep. That term had come to mind then, so Wyatt's words about silent shepherds starving the sheep had really hit home. Even when in church full time, this stuff, this last-days message, hadn't been preached.

She looked straight ahead rather than at Wyatt. "He really does know how to draw us in." Her heart sank as she understood how easily the enemy had used her hurt and resentment toward her dad against her.

"Do you want to ask questions," he said, "about what Echo told you before I joined you? I told him to take it easy on you. I guess I should have defined what easy is."

"I didn't think I wanted him to take it easy. I'm afraid maybe that was him taking it easy."

"I don't see the need to dump it all on you in one load," he said. "Honestly, there's so much to tell that we can't possibly scratch the surface in one conversation. I still learn something every day: new players, darker agendas, and deeper deceptions. It's too much for me. It's too much for you."

"How do you do this?" she said.

"I've learned to keep looking at the bigger picture rather than the pieces. That keeps me focused and on point. The scope of all that makes up the image of the tribulation was really dragging me under."

"And now?"

"Now I keep focusing on what's coming next for us, not all the ways it's falling into place for when we're gone."

"So you keep focusing on the rapture? That really works?"

"I do, and it does. If not for my faith in that, I'm pretty sure I would drown in all of this." He glanced at her and back at the road. "I went through a really tough time a few months back, like I was staying in a truly hopeless place. I felt the Lord warn me that I was spending too much time looking at the darkness rather than the Light. We truly have to keep looking up rather than at what's ahead of us here."

"I can see that," she said with lungs burning like they were filling with water. "So," she said, "millions are leaving, and billions will be left behind."

He only nodded.

"But even before then, before the rescue, a one-world order is already forming?"

"Right before our very eyes."

"What will that mean for America?"

"I honestly don't know. If I had to guess, I think they'll crash our economy to destabilize us and leave people helpless. I'm not sure how much more could happen here before the rapture. We're an armed people accustomed to freedom. I don't see men and women of this land willingly giving up their arms and properties for anything that even remotely resembles their early stages of socialism."

"I don't either," she said. "Can you see any good ol' Georgia boy handing over his weapons?"

"That's my point." His tone was firm. "There's no way we can guess how this will all play out. That," he said with a distinct nod, "used to keep me awake at night, me trying to figure out the enemy's next moves."

"And now?"

"I try to keep my eyes focused on the here and now rather than the then and there. I ask myself: What can I do today to advance the kingdom and weaken the darkness?"

"I'd like to adopt that attitude, but I'm not so sure I can keep from focusing on what Echo has shown me."

"I really do understand."

"Did you feel like this when you first knew?"

"I did. I spent all my time researching, following the trail of what was coming and who was taking us there. There were times I had to stop and take a step back from it all. Your dad was good for me and always reminded me to keep my eyes on Jesus and His promises."

"I know you said I can't spend time in regret, but I wish I would have listened."

"God's timing is never off: never early, never late. You weren't ready until now." He paused a few seconds. "You may not realize it, but you are ready. You just need to make sure you're standing on the right foundation. Focus on that."

"You mean focus on the rapture rather than the tribulation?"

"Yes. You get that settled in your heart, and you'll be able to withstand whatever comes."

Paige sure wanted to believe that. "Do you think we will face persecution here in America?"

"To some degree, I think so." His tone became softer. "But, Paige, whatever does come, you're not alone. We are here for you. That's why telling people what's coming makes all the difference. We're stronger together." He rolled his eyes. "Another phrase that's been hijacked by the wrong side. But we, as believers, can and do know strength in numbers. We have to band together."

She nodded at that but never replied. What she didn't want to voice aloud was that if she didn't find her dad, then she would be living this out alone. A group of strangers wasn't family, even if her dad had given one of them "lemonade" to assure her he was safe.

Sorrow

Day 2, 1:34 p.m.

A pit stop for a bathroom break and a drive-thru later, and the two were underway again.

"I thought you said we wouldn't stop." Paige unwrapped Wyatt's burger and passed it to him.

"You slept until lunch." He held up two fingers. "Then gave me little time to get ready."

Paige grinned. "That's the most fun I've had in two days."

"You're almost exactly like I thought you'd be."

She took a bite and licked the special sauce off her finger. With mouth still full, she said, "Yeah, how's that?"

"You're like a girl version of your dad, quiet and reflective one minute, then outspoken and bold the next."

"My mom always said I'm just like him."

"It's a compliment to be like him." He hesitated. "I'm sorry you've been apart from him. I know he's been sorry too."

"I'm still kind of ticked off. He could have told me. Even when I didn't want to hear, he could have kidnapped me and brought me to Overwatch. Can't y'all use toothpicks or something to keep people's eyes open to watch the big screen?"

Wyatt chuckled. "I've never tried that technique."

"I wish he would have made me listen."

"You can't make anyone listen, Paige. What little he did tell you drove you away."

"Him leaving me drove me away."

"Well, you two can work through all that with a counselor or something when he gets back. I'm not getting in the middle of a Donovan dispute."

Paige heard the doubt in her own voice. "He's coming back, right?"

"I'll do my best to get your dad home." After a second he smiled and said, "I now have a partner to make that happen."

For a moment Paige wouldn't allow herself to look at him or her ringless finger. Finally, she said, "Since you know all about me, I think it's fair that I get to know my partner."

"I'm from Florida mostly, though we moved a lot when I was a kid since my dad was in the Navy."

"That's why your dad was in and out of the picture?"

"When I was a little kid, yeah. Later on," he paused and looked ahead as he drove, "he wasn't healthy, so my mom wouldn't let him come around."

Paige assumed it was drugs or alcohol but didn't ask. "I'm sorry. That's tough. Do you see him now?"

"No, not in years. I've talked to him a minute here and there."

"What about your mom?"

"I don't see her much. She got remarried when I was in middle school and had a couple more kids. I've never felt like a part of her new family."

"So, my dad and the guys are your family?"

"They are. They're enough." With a good-natured chuckle, he said, "Sometimes way more than enough. We're up in each other's grill too much at times."

The fact that her dad practically had a son and she didn't know didn't bother her as much now. Clearly, Wyatt needed her dad, and her dad was there for him.

"Did you ever meet my mom?"

"I did meet her. She was a great lady."

"Yeah," Paige said with a longing heart. More than missing her mom these days, she wanted to know the Catherine who had an entire hidden life. Paige had so many questions, and unless she found her dad, they would go unanswered.

"Your dad kept the team away from Savannah, away from your home, on purpose. I only met your mom because she came with your dad to D.C. a couple of times."

They rode a few minutes more, Paige's heart growing heavier. "You said when you learned what was happening in the world, that you had to grieve what seemed like loss of what you planned for your future. You said 'then.' Do you feel that loss still? Will it get easier?"

For a long moment he was quiet as he considered her question. "It's not the same as then. I don't feel the loss of it. I know now it's what needed to happen at the time."

"You were seeing someone at the time?"

"I was. And she wanted all the things I knew I couldn't give her and do what I'm called to do."

Paige nodded. Since that conversation, the thought had tried to surface, but each time she pushed it away. She wouldn't likely have those things she dreamed of either: a husband and kids and a couple of dogs–not now. How could she ever go back to any semblance of a normal life knowing what she now knew?

"I won't say it gets any easier," Wyatt said. "You just grow acclimated in some ways to a new reality."

When she was quiet for some time, he said, "I'm sorry. I know this is tough."

"When I go back home, I don't see how things can ever be normal again."

"Paige..."

His sympathetic eyes disclosed a truth she hadn't once considered. "Are you saying I can't go home?"

"I don't know if it'll ever be safe for you to. If we don't take Groves down..."

A meltdown was imminent no matter how much she tried to hold it back. "Stop the car."

"Why?"

"Just stop the car!"

The car had barely come to a stop when she unlocked the door and jumped out. Her heart was actually throbbing, and she couldn't catch her breath. All she could do was drop onto the roadside and bury her face in her hands. Once she began to weep, she had a sense she may never stop. At least internally, it was likely her heart would cry quietly until she died or was caught up or snatched away or whatever Wyatt's Bible-geek terms were.

Wyatt sat next to her without saying a word.

"Please wait in the car," she said through wracking sobs.

"I can't do that."

She could say no more. All she could do was sink deeper beneath the weight of the vision of her future, or lack thereof. It came to mind and she wanted to blame her dad, the one person she was most often able to point to as the source of her pain. If not for him and his work, she would be at home describing colors and architecture and climates on her keyboard instead of sitting on a roadside with nothing but dread and sorrow ahead of her. But it wasn't his fault. Only now did she understand how he had given her an extension of time to live in clueless bliss.

Her dad had grieved alone and kept his pain from her to save her from sharing in it. He had held onto their family and home and belongings after losing his wife and being forced to distance himself from his daughter. Now, in an effort to save innocent girls from pure evil, he was in trouble, maybe worse than that, and here she sat on the roadside crying like a girl.

She wiped her nose on her shirt sleeve, only now realizing Wyatt's hand was on her back, moving in gentle circles.

He moved in close. "Fix your eyes on Jesus, Paige, the author and perfecter of your faith. For the joy set before Him, knowing He would soon go home to His Father, He endured the cross." With a gentle tone, he said, "That's what we have to do now, keep looking at Him while we carry this temporary cross. I promise you, what's on the other side is worth what we'll endure here."

Her voice was barely audible. "I can't see Him at all right now."

"You'll get your vision back. I'll help you."

"I don't know if I'll ever be okay with this."

"The longer you know and see and believe what's on the horizon, the more readily surrender seems to come. At least it's been that way in my case. I was so angry at first, but eventually anger faded into acceptance, then acceptance into surrender. It's a process, one you won't experience overnight."

This was a waste of time. Her dad needed her, and here she was melted into a puddle on a Georgia highway. "We don't have time for this," she said and wiped her nose again. "I'm sorry."

When she tried to stand, he held her arm, forcing her to remain seated. "It's okay to feel and cry and mourn. Allow yourself that. If not, it'll come out at the most inopportune time. Sorrow will devour the soul who refuses to acknowledge its presence."

In acknowledging her sorrow, she was forced to admit, "I'll never have those things either, marriage and kids and a couple of dogs, but I can't imagine ever seeing it as anything but loss."

Wyatt slipped his arm around her shoulder. "Don't say never. I don't want to believe that. We may have a few years left here. I want to believe we will know good in the midst of whatever's coming."

Paige rubbed her face, the embarrassment of her breakdown dawning. "We need to get back on the road." She stood. "We're close now."

The ride was quiet. Wyatt's normally pleasant expression was now drawn and intense. Paige regretted her outburst in front of him. She hadn't been herself at all the past few days.

After half an hour of this, she reached for his arm and watched his muscles tighten beneath her fingertips. "I know you said it's okay, and I believe you mean that, but still, I'm sorry. We've got too much ahead of us for me to melt down like that."

At that she withdrew her hand, but he reached out and covered her hand with his. For a few seconds she watched him, anticipating a response. He didn't turn to look at her; he just drove.

Eventually, he said, "I've always wondered what it would be like, that day when you would have to find out. I never wanted to be the one to tell you." He forced a smile. "So maybe I regret you not listening to your dad as much as you regret it."

"Doubtful." She let out a long sigh and pulled her hand from his. Her emotions were raging, and his hand holding hers felt better than it should. It would be too easy to get confused in the tenderness of the moment.

"How are most of us missing it," she said, "and some like y'all aren't?"

"I think most people are so content living in the physical plane, that it's just easier to stay blinded to spiritual truths. The wonders of this world can easily dim vision, even in the saints."

"I should have been more dialed in."

"You are now, Paige. Even if you did know something wasn't right, it's no surprise that you didn't catch a glimpse of the bigger picture. It's strange how the mind works. We can look at one piece of this puzzle and think it's odd but no big deal. Then we can look at another and think the same thing. Early on for me, I had to keep snapping the pieces together over and over in order to adjust to the scope of all that's going on. Otherwise, it was too easy to dismiss it and pretend it wasn't connected."

When she didn't say anything, he said, "You can't stay stuck here, wondering how you missed it. Instead, you just begin from this point, trusting the Lord's timing."

Thoughts trailed through her mind, ones she had kept to herself for most of her life. "Can I be honest about something, even though I don't want to talk about it right now?" When he nodded, she said, "I'm not excited about heaven."

"When you are ready to talk about that, I'm here."

"Are you excited, really?"

His brows narrowed and he seemed to ponder her question. "I certainly don't dread it with all that's coming."

That didn't seem like a very heartfelt answer from a man looking forward to the rapture.

Wyatt pulled off the road and into Aunt Bertie's driveway. He slowed to a stop and nodded. "Thanks."

"For what?" she said.

"That was for Echo." He tapped a device in his left ear that Paige hadn't noticed him insert.

He turned to her. Once again, his words seemed measured. "I really don't know what's ahead for us. What I do know is that in a world only getting darker, we have to figure out how to shine a whole lot brighter. I hope you'll decide to shine with me, Paige."

"Like, part of the team?"

"Yeah. If you can't go home," he cast his eyes away and back again, "I want you to stay." Without waiting for her to reply, he started up the drive again.

Unsure of which excited her more, his words in light of the memory of her dream or the fact that she was going to her favorite place on the planet, Paige rode along the rutted drive, sorrow fading as her head bobbed and a semi-smile tugged at her lips.

Fireflies

Day 2, 2:40 p.m.

Wyatt came to a stop in front of the house and held her arm as if telling her to wait. Paige moved in closer to the windshield to take in the full view of the pristine-white, two-story Colonial, a vision of Southern elegance at its finest. Two tiers of spindled porches spanned the front of the old home and, as Paige knew, crossed the back too. No better place for sitting and contemplating the world.

A sigh escaped her. "This place..." Memories of arriving, jumping from the car, and running up those steps flooded her mind.

Wyatt looked to their left to take in their surroundings. "Settled on the marshlands." He paused a second. "I've never seen anything like it: Even with all the bugs and birds swooping and diving, there's an absolute stillness here."

"Yeah," she glanced at him, at his expression of wonder. This place did the same to her still, after all these years. "She has about ten acres, but since they're adjacent to the marsh, it's like being out on a secluded peninsula."

"I think I like that from a security standpoint. Does she have a boat?"

"I doubt it these days. She's seventy-two."

"And lives here alone?"

"She sure does. You'll understand when you meet her." Paige reached for the door handle. "Come on. I can't wait to get in there."

His nod showed his hesitation, but Paige got out of the car anyway. She wasn't scared. If anything, this was the first moment's peace she had known since Tuesday afternoon.

Everything about the place was exactly as she remembered. At the top of the porch steps, she stopped and turned to look back at the lush green grass. To the right was the spring-fed pond she had fished with her dad, and beyond that grew hedges of white azaleas just this side of the densely wooded marsh front.

To the left was deep foliage leading to more coastal marshlands. Aunt Bertie's green thumb was evident as the beauty of blood-red cannas and Southern blue flag irises speckled one massive bed.

"When I close my eyes, I can see fireflies and taste watermelon." She let out a long breath. "My mom and dad are rocking here on the porch while Aunt Bertie talks about Jesus."

Paige opened her eyes to find Wyatt there by her side, eyes closed.

"I'd give anything to see that sight," he said. When he did look at her, he smiled. "This is maybe the prettiest place I've ever been in my life."

She nodded at that and stood wishing she could go back to any one of the nighttime summer scenes she had just described. "I think it is for me too."

Wyatt's nearness was soothing. His kindhearted manner tended to bring her comfort. To know her dad cared for this man so much as to grow him up in the Lord softened her heart toward him in a remarkable way.

She turned and smiled at him. "I'll knock, but I'm guessing she's out back on a sunshiny day like today."

When her knocks went unanswered, Paige jogged down the steps with Wyatt on her heels, then the two walked around the pond side of the house to the back.

"I knew I'd find you here," Paige said.

The wide-brimmed straw hat raised and turned, the platinum hair beneath swinging as Aunt Bertie shook her head in slow exaggeration. "I think I might be in heaven and seeing an angel." She stood fast, still as spry as ever, her smile radiating the youthful energy of a woman decades her junior.

"I'm not sure I've ever been called an angel."

"Probably not. I'm giving grace, sweetie," she said with all the refinement of a proper Southern matriarch. She met Paige on the lawn and wrapped her arms around her neck. Then she held Paige back to look at her. "I know what a rascal you are."

Bertie took a step back and looked at Wyatt. "I suggest you get some better company, young man. This girl will get you a whooping fast."

Wyatt let out a soft chuckle. "Yeah, how's that?"

"She gets into my cookies and will cut a piece of cake intended for a church social. I can't take my eyes off this girl one minute when she's here. I can't get her to make a bed or pick up a dirty towel. And you can forget her cooking."

Paige batted her eyes. "I've matured since I was here last."

"I'm not sure I believe that," Wyatt said. "I've been cooking for and cleaning up after you the past couple of days."

With a quick grin at Wyatt, Paige said, "Maybe there's an element of truth to it."

The expression in his brown eyes kept Paige smiling. "Aunt Bertie, this is Wyatt."

"Nice to meet you, Wyatt." Bertie looped her arm through Paige's. "Come on inside. I've got half a blueberry pie I'm willing to share."

Paige felt a teeny burst of joy invade her heart, her first in countless months. "I'm up for that."

"And we might even give your young man a bite or two."

With cheeks flushing, Paige said, "He's not my young man. He works with Dad."

They climbed the back porch steps as Wyatt held the screen door open, a nod and a wink from Bertie saying she believed otherwise.

Paige shrugged her shoulders at Wyatt, and he gave a good-humored wink back at her.

"Aunt Bertie," Paige said while the woman busied herself with getting plates and cutting pie, "have you heard anything from my dad?"

"Not recently, no." She stopped and straightened, then turned to look back at them. "It's been a few months, since Christmas I guess."

Tears threatened to come since her dad had only sent her a card. "He called you at Christmas?"

"No, just a card this year. But he usually calls."

Paige tapped the well-worn oak table, a different one than the vintage table of her youth. "I hoped you had heard from him recently."

She glanced at Wyatt with blood rushing to her cheeks. He must think this a waste of time, following her hunch.

"He wouldn't have called, Paige," Wyatt said. "He would more likely have sent something."

Bertie set a piece of pie in front of each of them. "I'll go grab the mail off the table in the front hall. I haven't even sorted through it."

Wyatt's words gave Paige new hope. When Aunt Bertie left the kitchen, she said, "He only called me Tuesday night, so if he did mail something, it might not be here yet."

"That's my thought," Wyatt said. "Now that I'm here and see your connection to the place, I could see your dad doing something like that."

"Why wouldn't he have sent it to you at Overwatch?"

He shrugged. "I can't say for sure."

His eyes held evident discomfort, so she said, "Any ideas?"

"I've got nothing here out of the ordinary," Bertie said when she returned with a stack of junk mail that landed in the garbage.

Wyatt stood and got the third plate and brought it to the table for Aunt Bertie. Something about his exit from the conversation gave Paige a bit of a stomachache.

She said, "Would it be okay if we stay until tomorrow to see if something arrives?"

"We can go to a hotel if it's an imposition," Wyatt said.

Paige shot him a sharp glance just as Bertie reached out to slap his arm.

Bertie said, "That's a dimwitted suggestion from such a striking young man. I had a little more hope for you than that."

"I saw that coming," Paige said and then took a bite of her pie.

"I didn't want to intrude." This time he saw another slap coming and moved his arm in time. "But now that I think about it, I would love to stay."

"That's better." Bertie scooped a hunk of pie onto her fork. "I'll thaw something fattening for dinner."

"Fattening is my favorite, ma'am," he said, not expecting another light-hearted slap to his arm.

"It's Aunt Bertie, not ma'am."

Wyatt looked across the table at Paige. "Sorry, Aunt Bertie."

With her pie finished, Bertie sat back in her chair. "Is your dad in danger?"

Paige looked at Wyatt, remembering what Echo had said about him never lying, even undercover. She wouldn't lie either to someone she loved so much.

"He is in danger. I'm hoping he has sent something that will help us find him."

"So it's about Daybreak?"

Paige could hardly get the sputtering words out. "You know about that?"

"He calls me to check in from time to time."

Her tone was more biting than intended. "He's kept in touch with you more than his own daughter." Her voice grew a little louder. "He's told you about Daybreak and not me?"

Bertie held out a hand to shush her, so Paige did just that.

"Paige, he knows I see it, so we've had many a conversation. He's tried with you. We both have. The times I've mentioned what's going on in the world, you've not only shut me down but made an excuse to hang up. I stopped talking about it because you pulled away when I did. I didn't want you to stop calling me at all."

"I wouldn't have done that."

"I'm not so sure about that. Your dad agreed. We both knew we would never get through to you if we pushed you away entirely."

Paige lowered her head and rested it on her clasped hands, taking several deep breaths to keep from crying.

"He wasn't angry." Bertie reached out and stroked her back. "Me either. We just agreed you weren't ready to hear what we had to say. Only the Lord can ready a heart and open the eyes."

"And a gunshot on the other end of the line," Paige said when she looked back at Aunt Bertie.

"You think he was shot?" Bertie's eyes grew misty.

"I think maybe so."

Paige looked over at Wyatt, but he looked away.

Bertie said, "I'm not ready to let go of another one I love."

"I'm not ready to let him go either." Paige reached out and took Bertie's hands. "We'll do everything we can to find him."

Bertie nodded and stood. "I'll get this mess cleaned up. You two go get settled in." She pointed at Wyatt. "You're at the far end next to my room. Paige will show you."

Wyatt shot Paige a look that said that wasn't going to happen. "I appreciate you watching out for Paige," he said to Bertie. "That's my objective, too, so I'll have to be closer than that." His expression softened with his smile. "I promise you can trust me with her."

Bertie nodded and patted his arm where she had slapped him. "I can see that in your eyes."

Paige led Wyatt up the staircase when he came in from fetching their go bags. "These worn old wooden steps have carried the people I love to bed more times than I can count." She continued down the hall and stopped at the room where her parents used to stay. "This is you. I'm just next door."

"Do you need to rest a while?" he said. "Today has been a hard one."

"I'm not sure what I need right now."

"I'll be next door when you're ready to go back down."

"Okay," she said and closed the door behind her.

Paige tossed her bag onto the bed, the iron headboard rocking and creaking a little from the movement. Her mom and Bertie had painted that headboard white out in the back yard one summer when Paige's dad had been overseas for an extended tour. They had spent several weeks here that year, and Bertie had said she wanted to make one of the boys' old rooms more fitting for a girl.

After that, Paige had spent weeks here each year until she turned sixteen and got her first summer job.

A tap sounded on the door and Aunt Bertie entered with her arms loaded. "Here's some fresh sheets. I've gotten your young man settled in next door."

"He's really not my young man. I wouldn't lie to you."

"I've seen love look at me more than my fair share. Say what you will, but love is looking at you through those tender brown eyes, Paige."

Her heart fluttered at Aunt Bertie's words, but with her dad's life on the line, love was the last thing on Paige's mind. "Even if that were true, this is no time to pursue something like that."

"Every day is a day to pursue love. Our toughest days may be the best ones of all. The Lord knows what we need and provides."

"To what end?" Paige said. "With all that's going on in the world, we wouldn't have a future. There would be no joy or happiness or normal life with him."

Bertie grinned and sang, "But love sure would be a fun ride on your way out of this place."

Before Paige could respond, Bertie walked to the door. "I need to finish up in the garden. When you're done moping, come give me a hand."

"Yes, Aunt Bertie."

She grinned at her. "That's a good girl."

This was exactly where Paige needed to be at the moment, a place where Aunt Bertie ordered her around and fireflies would light up the night sky.

Joy

Day 2, 4:07 p.m.

Near the bottom of the stairs, Paige stopped and stood looking into the living room, a room she had intentionally avoided viewing so far. The furniture was well used, threadbare in a few places where family and friends had gathered over the years. How many times had she sat in that room with her parents and Aunt Bertie, laughing and playing games?

Now, under the circumstances of her current worldview, that level of happiness would never be a part of her life again. It wasn't just that her mom was gone and maybe her dad too. It was the scope of all that was going on in the world and what that would mean for her future. How could anyone ever live a normal life once knowing?

She stepped down another step, and the walnut floorboard creaked, a sound that brought a smile at the memory of Aunt Bertie's nighttime warning to keep herself in her room when she was boy-crazy.

Wyatt said from the top floor, "Where are you sneaking off to?"

That the squeaking board had alerted him made Paige laugh a little. "Just out to garden with Aunt Bertie."

"You can't be running off without me." He jogged down the steps and caught up with her. "I was on the phone and missed you leaving. I thought you'd stop by if you left."

"I'm sorry, Watchman Wyatt. I'll be louder next time."

On the way through the kitchen, Wyatt stopped at the counter and reached for the last piece of pie.

Paige pointed. "Forks are over there."

"Who needs a fork?" He scooped up the pie with his hand and carried it with him. "You really are a bad influence," he said as he took the first bite. "I wouldn't normally be a pie thief, but I think you've rubbed off on me." He took another bite. "This is definitely my favorite place on earth."

"I'm telling her you ate the pie," she said.

"I'll blame it on you. With your history I have a feeling she'll believe me."

"I know better. Rumor has it you don't lie."

Before opening the screen door, he said, "Never, especially to you."

The sunshine splashed onto Paige's face and gave her a little jolt of exhilaration. Aunt Bertie was kneeling with her back to them in a bed near the picket fence just to the left of the sagging old potting shed. "It's good to see her doing that after her knee surgery last year." She paused and watched her a moment. "It's good to see her at all."

Wyatt dropped onto a chair. "I'll give you some time with her. Let me know if you need any muscle."

"I'll do that," she said and walked down the three steps.

Paige kicked off her shoes to feel the grass beneath her feet and hesitated there for a minute wiggling her toes. This was life from ages ago, exactly what she needed today more than ever.

She turned quickly and glanced at Wyatt, his parting words still in her head, to call if she needed muscle. There was something about his presence that only made her grow more at ease with him.

Aunt Bertie's words about the way Wyatt looked at her had hardly left her conscious thoughts. It was a crazy thought, really, but his expression did look more like love than simple fondness.

"I've been waiting on you, favorite niece of mine," Bertie called out.

"I'm your only niece." Paige continued her trek to the flowerbed.

"If I had a dozen, you'd still be my favorite."

Paige reached the edge of the bed and dropped onto her knees, looking forward to doing something with such fond memories attached. "How do you know that?"

Bertie stopped digging and turned to her. "You're your mama's girl, so much like her." She paused and moved Paige's hair from her shoulder. "Then you've got your daddy all mixed in there too, a man I loved the very moment she brought him to meet me. You're the perfect combination of two of my favorite people in the world. How could you not be my favorite?"

"You make a good point," Paige said with a quick smile as she reached for a dahlia and placed it into the freshly dug hole.

"You're not out of practice," Bertie said.

"I'm surprised. I don't do this at home."

"You should. There's joy in the soil and the sunshine."

"I'm not sure I've known any joy at all since Mom passed. At least not much to speak of. Especially now, with all I see coming, how am I supposed to experience joy? It seems to be lost to me these days."

"I've lost a lot over the years," Bertie said, eyes swimming with understanding. "Parents and husbands and children and your mom. That's a whole lot of joy to lose over time. Thankfully, the heart has a wellspring of joy from the Spirit. It just looks different in every season of life.

"You have to find new joy, Paigie. It's not lost, just waiting to be rediscovered. I find it out here digging in the dirt, when a bird sings to me while I'm weeding, and when the sun kisses my cheeks good morning." She tapped her heart. "Joy is still here."

"I felt a little sprinkle of joy when I stepped outside to be with you just now."

"Then reach your hand out and capture as many of the sprinkles as you can and tuck them away in your pocket to jingle around later."

Paige glanced up at the porch to find Wyatt watching them. That man may have had a little to do with her sprinkle of joy.

Bertie chuckled. "That's a joy I've known in life, too, when love looked at me the way Wyatt looks at you."

Paige nearly corrected her again but didn't. She couldn't explain Wyatt's tender expressions toward her any better than that, looks of love.

"I don't know if you're right about him or not, but I do know this: From the moment I arrived here, I've felt love and happiness like I haven't felt since losing Mom."

"Then make sure to carry a pocketful of me back home with you along with your sprinkles of joy. You'll always have my love."

"I'm not sure I can ever go home. Wyatt says it may not be safe, depending on the outcome of all this."

"Home is where the people you love live. You can come back here if you need to. If you don't know it already, this is home." Bertie reached for her hand. "In case you didn't notice, I felt a whole lot of joy when I saw you round that corner."

Bertie's eyes grew heavy with compassion. "I know you're troubled about more than your dad. I remember what it felt like to see what you're seeing. I wasn't sad for me since I've lived my life–and part of someone else's." She gave a quick wink. "My son is grown and has lived his. Truthfully, I don't feel sorry for you or the young believers I know since where we're going is vastly better than what we're leaving. In case you haven't noticed, the Lord has sure allowed a world to emerge that's getting easier for us to let go of."

Bertie took her spade and began to dig a hole. "Nothing's the same: not shopping or eating out or church for most folks. Everyone's scared to get too close or hug or shake hands. This isn't how life is supposed to be. People thrive on togetherness and connection. Right now, that's not happening."

With a firm shake of her head and a glance at Paige, she said, "That's why you won't catch me out in a mask. I smile and greet people in the grocery store."

"You got the vaccine, though, right?"

"Absolutely not. And I won't. I've done a whole lot of research and read things they're not telling the public."

"Aren't you afraid of getting sick?" Paige left off the at-your-age part.

"Not a bit. I would rather take my chances with the virus." She pointed to the flat of flowers and motioned for Paige to plant one. "I know this: I'm not leaving this world even one day early, not until I finish what the Lord has planned for me to do. I'm going to finish out my call, and that's not me being foolish. I don't go stand in traffic. I just know He's telling me that I'm to trust Him and love people. I can't do that when I'm sitting in my house alone or with my face covered with pretty fabric."

"So what is your call?" Paige had been asking herself the same question and still had no answer.

"Today, I'm called to encourage you and speak truth. Tomorrow I'll do the same with anyone the Lord puts in my path." She kept digging the holes while Paige followed behind her, planting. "We're told to meet with one another and encourage one another." She stopped her digging and looked up at Paige. "The last part of that verse in Hebrews 10 says, 'and all the more as you see the day drawing near.' Sweetheart," she said with a little shake of her head, "the day is so near I can almost reach out and touch it."

"I'm beginning to see that too." Paige looked up at Wyatt and found him watching her. At that, her mind almost wished for a little more time to get to know him better.

Bertie sat back on her heels and said, "Still, there are folks I know who aren't ready, ones who won't listen to the truth no matter how I frame it for them."

"Like me?"

"No. I mean those who don't follow Jesus. You were just oversleeping a little."

"I had no choice but to wake up."

They were quiet for a few seconds, then Bertie said, "Gunshots, huh?"

"Yes, ma'am. I was hopeful when I knew Wyatt was hopeful."

"He's not now?"

"He hasn't said it, but I can tell he's not so sure anymore."

Bertie took her hand and squeezed. "We'll both hold on to this truth: He's still the same Jesus this close to the end and even at the sound of gunshots. Same goodness. Same love. Same nearness. Same power. Same God who wants people to know Him. Whatever you find out about your dad or this world, you keep looking at the Light and not the darkness. Will you do that for me?"

Paige looked up at Wyatt. "That's what Wyatt just said, to keep looking at the Light rather than the darkness."

"Well, you listen to us."

"I'll try."

"How about you will!"

She grinned. "Yes, ma'am, I will."

"That's better. Now we better get in and eat some supper. I'm thawing a casserole."

It was late. Aunt Bertie had gone to bed just after nine. Since then, Paige had been sitting on her bed reading her Bible. She had read all the verses Wyatt and Echo had shared with her so far, especially the rapture ones. She needed the reminder again.

Aunt Bertie's Hebrews verse had brought deep conviction over how she had given up "assembling together," knowing that had been her first stumbling step to get to the faraway place where she now dwelled.

At the moment, she was looking at the verse from Hebrews Wyatt had spoken to her on the roadside earlier in the day, that she should fix her eyes on Jesus, the author and perfecter of her faith.

Those words rang true with what Aunt Bertie had said in the garden about looking at the Light rather than the darkness. Paige was realizing that if she kept looking at what was to come, she would remain in turmoil. Now, in a rare moment since her dad's phone call, she found peace was extraordinarily present.

A knock on her door sounded. "It's open," she said.

Wyatt walked in with a bundle of bedding.

"What are you doing? You heard Aunt Bertie."

"I did but never agreed to it. I've got her blessing now."

"What did you tell her?"

"That I'm sleeping on your floor whether she liked it or not." Deep dimples accompanied his mischievous smile.

Paige's eyes widened. "You did not!"

"Nah, I didn't. I just explained that I won't be able to sleep at all if I'm not where I can keep an eye on you."

"So you're going to sleep on my floor?" It was pretty obvious as he made a pallet with his bedding.

"Yeah. I planned to sleep out in the hallway, but I couldn't get these three windows off my mind."

She slid down beneath the covers. "Are you going to be okay down there?"

"Totally fine. Soldiers sleep in all kinds of unusual places. A nice clean floor is a step up from most."

For a moment more she lay there, first feeling sorry for him that he was sleeping on the hard floor. Then the memory came of how real it had felt, even when wide awake, of Wyatt snoring next to her–more on her pillow than his. Anxiety and what could only be deemed anticipation rambled around, mingling in her chest. It wasn't concern for his current well-being exactly; it was alarm for herself that she was allowing the dream, and now Aunt Bertie's words, to stir up these outrageous ideas and images.

"Want some more blankets to pile up for a softer pallet?" she said.

"I'm good. Just get some sleep."

"You're so weird," she said, with those sprinkles of joy drawing her lips into a slow smile.

"Heard that before."

Paige closed her eyes and let out a soft sigh. How could she not fall someday for a guy so weird that he would sleep on the floor to keep her safe?

"Thank you for watching over me," she whispered.

His response was quiet too, "There's nowhere I'd rather be."

Tears stung her eyes at that. Only love could feel that way. She couldn't remember the last time she had actually felt loved.

Directive

Day 3, 7:25 a.m.

Though she wrestled against it, the smell of coffee pried Paige's eyes open. There was Wyatt, sitting on a straight-back chair next to the front window eating a muffin.

She sat up, rubbed her eyes, spotted the tray, and patted her lap. "Continental breakfast in bed. I really do have a good gig going."

Wyatt brought the tray and set it over her legs. "I can totally get used to this Aunt Bertie life. She brought this up a few minutes ago before going to a neighbor's." He sat on the edge of Paige's bed and picked up a plump strawberry. "If she's seventy-two, how old might an elderly neighbor be?"

Old-summer memories of fishing came to mind. "Ancient! Mr. Cox would be in his mid-nineties by now. You'd love him, though. He's a crusty old vet who still gets around like he's...," she smiled and said, "like he's eighty. He and Aunt Bertie have been friends for decades."

"Maybe I'll meet him someday."

She nodded at that and peeled the paper off her orange-cranberry muffin, her mind drifting back to a faraway better life. "I bet there are cookies down there by now."

His eyes lit up. "You think?"

"I'm sure of it. She bakes them but doesn't mention it, so I get to steal them. It's much more fun that way. We've been playing cookie thief since I was a kid."

"I wouldn't mind being a decoy while you swiped a cookie or two," he said as he sipped his coffee.

Echo's use of words about how they funded Daybreak came to mind. "Maybe I can do a little Robin Hoodery of my own, taking from the cookie rich to share with the cookie poor."

"You think like your dad," he said and ate another muffin in two bites.

"Who do you think used to help me get away with my crime?" She grinned, and her heart was overcome with delight that was rare these days. "When he was on leave and got to come here with us, it was our favorite pastime."

Wyatt's expression was one of almost sadness. Clearly their childhoods were in no way similar.

"Hey," she said and blinked a few times, "he was helping me learn to be covert even then. Crazy that it would lead to this, huh?"

"I don't believe in coincidences. God uses anything we give Him, even Robin Hoodery skills."

Paige nodded and looked away, the idea that she hadn't given Him much to work with lately stinging more than a little.

Wyatt made no move to leave but just poked his fork into the bowl of melon and ate a bite-sized chunk of cantaloupe.

She already knew since his tired eyes had given her a bit of a gloomy heart when she had first woken, but still she asked, "How did you sleep?"

"Better than usual. Once I knew you were asleep, I tapped out. That's rare for me."

"You were really worried last night? That's why you came in here?"

"More conscientious than worried. If anyone suspected this place, they would have been here waiting for us."

Another half-eaten muffin later, he said, "Echo ran thermal before we turned into the drive, so I knew we were okay."

"Thermal imaging?"

"Yeah. His drones are some of his favorite toys in his arsenal." With little expression, he said, "Echo heard from Bash. Your dad is nowhere on the compound, so that's good news."

Paige closed her eyes and thanked God, then looked back at Wyatt. "That means he has a chance then. All I could envision..."

"I know. Me too. Bash will stick around another day to see if he finds any other leads."

"How did he get in?"

"Networking with other security guys on Groves' team."

"Networking?"

Wyatt chuckled. "As he would call it, drinking a pint where they hang out."

"Smart. You guys really know what you're doing."

"We do. That's why you can trust us."

"I do trust you."

He refilled her coffee and sat now without eating while she added tons more cream. Finally, he said, "How are you this morning? I know from experience; this new reality is tough."

Her cheeks flushed at the memory of her roadside breakdown. "I'm better than yesterday."

"You never have to pretend with me. I hope you know that."

In hopes of pacifying his concerns, she said, "You take your directive too literally. I'm really okay."

"This has nothing to do with my directive. I care about you and can't stand to see you hurt. I know to you I just landed in your life a few days ago, but I've known about you for a decade. You've become an actual part of my life. There's nothing I wouldn't do to keep you safe." He cast his eyes away. "And to keep you from crying."

Paige hadn't expected such a heart-felt admission and found herself with a flicker of hope that what Aunt Bertie had said might actually be true. She couldn't help but do a little fishing: "Because of my dad?"

"Because of you," he hesitated, "because of who you are to me."

She cast another line: "I'm family because of how you feel about my dad?"

"You could say it that way." His jaw was tight and his expression tense.

She could tell he was using phrases that were true enough to keep from lying, yet not saying more than would actually answer her question. A little more bait: "How else might you say it?"

"Paige, I'm here for you for a variety of reasons." His eyes filled with evident compassion. "I know the toll these past years have taken on you. I've grieved with you over your mom. I've watched you close yourself off from the world and from church." His eyes grew misty, and his voice was soft. "I've never prayed for anyone the way I pray for you. Even though you hardly know me at all, I'm connected to you, bound to you in a way I don't even understand myself, well beyond my original directive."

He stood and set the tray on the table near the bed, then walked to the door. "I'll shower while you get dressed. The mail usually comes after lunch."

Paige sat looking at the door he closed behind him, her heart racing so fast she had to take a few steadying breaths. Every blink brought his image to mind, the look in his eyes as he had spoken such revealing words. Why had she pushed him that way?

She shook her head to clear her mind and jumped from the bed. The last thing she had the capacity to dwell on now was how his words had affected her and made her heart warm in such a way that it felt like fireflies glowed and fluttered within.

Fig Tree

Day 3, 8:47 a.m.

"There you are," Bertie said when Paige entered the living room. "I've been getting acquainted with your..." she paused and grinned at Paige, "your friend here."

"I hope you've learned more than I know about him."

"He loves Jesus. I'm not sure how much more you need to know than that."

Paige sat on the small settee next to Aunt Bertie and leaned her head onto her shoulder. "I think I already know that much."

Enough about Wyatt, Paige thought with cheeks burning and an unwanted appreciation of how handsome he looked in his fitted tan T-shirt and sand-colored camo pants. She liked how his curly hair peeked from beneath his sweat-stained ballcap and how he would sometimes move it to sit farther back on his head when he seemed to be thinking.

Paige blinked several times and turned her attention back to Aunt Bertie. "How's Mr. Cox?"

"Joe's got one foot swollen up like a honeydew. That skinny, old coot ain't ever gonna die. I've been taking him breakfast to save his daughter the early trip. Her back is out, so I'm trying to help her out."

Wyatt was in a chair nearby. With his statement he moved up to rest his elbows on his knees. "I hear he's a vet."

"He is, the Big One," Bertie said.

A conversation erupted over Mr. Cox while Paige sat and listened as a bystander. Wyatt hadn't exactly made eye contact since she had entered the room, so she was relieved to see him now so animated.

Her heart warmed afresh, and that little firefly flutter came again when his words from her bedside came to mind, how he had grieved with her and prayed for her. Even now she found it difficult to look at him without those words floating around and cluttering her mind. She glanced at him and back at Aunt Bertie. "Wyatt says he would like to meet him someday."

"Well, today might be the day since I'll be taking him lunch and dinner too."

"It depends on the mail," Paige said. "If something comes..." She looked at Wyatt whose expression was unreadable. "What if nothing comes? What if –"

"This was a sound hunch, Paige. Don't question yourself. This is ninety percent of my life, following up on the best leads we can get. This is a good lead."

For a moment they were both quiet and sat looking at one another.

Bertie spoke up. "We were just talking about the fig tree when you came down, and how we agree on its timing."

"You have fig trees now?" Paige said.

"No, the Lord's fig tree." She drew her Bible from the side table to her lap. "In many places in Scripture, He refers to Israel as the fig tree."

Paige didn't ask since she knew she would elaborate. Once that glimmer of the Word reached Aunt Bertie's eyes, she would spew a whole lot of Jesus around the room.

As much as she had appreciated her parents' teaching her God's Word, Paige had always been more drawn to Aunt Bertie's way of explaining it. Her excitement was contagious, especially the way she framed everything around how the Shepherd loves and tends His sheep.

"It's mentioned in Matthew as well," Bertie said, "but I like how Doctor Luke expresses it. In chapter twenty-one, he says, 'Then He told them a parable: "Behold the fig tree and all the trees; as soon as they put forth leaves, you see it and know for yourselves that summer is now near. So you also, when you see these things happening, recognize that the kingdom of God is near. Truly I say to you, this generation will not pass away until all things take place."'

"Some prophecy teachers disagree on this passage," Wyatt said, "but Aunt Bertie and I agree that this is the Lord specifically referencing Israel."

Paige said, "You mean them regathering in '48?"

Wyatt tilted his hat back in evident surprise. "You know about that?"

"Echo mentioned how, until Israel became a nation again, many last-days prophecies couldn't possibly be fulfilled."

"Exactly," Bertie said. "When it says, 'this generation will not pass away,' I believe it's referring to my generation since we are the ones who were born right when Israel was regathered."

"That's what Echo meant by a timestamp." Paige reached for the Bible.

Aunt Bertie said, "Some teachers believe the Lord isn't talking about those who see Israel's regathering being the fig-tree generation. When He mentions the fig tree, they think His parable is only indicating the generation who will see all the things in the above verses happen, the tribulation signs."

"Hold up," Paige said and scanned the passage. She was familiar with it: nation rising against nation and earthquakes and plagues and famine.

She looked at Aunt Bertie, then with hesitation to Wyatt. "So, y'all think that Jesus mentioning the fig tree means those who witnessed the regathering of the Jews in '48, that particular generation, will not pass away before the end of the tribulation? And others think Jesus used the fig tree as a more general illustration of timing and nature to indicate that those who see the signs He mentioned above are the generation who will not pass away?"

Wyatt nodded.

She read it all again twice more, to view it from each differing perspective. Finally, she looked up and said, "I can see it applies to either viewpoint. But, if He is referring to Israel's regathering," she grinned at Wyatt, "then this is some crazy amazing clue the Holy Spirit has given to us as a red flag."

He nodded again. "Seriously, what are the chances that the generation who was alive when Israel was reborn, when Israel was young again as a nation and putting forth new leaves, just so happens to be in their mid-seventies now, right when the one-world order is taking shape? Right when the world is turned upside down and technology is primed for the Antichrist? The timing is too precise. God is always intentional in His Word, never coincidental."

"Seems pretty likely to me," Paige said.

"Here's what you need to know, Paige," Wyatt said. "The study of prophecy is never a precise art, not for any man. Only God knows what little nuances mean and how it all ties together. We, as students, read the Word and try to link scattered last-days verses with one another. None of us are ever a hundred percent right. You need to know that when you read and study more, you'll always find differing opinions. This," he said with a soft smile, "is like reading a treasure map. We are all looking at the same map but sometimes see clues in a different way based on what we've been taught in the past and our own understanding of the Word. Ultimately, though, we don't major on the minors, and we don't beat each other up over differing opinions. It's okay for people to disagree over things like this as long as we agree on Jesus and salvation by grace and not works."

Bertie took her Bible back from Paige's lap. "It's fun to grapple with it when you find someone who'll listen." Her face lit up when she said, "This excites me. More than just the conversation about it, the idea that I might not check out before the rapture gives me great satisfaction."

Her eyes narrowed in on Paige's and flashed sudden urgency. "All the believers who've gone before us have wanted to be this generation, to see this, but what they didn't realize is that 'to whom much is given, much is required.' This follows our conversation from yesterday in the garden. Things will only get darker, sweetie, so you'll have to be a burst of starlight against the black canvas of this world."

Paige looked over at Wyatt, remembering how he had invited her to shine with him. Her cheeks flushed, but she couldn't seem to look away as his knowing expression told her he recalled his words as well.

"Like I told you," Wyatt said, "the rapture could be this year or several years from now. People who think this parable of the fig tree is based on the regathering of Israel will even disagree on the definition of a generation." He shook his head. "I just know with all that's coming, we hope for the rapture to come sooner rather than later."

With a slight pause, he looked at her with intention, as if heading off any doubts she may have. "Remember when we first talked about the rapture at your dad's house, we read in First Thessalonians where Paul was talking about us being caught up? He said for us to comfort one another with his words. I've had to read that passage time and again for comfort. We are waiting for Jesus to come and rescue us. Otherwise, it wouldn't be comforting at all to think we will be here for seven years of utter darkness."

"My pastor has mentioned that exact thing," Bertie said. "If Paul was referring to the tribulation, that would be terrifying, not at all comforting."

Paige nodded as if she agreed with them, and in some ways she did since she didn't want to be around for the bad, but the idea of facing a God she had intentionally chosen to distance herself from was more discomforting than comforting. While she hadn't intended to, the words popped out, "I need to work on this, to study on it more."

Misunderstanding her meaning, Wyatt said, "It's a cool trail of thought to follow, huh?"

"Crazy cool," she said with fake enthusiasm.

What did bring her excitement, however, was this small journey through the Word with Aunt Bertie sharing about the fig tree. This was like making her way home from that far-off place, and back to her love of the Word. And, too, she liked this journey with Wyatt more than made sense.

Unborn-Again

Day 3, 12:22 p.m.

The sandwich sat before her on the plate. Paige had taken only a few bites and now sat listening to the back and forth of Wyatt and Aunt Bertie's conversation.

To Paige's amazement, she found her seventy-two-year-old aunt to be way more current with the times than she was. Aunt Bertie told Wyatt the sites she viewed and preachers she watched for prophecy updates. Some they shared in common.

"I never miss Pastor JD," Bertie said of a preacher in Hawaii whom Wyatt mentioned.

Paige didn't feel left out of the conversation exactly. It was more that she felt foolish for not seeing what was evident even to her elderly aunt. People who chose to see did see. That was Paige's conclusion. Like Echo had said of believers in general, she had been blinded by lies and misinformation. And, too, she had to admit, she hadn't been in the Word much. She had never been willing to read the book of Revelation or do any in-depth study on the last days. The most she had read of it was whenever she had been directed there during a sermon, which, she reminded herself, was seldom, if ever. Of course she had missed it.

Now, as they discussed the regathering of Israel again, their conversation took a turn to include the building of the third Temple.

Bertie said to Paige, "In Daniel, we're told the Antichrist will desecrate the Temple at the midpoint of the tribulation. He can't do that unless a Temple is in place, right?"

"Everything needed," Wyatt said when he turned to look at Paige, "all the implements and materials, are ready to begin building. They have the priests trained and even their garments waiting. I've heard some say that it could be built in a matter of months."

"Where the Dome of the Rock sits?" Paige said. "How will they ever be allowed to do that?"

That set off a firestorm of debate between the two, leaving Paige to watch the volley of conversation.

"Just recently," Wyatt said, "I read where some Saudis have said it's not that important of a site to the Muslims, that Mecca and Medina are the most critical." His eyes grew wider. "Who would have ever thought we would hear that said by any Muslim? Could that open the possibility of a shared space where Israel might begin building soon, or Israel's new government may be open to more compromise with Arab nations?"

Aunt Bertie said, "A man was telling me at church recently about the possibility that the original Temple was built in the old City of David and that what they now consider the original holy site was actually the Roman fort. It seems unlikely, but it's intriguing nonetheless."

With a shake of his head, Wyatt said, "I've seen some archaeological evidence that's supposed to support that, but I just don't buy it."

The conversation wasn't as fascinating to Paige as it was to them since it meant the world was only one step closer to the end. "They'll all suffer so much," she said aloud rather than in her head as intended.

They both grew quiet, and Bertie nodded and reached for Paige's hand. "I think about that too. Some days it grips my heart so tightly I can hardly breathe."

"Is Mr. Cox a believer?"

"He is."

"I know people who aren't," Paige said.

Bryce's face came to mind along with those last nasty comments she had hurled at him when they had broken up. His behavior had been rotten, but nothing he had done would ever make her wish such a fate on him.

"We all know people. This is our time to reach out to them as best we can." Bertie gave a little shrug. "I've not had much success in that regard. People don't want to hear. They like wallowing in their sin better than walking away from it."

The Word formed and settled onto Paige. "Jesus said that people love the darkness rather than the Light because their deeds are evil. It's true. I'm only now seeing just how much evil is out there." Paige looked down at her less-than-half-eaten sandwich. "I know some, though, they are good people. Just lost. They don't see the Light at all."

"Those are the ones we try to reach. We give them what they'll need even if they refuse the Shepherd for now." Bertie's eyes held anguish that seemed to fade into delight. "The one thing I've found to give me purpose and hope is making plans for those unborn-again sheep."

Paige considered her words and noticed how Wyatt's eyes blinked rapidly as if considering the term as well.

"Once we're gone," Bertie said, "people, even some of those we've been telling the truth, will call upon the name of the Lord and be saved. They'll be His sheep someday; they're just unborn-again, not born again as of yet."

That term kept repeating in Paige's head: unborn-again sheep. She grinned at Aunt Bertie, not so surprised she had come up with it.

Bertie said, "That's been my focus as of late, getting my house in order. I heard a man recently say that our homes may very well be a refuge for tribulation saints. I've had that on my heart ever since then. I'm leaving food and water, Bibles and notes of encouragement, and a shotgun or two," she said as she finished with a wink.

Paige's own house came to mind, the torn-up mess that was now her home. "I don't have much of a home to leave behind."

Wyatt said, "We'll get someone in to clean up the mess and salvage what we can."

"Even if we do, what will I do with the place if I can't go home?"

"You'll know when we see how this all plays out."

"What happened to your home?" Bertie leaned in closer to Paige. "Did someone come in after you?"

"Not before this guy came to drag me out." Paige turned to smile at Wyatt. "If I never formally thanked you for that–thank you."

Bertie reached over, tears filling her faded blue eyes, and patted Wyatt's cheek. "I owe you one for taking care of this favorite niece of mine."

"My pleasure," he said more to Paige than to Aunt Bertie. In what was likely an effort to break their long gaze, he checked his watch. "If you don't mind, I'll walk down to the mailbox."

"You go right ahead while I clean up this mess, and you take this girl with you. It'll do her some good to get a long smooch of sunshine."

Wyatt didn't budge and said to Paige, "You need to eat something first. I'll wait."

By the time they were heading down the gravel drive, Paige was more curious than melancholy. The sun had done its job, giving her kisses on her cheeks as they walked along.

"You okay?" Wyatt said.

"As okay as I can be."

"It weighs on me too, knowing how many people will be left behind."

"When you told me about Daybreak, you said something that keeps coming to mind, how when daybreak ends, the world will suffer seven years of nightfall. At the time I wondered if maybe I might be one of those people left behind."

"But you know better now?"

"I do know better. I haven't been where I need to be, but I will be soon. I can feel Him drawing me near like before."

"I'm glad to hear that. I told you, I've been a little adrift in my faith before."

They took a few more steps before Wyatt said, "I've thought of this a few times, but only recently has it come into real focus. The Restrainer holding back the Antichrist is the Holy Spirit, but I can see it from another angle too. Every new daybreak is the restrainer, the Light forcing the darkness to flee for another day as long as the church is here. We, because the Spirit of Jesus dwells within us, are the light of the world. When that light is extinguished, there will be perpetual nightfall. The Spirit will be here, but we as the light will be gone. Every day will be another long, dark night for those left here to suffer."

Tears filled Paige's eyes. "How will they endure it, the people who figure out what's happened, that they've been left?"

"Maybe it's like Aunt Bertie said, they'll depend on us to have prepared the way for them." He paused as they drew near the mailbox. "I'm not sure what that looks like yet, but I like her idea to make a sanctuary for the saints."

"What she said was something, huh, about the unborn-again sheep?"

"Something so profound I'll have to give it some more thought." He began to walk again. "A term so tender that it hurts me a little."

"Yeah," she said as they took the final few steps toward the mailbox, "I know exactly what you mean."

Paige pulled the stack of mail from the box and sorted. There, third envelope down, was her father's handwriting. "It came," she said, as astonished that she had figured this out as she was relieved to have it in hand.

"Open it," he said as he took the remaining mail.

They began to walk as she tore into it. A key was taped to the inside of the envelope, along with a note for Paige. She stopped to read it aloud.

Paige,

That's my girl. I knew you'd come here, that you would remember. I'm sorry you had to get involved this way and that your life is very likely in danger (Ps. 23:4). I never wanted any other life for you than one where light eclipses the darkness. I'm afraid time is running out faster than any of us may know.

This key is for my safety deposit box: Bank of America on Light St. in Baltimore. I have you listed as authorized to access my box. The account number is in a separate mailing.

Keep Wyatt by your side. You can count on him always. He's a man after your dad's own heart.

Welcome to Daybreak, sweetheart. I know what you're made of.

Love, Dad

She looked up. "Is there another envelope?"

"Yep," Wyatt said. "Looks like we're heading to Baltimore."

They both began to sprint toward the house, Paige often struggling to maintain Wyatt's speed. "You know I'm a girl, right?" she said.

While at a steady pace of running, with what seemed like zero effort whatsoever, he smiled and said, "I'm a little surprised to hear you play the girl card."

"I'm not exactly a feminist. And I'm sure not a soldier." He slowed only a little, so she did too. "I couldn't even hang through a whole session of CrossFit."

Winded by the time they were in sight of the house, Paige slowed even more and looked up at the gleaming-white home. Something told her this might be the last normal-seeming day she would ever know again.

It wasn't a foreboding sense for Aunt Bertie's sake. Paige smiled at that, knowing that powerhouse of a woman would outlive them all. It was more about this place and the innocence of her long-ago childhood here. Today, something–or Someone–was ushering her into a new call. She felt it. Her father's words, "Welcome to Daybreak," had sent a quake beneath the foundation of her feet. There still seemed to be a rumbling beneath her shoes.

Wyatt fell in beside her. "You okay?"

"I'm ready to go find my dad, but leaving here is tough. Being here is the first sense of family I've known in years." Paige reached the steps and stood without going up. "I should have come more. I hope I get that chance."

"We'll make sure you do." When he held the door for her, he whispered, "I'll distract her, and you go for the cookies. We'll need them for the road."

The future was serious. Her father was in danger. Paige's stomach was often in knots. But everything about Wyatt lended levity to life's gravity. If a man like this did happen to love her, a man after her dad's own heart, she sure wouldn't put up much of a fuss about it.

"Call when you can," Bertie said with her arms wound so tightly around Paige's neck that she felt a little pop.

"I'll call plenty. I promise."

They hugged a long moment more. "I pray you find your dad. I believe you will."

Paige hugged her a little tighter. "I'll let you know."

Bertie held Paige back to look at her. Her eyes narrowed yet held a gentle gaze. "I know you two stole my cookies."

With a quick glance at Wyatt, Paige said, "I'm betting it was the new guy."

"Then why do I smell them in your bag?"

"I have no answer for that."

Tears filled Bertie's eyes. "I would be offended if you didn't steal them. I baked them while you slept just so you could."

"I kinda guessed that."

"I love you, Paige. You be careful. Let Wyatt watch over you." She hesitated and looked at him there in front of the car, then back at Paige. "Not that you can stop him." Her voice was quiet. "And be careful with the heart of a man who loves you that much."

"I will be."

Bertie met Wyatt in front of the car. Their hug was quick, and when Bertie stepped back, she pointed at Wyatt and said, "You got it! Nothing would make me happier."

Wyatt climbed into the car as Paige removed the plastic bag filled with cookies, then slung her bag into the back seat. "You've got what?" she said. "What'll make her happy?"

"I told her when she is ready to sell this place," he paused and leaned in to look up at the house through the windshield as Paige had done when they arrived, "to let me know."

Paige waved at Bertie as they made the loop around the drive. Once on their way, she said, "You mean you want to buy it?"

"Yeah. You need a place to chase fireflies and eat watermelon."

For a few seconds she just sat looking at him, trying to figure out if he was serious. "So you're buying it for me?"

"Why not? You love it here."

Her eyes grew wider as she tried to convince herself he was only joking. "I thought you didn't get paid."

"Just not paid for watching you."

Wyatt's phone rang, yet Paige was barely dialed in to his end of the conversation. Fireflies and watermelon? Did he really love her that much? That question faded, and one took its place: Would she someday actually live there and make it a refuge for the unborn-again sheep like Aunt Bertie planned to do? She turned to look at Wyatt, wondering if he planned to live there too.

"Yeah, we got it," Wyatt said. Then, "Have Halo waiting. We're heading back to Savannah now."

Connected

Day 3, 2:44 p.m.

The first hour of the trip was quiet, so quiet and unnerving that Paige rested her head back, hoping to fall asleep. The one time stress sleep was most warranted, she sat instead with her eyes closed and mind cluttered, filled with images of Wyatt's kind expression and telling words from that morning.

She snapped her head up and looked straight ahead. Reliving the moment was maybe more uncomfortable than the quiet ride. His silence made sense, though. He was likely just as uncomfortable after the things he had said as she was now knowing them.

"I can't do this," she said.

"Do what? Go to the bank?"

"I can totally go to the bank." She stopped and stared a second. "Can Echo hear us?"

"No, only when I activate the coms."

"Okay." She sat looking at him, biting at her lip, daring herself to ask the question. Finally, she blurted out, "Do you love me?"

He turned to look at her too long for a man driving. With a quick glance back at the road, he looked at her again. "You do know that's an unfair question, right?"

"I do know. But honestly, my brain hurts right now. I've got so much to try and figure out. I don't know my place in this new reality I'm living. I won't live out the future I saw for myself. And my dad..." She sighed and shook her head. "I'm used to him not being around, but I keep hearing it in my head; it was more like loud pops."

"Paige –"

"Please just hear me out," she said. "This one thing, the way you look at me and treat me, it weighs on me and maybe even confuses me a little. Aunt Bertie planted a seed, and your actions only make the thought grow. I don't want to allow these thoughts to become out-of-control weeds if I'm wrong. I've been wrong before and was left looking pretty stupid. All I'm asking is that you help me understand where you're coming from."

He looked straight ahead, his jawline now tense. "Do you think it's possible to love someone you've never met?"

That's a question that had come to her mind more than once since Aunt Bertie's meddling. "I don't know."

"I didn't either. For a long time I wondered. It seemed pretty crazy to me." He looked at her. "Then you came to Overwatch, and I didn't wonder anymore." He looked back at the road.

A minute passed. Then another. Paige kept looking at his now-relaxed expression. "So you're not going to answer?"

"Do I need to?" He took a quick peek in her direction. "Do you need to hear it? Isn't this weird enough already?"

"The epitome of weird."

Wyatt chuckled. "Then let's leave it at that." As if truly unaffected, he reached for the bag of cookies on the console and struggled with the zipper.

Paige grabbed the bag and got two out for him.

He took a bite, grinned, and cut his eyes to look at her. "You'll love me back someday."

She swallowed hard, and a knot formed in her stomach. "How do you know that?"

"I'm not sure how I know, but I do. I've known it for a long time, so I've just waited." He reached for another cookie but then tossed it back on top of the bag as he grimaced. "It hasn't been easy, especially when you were dating that," his face now contorted into a deep scowl, "that jerk Bryce." He shook his head. "Why would you date a guy who would treat you that way? Just to spite your dad?" He glanced at her. "If so, it worked."

"That's not why. He was smart and handsome." She paused and looked at Wyatt thinking how less true that was now by comparison.

"And pompous and egotistical, so your dad said."

"I knew my dad hated him."

"What did you expect when you introduced him to a guy who doesn't share your faith?" Wyatt's voice rose. "And a guy who belittled you in conversations, even with your dad sitting right there. He was lucky your dad didn't take him out then and there."

Paige blinked a few times, considering that expression. "You mean kill him?"

"Maybe not kill him, but the guy was lucky to walk away with his teeth." Wyatt shook his head. "You didn't see your dad. The next morning, he literally threw a rolling chair through one of the plate-glass windows."

"At Overwatch?"

He nodded.

"Come on," she said. "Bryce wasn't throw-a-chair-out-a-window bad."

"Your dad disagrees. I do too." He was quiet a second, then said, "Seriously, he was an atheist and antagonized your dad the entire night. Is that what you wanted when you introduced them, to get under your dad's skin?"

"He's agnostic not atheist."

"No difference."

"No, an agnos –"

"I know the difference between the terms," Wyatt said. "I just mean lost is lost, no matter the label you slap on it." When she gave no more response, he said, "So you didn't answer. Was it to hurt him?"

Her words were quiet. "It didn't start that way."

"But you saw it and enjoyed it a little?"

"I hadn't gotten his attention in so long. Maybe I did enjoy it a little."

A realization struck her, how all she had done and said to her dad had been not only mean-spirited, but she had intentionally hurt the one person she loved most. It was possible that would be the last he knew of their relationship.

Paige's words were barely a whisper. "He didn't say a word to me about not liking Bryce."

"He knew better," Wyatt said, his tone softening now too. "But he had us do a dive on him."

"A dive?"

"Check into him. Watch him."

The blood reached her cheeks at the memory of how humiliated she had been. "So you know?"

"That he cheated the whole time? Yeah."

They both grew quiet. Paige was lost in the memory of how everything seemed to fall apart when she had found out. At the time it was similar to what she now felt, knowing her world wasn't at all what it seemed.

Wyatt did that thing again, keeping his eyes on her and not the road. "Did he hurt you?"

"Of course he hurt me."

"Did you love him?"

"I'm not sure it was love, but close enough." She hesitated as a question came and the firefly dance erupted in her tummy. "Did you have feelings for me by then?"

His jaw tightened like before, and he gave only a slight nod. "Yeah, I'd say so. I still can't make sense of what I've felt; I just know something has connected me to you."

It made no sense to her either, but Paige could see it was something meaningful to him. Stranger to her or not, she wouldn't belittle what he felt or take his affections for granted. To live on the outskirts of someone's life as he had hers, to grieve with them and pray for them, clearly had the power to form a bond that was real to him.

Wyatt's feelings for her were already deeper and truer than Bryce's had proven to be. What had ended their eight-month relationship was a text she had received from Bryce that was intended for someone named Club Girl, a woman, she found out later, he had met while out with his friends at a bar. That was actually how he had titled his message, "Hey, Club Girl, wanna hook up later?"

What made the text even more hurtful, was that Bryce had sent it while out with her at a restaurant when Paige was gone to the restroom. She only saw it when they got back to the car and she checked her phone. Of course she erupted when he denied sending it. When she demanded to see his phone, he had refused. Even the next day he kept calling and denying it, saying someone had spoofed his phone to cause trouble.

Now, looking at Wyatt's profile, Paige's mind began to click until finally it dawned on her: "Did you reroute his text to me, so that I would find out he was cheating?"

"I don't have the tech skills to pull that off," he said with his first smile since the topic of Bryce had come up.

"I'm guessing Echo does."

"I'm guessing Echo does too."

"Was it my dad's idea?"

"Not exactly."

"Yours?"

"What was I supposed to do, Paige? She wasn't the only one. I knew you would only get hurt worse as time passed."

More than a year past the incident, she did have to admit, their means of intervention was really pretty clever. "So I'm now part of a team who does really shady things?"

With a slight shrug, Wyatt said, "Seems like the perfect place for a cookie thief to land."

She grinned at that. "Did you have anything to do with his job offer in Atlanta?"

"That was all Evan Donovan."

"I'm glad you did what you did," she said. "Thank you."

"I will always watch over you."

"Like it or not?"

"Like it or not," he said.

Whatever had created his sense of being connected to her was something Paige would have to ponder since that same elusive thing may be inviting her to form her own connection.

Moments later they pulled into the DQ drive-thru. Wyatt ordered without asking what she wanted. On the way to Overwatch, he drove with one knee and ate his Blizzard at the same time. "You really have changed my life with this," he said with a mouthful.

Twice Paige reached for the wheel as the car often weaved and swerved. "You've done a little destruction to mine too."

His smile was sweet. "I meant in a good way."

"I did too. Well, until you kill us both." She kept her eyes on the road rather than him in case she needed to take over again.

Since she knew an airport would be too risky, that would mean an hours-long drive with this maniac. "I'm driving to Baltimore," she said.

"I'd really like to see that."

The bay door opened for them to pull through. "You'll meet Halo today. He's a better driver than me. Promise."

Daybreaker

Day 3, 3:17 p.m.

Wyatt hit the button to kill the ignition, so Paige reached for his arm. "Thank you for having that conversation with me. I'll never take advantage of your feelings for me."

"You can if you ever need to." His smile was warm. "And just so you know, I'm okay with where we are. I'm not embarrassed. Honestly, I'm relieved to have it out there. There's no pressure on you. I may be wrong. Maybe you never will feel the same for me, and that's okay." With a quick grin, he said, "But it's only been three days. I'm guessing I just need a week or two." He got out of the car.

Paige sat looking at his empty seat for a second then through the window as he walked toward the door. Finally, his cocky little strut made her burst out laughing. She had been feeling kind of sorry for him, as if baring his soul had left him feeling vulnerable. Instead, he seemed pretty confident he could capture her heart within a week or two. Oddly enough, she thought as the dancing fireflies moved from her tummy to her heart, she wouldn't bet against him.

It was the first time the thought came: Did her dad see this man for her future? Was he so intuitive to know Wyatt would someday be the man for her?

Wyatt shouted for her and ended her wondering. She jumped out of the car and followed him to the elevator. Once inside the loft, they approached the bedroom hall door where Wyatt allowed his eye to be scanned. "Why do you have this here inside considering we've already been through two security doors?"

"This," he said as he opened the door, "leads to three ways of escape. If you were ever in trouble, you can get to a safe room, emergency exit, or to the roof."

"Very James Bond of you."

"This is the most advanced of all our locations, but since your dad mostly operated out of here, the additional security seemed warranted, and..." Wyatt stopped at his room. "I'll gear up and meet you back out in the main room with Echo."

"And what?"

With a more tender-than-usual expression, he said, "And he hoped you'd be here someday."

Paige smiled at that and looked inside her now open doorway at the room her father had made for her. "And here I am." She couldn't help but believe Wyatt had shared in that same hope. "I'll get packed."

Wyatt was already waiting when Paige joined him and Echo. "Ready when you are," she said.

He looked at his watch. "Halo is five minutes out."

"Any thoughts from yesterday?" Echo said and rubbed his chin with a sinister grin. "I would think you bugging out of our conversations to go on a mission was a well-planned escape if you hadn't come back with a key."

"That may have been a total accident."

Wyatt shook his head. "Don't sell yourself short. You have good instincts."

"I agree with Wyatt. That key was a huge find. The fact that you put it all together with the word lemonade validates your dad's confidence in you." He grinned. "You'll be a Daybreaker before you know it, if you're not already." He kicked a chair so that it rolled closer to her. "Now that you've had a day for things to sink in, give me a recap of what you've learned."

She spun the chair around and sat with her chest facing the back as Wyatt often did. "I'm seeing people really aren't who they seem to be. The same people whose goal it is to use the pandemic to unite the world in a global economy were the main sponsors of a 'simulation' of how a corona pandemic might play out." Her words were soft. "And that's how the media and government responses played out only months later. What are the chances of that being a coincidence?"

"Unlikely if you ask me," Echo nodded hard. "And..."

"A really scary agenda is shaping up, especially with vaccine passports being required in some places, an agenda I'm not wanting to be a part of. This," she paused and looked at Wyatt, "all this virus stuff was really no accident."

Wyatt leaned against Echo's desk, crossed his arms, and said, "You're waking up to the truth that others refuse to see. The virus is merely another stepping stone–a huge one–of a demonic agenda to get the world to go willingly where the Antichrist plans to take them."

"I've been lied to." She paused and scowled. "That really triggers me to be played like that. I wasn't ever afraid of the virus for my sake, but I see what it's doing to people I care about. Beyond the unnecessary deaths, people have been locked down and separated."

"Why do you think that is?" Echo said.

"If people aren't communicating, then they're not as likely to figure out what's going on. In addition to that," she trailed one finger from her lips forward, "if our mouths are covered, we can't speak forth. That's what we're supposed to be doing, telling others about Jesus."

When he said it, Wyatt took a step closer, "That's a compelling phrase. And you're right; we are supposed to be speaking forth. Jesus is coming soon, and few are out there warning the world."

"Closed churches have hindered people so much," she said. "Even me. The more I didn't go, the easier it was to just watch online even when it did reopen." The Hebrews verse came to mind again. "We're not supposed to give up assembling together and encouraging one another..." The rest of the verse came as more of a blow than a memory, "especially as we see the day drawing near."

Paige rolled back in her chair, and with eyes widening, said, "That's what they've done to us, forced us to stay apart because they know the day is drawing near."

"You're exactly right," Echo said. "It's not just near."

She nodded. "It's here."

"And there you have it!" Echo said. "Another Daybreaker is born."

Her stomach twisted in knots at those words. She still had so much to overcome before she would ever know the team's level of boldness and belief.

A sound overhead got Wyatt moving. "You can continue your recap with me." He grabbed both of their bags and moved toward the bedroom hall door, so Paige jumped to her feet and followed behind as the sound of the helicopter grew louder.

She hesitated only long enough to look back and say, "See ya, Echo."

He nodded, his expression more concerned than he likely knew. "Be safe."

Wyatt led her through the door next to his bedroom, up two flights of stairs, and through a massive steel door. Once on the roof, he handed her one bag, grabbed her hand, and they both walked bent over beneath the downward pressing air of the blades.

When Paige was settled in the back seat and buckled in, Wyatt closed the door and buckled in himself.

"Welcome to my bird," the long-haired, bearded pilot said.

"Paige, this is Halo, our missing Daybreaker from our call the other day."

"Nice to meet you, Halo!" she shouted above the roaring sound of the propellers.

Halo turned his attention back to his controls, and soon blaring rock music sounded as they lifted off the ground. It wasn't at all what she expected. No more were they in the air than they began their descent to a private airfield adjacent to the airport. Jumbo jets taxied on runways off in the not-so-far distance.

Once Halo's bird was settled onto the ground, the three exited and made a quick dash over to the waiting private plane. Wyatt hovered near and almost over her as she jogged up the stairs. Halo entered and closed the door behind them, and only hesitated a second to say, "We'll taxi and take off soon. Get buckled in." His eyes smiled as he said, "We'll find your dad, Paige. He's always got a plan."

She nodded. "Thank you for saying that. I need a little hope right now."

"Wheels up!" Wyatt said with a near bark.

Veritas

Day 3, 4:04 p.m.

Finally in the air, with Wyatt sitting next to her for the hour and a half flight, Paige said, "Do you still believe there's a plan, that my dad might be alive?"

"I won't believe otherwise until I know different."

Paige nodded and looked out the window at the expanse of nothing but misty-white clouds surrounding them. Tears were nearby, but she didn't want to break down in front of Wyatt again. If he thought her so emotional, he may be alarmed and unwilling to let her go into the bank.

When she had joined him with Echo earlier, she had heard Echo ask what other option they had than for her to go. Clearly, Wyatt was taking her along only because it was her name on the account.

"Let's talk more," Wyatt said. "Follow this trail: A virus travels around the world in weeks. All cheap and effective treatments are rejected. Economies are ruined and people are convinced they need a vaccine in order to get back to normal." He paused. "Who stands to benefit from that scenario?"

"Drug companies," Paige said.

"That's right, a trillion-dollar industry."

"I have a friend who lost her husband," she said. "It was tragic for their family and devastating for her. Are you saying his death was really preventable?"

"Very likely, yes. Nationwide, there are doctors effectively treating Covid patients with a variety of medications, yet some of those doctors have been removed from hospital positions and their reputations discredited. Still, they are vocal about the success of early treatment and have formed worldwide networks of doctors who are sharing their protocols with one another. Many of those doctors have never had a hospitalized case." He leaned in closer. "Paige, when someone has everything to lose but sounds the alarm anyway, those are the people we need to listen to."

"If you're right," she said, still hard pressed to believe the medical community would withhold treatment, "then that's mass murder."

"I am right, and that's exactly what it is, crimes against humanity. I'm telling you: The ones behind this massive deception will stop at nothing.

"Because health organizations are saying there are no early effective treatments–a blatant lie–mainstream doctors are telling Covid patients to stay home and do nothing until major respiratory distress is present. That's the absolute worst advice.

"Hydroxychloroquine has been safely used for over sixty years. It gained national attention as an early treatment but was immediately deemed ineffective and potentially dangerous. After that flawed study was disproven, the retraction by the medical journal that published the original findings was so low profile that the public never heard about it. The false narrative gained national attention, but the truth was hardly reported."

Paige nodded. "I listened to a video about that the other day."

"I took Hydroxy," he said. "By the next day my fever and body aches were gone. I had little more than a lingering cough after that, but I also have a hyped-up immune system. That's why I've been after you to take vitamins."

"You said we have natural immunity once we've had Covid."

"We do, but beyond the mutations of the virus that are already here, I can't help but suspect that more will come. I want to be prepared. We need our immune system in its best possible condition."

"You're sounding crazy again."

"Duly noted," he said, not missing a beat. "Let's talk a little about what they're calling vaccines." He paused. "I won't go into the science of it, but these shots aren't even vaccines. A true vaccine uses an actual portion of the targeted virus to create an immune response in the body. These shots don't do that. But calling them a vaccine, though, reassures people who are already familiar with vaccines. I'm not kidding when I say this: They have actually changed the definition of vaccines in online dictionaries because so many doctors and virologists have been telling the truth, that these aren't vaccines.

"True vaccines usually take many years for development and testing. Since there have been years of research and trials done on coronavirus vaccines in the past, they did use that research to build on for these shots. But still, if none of the previous attempts at this type of vaccination have ever been successful, how did they suddenly get it right in ten months? Why should we trust new technology that has no proven track record?"

"I don't know," she said. "It's crossed my mind how quickly it was produced, so I had decided to wait."

Anger flashed in his eyes. "People are the guinea pigs since animal trials for this current vaccine were skipped. They did that for good reason. I've heard too many doctors' and virologists' warnings. All the animals in the previous coronavirus research trials either died or were critically sick when later exposed to the natural virus after injection, something called antibody-dependent enhancement. Those experts are saying the same thing: We have no way of knowing what'll happen a few months or even a few years down the line after someone receives the shot.

"Even a doctor who was part of inventing the mRNA technology warns that for the people who've had the shot, the virus can be more infectious or even deadly. When real numbers are viewed, breakthrough cases for those who've been vaxxed are as high or greater than the unvaxxed in some countries, Israel specifically.

"Paige!" he said with a broad shake of his head. "Israel has been the leader in pushing shots on their people at unprecedented rates." He paused and sat looking for a few seconds. "Israel, Paige. When we see Israel on center stage of the news like this, we can know there are prophetic implications. They're being deceived as a setup for what's to come. Israel has always been Satan's target because of who they are to God.

"Manufacturers are lying to them, to all of us, telling us their products are safe. Tens of thousands have had terrible reactions to the shots. Thousands have died, more than all the deaths from all previous vaccines combined since they began tracking. In years past with other trial vaccines, when a small number of people died, they stopped the program. Why haven't they stopped this when the death toll was over eighteen thousand the last time I checked? And that's a grossly underreported number. Have you heard much about that on any news source or social media?"

Her eyes grew a little wider. "No, hardly anything about it. Echo says they're censoring what we're seeing."

"They really are. That's not a conspiracy theory, Paige. If something is based on fact, then that's an actual conspiracy, not a theory. A video will be uploaded of someone sharing their own personal adverse reaction after the shot, then the video will be removed. Same with doctors and scientists trying to warn the public. These people and their true stories are actually being censored so that the public is never warned or able to make an informed decision. Wouldn't you call that a conspiracy?"

Rather than waiting for an answer, he said, "If you'll notice, people are suddenly dying from natural causes again." His frustration was evident as his voice grew louder. "Such hypocrisy! In 2020, Covid case numbers and deaths were overinflated to drive fear. Then they changed the official Covid reporting method so that case numbers were more accurate, much lower. That change in reporting coincided with the rollout of the shots. And now that the shots have failed and vaxxed people are getting and spreading Covid, they're changing the method of reporting yet again."

"So you think they wanted the case numbers to look lower to prove the vaccine was effective?"

"Absolutely. They now admit the PCR tests are flawed. Since there were hundreds of thousands of false positives, the numbers of cases and transmissions were never as bad as they made them out to be. But they needed to push for a vaccine, a "shot in every arm" on the planet. They reported skewed numbers of deaths. Now they're doing the exact opposite, downplaying shot-related deaths.

"It's proven through breakthrough cases that the shots failed and never did prevent contraction or transmission of Covid. But the government and media are now beginning to point the finger at the unvaccinated, as if we're to blame for infections in the vaccinated. The more likely scenario is that the withholding of early treatments and the compromised immune systems of those who've been jabbed are the issue.

"For people like us who refuse the shot–you mark my words–this blame game will be the tightening of the noose, their next step in putting pressure to get every person injected. Infected people who've had the shot will believe we're to blame, which will create more social pressure and bullying."

"What about the people who've already been vaccinated? If the shot is dangerous, what can they do?"

"They can *not* take the second dose if they've only had one. They can *not* take it again when boosters are required. They can amp up their immune system. Other than that, I'm not sure. We are in uncharted territory, listening to a medical community who is hiding the true statistics."

"This is terrifying," she said. "I have friends who've taken the vaccine. Some had pretty serious issues; others haven't."

"Another prime question we should ask is: Why are they pushing a shot on people so heavily for a virus with nearly a one hundred percent recovery rate? Why would they insist that those who've had the virus and have natural antibodies against Covid take a shot? Why would they want you to take this drug at all if there are inexpensive treatments, like, twenty-dollar treatments?" He paused. "We have to keep asking those questions and keep looking at the mounting evidence that gives their agenda away."

She said, "You're saying it circles back around to all the money to be made on vaccines for some and sets the stage for the one-world order for others?"

"That's exactly what is happening.

"Paige," Wyatt's voice was lower now, filled with intention as he looked her in the eye, "call me crazy all you want, but whether you want to admit it or not, this is a massive conditioning and control exercise, a diabolical plan that has been years in the making. Nations were shut down and economies destroyed. People were told to stay indoors and wear masks when out. For a time," he paused, "the enemy was successful in ending real communication and togetherness, thereby reducing the risk of an uprising of thinkers. I believe the masks were just the beginning, the testing of the waters of the general population to see how submissive we were. Social pressure alone did much of the policing.

"Same thing is happening with all the pressure and mass media campaigns to shame and intimidate everyone–all the people in all the world–to get the shot. Superstars and influencers are posting their photos of getting the shot and telling all their followers to get it. This is an enormous campaign of lies, an exercise in control.

"The one person who would most gain from the control of the world's population is who?"

When she sat looking at him, he said, "Say it."

She swallowed hard. "The Antichrist."

"That's exactly right." His eyes were trained on hers. "Who, but the father of lies, has more incentive to suppress the truth? Truth," he said with a burst of passion, "truth resides within the believer. Jesus said He is the way, the truth, and the life. In that case, He is truth in us. *Veritas* in Latin. It's a word that rings in my head and hardly ever leaves. We have to see truth and then live it. We can't fall to the pressure of this world no matter what culture is telling us. That applies to these shots, no matter what penalty we pay for not getting them."

"I see it now," she said in a near whisper. "It really is a part of what's coming."

She felt it, the color draining from her cheeks. The things Echo had said about vaccine passports came to mind. "Echo was right: The vaccine and the passport will somehow be used in conjunction with the mark if people can't buy or sell without it?"

"Eventually, yes. I'd bet my life on it. It's not now." His words were soft. "Remember, you can't have a mark of the beast without the beast. We won't be here for that. But I think it'll all come together to become what the Antichrist and false prophet will use as the mark. What better way to get the world to comply than to link the mark with fear over their health? For now, the proof of vaccination would be on people's phones, but when phones are so easily stolen or fraudulent paper passports are created, that will open the door for the masses to be chipped." He shook his head. "When we see the evil intentions now, how it's harming and killing people and how it will be used for even more evil in the days to come, we can have nothing to do with it."

Paige only nodded. The verse came to mind to avoid even the appearance of evil. This was all becoming too much for her, and her stomach cramped.

He rubbed his face. "It's just all coming so fast. I can't believe how few people see it for what it is."

"I understand what drives them," Paige said. "People want normal life back so badly that they are standing in line to get the shot."

"People are being lied to."

Paige could truly see piece after piece of the puzzle falling into place. "Echo and I were talking about it. They're conditioning people for the chip now by taking temps on the wrist and on the forehead. Later, they won't think anything about extending their hand or having their heads scanned."

"Exactly," he said. "It doesn't even have to be a chip to be scanned. The technology already exists, something called a Quantum Dot Tattoo. Medical and financial records can be stored within an applied tattoo that's readable with a scanner." He threw his arms out wide. "You can't even make this part up: The material that makes it readable is something called luciferase. I kid you not," he spelled it out, "L-U-C-I-F-E-R-ase. I hate to tell you this part, but it's made from what allows lightning bugs to glow at night. Lucifer means light-bearer. That's how in our face he is so close to the end."

With heart pounding violently, Paige drew in a sharp breath. "Stop! Just stop it. I can't take anymore."

Wyatt's eyes took on immense tenderness as he reached for her hand. "I'm sorry. I'm moving way too fast. Remember, you won't be here for that."

"I know that, but people I love will be."

"That's why we have to speak forth, Paige. Give them truth–the *veritas*–they need."

From then on both were fairly quiet. This recap with Wyatt brought such deep grief that Paige spent the next few minutes with eyes closed tight in prayer. Her words of pleading with God to deliver the people she knew soon shifted and took on a different tone. All she could ask was: What can I do? Those words resonated over and over in her mind like the clanging of a cymbal until a headache formed.

The phrase clanging cymbal brought the love chapter to mind from First Corinthians. She could have all the insight and understanding in the world, but if she didn't love, it meant nothing. Love speaks forth. Love tells the truth. Wyatt's word *veritas* seemed to whisper a challenge in her heart: Tell the truth. That's all you can do.

Her eyes snapped open, and she said aloud without intending to, "I really need to become a Daybreaker."

Wyatt didn't seem at all surprised by her admission. "Yes, Paige, you were always meant to be a Daybreaker."

His acknowledgement should have reassured her, but that wasn't the case. If anything, she felt even more unequal to the task. All this craziness she was discovering, no one would believe her if she did tell. She hadn't believed until those gunshots were fired; only then was she forced to listen.

She spoke the one thing she did believe, "I won't be here for what's coming." Her next words were quiet. "I want to take as many people with me as I can when I'm caught up. No man left behind."

Deep dimples formed when Wyatt said, "I always knew you would get to this place."

This stranger who loved her affected her more than made sense. "Thank you for coming for me."

Emotion-filled, his words were quiet yet emphatic. "I will always come for you."

Proposal

Day 3, 6:13 p.m.

From the moment they had landed and transferred over to a dark SUV, Paige had been surrounded by protectors. Cade drove with Bash riding shotgun. Serious and on high alert, neither man was now as warm and friendly as the day she had met them online. Hank followed behind them, and Halo drove the SUV in front. Wyatt had ridden in the backseat with Paige, always watching around them for a tail. All wore a solemn expression at the gravity of the situation and the potential danger of Paige entering the city where Groves possessed such far-reaching power.

Still surrounded by those fully armed men, she had been ushered through the lobby of the Hyatt into the elevator, then to a room situated between two rooms housing the team.

One room with two queen beds wasn't a concern for Paige. It wouldn't have mattered anyway since Wyatt hadn't given her an option.

He said little and still wore an intense expression as they entered their room. "Take the far bed," he said.

Paige tossed her bag on the bed and sat. She didn't ask questions. By the team's conduct, Paige, too, had sensed danger lurking around every corner, a reality that should have her on edge. She should be terrified, but, instead, she was more focused on the change in Wyatt since their conversation on the plane. From the moment of descent and even up until now, he was a changed man. This Wyatt was an alert soldier who seldom looked at her while watching over her methodically.

The verse her dad had written in the note came to mind again. Maybe that was where her unusual sense of well-being had stemmed from. She hadn't even looked it up since she knew it by heart: "Even though I walk through the valley of the shadow of death, I fear no evil, for You are with me; Your rod and Your staff, they comfort me."

The familiar words reminded her she wasn't in this alone. Wyatt and the guys with her were God's very rod and staff of reassurance and protection.

Wyatt's expression at the moment certainly didn't exude peace. She watched him as he did the same as her and sat at the foot of his bed. Still, he wasn't looking at her. Finally, he said, "This was a mistake. The city is swarming with traffic cams. If they've tapped in..." He looked at her. "I should have found someone to pose as you and go to the bank. This could be a setup."

Paige said nothing, though she had thought the same thing about it being a setup countless times on the plane.

"You can stay here, and I'll –"

"I'm going to that bank," she said. "How else would you gain access?"

"I'll go." He covered his face and rubbed, then let out a long sigh. "I don't know. I'll figure something out."

"You can't go. The account is in my name."

He jumped to his feet and started to pace. When he stopped, his eyes bright with what must be a clever idea, he said, "I'll tell them you're my fiancé."

"What? That's ridiculous." With a bit of a smirk, she said, "I thought you didn't lie."

Wyatt stood looking at her, his expression so firm that he hardly resembled the easygoing man she had stolen cookies for at Aunt Bertie's.

"I won't lie." He took another step, hesitated a second and stood blinking, then closed the final distance between them.

When he dropped onto one knee, Paige's eyes grew wider and she sat staring at him. Her mouth had gone suddenly dry and her hands trembled enough that she had to sit on them.

"Paige Donovan," he said, "will you –"

"This isn't even funny!" She tried to stand, but he placed his hands on her knees.

"I'm not joking. Say you'll marry me someday, and it'll be official. I'll say I'm your fiancé at the bank and that you're sick. We can have you on a video chat, and you can show your ID." He didn't move. Instead, he only looked at her with greater intensity. "We'll figure it out."

"You have lost your mind!" She removed his hands from her knees and stood. "I hope you've found it by the time I get out of the shower."

While she rummaged through her duffle bag, Wyatt stood and went to the window, separating the drapes only a little. "Why would he do this, put you in danger this way?" he said. "Why didn't he put my name on the account?"

"Look, favorite son..."

Wyatt's head snapped around at that.

"I have no idea. I just know that it's my name and my key. This is my lemonade trail to follow. I'm going to that bank tomorrow. Whatever is there may help my dad. I'll get it, and then we'll decide our next steps."

"Why did he send it to you?"

She stopped searching for the toothbrush she may have forgotten. "I don't know, Wyatt," she said in a sharp tone. "Maybe he believes in me, believes I can do this."

His face fell, and he moved to her side before she could get away. "Of course he believes in you. This isn't about that at all." He became quiet for a few seconds before reaching for her arms. "I didn't mean it that way. I believe in you too. I'm just afraid for you. I can't let you place yourself in danger by walking into that bank."

"I'm grateful for the way you've watched over me. If not for you..." She shook her head, not wanting to consider what those men might have done to her if not for Wyatt. "So don't take this as me being ungrateful: But you don't get to tell me what I can and can't do. I will walk into that bank first thing in the morning. And I will access that box to find out what my dad has on Groves. If it's proof he's been harming young girls, then it's worth the risk. You're welcome to come with me if you'd like."

She stepped around him and went to the bathroom, then paused at the door. "If you want to do something to help, find me a toothbrush."

Paige washed her face and showered. After their conversation, she had anticipated being shaken by it. Oddly enough, she wasn't at all. She had stood her ground, knowing what she had to do. It wasn't like a shot would ring out from some far away window when she entered the bank. They were more set on capturing her, a thought that caused a pit to form in her stomach. It didn't seem probable that they would follow her into the bank and grab her there.

Wyatt wasn't likely mistaken in his concerns, but he was certainly allowing his feelings for her to overdramatize the situation. Good grief, had he actually dropped onto one knee?

A tap sounded. When she cracked open the door, only a hand and a toothbrush appeared. She opened the door enough to peek out and look at him. "Thank you."

"I've found my mind," he said with a sheepish grin. "Well, at least pieces of it, so it's safe to come out when you're finished."

She grinned at that. "I found a piece in here on the counter. I'll bring it when I come. In the meantime, I'll let you borrow Psalm 23:4. Or better yet, maybe my dad sent me the key and you the verse."

Wyatt nodded and took a step back. "Maybe he did. I don't even need to look it up."

Paige closed the door and wiped the condensation from the mirror with her hand. His willingness to laugh at himself would hopefully alleviate what was sure to have been an awkward night stuck in the room together after his proposal. She grinned at her reflection, especially as she pictured that lunatic dropping onto one knee.

Closed Door

Day 3, 11:11 p.m.

Paige's eyes fluttered open, and for a few seconds she lay there trying to figure out where she was until the memory of the flight to Baltimore came.

A glance at the clock said it was only a little after eleven. It was coming back to her, her dinner with Wyatt in their room together with them both trying to make casual conversation after his stupid fake proposal. Not long after that, as Wyatt had showered, Paige had only intended to rest on her bed until he was finished. Four hours later...

Something else began to surface in her mind, the images she had encountered just before waking. Her father had been off in the distance speaking to her, but she couldn't hear him. More of the dream reemerged as Wyatt was suddenly standing with her dad speaking to Paige as well. She had kept shouting to them that she couldn't hear. Her final words had been, "I'm too far away!"

Paige sat on the side of the bed trying to steady her now racing heart. Her chest was tight, and her breath came in rapid bursts. Wyatt's steady breathing nearby in the other bed, something that seemed nearly familiar since her dream of waking with him sleeping on her pillow, only made things worse. Her cheeks grew warm at the memory.

Words came and began to mingle with her thoughts, offering insight that didn't surprise her so much. Rather than fight their invasion, she decided to meet the words head on for the first time in a very long time. She reached for her duffle bag and drew out her Bible. With it in hand, she sneaked past Wyatt's bed and to the bathroom.

After drying out the water in the bathtub, she rolled up another towel and stepped into the tub, then stretched out and tucked the towel behind her head. Better than the toilet, she thought as she flipped to the Gospels and began to read.

Not more than ten minutes later, a light tap sounded. "You okay? Are you sick?"

"I'm fine."

A few seconds later, with growing concern in his voice, he said, "Are you sure?"

"You can come in and see for yourself."

The door opened slowly, and just as she had expected, his lips were drawn into a grimace. Then once seeing her, he actually laughed out loud. "I didn't expect this."

"I didn't want to wake you."

He came and squatted down next to the tub. "You can come back out and read. The light won't bother me."

"I'm good right here," she grinned and added, "trying to cleanse the temple."

With another soft chuckle, he nodded. "I like Bible humor."

"With the way I've been running," she said, "I'm not sure I'm being funny."

Wyatt sat and wrapped his arms around his legs. "Let me guess, you're reading about the prodigal?"

Paige looked at the open Book and back at him. "Good guess."

"I see shame written all over your face." He paused. "It's not like you've been out running amuck."

She arched an eyebrow. "Who says that: running amuck?"

"My granddad did. I spent a lot of time with him when I was a kid." His eyes filled with mischief. "I did a whole lot of running amuck back then."

That was an image easy to conjure up, this now incorruptible man once running amuck as a boy.

She grinned at him. "No, I've not been out running amuck, but I've sure ignored a father," she pointed up, "and a Father who both tried to get my attention." Her heart sank. "How can I ever be what I'm supposed to be if I haven't been who I should've been?"

"There's a way back for you. You'll find it right where you're looking." He tapped her Bible with his fingers. "Personally, I think you're reading the wrong story."

"What should I be reading?"

"Let's hammer this out together." For a few seconds he cast his eyes up and to the left. He did a little scratching on his beard. Finally, he nodded and said, "Maybe when your mom died and your dad took off, you got tossed into a well, then sold into slavery."

"Slavery to what?"

"You tell me."

With a pucker of her lips and a few taps on her chin, her thinking face, she finally said, "Anger and resentment." She blinked long. "Grief, pain, and loneliness. It's held me hostage for years now."

"Add to it fear of sickness," he said, "and all the lies and ways you've been manipulated by the world."

"I was never really afraid for myself, not of the virus."

"But you were isolated nonetheless." When she nodded, he said, "Maybe I can see something broader than you can see for yourself. Joseph was held hostage by the world too. All that time, though, and all those painful experiences were his training ground. God was getting him ready for a mighty work."

Paige had to look away from his calculating stare. "Don't say that of me. I don't see how I can make much of a difference."

"I know you can. I'm not sure you will until you get back in tune with God. It doesn't take a shrink to figure it out. You associate God with your dad. So when your dad left, you left God. I'm sure you've heard people say, 'God doesn't move, so it's you who stepped away'?" At her nod, he said, "That's only true in part. It is us who takes the step away." Wyatt smiled and pointed up. "But He goes too. Jesus goes where we are. We may feel like we've run or that we're not in intimate touch with Him, but He never lets us out of His sight. No one takes us out of His hand; even we can't take ourselves out once we're in His grip of grace."

His words brought peace, proof already that Wyatt was speaking truth.

"Think of your house, Paige, that little nook where you write. I can see you sitting there, typing away while the Lord sits in that flowery chair in the corner nearby."

"Paisley," she said. "It's paisley, not floral."

He cut his eyes away and back. "Paisley chair if we have to imagine it literally." He smiled when she did. "That's been the image of you, your back to Jesus and looking at the world, at least the world through your computer. You've lived absorbed in your colors and buildings and scenery while He sat close by waiting for you to turn back." He hesitated a second. "That's really all it takes. Don't make this complicated. Just turn back around."

Paige sat thinking, then said more to herself than to Wyatt, "I haven't done that over the past few days."

"Done what?"

"This thing I do in my head, a rambling of colors and descriptions."

Wyatt's soft sigh indicated he thought she had missed his deeper meaning. Still, with understanding, he said, "You've had plenty to keep your mind occupied."

"I don't think that's it. Since my dad left, that's been my way of not thinking about my parents and...." Truth was stirring within so that it all made perfect sense now.

"And God?" he said.

"I was going to say the Word. If I had words continually floating around in my head: colors and descriptions, then *the* Word didn't have room to invade."

"You've just proven my point, that this started with your dad. You stepping away from the Word and God correlates to that."

"It really doesn't take a shrink to figure out, huh?"

"But you've known this, really."

"I have."

"For the record," he said, "you're not alone in your response. There's a verse in Jeremiah where God says His people's backs are to Him and not their faces. Many believers are living like that." He shrugged. "I have. We get saved and make little progress in our walk with the Lord, so we end up turning our faces back toward the world we know, looking for something–we all have our something–rather than looking to Him.

"Figure out what your something is, Paige. Then realize whatever it is you're looking for, it's found only in Jesus. Sounds too simple, but it really is. Even the fulfillment I found in physical relationships," he paused as his cheeks flushed. "That physical yearning was just a symptom of a spiritual need. What I really needed was a deeper fulfillment in Him, to be satisfied in a spiritual way that I hadn't been as an early believer."

Paige sat looking at Wyatt. This was deep talk, things she needed to consider for herself, but at the moment she could only focus on her stomach, and how when he had mentioned physical fulfillment with other women, it had done this funny little thing, a little flip and flop. His words didn't sit well with her.

"You missed your dad," he said. "When you could have turned to God to meet the need his absence created, you instead turned away to punish Him like you wanted to punish your dad."

"That's exactly what I did."

"Remember," he said with a soft tap on her arm, "it's easy. Just turn back."

She was sincere in her next words. "I will. I am."

"Good for you. I'm here if you need to talk more." He grinned. "I don't want things to be as awkward between us as they were tonight. I acted like an idiot."

Paige nodded. "That knee drop was..." She shook her head and thought. "I'll go with totally insane rather than really stupid."

He didn't smile. "I'm not afraid of anything–ever–but riding in that car today," he paused and glanced away, "I really was. I don't know how to process fear."

"You're really never afraid?"

"Never. And it's not some holy trust in God. I was like that even as a kid." He now grinned. "I broke so many bones on bikes and falling out of trees, the police once questioned my mom at the ER thinking maybe I was being abused. I literally don't experience fear. I've always thought something was broken in my head."

"But today proved otherwise?" she said.

He chuckled. "Let's just say I'm not so broken after all. Fear made me do something totally insane and really stupid all rolled up into one. Besides the obvious down-on-one-knee thing, I made you think I don't believe in you. I genuinely do. I'm just so afraid I'll let you get hurt. That would wreck me."

His final words nearly brought tears to her eyes. She said, "I have to do this."

"I know you do. And I have to trust the Lord and do some Psalm 23-ing over the situation. I'm so proud that you're even willing." His smile showed his embarrassment when he said, "I'll be right there by your side in the bank as the guy who works for your dad."

"You're more to me than that."

Wyatt stood. "I'll let you do a little more bathtub reading. If you want to talk, I'll be the guy on the other side of that door."

Paige stared at the closed door. A sound resonated in her mind, bringing with it a memory of the day she had found her dad's house empty and for sale. That final time she left, she had slammed the door so hard behind her that the windows rattled. Nothing was ever the same after that.

Her dad and Jesus had both been locked on the other side of that door since then. For now, she couldn't fix things with her dad, but she could with Jesus.

Paige turned to Revelation and scanned the letters to the churches. There in the last one, Jesus said,

"Behold, I stand at the door and knock; if anyone hears My voice and opens the door, I will come in to him and will dine with him, and he with Me."

In these words she saw a spiritual application for her own life. Paige whispered aloud, "My door is open, Jesus."

She would believe Wyatt that it was just that easy to turn back.

Paige closed the Bible and looked again at the door. Understanding came with an enormous surge into her heart. She smiled. All that time she had felt so alone, her Father had been there waiting on her. So had her dad.

A gentle flutter began in her heart and made its way to her belly, the truth now more fully dawning on her, how both her spiritual and physical worlds were so intertwined. Wyatt had also been just a closed door away, his love for her a portrait of Jesus' love for her. The distance she had created between herself and Jesus hadn't hindered His affections for her at all. He had waited right there in that paisley chair.

Like a warm breeze blowing, the comparison stirred within: Wyatt, like her Groom, had loved her and watched over her from afar. Knowing came with a sudden gust: She would love that man someday. She didn't yet, but something was present already, maybe the first stirrings of affection. She could only wonder if this awareness in three days was any more preposterous than him loving her from afar. There was only one way to find out, and that was to let Wyatt, like Jesus, walk through that closed door too.

When she entered the darkened room and heard a little snore, Paige tried to tiptoe past his bed. For a man who didn't sleep much, he was getting plenty of sleep that night.

Wyatt sat up, turned on the light, and rubbed his eyes. "I dozed; I think."

"I'm sorry I woke you again."

"It's okay. I've got to go to the bathroom anyway. It was occupied before with some weird girl in the tub."

She smiled and went to sit on the side of his bed. "You've been able to sleep tonight," she said.

"Yeah, I did at Bertie's too. I'm figuring out I can sleep when you're close and I know you're safe."

He rubbed his eyes again, and Paige looked at his left hand, her dream of him sleeping so soundly next to her invading her thoughts.

She sat looking at him so long, he finally said, "What?"

A little grin tugged at her lips. "I think I just might marry you someday."

There was a long moment where they sat looking at one another. She wasn't sure what she read in his eyes, a mixture of what seemed to be relief and surprise, maybe even a little excitement.

Paige stood and went to climb back into her bed, then reached for the light and switched it off.

Wyatt went to the bathroom and came back.

She heard him settle in and fluff pillows. Then with a soft chuckle, he said, "That was easy. And only day three."

"That was a maybe," she said.

"Close enough for now."

"Go to sleep, Wyatt."

"Already drifting." A quiet moment passed when he said, "I know you haven't felt very loved here lately, but you have been."

His words expressed her earlier understanding of how much love had resided on the other side of that closed door. With a soft smile in the darkness, she said, "That was pretty close to you actually saying it."

"Close."

Nothing more was said. It didn't need to be. She whispered a whole lot of thank yous to the Lord: for Him waiting in her paisley chair, for her dad watching over her. Her heart beat a little faster when she whispered aloud, "and for Wyatt."

Her last prayer for the night was, *Please give me the opportunity to tell my dad I'm sorry and that I love him.*

Lock Box

Day 4, 6:10 a.m.

"Morning," Wyatt said from his bed.

Paige squinted and raised her head just enough to see him sitting on the foot of his bed. "Did I oversleep?"

"No. It's early still if you want to get a little more rest."

"I'm fine." She sat up and ran her fingers through her matted hair. "Starving."

"I'll order something."

He was different, now the soldier Wyatt who had accompanied her to the hotel. "You're worried again," she said.

"If your dad had his phone on him when he went into that bank, then they may know we're coming."

"Would you leave your phone on if you were him?"

"No."

"Then trust that he knew what he was doing."

He didn't look at her. "He always knows what he's doing. I still don't like this."

"We have no other choice," Paige said. She swung her legs over the side of the bed and sat looking at him. "This, Mr. Running-Amuck Wyatt, is what the rest of the world feels. Fear can be debilitating if you allow it."

"You have to be scared too," he said.

"I'm trying to push that aside. I care more about my dad than anything else right now. If this is what it takes to help him and take Groves down, then I'm willing."

His voice was low. "I'm proud of you."

Paige nodded, his words meaning more to her than made sense. There was a small part of her that kept from panicking just for Wyatt's sake. She wanted him to see her as the strong woman she had always been rather than the blubbering mess he had known these past few days.

"I want to ask you something," she paused and looked him in the eye, "and I need you to be totally honest with me."

"You know I'll be honest."

"I know you're honest, but often you tell me a shade of the truth but not the whole truth. You hold back. This time I need the whole truth."

He nodded.

"Do you think my dad is still alive?"

His hesitation was his answer, still, he said, "I honestly don't know anymore. It's day four. I can't imagine anything other than him being seriously injured," he paused and sighed, "or dead that would keep him from checking in to see if I got you out in time. Nothing would matter more to him."

Paige gave a little nod of her head. "That's my thought by now too. I fear this may be a recovery effort and not a rescue."

"I don't want to believe that," Wyatt said, his words filled with evident sadness.

"It wasn't right, how he did this," she said. "If he had told me he was staying away because his work would place me in danger, at least I would have seen things in a different light. His secrets were what erected the wall, not just my anger."

"Honestly, I agree. I told him as much." Wyatt leaned forward and propped his elbows on his knees. "You would have handled that better. But like you said, your dad really was different after your mom died. He never went back to being the man either of us knew."

"He didn't?"

"No. He never said it, but I think much of what drove him was guilt. I think he had a hard time looking you in the eye since he blamed himself for your mom's death."

"Or maybe he saw my mom when he looked at me."

"Whatever it was, Paige, I know it has hurt you deeply. I think you have a right to feel that. I'm just asking you to remember that something shifted within him when he discovered what really killed your mom." Wyatt straightened. "After all you've seen, Sentinel and Overwatch and how he's had me watching over you when he couldn't, that has to help you know how much he loves you."

"I do know that now." Tears floated in her eyes. "It helps and gives me back the dad I remember."

"We won't give up looking. You can believe that." Wyatt nodded and stood. "I'll order something to eat if you want to get dressed. We'll leave here a few minutes before nine since it's just down the street. I'm hoping it won't be busy on a Saturday morning. I want to get you in and out fast."

"I'll get dressed." She stood and then hesitated at the foot of his bed. "I'm scared too, Wyatt. Not so much about today as I am over where it'll leave me if my dad is gone."

"If he's gone, I'll help you get through it."

Based on the pain so evident in his eyes, she said, "I think you'll need a little help too. I'll be here for you."

The transport to the bank was the same as to the hotel. The three vehicles remained bumper to bumper traveling the few minutes down Light Street. Its name wasn't lost on Paige and made her wonder if her dad had chosen this bank specifically for its street location.

They came to a stop in front of the bank, and Wyatt reached for her hand. "You sure about this?"

She forced a smile. "Come on, with a name like Light Street, this'll be a piece of cake."

"I was just wondering if your dad chose this location for that reason."

"Me too." She gave his hand a little squeeze. "Let's get this done. We have to finish what he started."

Paige remained seated until the team was in place on the sidewalk. Wyatt took her hand and helped her from the car. The five men walked nearby. At the bank entrance, Halo and Hank moved to stand at either side of the front doors while Bash and Cade walked one behind and one before Paige and Wyatt into the bank.

The wait for someone to allow her entry into the vault was only a few minutes. Bash and Cade hovered nearby but not so close as to be conspicuous. Wyatt was never more than an inch away from Paige's side. Everywhere she looked, every face that looked at her, seemed to be a source of potential danger. With each breath she forced a steady rhythm so that she wouldn't resort to panic as the situation warranted.

"I'm Clarice," the woman said and held her hand out to Paige.

"Paige Donovan." Paige had her ID ready.

"Wyatt Fletcher," he said, "Paige's fiancé."

Paige turned to look at Wyatt, his smirk making her smile amidst a tense situation. It wasn't as much that he introduced himself that way; it was that she hadn't even known his last name until that moment. How could she be maybe-someday engaged to a man and not even know his last name?

"Sounds crazy to say it out loud, huh?" Wyatt said to her, his relaxed manner now totally unlike the high-strung soldier who had escorted her in.

To Clarice, he said, "We just got engaged last night, so it's still a little surreal."

His playful tone calmed her. Paige flashed a wry smile. "I seem to recall saying maybe."

"Maybe is as good as a yes to me." He winked at her. "Once I get the engagement ring, it'll be official."

"Don't you dare get me a ring."

Clarice said, "What? Let this man of yours get you a ring."

"I'm not a ring kind of girl." She grinned and looked down at her bare finger. "I think I'm more of a plain-gold-band girl." She blinked a few times and considered that maybe Dream Paige had left her engagement ring on the dresser like her mom used to do.

Her head flew up and she looked at Wyatt. "Now I've lost my mind."

With a sweet grin, he said, "I'll help you find it."

Paige filled out the signature card, and they followed Clarice to the vault. In route Paige whispered, "You better not get me a ring."

Wyatt lowered his head and whispered back, "I may not lie, but I never said that I mind very well."

At the thought of Wyatt actually showing up with a ring, Paige said, "We're not really engaged."

"You may not be."

They entered the room, and all the joking now seemed suddenly out of place. It wasn't lost on her that Wyatt had likely kept her mind occupied for just this reason, because he knew how real the situation would feel once she opened her dad's lock box.

With the two of them now left alone at the table where the metal box was placed, Paige noted how Wyatt's expression had changed as well. Once again, he was the solemn soldier from her caravan.

Her hands trembled as she opened the box. She glanced up at Wyatt to find he had noticed. He nodded, and she reached in to take the envelope from the box.

"Let's just take it and go," he said in a low voice. "We'll open it once we get you out of here."

Paige raised her head and flashed a brilliant smile toward the waiting Clarice. "That's all we need for today."

Getaway

Day 4, 9:20 a.m.

As easy as that, Paige and Wyatt walked out the door with Bash and Cade once again behind and before them. When they exited, Wyatt reminded her, "Head down."

Halo held the door open for them, then all the team dispersed into the three vehicles once Paige and Wyatt were loaded into the back of the middle SUV.

When the door was closed and the caravan was underway, Paige let out a loud gush of air. "See, piece of cake."

Wyatt fell back hard against his seat and rubbed his face. "Well," he said, "let's see what we just risked your life for."

Paige opened the envelope with now-steady hands and pulled out a flash drive then a note. When Wyatt took the drive, Paige opened the folded sheet.

> Paige,
>
> This should be everything you need to stop Groves. Don't trust the local authorities. Take the drive to where the grass is greener. Honestly, I don't know who you can trust, so be wary of everyone outside the team.
>
> Paige, you are your father's daughter. Never doubt your strength or the strength of the One who sustains you.
>
> (Psalm 28:7)
>
> Love, Dad

Wyatt's puzzled expression amused Paige. Only now did he seem to relax a little.

He scratched his head. "Where is the grass greener?"

"I know exactly where that is," she said. "Arlington. My dad's old friend from Hunter took a Pentagon position. He always told my dad the grass really was greener out of the sandbox." She thought of his daughter's recent post on Facebook. "He's a Brigadier General now, Allen Gwaltney."

"He could be surveilled."

"All we can do is reach out. I'm not sure how much he can help, but if nothing else, he will know of someone at the FBI who can be trusted."

Wyatt's apprehension was evident. "Have they stayed in touch?"

"I don't know how much the past few years. We used to do a lot together as families, but that's been many years ago."

When Wyatt only nodded and sat looking at her with a mind that was clearly calculating odds and risks, she said, "We have to do this."

She looked again at the note and said, "I don't know this verse."

Wyatt said, "'The Lord is my strength and my shield', a favorite of your dad's here lately."

A smile tugged at her lips, at how her dad had included an encouraging verse with both notes. "He was today, wasn't He?"

"Yes," Wyatt said, "He certainly was. That could've really gone sideways."

He tapped his earpiece. "Set a course for Arlington." Wyatt then grinned and said to Paige, "Echo says congrats on our engagement."

Her eyes grew wider, and before she could say anything, Bash turned in his seat. "You should have a ring. Every girl deserves a ring."

Cade glanced at her in the rearview mirror. "A big, fat diamond. I'm thinking a princess or emerald cut."

"We're not engaged!" she said, with only laughter in response from the front seats.

"I'm engaged." Wyatt's words were soft, and he wasn't smiling.

With cheeks burning, intending to redirect the conversation, she said, "So everyone has coms but me?"

"You'll get your own next time." He reached over and took hold of her hand. "You did good. Your dad would be so proud of you."

She blinked and held her eyes closed a few seconds longer than usual. When she looked back at Wyatt, she said, "Something tells me we'll find him."

He gave her hand a little squeeze. "I believe you're right."

Paige knew Wyatt would never say that if he didn't believe it. This time her long sigh allowed more than nervousness to escape her. It was her purging her recent loss of optimism. Truly, hope filled that space and gave her reason to believe again.

The drive through the city to the airport allowed Paige a moment to reflect. She could have very well lost her life. That thought should terrify her, but it didn't. There had been something about that team of massive soldiers surrounding her, like an army of the Lord who would have died rather than allowing her to be captured. It made no sense whatsoever, how in the midst of the most difficult time in her life, with her dad missing and danger looming around her, that she experienced such a sense of belonging with this group of men who cared enough to be the Lord's rod and staff.

Wyatt leaned over and said, "Fletcher."

"Yeah, I know that now."

He grinned. "Donovan is a great man's name. I'm sure you'll want to hyphenate."

While he was likely joking, his words caused her to choke up a little. He was right. When she did marry this crazy soldier next to her, she would definitely keep that great man's name. "Look what you've started with the guys," she said. "I only said maybe."

"It's just day four."

Paige was about to reply but remained quiet when she noted the change in Wyatt's demeanor. His eyes darted around, and he said, "Check your six."

"Got it," Cade said.

She didn't ask, but the sudden altered mood in the car didn't necessitate the question. Someone was following them. Traffic was heavy, so gaining speed to evade the tail wasn't possible. Cade began to weave in and out of cars when even the smallest space was open. Horns blared.

Halo, in the SUV in front, was running interference, blocking the flow of a lane when he could to allow them to get through. For a few seconds they ran side by side with Halo until he swerved, cutting off a minivan, in order to get in front of them again.

Each of the three soldiers now had weapons drawn, Wyatt's resting on his right thigh.

Paige turned to look behind them as Wyatt was now doing. Hank was trying his best to block the approaching dark sedan. Finally, just before crossing through a traffic light, he rammed the car into a light pole then pulled back into the intersection and soon caught up with them.

It was all happening so fast that she couldn't keep up with the conversation. At times Wyatt would talk to Cade and then to the escorting drivers. Once, she was pretty sure he was talking to Echo since he was asking about an exfil and flight plan. Most notable was how none reacted with raised voices. Their tones remained steady and calm, this clearly not their first escape.

Wyatt reached for Paige's hand but never looked at her. "Break away, Halo. We'll lose the tail. Be ready for a hot entry."

"Another on your six," he said to Cade.

"Hank, do what you've got to do. We've got to lose him before heading to the airfield. Echo has taken down the cams. If we can duck out, then maybe we can squeeze in unnoticed."

With her attention focused behind them, Paige didn't understand the implications of Bash yelling, "Nine!"

The impact near her side door and the side air bag deploying flung her toward Wyatt. But still, Cade didn't stop and now drove half on a deserted stretch of sidewalk.

"The nine is disabled," Bash said.

Her ears were ringing, and the world took on a dream-like quality where voices seemed distorted and faraway.

Wyatt reached for her, placed one hand behind her neck, and pulled her closer. She was pretty sure he said, "Are you okay?"

Paige only stared at him wild-eyed.

"We'll get you out of here." His words were a little clearer now, and his forced smile exposed his uncertainty.

Wyatt sat back, then said to Cade. "Hank sidelined the tail. Get us gone."

The last mile toward the airfield was no less tense. Though the two remaining vehicles traveled unhindered and at top speed, not one word was said other than Wyatt's one interaction with Echo.

Paige was silent, her piece-of-cake mission now leaving her truly shaken and more than likely bruised. Wyatt held her hand, often giving it a little squeeze for reassurance. The way he kept looking over at her, his eyes filled with concern, she didn't dare mention the pain in her left hip since it wasn't likely anything serious.

Their vehicles pulled right up to the open steps of the jet on Wyatt's side. He stepped from the SUV and held out his hand to keep her in place. Once the team surrounded the open door, Paige was ushered from the car, up the steps, and into the plane.

Fastened in and taxiing down the runway, only then did she trust her voice to speak. "If they all come with us, then who will be here to look for my dad?"

"We are doing what the Apex would direct: watching over his daughter."

Paige didn't back down. "Bash should stay since he's on the inside."

"He's coming."

"But –"

"Don't!" The look in her watcher's eyes left no room for debate. "I'm in charge when the Apex isn't in command. They're all coming." Wyatt sat back in his seat next to her and closed his eyes. With one hand he covered his mouth and rubbed his chin. The other reached for hers.

A quiet moment later, he whispered, "I would die before I'd let them take you."

That was it. Tears came, but Paige refused to weep aloud. Instead, they trailed down her cheeks, so she turned to look out the window at the disappearing ground as the plane made its ascent.

Wyatt leaned in close, his face near her ear. "It's okay. We got away." He moved even closer until his lips grazed her cheek. Then he pulled her over to him and held her. "He is our strength and our shield."

Release

Day 4, 10:10 a.m.

Miles away from Baltimore now, Paige's emotions had settled until she was currently more in denial of what had taken place than she was in fear. When the memory of the car chase threatened to surface, she remembered instead Wyatt's soft words of comfort, that he would die rather than allow them to take her.

"You are our strength and our shield," she whispered aloud to the Lord in reflection.

For some time they had sat huddled together, and when he had turned her loose, Wyatt's eyes had conveyed indescribable tenderness and bewildering love. Those were the things she now held close to deflect anxiety over what may come next. The love of this near stranger gave her every reason to believe in her safety.

Currently, Wyatt was in the rear of the small plane speaking to the team in hushed tones.

Paige didn't try to overhear; she didn't want to know whatever he felt needed to be withheld from her.

Wyatt came back and took his seat. "Echo has been checking into the Brigadier General. He has routines we can leverage."

"Leverage how?"

"He runs at Gravelly Park every Saturday afternoon. I'll make contact with him there."

Paige stared at him for a few seconds. "You mean I'll make contact?"

"Absolutely not!"

"He doesn't know you," she said. "I've known him since I was six."

"I'll tell him I work with your dad."

"We're not doing this again," she said.

"After what just happened, you don't see how dangerous this is for you?"

"I do see. I knew it was dangerous going to the bank. Just because we were tailed doesn't change our mission. We have to do this to find my dad."

"We weren't just tailed, Paige. Someone crashed into us. You could've been hurt or taken." The shake of his head was adamant. "I'm sending you back to Overwatch with Halo. Echo will be waiting for you –"

"Why do we have to keep having this same argument? You may be in charge of the team with my dad gone, but I'm not under your command. I'm going to see Allen."

Wyatt let out a loud breath, leaned up, and rested his elbows on his knees. For the longest time he sat with his chin propped on his clasped hands. He didn't speak. He never looked at her. Eventually, he got up and moved to the back section of the plane again.

The flight was just over half an hour, so when they began their descent, Wyatt moved back to his seat and buckled his seatbelt. Still, he was quiet.

Once they landed and as the others deboarded, Wyatt held Paige's arm when she unbuckled her seatbelt. "Wait," he said, with a soft voice.

When only they remained, he turned to her. "I'm sorry. I won't keep having that same argument. I won't be that guy and keep undermining your confidence in what you're here to do."

She blinked a few times, noting the evident difficulty he had in saying the words.

"You did great at the bank," he said. "You didn't panic during the chase, and just like any other Daybreaker would do, your first concern when we all boarded was not for yourself but who would be left to look for the Apex." He paused. "Your dad believes in you. I believe in you. And," his eyes narrowed, "George Whitefield once said, 'We are immortal until our work on earth is done.' So that means that you've got time here, Paige. You have a job to do. I have to trust God with you. You are His Daybreaker–not mine. I release you to Him." With that he stood and waited for her to do the same.

Paige stood, masking the pain in her hip, and stepped out into the aisle.

Wyatt said, "This is your op, and you have a place here. But," he reached and took her fingers in his hand, "I hope after this, you'll be a word Daybreaker and not a field Daybreaker."

"Thank you for believing in me." She forced a smile when she looked up at him. "After all this, I think I'll be glad to give up being a field Daybreaker. Maybe I'll just make coffee for the real Daybreakers."

"You are a real Daybreaker, Paige. Even when you don't see it, I do."

Vehicles awaited them like before when they exited the plane. It was almost a copy and paste version of their morning caravan ride.

Wyatt said, "Hank has found us a place to lie low until this afternoon. City cams might be tapped here as well. That's the only way you could've been spotted in Baltimore."

Her brain was clicking. "So that's why Hank is called Fortress?"

"It is. He finds secure locations wherever we operate." Wyatt checked his watch. "We have a few hours to kill, and I didn't want to do it sitting there exposed on the tarmac. We'll get you something to eat," he said with a grin, "and your coms when we get there."

Paige only nodded and peered out the window as they rode. Once again, she wasn't as frightened as would make sense, but she certainly didn't take this as lightly as when she had been in route to the bank.

The crash had left more than her hip sore. She had once been in a fender bender and remembered waking the next morning feeling as if she had been hit by a train. That would likely be the case tomorrow.

"You okay?" Wyatt said.

She turned and gave him a reassuring smile. "I'm okay." That wasn't exactly true, but she would be. The sight of the man's face as he had plowed into them flashed before her eyes, and her heart raced. "Just ready to get off the road."

He leaned closer. "It'll fade."

Paige nodded and watched her surroundings until they pulled through a warehouse door. The vast emptiness hardly resembled Overwatch. While barren space for the most part, there were some makeshift areas separated from one another.

Wyatt led Paige to the remotest space behind a partition. "There's a restroom back there," he pointed, "but I'm guessing you're looking for that." He nodded at the single bunk with a blanket and pillow.

Paige smiled and tossed her bag on her bunk. "It crossed my mind." She looked at the bed, more than a little tempted to escape from the day. "I think I'll grab a bite with you guys instead."

Rather than moving back toward the common area, Wyatt sat on her bed. "I meant what I said today. I'm proud of you. Many aren't reporting for duty these days because they're scared or feel unqualified. You've really stepped up."

She sat next to him. "Because of my time away from the Word and the Lord, I know I'm unqualified."

"But?"

"But I'm not going to let the enemy psych me out. Even though I can feel it, some level of hesitation I don't understand myself, something tells me I'll get past it. I am stepping back into Jesus. I know that's where I start." When she grinned, she leaned a little closer and nudged Wyatt with her arm. "I hear He's been waiting right there in my flowery chair."

"Paisley," he said.

"Paisley, if we have to be literal." She sat a moment. "It's something," she said. "My greatest weakness throughout my life of faith has been exactly this, the last-days stuff. That and letting go of this world. Now here I am in the thick of things, and all I can do is wonder how I can help people. That one thought is ablaze within my heart." With a little shake of her head and a long blink, she looked back at Wyatt. "And it doesn't escape my notice how God has now given me a new world that's easier to let go of."

Wyatt stood and looked down at her. "I would have said that too a few days ago." With that he turned and walked away.

Paige sat watching him for a few seconds before standing to her feet and hobbling the first few steps to ward off her stiffening joints. She slowed and moved her waistband out to peek at her hip. No more than redness so far, but a bruise was coming. When exiting the car at the warehouse, for Wyatt's sake more than out of pride, she had forced herself to walk as normally as possible. He would take her pain way too personally.

That thought stopped her in her tracks. His care and concern for her were things that clearly hindered his judgment at times, a thought that actually scared her for him. Aunt Bertie's words came to mind, how Paige should be careful with a man who loved her so much. What should be a reassuring thought was now creating a sense of alarm in her belly–for him–not for her. A man who would die for her was not to be taken lightly.

Wyatt not being as willing to let go of this world as he had been just days before gave her reason to suspect that what he had said on the plane about releasing her to God wasn't exactly true, even if he didn't know it himself.

Cade calling for her from the outer area, asking what she wanted on her pizza, was a welcome distraction and got Paige moving again.

General

Day 4, 2:07 p.m.

Fitted with a mic in her ear, Paige sat on a park bench with her team scattered in various nearby positions. Wyatt was supposed to be reading a book, but he hadn't once looked down. She said, "You're not very convincing with your reading, Arrow."

He was close enough that she could see his grin. "I'm reading the situation and people."

Bash chuckled. "You haven't looked at a situation or person but Paper since you sat down."

"I've got eyes on the prize," Hank said, giving advance warning from his forward position.

Her heart pounded hard as she watched the familiar face come into view. When Wyatt said so, Paige stood and moved in Allen's direction. Even before she could speak, Allen began to slow and then stopped.

"Paige!" His eyes were wide.

"Hi," she said and stepped into his open arms. "It's good to see you."

He stammered at first and let her go, saying, "What are you doing here?"

When she formed the words to tell him her dad was missing, she said instead, "My dad sent me."

"Where is your dad?" His eyes narrowed. "Is he here with you?"

Something about his question made the stubble on her legs prickle. "No, he's out of town and couldn't make it. He asked me to reach out to you, to see if you can help."

Allen looked around, then back at her. "What can I do to help?"

"We need a name at the Bureau, someone who can be trusted with information."

His voice was a little unsteady, and his eyes darted away and back again when he said, "What kind of information?"

"Just something that needs to be investigated." Her next words weren't her own: "I don't have it with me. It's in a safe place," she said, both of which were true since Wyatt had the drive with him.

"I can get you a name." He looked around again and swallowed hard before saying, "You can come by the house later, and I'll have something for you."

Nothing about this familiar man was usual for him. While he didn't show it necessarily, she could almost feel his apprehension.

She looked him square in the eye to see his reaction to her question: "How are Allie and Steph?"

He didn't smile. "Steph is married now and living on the West Coast, and Allie is still working on her degree." He blinked long as if considering his next words carefully. "You'll get to see her. She's at home this weekend. You know how she is, always needing time with Mom and Dad."

"Yeah," Paige said with an understanding nod, "sounds like her."

"Well, you stop by later and bring what you have with you. I'll take a look at it."

"I'll do that," she said and reached out to hug him. "Thank you."

"You know I'd do anything for you and your dad, right?"

Tears nearly came, so Paige blinked long. "I do know that."

"I can see you all now," he said, "you girls playing on the lawn together, spraying each other with water guns and tossing balloons."

"I can see it," she said.

He moved in for a hug and whispered, "Take care, kid." His look was somber when he jogged away.

Paige ignored the yelp of her stiff hip, broke into a run, and never stopped when she reached Wyatt. "We need to get out of here. He's been compromised."

Wyatt didn't ask; he just fell in beside her as they made their way toward the SUV. The rest of the team were right behind them.

Once loaded into the car, she said, "Someone was listening to our conversation."

"How do you know?"

"They've got his family at home. Allie is the least dependent person on the planet."

Wyatt sat in the seat next to her nodding. "That's why he mentioned the water guns; they're holding his family." He paused. "They've instructed him to keep his normal routines in case you reached out."

Paige's breathing was still unsteady. "We have to go to his house."

"You have lost your mind," he said. "I'm not taking you to where I know Groves' men are waiting."

She didn't want that either. "Then you'll have to go. We're not leaving them to die."

"No, Paige, we won't leave them. I would never do that to a man who would risk everything to warn you."

With a soft sigh and pounding heart, she sat back in her seat and began to pray.

Wyatt said to Cade, "To the airfield." Then, "Echo, set a course for Greensboro."

Paige's eyes flew open. "But you said –"

"I'm doing what I said. The team will be at the General's house tonight, but in the meantime, I'm getting you out of Arlington."

"Why Greensboro?"

"I have a safe place there."

"I won't argue, but I do need my bag from the warehouse. I need my Bible."

"Fortress, make a stop and meet us at the plane."

Paige reached for Wyatt's hand, the first time she had ever done so except to help him up from the floor that first day. "Thank you for helping Allen. They're family to us."

"I see now why your dad trusted him with you. That he would give you a clue like that and risk his family makes him a man worth saving."

"They will, right, save them?"

"I have no doubt."

"Wyatt..." she hesitated, "that fleeting hope is gone now. I'm not so sure we'll find my dad alive."

"And I'm not losing hope," he said. "Not yet."

He wouldn't lie, so his hope rekindled her own. She let out a quiet sigh. It wasn't confident hope, but at least there was a glimmer.

Booby Trapped

Day 4, 3:49 p.m.

Little more than an hour and a half later, Paige rode next to a quieter-than-usual Wyatt. He had been the same during the flight. Her mind was occupied anyway, so the time to ponder was welcomed. Her dad was right about her, particularly today; the Word really did fall onto the Paige. Verse after verse formed in her mind, ones never forgotten, reminding her that turning back had really been as simple as Wyatt had suggested.

One urgent phone call had opened her eyes to two new realities: the earthly darkness and the soon-coming Light. With that in mind she recited rapture verses often, her favorite being how she would be caught up in the clouds to meet Him in the air.

This continued, the bouncing in her head through the Scriptures as she rode along in the pickup on the deserted stretch of highway. Wyatt's pinky finger was looped around hers; his touch, something that now felt natural to her, assured her that wherever he was taking her was for her best.

Paige wasn't sure anyone had ever reminded her more of Jesus than Wyatt. That observation led to another: On this journey, God could be trusted even more. If any truth needed to be imbedded into her belief system, it was that one. Her study of the rapture, that the insanity of this world was leading to His coming, didn't bring dread with it as it used to. It was more that she wondered what would happen if the Lord didn't come for them soon. With all that was coming against them, the thought of not being caught up and removed from the horror of it was enough to paralyze even the bravest of Daybreakers.

She stopped and considered that, herself as a Daybreaker. After her meeting with Allen in the park, though, she knew she was in training to be one. That was a test she had passed.

Brave. She tossed that word around in her head a few times, admitting she wasn't brave at all. If not for searching for her dad, Paige wouldn't likely be doing any of what she was doing. Her secret aches and pains reminded her that Wyatt was right. If she became one at all, she would need to be a word Daybreaker rather than one in the field.

When they turned off onto a long, narrow gravel road, she glanced at Wyatt and noticed how his jaw tensed and relaxed over and over. Wherever they were going didn't seem to bring him a sense of ease, not with the intensity she felt radiating from him.

Her heart beat a little faster, and not from the anticipation of where they were going. She looked down at their hands. At least she knew one thing riding beside this brave soldier: Her conclusion from the day before wasn't accurate at all. If her dad wasn't okay, she thought with a sinking stomach, at least she wouldn't be left living this out alone. That little pinky holding hers gave her all the reassurance she needed.

"You good?" he said.

"I am good." She looked up and blinked a few times. "It strikes me, though: This is our fourth city since yesterday if you count our trip back to Savannah."

Still, he wasn't smiling. "I've done more in less time."

Before she could respond, Wyatt slowed the truck, turned onto a gravel patch of ground, and came to a stop before a heavy chain cordoning off what seemed like nothing more than a trail leading into woodlands. Several warning signs were posted to keep out.

"I need you to stay right here. Got it?"

His forceful tone led her to only nod.

"No matter what happens next. You stay right here. Don't move. Just sit still." He didn't wait for her to respond this time and stepped from the truck and started walking with his arms held up in the air.

A shot rang out and hit the dirt in front of Wyatt, so he stopped dead in his tracks. She watched his care and hesitation as he slowly removed his ball cap and once again held both arms high in the air.

He stood motionless as if waiting for something. A few seconds later, Paige watched an armed man dressed in Army fatigues appear from the thick brush. He stopped and stood with rifle pointed squarely at Wyatt. Then, as Paige watched with a held breath, the man lowered his weapon and began to advance toward Wyatt, an act that was either a sign of aggression or anticipation.

When he reached Wyatt and wrapped his arms around him, only then did Paige understand: This was Wyatt's dad.

Once the two men stepped back from their quick embrace, they stood for only a few seconds talking. Then Wyatt came back to the truck and opened

Paige's door. "We'll have to make part of the trip on foot. Stay right by my side every second."

Paige didn't even nod; she just slid out of the truck and stood waiting, wild-eyed when he reached for her bag.

"You're safe here," he said. "I just mean the land is booby trapped." Wyatt took her hand and led her along.

They walked in silence through a large gate, then toward the hillside from where the man had descended. Paige struggled along behind Wyatt as they climbed the hill. Occasionally, the senior Fletcher would point, and they would all veer onto an alternate path. He never once spoke. The only words ever said were Wyatt's brief warnings to Paige to watch her step.

Once, as she struggled to keep up and limped a few times on a leg she feared may give out on her, Wyatt said low enough so only she would hear, "Are you hurt?"

"Just sore."

"Paige..." he sighed and kept moving in step behind his dad. "You should have said something."

"I'm fine. Don't worry."

Just then, they came to a small clearing where an old green pickup waited. When Wyatt opened the door for her, he said, "Not much longer now."

Waylon

Day 4, 4:17 p.m.

Paige rode in the middle seat of the truck between the two silent men. Only once they were within sight of his home did Wyatt's dad seem to relax. All along the unnerving drive, she had only looked straight ahead, so now, in her peripheral vision, she noted how his grip on the steering wheel loosened.

Wyatt had been no different. His hand had held to hers nearly painfully so since they had climbed into the truck.

While Wyatt opened a metal gate, his dad said, "Waylon."

"I'm Paige." She looked at him fully now for the first time. His son so resembled him that her tight shoulders relaxed in his presence. Besides their thick, curly hair, their eyes were the same, dark brown, conveying tenderness even when they didn't likely know it. How could she not trust the man who had fathered such an incorruptible arrow?

"Thank you for letting us come here," she said.

"You'll be safe."

During the remainder of the drive to the house, the two men spoke briefly about fishing and the current shortage of ammo. Wyatt's demeanor with his dad was respectful but not warm, more like a conversation between two soldiers than father and son.

It was clear now, how when Wyatt had said his dad wasn't healthy, he had meant mental illness. This place, so far off the grid and rigged with explosives, was evidence of that.

They now passed a group of buildings and barns and what was likely a smoke house. A bank of solar panels was to the right of the modest stone cottage, and a well was not far from the side of the house.

Waylon dropped them off in front of the house, then stayed in the truck.

Paige followed Wyatt up the steps, him holding her hand and watching her make her way up. "Are you sure you're not injured? You took a pretty hard hit."

"Positive. I wouldn't lie to you. I'm just sore."

"It'll be worse in the morning."

"I'll be okay."

"You don't have to be afraid of him," Wyatt said as he opened the door for her.

"I'm not."

"He's been stable for years now."

"I'm really not worried."

Wyatt hesitated just inside the door. "He's quiet except when he talks about the things he knows."

"We'll be fine."

"You will be." His eyes softened as he looked at her. "I need to be back in Arlington before dark."

"What do you mean? You're leaving?"

"I have to." He reached into his pocket and handed her the flash drive. "I don't know what the team will be walking into, especially now that Groves thinks you're in town." He paused and looked at her with determination. "The General risked his life for you. I'll risk mine for his family."

Tears filled her eyes. "I don't want you to go."

"You'll be fine here. I promise."

"That's not it at all."

Wyatt lowered his head and rested it on hers. "I'll be okay. I'll come back for you." He raised his head and scanned the small room. "I just needed you to be somewhere I know you'll be safe so I can keep my mind in the field. An army couldn't breach the place and make it to this house before I get back."

"Wyatt..." She stood for a few seconds looking at him. Finally, she whispered, "Just be careful. Come back soon."

"I told you: I will always come for you." With that, he took a step back through the doorway and onto the porch.

Paige followed him out, and before Wyatt reached the bottom step, said, "Do you really plan on marrying me?"

His stop was abrupt, and he turned to look at her. This was the first time he smiled since they had landed. "When you're ready, yes."

"Is that what my dad wanted, me to be with you?"

"He hoped."

"He said that?"

"Yes."

"It's only day four," she said, "so I'm not committing, but I think my dad's a pretty intuitive man."

"I know that to be true." He climbed the two steps and approached her. With his hands on her cheeks, he kissed her forehead and then pulled her close. "You really are making this engagement thing easy."

Paige couldn't force herself to joke. All she could do was hold on to this no-longer-a-stranger even tighter. What if he didn't come back? What if she never saw him again?

"I'll be okay," he whispered near her ear. "I hope to be back before daybreak."

This time when he moved down the steps, he only hesitated and glanced back when he said, "I would kind of like a real kiss once the engagement is official."

Only now could she smile even a little. "I don't think I would mind that much at all."

When the truck was out of sight, Paige stepped back into the house and scanned the one room made up of the kitchen and living area. There were two closed doors at the end of a small hallway, a bedroom and a bathroom she supposed.

Books lined the walls on shelves that reached the ceiling. Books were stacked on tables and the floor near the camo-fabric recliner next to the fireplace. The only other large piece of furniture in the room was a couch with gold and rust-colored tweed fabric from the '70s. Small, hand-built tables were on either side, both containing more paperback books.

Paige wasn't sure what to do with herself but to sit and wait for Waylon. The drive to the house had taken nearly twenty minutes as they had bobbed and weaved through the woods on what could hardly be called a driveway, plus the ten-minute walk, so she didn't expect him back for nearly an hour.

Finally, she removed her Bible from her bag and sat on the sofa to continue to catch up on what she had missed in her absence. Open again to the dreaded book of Revelation where she had been reading off and on the past two days, Paige read chapter seven. Even the section header, The Multitude from the Tribulation, made her want to read somewhere else. Psalms was a nice book, she thought, or Esther's story–anywhere but the tale of what was to come for the lost people in this world around her. It was a thought she seldom pondered without her stomach burning and her heart sinking.

One verse in particular captured her attention now. In verse seventeen she read,

"...for the Lamb in the center of the throne will be their shepherd, and will guide them to springs of the water of life; and God will wipe every tear from their eyes."

Paige read it for a second time when Aunt Bertie's phrase, unborn-again sheep, came to mind. How many millions, maybe even billions, of unborn-again sheep would come to their Shepherd in the midst of the chaos? How would they learn? How would they grow and teach others?

The idea of Aunt Bertie's to prepare her home to be a refuge for tribulation saints was absolutely inspired. Maybe Paige wouldn't have a home to go home to, but wherever she landed in this new world of hers, she would do her best to leave supplies behind and maybe spiritual food to help feed the Lord's to-be-born-again sheep.

She let out a little sigh, knowing she first had work to do herself. After her time away from the Lord and His Word, this was what she needed most, to renourish her starving-sheep self. That's where she would focus for now. As Wyatt had called it, getting back in tune with God.

A scripture came to mind at that thought. Similar to the last one her dad had given her in the note calling God her strength and shield, the one she recalled now was about God being her strength and song. In order for her to get back in tune with Jesus, she needed to learn to allow Him to become her song again.

She tilted her head, wondering what exactly that might mean. God as her strength and her shield made sense in a protective way. But her strength and song, what exactly did that mean?

Paige flipped around in her Bible but couldn't remember where the verse was located. Her phone had sketchy reception here off the grid, so she would just have to ponder this one until she got back to civilization.

What did come to mind was the verse in Matthew about "in the days of Noah." To most people these days, life was normal except the virus craziness. They were eating and drinking, and like a close friend of hers, marrying and giving in marriage. They were living lives apart from God and had no clue what was to come.

It came again, that question that had sounded in her head so many times that it now brought with it angst and a tightness in her chest: What could she do?

She turned to the days of Noah passage, this time fresh understanding dropping onto her head like dew. Paige felt suddenly warm all over, loving when that sensation came at the Word's unveiling.

This passage didn't mention it, but she knew from the Genesis story that Noah had not only built the boat, he had also preached the warning long before the flood. He had warned them until the Lord closed him and his family in the ark.

While the ark as a symbol of the rapture brought peace for the believer, the flood symbolized catastrophe for the unbeliever. A flood for the lost was just as imminent as the rapture for the found. Until it came, she whispered aloud, “I have to warn people.”

With eyes closed as she waited for Waylon to return, Paige rested her head on the back of the couch to pray and contemplate. How could she do that and not sound like a nut? Noah did. She would. She knew it. How could she embrace her inner nut and tell anyway? There had to be a way.

Waiting

Day 5, 7:12 a.m.

Her eyes fluttered open and Paige's first sight was of two deer heads looking at one another from either side of the fireplace. She raised her head and found Waylon in his recliner reading near one of the two lanterns in the room.

"I'm sorry." She wiped her mouth and blinked a few times. "I must have fallen asleep."

He never looked up. "No reason to be sorry."

She had fallen over onto the armrest of the sofa at some point, and there was now a wool blanket over her. The stiffness in her neck and shoulders was likely a mixture of her sleeping position and the crash. She sat upright, sore all over, and scooted to the edge of her seat. The blinds were all drawn, so even while squinting, she couldn't see the mantle clock. "What time is it?"

"A little after seven." He rested his book on the arm of his chair. "You must be hungry."

"We grabbed something on the way," she said, "so I'm fine."

"That was yesterday. It's seven a.m., not p.m."

"What?" Paige stood and looked at the closed doors at the end of the hallway. "Did Wyatt make it back? Is he sleeping?"

Waylon stood too and began opening the blinds. "Not yet."

His not looking at her only gave rise to her unease. Was he hiding his concern? Was he just awkward? She wanted to pace, but the small space didn't exactly allow for that, so she wasn't sure what to do to expel this nervous energy. "He said he should be back by daybreak." She wrung her hands. "What if something went wrong?"

"He'll make it back. Want some tea?"

Tea? How could she drink tea when Wyatt may be hurt or worse?

"I would love that," she said in a voice that masked her internal state of panic.

Paige followed Waylon into the small kitchen.

The small, rustic kitchen, created for the man's man, is practical and... Stop it, Paige! It's okay to let yourself feel.

For a moment she allowed herself that, to feel the fear of losing the man she was coming to care for, the son of the man now busy making her tea. Her heart thudded. "Mr. Fletcher," she swallowed hard, "what if he isn't okay?"

"Call me Waylon," he said, then, "He's a strong man, a good soldier." He never looked at her but went about his business of pouring water from a jug into a kettle, then adding wood to the vintage stove.

Paige dropped onto the chair and bowed her head to pray. When she did look up, she nodded at no one really. She agreed: Wyatt was a strong man and a good soldier. Her dad was too. Worry would only cripple her. And too, she didn't want to crumble in front of Wyatt's dad. If he wasn't worried, she didn't want to be the reason he did.

"Your stove is beautiful," she said.

He didn't reply.

"Wyatt says you don't talk much. Is it okay if I do, or do you prefer the quiet?"

"You can talk," he said with his back still to her.

"Your son is a wonderful man."

With a quick nod and only a glance her way, he said, "Agreed."

"I see he gets his survival skills from you."

Waylon turned and smiled. "I don't think he would much like this life."

Paige nodded. "I'm with him. I would starve without takeout."

His lips formed into a deep scowl. "It's not good eating all that junk."

"I know," she said with a slight shrug. "I eat a salad here and there for good measure."

He almost smiled at that, then turned his attention back to his kettle. "I live mostly on chicken, fish, and eggs. And I eat oatmeal every day."

"Oatmeal is good for you. I like it too."

He turned and looked at her with a troubled expression. "Will you eat some now?" His eyes narrowed. "Wyatt told me to make sure you eat. I have pure maple syrup."

"I'm not sure I can pass that up."

She sat and watched him as he made her oatmeal, noticing his discomfort with having a guest.

"Thank you again for allowing me to stay here until Wyatt returns." A pit formed in her stomach, so she closed her eyes and whispered another prayer for his safety and her dad's.

When she opened her eyes, she found Waylon looking at her.

"You worried?" he said.

Paige nodded.

"Don't be. He'll be back."

"I wish I knew that for sure."

"He's doing the Lord's work." Waylon pointed up. "He'll watch over him."

Paige's heart began to slow, and her shoulders relaxed. "I believe that too."

He turned back and stirred the pot on the stove. "He says your dad is missing."

"He is, has been for a few days."

"I know he's been good to my boy."

"That's what Wyatt says."

The fact that she hadn't met Wyatt before this week still bothered her. If she could go back and work toward a better relationship with her dad, she would. Now, watching this eccentric man move about in his isolated home, Paige could only wonder if Wyatt wished the same with his dad.

She said, "I haven't seen my dad much these past few years. Things have been tough between us."

"I hear that."

Her voice was soft. "I'm realizing life is too short. Sometimes it's even too late when you do want to make the connection."

Waylon set her tea and oatmeal before her, got his own, and then took the seat across from her. Him bowing his head surprised Paige, so she dropped her head as well.

"I ask You, Lord, to protect my boy." He paused. "Thank you for oatmeal and for freedom."

Paige stirred her steaming oatmeal and blew on it.

"I'm better now," Waylon said. "Did Wyatt tell you that?"

"He's never really told me what was wrong before."

He scratched his chin. "Can't say that I blame him."

"If you're better now," she said, "then isn't that all that really matters?"

With a quick nod, he stood again, clearly more comfortable when in motion and not sitting face to face.

"All these years they thought I was crazy. I guess they see now I wasn't too far gone. It's this world that has gone crazy."

"I can only agree with you on that."

Waylon brought her a half-full bottle of syrup and sat again. "A friend in town gave me this. Best I've ever had."

Paige stirred the syrup into her oatmeal and ate a few bites. Between thoughts of her dad and now Wyatt, she wasn't able to eat much. "It really is good. I'm just..." She closed her eyes and shook her head.

"Just pray, Paige. That's what I keep doing."

"I am. I will."

Waylon stood and left the room. Paige ate only a bite more then took the bowl to the trash to scrape out the rest.

"Save that," Waylon said behind her. "I've got a raccoon that loves oatmeal." A slight smile tugged at his lips. "I think it's more the syrup he likes."

He glanced toward the window. "Now that the sun's up, I figured we could do a little fishing."

"I would like that." She paused. "I might need to clean up a little first."

"Bathroom's in there. I'll meet you outside."

By the time Paige went out to meet Waylon, it was nearly eight. Every minute that ticked by in the waiting formed a new knot in her stomach. She would do everything she could to stay calm and remember Who was watching over that man she just might marry.

Around the side of the house, Waylon was holding two rods and a bucket. He didn't speak when he handed her a rod, reached for the handle of the cooler next to his feet, and took off walking. Paige didn't either. The quiet gave her more time to pray instead of worry.

A few minutes' walk led them to a clearing with a large pond. Surrounded by dense forest and swarmed by small insects, the only man-made presence was a narrow wooden bridge that spanned the water's surface. Waylon led the way and stopped in the middle of the bridge.

"Can you bait a hook?" he said when he held up the small pail.

"Of course I can bait a hook. Do I look like a city girl?"

He let out a soft chuckle. "A hundred percent city girl."

"Okay, I'm totally a city girl, but I know how to bait a hook and fish."

"I don't mind a city girl who can do both of those things."

Re-Zoning

Day 5, 10:17 a.m.

Paige sat with Waylon on the bridge, their legs dangling over the side. A couple of mostly quiet hours had passed. In the fresh air and sunshine, it had been nearly easy to forget her body aching and her hip hurting. Or more likely it was her mind tormenting her, trying to convince her to worry about Wyatt, that kept her attention off the dull aches.

Over and over, she had cast and waited, but never once had she gotten even a nibble. "Are you sure there's more than one fish in here?"

"You better hope so." He tapped the cooler containing his one caught fish. "It's what we'll have for lunch today."

She let out a soft sigh as tears threatened to come. Lunch? Would she be here without Wyatt that long?

"I'll throw in three potatoes to roast," he said.

"You're hoping Wyatt will be here by then?"

He didn't turn to look at her. "I know he will."

Waylon's next movement, him giving a quick tug on the line, indicated they would both eat today, maybe all three if he was right about Wyatt. "How do you know he'll be back in time?"

"I have my ways," he said with a slight smile.

More time passed. Waylon caught another largemouth, but still Paige caught nothing. She reeled in and cast again, letting out a sigh when she released this time.

"Hear that?"

She sat still and listened, but nothing beyond nature noises caught her attention. "Hear what?"

"Footsteps of a soldier coming for his girl. He'll be making that clearing in a few seconds."

Paige handed Waylon her rod, then struggled to her feet with a little groan over her aches and pains. Sure enough, only a few seconds later, she caught sight of Wyatt stepping into the clearing near the shore of the pond.

At a full run, Paige moved toward him while Wyatt's pace increased as well. They didn't meet; they collided there just before the entrance of the bridge. Paige jumped into his waiting arms and wrapped her arms around his neck.

"Thank God!" she said. "I've been praying and trying not to worry." It was all she could do to hold back tears.

"I'm fine. The General and his family are all safe." His words were soft as he held her almost too tightly.

"When I woke, and you weren't here..." She stepped back to look at him and only then saw the wound on his cheek. It didn't look too serious, but it had clearly been bleeding. In a way too familiar for her acquaintance with him, she traced her fingers along his jaw. "What happened?"

"Just a graze."

Paige's eyes widened. "You mean a bullet hit your face?"

He blinked long and looked back at her. "It's just a scratch."

"Do you know how close that came to..." She stopped and drew in a long breath.

"I'm okay."

She swallowed hard and nodded, trying not to think of how tragically that might have ended.

"Have you heard anything about my dad? Has he checked in?"

Wyatt only shook his head.

She wanted to ask more, but before she could, he glanced ahead of them. "How's it been with my dad?"

"I slept through yesterday." She half grinned and shrugged when he didn't seem too surprised by that. "It's gone well today. He's been kind and hospitable."

With a raised brow, he said, "I'm not sure I've ever heard those words used to describe my dad before."

"We had oatmeal for breakfast, and we're catching fish for lunch."

"I can believe both of those." He took her hand and led her toward the bridge.

When they drew closer, Waylon stood. "I didn't hear an explosion after my sensor tripped, so I figured you had remembered the path."

Wyatt smiled. "I white-knuckled it all the way here." He looked down at Paige and back at his dad. "Thanks for looking after her."

"I don't dislike her," he said without looking at Paige.

Paige grinned at that. "I don't dislike him either."

The two men exchanged a look, then Waylon said, "I'll get these fish cleaned."

Wyatt took the poles his dad offered him, then handed one to Paige. When he moved to sit, she did too, noticing something seemed off about him.

"So everything went okay with the General? The team is all safe?"

"Yeah. The General got hit, but it was nothing serious. I went with him to the hospital. We got his family relocated, so you don't need to worry."

Paige had not yet cast her line as Wyatt had, so she set it next to her on the bridge, drew her legs up, and wrapped her arms around them. "That could have all gone so wrong."

"But it didn't," he said without ever turning to look at her.

This wasn't the same man she had come to know the past few days. He seemed distant from her now. "I'm sorry," she said, "for insisting you help. I should have at least been there."

"Of course I helped. And no way would I have let you be there."

They sat for some time without speaking. Finally, Wyatt said, "I've had a tough time since I left here. I don't think I'm honoring your dad."

"Why do you say that?"

For a long moment he sat looking out at the water. Once, he reeled in and cast again. Paige just sat waiting, certain by his expression that he had something heavy on his mind.

"I never answered your question that day." He turned to look at her. "Yes, I do love you." When he turned back toward the water, he said, "I would rather you not respond to that. I know how crazy it must seem to you. It's crazy enough to me." He blinked long and looked back at his line. "I keep thinking back to when it all started, when your dad assigned me to watch over you. Those first months it was just an assignment." With a slight pause, he gave a little shake of his head. "Not exactly that simple because of who you were to him, but my head was in the right place. Then I started to feel things. At first I thought it was my mind playing tricks on me.

"I spent a lot of time praying about it. Soon enough, I realized prayer was what had clouded my feelings in the first place. All those early months of watching you grieve and praying for you truly formed a bond." His smile when he glanced at her was warm. "That makes sense since we're called to pray for others, even for our enemies. It's hard to take someone before the throne and not come to love them, I suppose. So that understanding settled my concern for a while." He rubbed his face and looked back at her. "'Til one day I made a colossal mistake."

She sat watching his profile and what appeared to be a pained expression. His grip on the fishing rod was tight, white-knuckled just as he had said he was while driving through the maze of landmines.

"You went to the farmer's market one Saturday. I was at Sentinel when you left, so I told your dad I would keep an eye on you.

"You wore a white sundress with big black and yellow flowers." His lips drew into a soft smile. "I'm not sure what I was more thankful for on that muggy day, the way the gentle breeze cooled me down or how it made the yellow ribbon in your hair ripple across your shoulders."

He sat for a few seconds more, his face taking on a more cheerful appearance.

"I got in line behind you and bought the same artisan bread you did. Then I bought the same honey as you at the next tent. All the while, I watched you interact with vendors and other shoppers." He turned and looked at her for a long moment. "I blame it on that smile of yours. You don't just smile; you light up. It's like the sun shines on the people you interact with."

Paige's heart beat a little faster at his vulnerable expression and tender words.

"Then," he said, "being the stalker that I am, I sat way too close to you on a nearby bench. I nearly laughed out loud when you tore off a hunk of bread right there and drizzled on some honey while you people watched. I did the same and watched you, how after you licked the honey off your fingers, you tapped them on the bench and sometimes your leg. I suspected you were writing in your head about the things you were seeing."

He chuckled. "Your phone rang, and I listened in. Whatever was said on the other end of the line made you break out into the cutest laugh I've ever heard." His smile faded, and he shook his head a little. "The craziest thing happened." He stopped and turned to look at her. "I listened to you laugh and knew I wanted to hear that every day for the rest of my life."

She let out a soft exhale, everything inside of her wanting to love a man who would profess his love with such sweetness and sincerity.

"That was in the spring," she said, "after my mom died."

He nodded. "I'm not sure that I ever really saw you smile before that, at least not a real smile."

Paige remembered the day well. "The night before, I had dinner out with friends. A waiter spilled water down my back, and I squealed and danced in my seat."

He seemed to force a smile. "I always wondered what was so funny." His face took on a more solemn expression, more likely reflecting his actual mood. "When I knew my feelings were out of line with my mission, I went to your dad."

"You told him you were falling for me?" At his nod, she said, "What did he say?"

"A lot at first." With a quick grin, he shrugged. "You know your dad, a lot of really loud words and phrases. He wasn't, like, throw-a-chair-out-the-window angry, but he wasn't happy about it and threatened to pull me from your detail."

The idea of her dad's eventual approval of this man's love for her stirred something within her. She could only trust Wyatt more. She could only find her heart caring more. "What made him change his mind?"

"I made a commitment to him. The one thing he asked of me was that I always put what is best for you above my own feelings."

"And now you don't think you're honoring that promise?"

"I haven't honored him or that promise since you asked me if I loved you."

"I don't know how you could have sought what's best for me any better than you have already. If you mean allowing me to go out with you into the field when I insisted –"

He shook his head. "It's not that at all. I have no doubt that this, you being out here in the field, is exactly what your dad had in mind. Otherwise, he wouldn't have listed you on the bank account." Wyatt let out a long breath. "It's more the things I've said and done."

"I think you kidding around has made a tense situation more bearable."

"Maybe, but I wasn't kidding. I really do believe we can have something together, but it wasn't right of me to say it, not now. You're living out the most difficult days of your life. With the wait to hear about your dad and the danger you've faced, it would be easy to focus your energy on me as a distraction. That's not what I want. I want your heart, not some emotional attachment due to our circumstances."

In a way that made little sense to her, his words caused her heart to soar. She believed the same thing, that they would likely have a future together. Something about it felt right no matter how ridiculous it seemed, considering how little she knew him.

And, too, his concerns resonated with her. Like him, she could also see the danger of her heightened emotions and how they could easily cloud her judgment.

"So," he said with a soft sigh, "I'm friend-zoning myself and friend-zoning you. I won't joke around anymore about engagements or somedays. You don't know this yet, Paige, but I'm already your closest friend. And you're mine." He hesitated and seemed to force his next words. "Let's just be that."

She nodded, maybe a little disappointed to let go of his crazy declarations of devotion. "I can agree to that."

"Friends are there for each other," he said, "with no hidden agendas, so that's what I'm going to be. That's what you need right now more than ever. I fear even tougher times are ahead for you." His eyes filled with notable sadness. "It's been five days. That can't be good. Your dad would walk through fire to find out if you were okay. The fact that we haven't heard from him gives us reason to think he may not be coming back."

Paige turned away and began to cry. Hope was all that had gotten her through so far, that and Wyatt's presence and care for her. Now, here on day five, she would have to accept the fact that she had no one anymore, no parents. At least a faraway father had given her someone to hold on to.

Wyatt slipped his arm around her. "Re-zoned friends do this, right?"

She nodded and rested her head on his shoulder. "They do."

"And close friends know what you're thinking: You're not alone, Paige. I'm here and not going anywhere."

She wrapped her arms around his waist and cried harder. "I need that most of all right now."

Several quiet minutes passed. She never did grow hysterical in her crying, but she did allow herself the release her tears brought. The loss of her father had begun so long ago, this now felt more like the bereavement of what had actually happened to them the day her mother died. More than loss, regret fed her stream of tears.

Wyatt cleared his throat and moved her back to look at her. "There's something your dad has driven into us all: Whatever happens, whoever comes or goes, the ones who remain finish the mission. We still have a mission, Paige."

She nodded at that and wiped her cheeks. "I want to take down Groves. I'll grieve when that's done."

"I'll grieve with you," he said. "Then after that, you keep exposing the darkness with me. Will you do that?"

"I'm not sure how I can help, but you better believe I'll figure it out." She grew quiet for a second. "My heart feels like it's on fire at times when I think of what's coming, what will happen to unsuspecting people. I've got to do something."

Sighting

Day 5, 11:31 a.m.

The walk back to the house had eased some of Paige's stiffness. That's what she needed, movement to ease her aches and pains. When they rounded the house, Paige and Wyatt found Waylon near the front porch cleaning his filet knife and blood-stained cutting board.

Wyatt held up his string of fish. "You'll have dinner for tonight too."

"I'll fry this mess of fish up and clean that later."

"I haven't eaten," Wyatt said. "I wouldn't mind eating soon." He looked at Paige and back at his dad. "We have to get back on the road before long."

Paige watched Waylon's face for any hint of disappointment but found none.

He said, "You can leave your girl here for safe keeping if you need to handle business."

Wyatt glanced at her again and back at his dad. "She's my friend, not my girl."

"If you say so," Waylon said with a doubt-filled shrug. He reached for the heavy iron skillet and set it on a grate over a low-burning fire. Potatoes were wrapped in foil and nestled amidst the embers. "I'll do the frying out here."

Paige busied herself in the small kitchen, setting out plates and cups for each of them. Wyatt dozed on the sofa while the food was cooking, allowing Paige to limp a little here and there in secret.

Occasionally, she would peek in at him. Though she couldn't see it from this angle, the memory of the grazed trail on his cheek made her a little nauseous. She could have lost the man who seemed to already belong to her.

Since their conversation on the bridge, she had thought of little else but of a man who loved her so much that he would friend-zone himself for her best. That made her smile and shake her head. She was pretty sure his earliest warning was right on: All he needed was a week or two to make her love him.

The front door opened, interrupting her thoughts and Wyatt's sleep. He jumped up and looked around as if to gain his bearings.

Waylon passed by Wyatt and moved into the kitchen. Paige watched what appeared on the surface to be the two men's indifference toward one another. She knew better. Affection was there on both sides, though neither likely knew how the other felt.

While Waylon went to the bathroom, Paige said to her new friend, "You need some sleep."

"I'll rest on the flight back to Savannah."

She only nodded and slid into her seat. Wyatt sat next to her, across from where his dad came to sit. They loaded their plates with fish and potatoes, then Waylon bowed his head as he had done over their oatmeal.

Wyatt's eyes grew wide, and he sat staring at his dad rather than bowing. Paige watched Wyatt. Waylon's "amen" seemed to break Wyatt from his trance. From this, Paige had to assume Wyatt didn't know Waylon was a believer. Did the two men ever discuss anything but fishing and guns?

Waylon didn't look up and said while still chewing, "Did you see what the DOD released?"

Wyatt sat up straight, his jaw muscles now seeming to contract and relax and contract again. "Yes, sir."

"Videos by Navy pilots."

"I saw that." Wyatt cut his eyes to look at Paige and said, "The Department of Defense has released some footage of UFO sightings."

"I saw that on the news," Paige said, unsure of why this was making the list of conversations between the two usually-quiet-together men.

"I lost my family for saying what they're saying." Waylon stood and went to the counter to pour more sun-brewed tea.

Wyatt said nothing and only took another bite.

It was only now coming together, how Wyatt had said his dad hadn't been healthy. He must have seen something all those years ago, and no one believed him. Paige looked at Wyatt who wasn't looking at her, his expression less intense now and more filled with regret. If anyone knew that look, Paige did.

Waylon sat again. "I figure it's about time they make it public. I'm guessing aliens is how they'll explain it when believers disappear."

When Wyatt said nothing, Paige said, "That makes perfect sense, doesn't it? That's how they will deceive people."

She wasn't just going along with Waylon to humor him. It really did fit their playbook. Her dad had always said that aliens were no more than demons. Now, with her recent acceptance that a rapture would come, she could see how the Antichrist would need to give an alternate explanation to Jesus coming for His church.

Wyatt moved his chair back in clear discomfort and seemed about to stand, when Paige reached for his arm to keep him seated. She said to Waylon, "Their lies have injured so many. I'm sorry you were both hurt."

A quiet moment passed while the two men looked at one another. Finally, Wyatt said, "I didn't think I had any reason to doubt her."

Waylon looked down at his plate, his words quiet. "I didn't either until she took you away from me."

Neither said any more, but the undercurrent of emotion between the two regret-filled men brought tears to Paige's eyes. She wasn't the only one at this table masking their pain. Now, both men sat eating as if nothing had transpired.

She blinked long and said a prayer for them. When she opened her eyes, she found Waylon looking at her.

With what was nearly a smile, he said, "Good fish, huh?"

Paige nodded and looked at Waylon. "It's great."

"No thanks to you." He chuckled and went back to eating.

That was it. No more conversation than that between a father and son who clearly needed healing.

An hour later, Paige stood next to the truck door with Waylon in front of her. Wyatt had said a quick goodbye to his dad and was now in the truck.

"This can be a refuge if you ever need it," Waylon said. "If you're ever in trouble, come. Do what Wyatt did: Park and wait. I'll come for you."

"I hope if I ever do show up at that gate you won't shoot at me."

A slow grin came. "Wouldn't think of it."

Despite his soft smile, Waylon's eyes held evident sadness. Wyatt's had, too, when they had parted with little more than, "See ya." Since Wyatt hadn't, Paige leaned in and hugged Waylon. "Thank you for letting me come." When he only nodded, she said, "I hope to see you again here on this side."

"I hope so too. Be safe." He opened the door for her and then closed it without looking at Wyatt.

She rode with a silent Wyatt, the truck rocking and bumping along the uneven terrain. They weren't far from the house when she said, "If I could see my dad, I would sure do what I could to make peace with him."

He said nothing.

A minute later, she turned to him. "As your closest friend, I strongly suggest you turn this truck around and go say a proper goodbye to your dad."

Wyatt stopped, shifted into park, and sat looking ahead. "I don't know that he wants that."

"He was glad to see you when we got here. He hugged you. Clearly he wants to bridge this space between you."

He let out a long sigh, his struggle evident as he tilted his hat back on his head, then sat rubbing his beard.

"You need to end this visit on a better note." She paused. "We have no way of knowing what's to come for any of us. Don't leave it like this."

"Paige, the things he said back then..." He closed his eyes and shook his head. When he looked back at her, he said, "It wasn't like he claimed to be abducted, but he wouldn't back down on what he said he saw while on duty. The more he stuck to his story, the crazier everyone made him out to be. I think that's what sent him over the edge. My mom was scared of him, scared of me being around him. I was young, so I didn't understand."

"From what you both said at lunch, I think he sees that. He knows you were swayed by your mom." Paige reached for his arm. "He's your dad. No matter what's happened up until this point, I think all he wants is for you to believe him now."

"I do believe him."

"Then go tell him. Hug him goodbye. Say you'll come back to see him."

There was a long silence while Wyatt sat staring straight ahead. Finally, he said, "He used to pray at meals like that when I was kid, like my granddad. I've wondered all these years if he had lost his faith. The few times I've talked to him, when I brought up God, he didn't much respond."

"I don't think you have to worry about that now." Her urging was soft, "Just go."

"I can't safely turn the truck around on this narrow path. I'll run back if you'll sit tight."

"I'll wait."

"Don't move." He glared at her. "Do you hear me?"

"I won't. Just go say goodbye to your dad."

Wyatt reached for the door handle, then turned to look at her. "My world used to revolve around that man. He was such a hero in my eyes."

"Tell him that too. Tell him you're sorry you ever believed otherwise. You were just a kid then."

Paige watched him in the rearview mirror. Because of her feelings of guilt over her own dad, she knew Wyatt would never regret the jog he was making back to his dad's place.

She closed her eyes and wondered about her dad. Did he die somewhere alone? Was anyone looking for his next of kin? One question she didn't have to ask was if he had thought of her in what may have been his final moments.

"I just ask for this one thing, Lord: Whatever happened to him, wherever he is, let us find him. I need to know."

The door opening a few minutes later caught her off guard.

"Thanks for that," he said. "You were right. He did need it."

"I'm glad you went back."

He sat for a few seconds more without putting the truck into drive. "We'll come back someday. I promised him that."

Paige nodded. "I'll be happy to come back with you. Stupid fish. I didn't catch even one."

With an easy smile, he said, "I'm sure it wasn't the fisherman."

"It wasn't the fisherman!"

They were again underway when Paige said, "What your dad said really does make sense, huh, that they'll say aliens abducted us?"

"I thought of it when I saw news reports about UFO sightings." He was quiet a second, then said, "I don't know what the devil will use to explain it away, maybe not aliens. But since he doesn't know when the rapture will happen, he has to have everything in line for when it does. So much is coming together so fast, I don't see how it could be much longer."

If it was coming quickly, Paige wanted to live all the life she could until the end. With a glance down at her ring finger, she felt an unwelcomed trace of disappointment that she wasn't engaged to this remarkable soldier. That would be a great way to end this life.

Reconciliation

Day 5, 3:10 p.m.

Wheels up and en route to Savannah, the flight was underway as Paige sat quietly and Wyatt slept next to her. They hadn't been in the air more than a few minutes when he had leaned his seat back and drifted off. She watched him on and off, remembering what he had said, that he found he slept better when she was near. Her first understanding had been that it was because he knew she was safe, so he could allow himself to rest. She didn't think that anymore. He was at peace when he was with her. She felt the same.

On occasion she would move and stretch to alleviate the tenderness in her hip, always careful not to wake and concern him.

Since they left Waylon's, she had been thinking mostly about her dad. She prayed often and teared up a few times. If she never had a chance to tell him how sorry she was, she would always live with this soul-searing regret. And, too, if she didn't get a chance to confront him about shutting her out of his life, she would likely always battle bitterness. He did the wrong thing–they both had. The painful loss they had both experienced was to blame, but still, it could have all been handled so much differently.

The same could be said of Wyatt and his mom and how they had responded to his dad's claims. She could hardly blame their doubting him, though. Even a week before today, if Waylon had said what he did about aliens, Paige would have not just doubted him, she would have thought him a total nut. These days, nothing seemed impossible or implausible. The world they lived in truly wasn't at all what it seemed. Why stop at aliens?

Wyatt jumped up and reached for the ringing phone in his pocket. "Mac? You're kidding?" he said. "Put the call through."

He stood and walked to the rear of the small plane, leaving Paige to wonder if maybe it was a call about her dad. Next thing she saw was him breezing by their seats to the cockpit. Now she was more than curious. Just as she began to unbuckle, Wyatt reappeared, the look on his face unusual, one she didn't understand until he sat next to her.

"It's my dad, isn't it? You've found his body?"

"Not his body."

Her heart raced. "So he's alive?"

"Barely." He blinked and looked back at her, then took her hand. "It's bad, Paige. He's not going to pull through."

She dropped her head and began to cry. "Take me to him."

With arms drawing her into him, he said, "Already on the way."

A few seconds passed, and Paige moved back from him. "What happened? Where is he?"

"Outside of Baltimore. He took a few rounds the day he called you. Mac found him Thursday," he hesitated and blinked a few times, "and has been trying to contact me. Your dad is in a coma."

"And he won't make it?"

Wyatt shook his head. "No, Paige."

She sat for a moment. Finally, she said, "Who's Mac?"

"We served together under your dad."

"So my dad is in good hands until we get there?"

"Best medic I've ever known."

Paige nodded and sat back. All she could do now was try and prepare herself for what was to come.

"It won't be long." His eyes filled with compassion. "Maybe you can get some rest."

The location wasn't at all where Paige had expected to find her father. Dumpsters and debris littered the alleyway where Wyatt drove with evident hesitation.

"One way in and one way out; I don't like this," he said as he looked ahead at the brick wall before them. "If it's a setup..." He hit the brake and put the SUV into reverse. "We're not doing this."

Paige reached for his arm. "Do you trust Mac?"

He sat looking ahead, then nodded a slow nod. "With my life."

"Then we have to do this. This has been my mission, finding my dad. I need this, Wyatt."

He said nothing and only shifted back into gear and crept along until they reached the last door. The entrance to the small urban clinic was marked only with a small medical cross.

Wyatt said, "Stay where you are," then he stepped from the vehicle. He walked around to her side, looked up and around, then opened her car door.

"No cameras that I can see. Still, pull your hood up and keep your head down."

Wyatt led the way as Paige held to his hand and watched her feet move along the cracked and filthy bricks.

"You're okay now," he said when he closed the door behind them.

A man in scrubs met them there, wearing a solemn expression. "This way. Mac's been with him since we found him."

Paige didn't speak and only lowered her hood. Her mouth was dry, and she was trembling on and off, the exact sensation she had experienced when called into her mother's room to say goodbye.

From the small waiting room filled wall to wall with plastic chairs, they followed the man through a security door and down a narrow hallway to a door with a hand-written restricted sign posted.

At the entrance Wyatt reached for Paige's arm. "Are you okay?"

"Not really." She glanced up at him and nodded. "Let's go in."

Nothing could have prepared her for the sight when she walked through that door. It wasn't at all like the high-level care her mom had received. Everything, all the equipment, was outdated with chipped paint and faded lettering. The exam room turned critical-care room was hardly the place for this dying man Paige barely recognized as her father. His face was covered with medical tape holding a tube in his mouth, and there were smaller tubes up his nose. Machines gurgled and hummed. The faint peaks on the heart monitor stole the last shred of hope she had been clinging to.

"Hey, Mac," Wyatt said to the dark-haired woman who stood near the bedside.

"Hey." Her soft tone matched Wyatt's. Then she moved to meet him at the foot of the bed.

The two stood staring for a few seconds, but Paige lost track of all else in the room but her father. She went to his side and touched his silver hair. "Hi, Daddy." Tears didn't come even when she bent over to kiss his forehead. Instead, she just stood looking at the lifeless, colorless face of this man she adored.

A quick glance around assured her, her dad was already a dead man if not for these machines. It was only then that it dawned on her. That's what she was there for, to witness the end of his life when the machines were turned off.

Paige looked at Mac. "How long have the machines been keeping him alive?"

"Since the early hours of Thursday morning."

She reached for her dad's cool hand, the one where his wedding ring rested. "There's really no hope?"

"No. I've just been waiting for you, Paige. It's what your dad asked of me before he slipped into a coma."

Tears stung her eyes now. "He did?"

Mac nodded. "We didn't have much time, but he did say that much, that he wanted you to be able to say goodbye. I promised him you would get that opportunity." She looked around. "I brought him here and have been trying to get in touch with Wyatt ever since."

Wyatt said, "Your dad didn't have his phone. He wasn't able to communicate enough to tell her how to contact us. Mac finally tracked down a buddy of Echo's."

"Thank you," Paige said to Mac, "for going to all this trouble, for keeping him alive until I could get here."

"He would've done the same for me." Mac let out a soft sigh and moved toward the door. "I'll give you time alone."

Wyatt pulled a chair over for Paige. "I'll be right outside if you need me."

She nodded and sat, still holding onto her dad's hand. With Wyatt gone and the door closed, she looked at the man who would soon be lost to her, the man who had already seemed lost to her.

"You could've told me you feared putting me in danger. It would have changed everything." Paige rested her head on the bed rail for a few seconds, then reached to unlock and lower it so that she could rest her head on the mattress next to his shoulder.

Was that true? Would she have believed the truth? Or was her father right to give her time to live in a world where the last days weren't so evident to her? Right or wrong, it couldn't be changed.

"I'm sorry for how angry I've been with you." Tears fell onto her cheeks. "I thought you didn't love me anymore. I couldn't figure out why you wouldn't love me just because Mom was gone."

Paige cried harder. "But I know that's not true now. You didn't leave me all alone. I saw your house and all our things from home. You've been right there with me or had Wyatt watching over me this whole time."

A thought came and fresh understanding exploded in her heart. "I'm not sure any dad could more resemble God the Father. You sent the son you love to watch over me and save me when those men were coming for me." She sniffled and wiped her face. "You are so much like Him. Thank you for always showing me God and for teaching me about Jesus." Paige closed her eyes. "Thank you for living the Word before me so that it has seeped into every crevice of who I am."

With a quick glance at the door and back, Paige said, "He's fabulous. No wonder you love him so much. It's evident you do and that you trust him with me. I get it. I trust him too." She blinked long and slow. "I'm scared, Daddy. What they've shown me scares me to death, especially knowing you won't be here with me."

Paige heard voices on the other side of the door, then a light tap.

Wyatt opened the door and handed her a cup. "Here, I thought you could use this. It'll be a long night."

She reached for the coffee, trying her best to hide a wince of pain. "Thank Mac again for me. This is what I needed, a long-overdue reconciliation."

He looked over at her dad, the distinct pain in his eyes likely mirroring her own. Her words to her father came to mind about how much he evidently loved Wyatt. Wyatt loved her dad just as much. Paige had been so focused on her own grief that Wyatt's had been lost on her. Only now did Mac's gesture when she had moved close to Wyatt mean as much. She had reached for his arm and mouthed the words, "I'm so sorry."

Wyatt moved as if to leave when Paige said, "Don't go. As my dad's favorite son, this is the night for you to grieve as well. This is something his kids should do together."

Tears filled Wyatt's eyes. "I wouldn't be the man I am today if not for him."

She reached for his hand. "Then that's yet another thing I love my dad even more for."

"I feel the same way," he said with a soft smile and a slight squeeze of her hand. "He sure did a great job with you."

"Grab another chair. Let's take advantage of our night with this great man."

Union

Day 5, 9:18 p.m.

Wyatt sat on the opposite side of the bed from Paige. Like her, he had lowered the bed rail and now sat with elbows resting on the mattress, head bowed in a posture of prayer. For hours they had sat in a room filled with unnatural noises, rarely speaking.

It wouldn't likely be evident to others, but Paige could nearly feel the deep emotion Wyatt was suffering. The times he did look up, his eyes conveyed such sorrow that Paige's eyes would fill again with tears, causing her to blink to chase them away. She couldn't help but wonder if it was possible to love a man simply because of his love for her father. Something was stirring in her heart, or maybe it was more in the realm of spiritual revelation.

If only her dad could view this sight, to see his only daughter and the man he had nurtured as a son there by his side, then his departure would take him home in peace.

That wasn't the fullness of the revelation, though. It was more that her seeing this sight was her father's intention. He had known when he had called her that Wyatt was coming for her. This man was clearly her father's choice for his only daughter. He wanted her to see what he saw, them coming together someday, their union.

Odd as it may seem, that's what she already felt with Wyatt: a union between them in their love for her father, a union in their mission to complete her father's objective, and a union of their lives and what would become a future together. The only thing that scared her about it was that it didn't scare her at all. It should terrify her that falling for a man in less than a week seemed so perfectly natural.

Paige rubbed her father's arm, and she looked across at Wyatt. "He's fought to stay here for our sakes."

Wyatt nodded. "He knew you needed this time."

"I did need this time to tell him how sorry I am for how angry I've been." The way Wyatt sat looking at her dad prompted her to ask, "What did you need to tell him?"

"Thanks, mostly, for so many things." A small sigh escaped his lips. "I'm thankful he saw something in me that made him take me under his wing."

"I can see what he saw in you."

"I can see what he saw in you, Paige. I understand why you were the light of his life."

They both sat again quietly. She noticed him glance at the clock a time or two. Just before ten, he said, "When daybreak comes," he paused and looked at her with regret-filled eyes, "we'll have to let him go. They need the space back for the clinic."

Paige nodded and wiped away tears. "Whatever happens, don't let me fall asleep. I don't want to miss one minute of my dad being in this world with me."

"I won't. It'll be a busy night. The team will all be here to say goodbye."

Something about his statement was like a jolt to her system. It was a deepening of the revelation from before. Her father's intention wasn't only to hand her over to Wyatt, he was placing her under the care of his team. Paige wasn't alone. This new family of hers, men so devoted to not only her father but to Jesus, would see her through whatever was to come.

She heard voices in the hallway already. "Do you want a few minutes alone with him before they come in?"

"Would you mind?"

"Not at all, but just don't lie to him."

His eyes widened and he nearly stammered. "Why would I do that?"

"I have a feeling you'll tell him you've not honored your promise. That would be a lie. The way you've cared for me has been what's gotten me through this so far." She looked at her dad and at the clock, then back at Wyatt. "It's what'll get me through what comes next." She stood and kissed her dad's cheek.

The moment Paige stepped into the hallway, Echo reached for her and pulled her to him. "I'm so sorry," he said.

"I'm sorry for you too." When she stepped back, her hip nearly giving way, she reached for the wall to steady herself and said, "I'm giving Wyatt a few minutes alone with him. I think we all need that."

Echo looked away, his expression filled with more than grief. "I have plenty to say to him."

"You didn't fail him."

"But I didn't find him either. If Mac hadn't tracked me down..."

"You can't blame yourself. He will die just as he lived, in service to others. He would have done nothing less than risk it all to rescue that girl."

"I know that. That's why I would've followed him even into a losing battle."

His words were said with such conviction that Paige's own heart was reminded of its recent commitment. "This wasn't a losing battle, Echo. I'm not so sure any of this was an accident."

"Meaning?"

"I was supposed to be a part of this search long enough that my heart would engage. If you had found him earlier, I'm not so sure I would have believed any of what you've told me or know what I know right now."

His eyes locked with hers as he asked a question he seemed to know the answer to. "What do you know?"

"Where I belong."

His eyes smiled even when his lips didn't. "Codename: Zenith."

She studied his words but then shook her head. "What's that supposed to mean?"

"Like Apex, Zenith is another word for the top. That will be you someday."

"You better come up with something that means a rung near the bottom."

"I'm not so sure about that. I'm seeing already you're a chip off the old block."

She grinned at that. "I'll take Chip over Zenith."

"Time will tell," he said.

Behind Echo's back, Paige saw Mac move through the security door toward the front of the clinic. "I'll be right back," she said.

Mac sat alone at the bank of chairs near a water fountain with an out-of-order sign.

"May I join you?" Paige said to a woman who was clearly exhausted.

"Please do."

Paige lowered herself onto a chair not trying to mask her pain so much with Wyatt out of sight. "I can't thank you enough for taking care of my dad."

Mac's gaze was filled with compassion. "He loved you so much. He always talked about you. Back when I served with him, and even recently, you were his favorite topic of conversation."

Paige's heart felt more warmed than grieved at hearing that. "We've struggled these past years, but he's almost always been one of my favorite topics of conversation too. I've been so proud of him all my life."

"I would be proud to have a dad like him too," Mac said with a trace of sadness. She sat for a second before saying, "This was my fault. I'm the one who got him involved in this in the first place."

"I didn't know that."

"No one did. Your dad never mentioned to Wyatt that I brought him in."

There was something telling in Mac's eyes when she spoke Wyatt's name that brought back their tender moment when Paige had first entered her dad's room. Her heart beat a little faster as the understanding came: Mac had feelings for Wyatt.

Paige blinked, trying hard to get the image out of her mind of those quiet seconds when Wyatt and Mac had stood looking at one another. It was evident only now, away from the emotion of seeing her father: Wyatt had feelings for Mac. That did something to Paige, struck an unexpected nerve.

"How did you get my dad involved?"

"I called him and told him about some missing girls from a mentorship program where I volunteer. I wouldn't have noticed the pattern if one girl in particular hadn't gone missing. I knew her. She was serious about getting her life back on track. Tia, she was different, too grateful for the program to bail."

"You suspected Groves had something to do with her disappearance?"

"It didn't cross my mind at first. He was the founder of the program but didn't seem to have any more to do with it than as a sponsor. It wasn't until I put together Tia's absence and the timing of his crew shooting fund-raising videos at our location. His organization had done that in the past, filmed some of the kids telling their stories."

Mac paused. "Even at the time something didn't sit well with me. I noticed how different they were when they questioned the boys and some of the girls. They would let them ramble and hardly pay attention to their stories. But when Tia and Imani were filmed, more pointed questions were asked, as if the girls' histories were of greater interest. I was there when Tia told hers. It struck me later how she mentioned that she was all alone in the world except for the counselors at the center." Mac shook her head. "That made her a perfect target."

"They were scouting for girls who wouldn't be missed."

"Yeah." Tears floated in Mac's eyes. "Both were biracial, beautiful and exotic, but Tia was clean where Imani was still struggling. I think that's why Groves chose Tia.

"When I began to dig into the center's history, another volunteer helped me piece it all together. A pattern emerged: Not long after being videoed, girls with a similar look and history were presumed to have returned to the streets when they never came back to the center.

"The crews in the past were never the same. Groves was the only common denominator." Her voice grew softer. "Darryl, the vet who helped me research the other missing girls, was found dead in his apartment after an overdose. He'd been clean for over a decade."

Paige's heart sank. "You think him poking around got Darryl killed?"

"I do. I got him into this and then your dad."

"It's not your fault about my dad. I can't imagine him walking away if he had any hint of young girls being harmed."

"I just knew I couldn't go to the police. Groves' hand is in most every pocket in Baltimore." She shook her head. "I'm not even sure what to do now. I have a friend in the DA's office who may be able to help."

"We have the evidence my dad collected against Groves."

Mac looked at Paige and blinked as if trying to decide if she should say more. Finally, she said, "And Tia, we have her."

Heart racing, Paige said, "You mean my dad got her out?"

"He did. She was with your dad, trying to care for his wounds when I found them. They were in an abandoned building together. He was burning up with fever and incoherent most of the time. She was terrified of taking him for help.

"That girl will never be the same after what Groves did to her," Mac said, "but at least she's alive."

Before Paige could ask anything more, the door opened and Cade, Bash, and Hank came barreling in. They each hugged her in a painful grip and told her how sorry they were as they walked with her to her father's door.

Wyatt was in the hallway talking to Echo when they neared, the sad look in his eyes much the same as when she had left him.

The men all talked in hushed tones while each took his turn going in to say goodbye. Just after Cade stepped into her father's room, Paige said to Wyatt, "Can we talk?"

They moved together through a doorway leading to a small storage closet. Once alone, he said, "How are you?"

"I don't know yet. But what I do know is that we have to do something about Groves. If he gets away with what he's done, no telling how many more girls will suffer."

Wyatt said, "You talked to Mac?"

"I did. My dad saved the girl."

That seemed to be news to him as he blinked and tried to process her words. "She isn't safe, then, as long as Groves goes unpunished."

"No, she's not." Paige looked at the door, knowing that on the other side of it was a mountain of a task that she would have to face before she could finish her father's work.

Wyatt took a step closer. "We'll find a way to make him pay."

"Whatever's on that flash drive, we need to make sure it goes public." She hesitated, then said, "I know of a newspaper editor who would jump at the chance to break the story."

A scowl came as Wyatt said, "You mean your ex?"

"Yeah."

"No way! Not him."

His reaction wasn't so surprising. "Mac knows someone who might be able to help, but we can't be sure we can trust anyone here locally."

Wyatt's words were soft. "We'll cross that bridge tomorrow. For now," he reached for her shoulders, "we need to get through tonight."

Paige stepped into Wyatt's embrace and rested her head on his chest, his heart's steady rhythm a soothing tempo after the nerve-wracking machines of the afternoon.

With arms around her, he whispered, "We'll do this together. You're never alone. Hear me?"

She nodded, now filled with that certainty: Their union was by design and for more than a just cause.

"Then tomorrow," she said with a fire growing in her spirit, "we'll make sure that evil man never hurts anyone else."

Incorruptible

Day 5, 12:06 a.m.

The late-night hours had progressed with the rest of the team arriving. Much of the time they all congregated in her father's room telling stories. It wasn't lost on her how all the years growing up, when her dad was apart from her and her mom, he had been building relationships with men who would someday become her family. There was a closeness between these men, and already Paige felt she belonged, simply because of who she was to her dad.

Dollar–Dylan–was said to be the newest member of the team and was the youngest present except for Paige. More than once he had spoken to Paige, small talk mostly. She had noticed, though, how Wyatt never took his eyes off of Dylan when he was near her. He didn't seem to be jealous, just more watchful than seemed necessary.

Landon, the former CIA operative dubbed Intel, arrived later than most and since then had shared many stories of working with Paige's mom. Only a few in the room had known her mom. It was fitting that the memory of the woman her father had so adored be present for his final farewell.

The last half hour, Paige had found herself tuning in and out of the conversations. Gunny had just told a story about her dad that involved live rounds of ammo and a cigar in a now-incinerated warehouse. The story elicited roars of laughter, but she hadn't caught the entire gist. Specifics didn't matter so much. What mattered was that this was exactly what her dad would want in his last hours, all the people he cared for most remembering the good and not crying over a man destined for heaven.

During a lull in their string of stories, a thought struck her, so Paige said, "All I can see in this world right now is how the enemy is attacking in every way imaginable. It's like arrows are flying from all directions. I'm so glad you guys work with my dad fighting back." She looked at Wyatt. "I suppose it started with you, Arrow; you were a way he could fire back."

Wyatt nodded. “He once said something similar to that.” He scanned the room. “Your dad assembled this team knowing what this world needed. I’m honored to be a part of it.”

“Same here,” Bash said.

The others all chimed in with their agreements, then the room grew unusually quiet. Soon one then another filtered out into the waiting area.

Eventually, Paige and Wyatt were left alone in the room. They sat close, and he reached for her hand. “You know what your dad is saying right now, don’t you?” His eyes were fixed on hers when he said, “Have I not commanded you? Be strong and courageous! Do not tremble or be dismayed, for the Lord your God is with you wherever you go.”

Her heart grew warm as Wyatt’s words sounded more like her dad’s as they were translated in her mind. “I can be strong because of the strength surrounding me. I needed this tonight, to have the team here and see what my father has spent his last years building.”

“Those men,” Wyatt nodded toward the door, “would each give their life for your dad. And for you.”

“I believe that.”

He gave her hand a little squeeze and leaned in a little closer. “You sure you don’t want some time alone?”

“Not at all. I want you here.”

Paige watched the clock, fairly certain it dragged at times and raced ahead at others. A few times she got up to move around the room, each time feeling less pain and tenderness in her hip. Bruises were beginning to form, but they would fade soon enough, leaving the car crash in her past.

She and Wyatt were alone now in the room. Only on occasion would Mac peek her head in to see if they needed anything. Paige tried not to notice the caring looks often exchanged between Wyatt and Mac in those brief moments.

The sound of the machines had become so much a part of the backdrop, that Paige once found herself repeating its rhythm in her head: swoosh and pause and swoosh and pause. Her heart faltered a second at the thought: When their cadence stopped, her father’s life would cease with them.

Presently, Wyatt was sitting next to Paige on the edge of his seat with his elbows propped on her father’s bedside. His head was bowed and resting on his folded hands.

Paige sat with her legs propped in her chair and her open Bible in her lap. From Ephesians five, she read about walking as children of Light, the Daybreak passage and admonishment she now received with greater urgency. Her heart caught fire when the Word went on to speak of her father's enemy, now her enemy, and how the man whose deeds were too disgraceful even to speak of must be exposed.

Not only for her father's sake, but for Tia's fractured future and those girls who had gone missing with no one to even notice or care, Paige had every intention of making the man pay. She would expose his dark deeds.

Her reading led her to the familiar passage in the next chapter illustrating the armor of God. Then she saw it at the close of the chapter, a phrase that nearly brought tears to her eyes in its modest beauty, Paul's parting words:

"Grace be with all those who love our Lord Jesus Christ with incorruptible love." (Ephesians 6:24)

What a fitting picture of the man sitting before her now, praying to the One who is incorruptible. No man she could ever choose for herself would compare to this man that her father—and her Father—had clearly chosen for her. No one thing in her life had ever become as apparent so quickly or precisely. She didn't just want to marry this man someday, she wanted to marry him soon. The time they did have left on this earth, Paige wanted to spend it growing in love with this fabulous, incorruptible man. She loved him already with a kindred-spirit kind of love. She loved him with brotherly love. She especially loved him for loving her dad. What she felt in five days was enough to assure her he was safe to love and that she was safe in allowing him to love her.

Love would only grow over time: every morning waking together with his head on her pillow, an after-dinner trip for a Blizzard, or the shared mission of being children of light.

With heart beating faster, Paige sat up and rested her hand on the back of the man who would soon be her husband. "May I have a minute alone with my dad? I need to tell him something about you."

When he sat back in his seat and looked at her for a few seconds, he said, "I hope you're not going to lie to him about me." He smiled.

"What might I lie about?"

"I don't know, maybe about my driving."

Paige broke into a smile. "Now that you remind me, that's for sure on my list." When Wyatt moved to stand, she reached for his arm. "I'm thankful he knows you so well since I would never be able to express how thoughtfully and tenderly you've watched over me these past few days."

Wyatt nodded and stood. "I'll be just outside."

"I really only need a minute. Come right back." She looked at the clock. "It's nearly time."

He lowered his head and kissed her on top of hers. "I'll be right back."

Once alone in the room, she said, "I can't thank you enough for that man. He's kind and compassionate, strong and bold. I'm not sure it's possible, but I think he may even be as stubborn as you. I can't imagine a better man for me than one so much like my daddy."

Paige looked at the chair where Wyatt had sat praying. "I want you to be here to walk me down the aisle. I don't want to do this without you." She took her dad's hand and removed his wedding band. "At least I know you approve and that your heart is in this with me. I can see why he's a man after your own heart."

For some reason tears didn't come as she removed her gold chain and slid her dad's ring on it, allowing it to nestle with the small gold cross her parents had given her the year she had graduated college. Most every good memory she could recall had both of them in it. Now, like she had been forced to do with her mom, she had to let her dad go too. This night had given her the strength to do that. Her dad had known exactly what she needed, what she and Wyatt both needed, and had fought to stay alive for just that reason.

"I'm glad you get to see Mom and Jesus." She hesitated a second. "Daddy, please tell Jesus to come soon. It sure is a dark world you're leaving us in. I don't know that I have what it takes to be a Daybreaker."

Wyatt poked his head in. "You good?"

She nodded and stood. "I'll give you a final minute before the guys come back." She smiled a soft smile when she passed by him. "I think there's a question you need to ask him."

He grabbed her arm to stop her, and for a long moment stood looking at her. Finally, he whispered, "I'll never let him down where you're concerned, never intentionally."

"I know that."

Paige stood in the hall with the entire team. She had rounded them up and insisted they all be there to say goodbye. When Wyatt opened the door, they all filed in. Each man entered and slowed long enough to salute her dad, a sight that brought tears to Paige's eyes. She was proud to be a part of this man's legacy and proud to stand among his Daybreakers.

Mac was the last to enter and salute. She stopped before Wyatt and reached for his hand. "He was a great man. I'm so sorry."

"Don't be. This wasn't your fault."

She only nodded and went to the side of the bed across from Wyatt and Paige.

Wyatt held Paige's hand, his grip so tight her fingers were becoming numb. He lowered his head to say, "You are never alone."

"I know that," she said to her incorruptible soldier.

He nodded at Mac who began flipping switches. Soon, silence filled the air as the machines concluded their life-saving labor.

Paige watched her dad with a small shred of hope that he might somehow breathe on his own. There was no more movement of his chest, though. He lay perfectly still, his ashen body nearly void of life. The lines of the silenced heart monitor decreased in height, peaks and valleys becoming less defined until eventually a flat line formed and remained.

Paige's voice was barely a whisper as she sang the song her dad had requested be played at her mother's funeral. "Oh, Lord my God, as I in awesome wonder, consider all the worlds Thy hands have made."

Voices joined in and soon the room was filled with booming praise. "I see the stars, I hear the rolling thunder, Thy pow'r throughout the universe displayed. Then sings my soul, my Savior God to Thee; how great Thou art, how great Thou art."

Groom

Day 6, 10:01 a.m.

The hotel room was quiet and only semi-dark with daylight peeking through the drawn curtains. Life was normal for only a few seconds before Paige's mind fully awakened, bursting with those final moments with her dad. She could hear the sounds of the machines and then the flipping of switches as they were being turned off. While she hadn't consciously noticed at the time, her recollection now brought with it the soft sound of Wyatt's sigh next to her when the flatline was visible. That's what she had felt too, the breathless sorrow of that unresponsive line.

Sadness surfaced now, but with it a small sense of relief as well, knowing her dad had held on for their final goodbyes. If she had never found him and had to live her life wondering what had happened to him, that would have been far more tragic. At least he hadn't died alone. Nothing could give her more comfort than that. All those he loved the most were there by his side, just as he would have wanted.

Her eyes were heavy, and she wasn't as sore this morning, so she was tempted to drift off again after getting only a few hours of early-morning sleep. The sound of the window unit humming near her bed was offering to lull her back to sleep. Wyatt always insisted she take the bed farthest from the door, something she didn't mind since she loved the racket.

A soft smile reached her lips, and she was suddenly a little wider awake as the recollection came that her union with Wyatt had been her dad's ultimate intention. She almost chuckled aloud as she wondered what her reaction to that discovery would have been just seven days ago. Now, six days after Wyatt's two-minute warning, marrying the man who was probably waiting for her to wake seemed like the most natural thought in the world.

Paige rolled over in bed to find Wyatt on his bed looking at her.

"Hi," he said.

"Hi."

He didn't move. She didn't either. For a few seconds they lay there looking at one another.

Finally, he said, "You okay?"

"You ask that a lot. And yes, I'm okay."

His eyes narrowed. "You're not just saying that, so I won't worry?"

"No. I mean, it'll be a process. I'm not sure I've even wrapped my mind around it all yet."

"Just know I'm here for you."

"And I'm here for you."

Neither moved or spoke for a minute. Paige scanned his face, the mixture of tender care and concern evident. "I'll always regret it. I was so mean to him the last time I saw him." A tear fell, so she moved to wipe it away. "The things I said..."

"You kissed him goodbye. You held his hand. Your last words to your dad were to sing a song of praise." He paused. "Until we get there," he pointed up, "those are the things you did the last time you saw him."

"I don't want to do something else I'll regret." Her pulse raced a little faster when she said, "When this is over, will you do something for me?"

"You know I will."

"Will you un-friend-zone me?"

His lips drew into a soft smile and he sat up on the side of his bed. "You sure that's what you want?"

"I know it is." She climbed out of bed and moved to sit next to him. "You loving me isn't confusing at all; it's comforting."

"You're vulnerable," he took her hand, "especially now."

"Like my dad, I trust even vulnerable me with you, maybe especially vulnerable me with you. It's like a soft whisper in my heart that says 'you're safe'."

"Always." He reached for her face and allowed his fingertips to trace along the skin of her cheek. For a second he closed his eyes. When he looked back at her and glanced quickly at her lips, Paige could tell he wanted to kiss her.

Instead, he said, "Let's get today behind us. After that, how about I take you to the farmers' market for our second date? We'll eat bread and honey and do some people watching."

"I think I'd like that, to actually be on the date with you this time." She grinned. "Maybe we'll find that same dress in the mess at my house."

"And the yellow ribbon?"

"For sure."

Wyatt's phone vibrated on the bedside table with Mac's name flashing on the screen. When he answered, his gentle hello caused Paige's stomach to sink, so she stood and walked to the bathroom. A few seconds later, Wyatt said through the closed door, "Mac got in touch with the guy from the DA's office. We're a go to meet with him this afternoon."

"I'll get a shower," she said, reminding herself that Mac was Wyatt's past and not his present no matter their tenderness toward one another.

"I'll get Hank to bring us something to eat."

By the time Paige showered and dressed, Wyatt was dressed and waiting with breakfast.

"I hope you're hungry," he said. White foam containers were stacked on the small desk.

"Not too much. I'm more interested in coffee."

Wyatt opened a container with pancakes and bacon, then handed it to Paige. "Eat anyway."

Paige filled her coffee with one after another of the little containers of creamer from a paper bag filled with them. "You know me well."

With a sip of his piping-hot coffee and a nod, he grinned. "You're pretty easy to figure out."

"I can't say the same about you."

Already into his second pancake, Wyatt paused long enough to say, "What's that supposed to mean? I've been an open book with you, at least recently."

"May I ask the open book a prying question?"

"Sure."

"Do you still love her?"

He stopped chewing and sat looking at Paige. Finally, he said, "I guess I always will to some degree, but it's not like it was back then."

"She's who you were seeing when you thought you would marry someday?"

His expression seemed to be one of guilt or heartbreak or maybe both. "She was."

"You said you saw it as loss then."

"Then, yes." His emerging smile was nearly a shy one. "Now?" He gave a quick shake of his head and wrinkled his nose. "Nah."

"Why not now?"

"I didn't lose what I thought I lost. At the time it seemed as if I should give up the idea of marriage altogether. I couldn't imagine heading toward a darkening world with her. It took years for me to figure out that I wasn't supposed to give up on the idea of marriage, just defer it." Dimples formed when he said, "Now, I can't imagine heading toward a darkening world without being married to you."

Paige bit at her lower lip and glanced away, her cheeks flushing in her excitement. His words came to mind from the day they had sat on the roadside with her weeping over what she then saw as her lost future. "You told me not to say never, that you believe we will know good in the midst of whatever's to come." When he nodded, she said, "You meant us?"

"I did mean us."

Paige sat looking at her now soggy pancakes, a pit forming at the thought of how they both once said they had envisioned marriage and kids and a couple of dogs. "I'm not so sure we can have the other."

Wyatt let out a soft sigh. "I can't imagine bringing kids into the world as it looks now."

"That's a tragic loss. I've always wanted to be a mom."

He still wasn't eating but sat looking at her thoughtfully. "It is a tragic loss. I guess we just need to figure out how to have spiritual kids."

Even a thought as sweet as that didn't take the sting away over letting go of a lifelong dream. With forced enthusiasm, she said, "I'm guessing I would be up for the couple of dogs part in this still hypothetical scenario."

"Me too." He closed the lid to his unfinished food and set it aside. "I'll admit, you give me cause to hang onto a world I was ready to let go of not so long ago. I want a little time with you. I'll take even one glorious day of being married to you before the rapture comes–hypothetically speaking, of course." He grinned. "Then, I'm ready. If I don't get that chance, I'm still ready."

He locked eyes with her. "I want the same for you, Paige, for you to be ready and excited about the rapture. It's something I want us to look forward to together."

She let out a soft sigh. "When I run across sites where they don't believe in the rapture, I feel kind of sick at my stomach. What if He doesn't come? What if we have to face it all? I ran across an article the other day." She swallowed hard. "The guy says we'll all be here through the tribulation, that the people who believe in the rapture are fooling themselves."

Wyatt said, "I've read sites from people who believe that. Each time, it makes me stop and question what I believe. I go back and review the verses that speak of the rapture to confirm what I know. The testing of our faith that James talks about doesn't always mean us enduring sorrow or being led into temptation. That testing can be a good thing, something that makes us grapple with what we believe and prompts us to prove the truth of it to ourselves time and again. That builds our faith, which produces endurance."

"It all feels so out of my control."

"It is out of your control. Mine too. All we can do is take this one day at a time." He moved in closer. "Listen to me, Paige," his eyes held tremendous intensity, "that's all we can do right now, live in this moment with today's Jesus. Don't look ahead. Just live right here, right now with me and with Him."

She nodded as tears filled her eyes.

For a few seconds he was quiet. Finally, when he spoke, he reached out and moved her hair from her eyes, the back of his hand tracing along her cheek. "Here we haven't even made it to our second date, yet I can easily think of you as mine already. It's crazy, but that's been the case since I developed feelings for you. I've always felt as if I'm waiting for you, not watching over you for your safety." He blinked long and looked back at her. "I'm right here waiting."

Before she could reply to that, he held up one hand. "I say all that to say this: Jesus is waiting for that moment when it's time to come for us, waiting for the Father's, 'Go get Your bride.'" He shook his head a little. "Because of my feelings for you and how I see you as mine already, I can refute this now more than ever: For those who believe we won't be raptured prior to His wrath, I would say to them that they clearly don't comprehend the love of a groom for his bride."

Wyatt paused and his eyes grew misty. "I would come for you. I would never leave you to suffer. I would walk through fire for you, literally speaking, and claw my way through rubble for you." He blinked long and looked back at her. "I would. Yet my love for you is but a pale expression compared to the love Jesus, the Groom, has for us. How can He not come? I know Christians have always suffered persecution at the hands of men, but what's coming is God's intentional wrath poured out on an unbelieving world. That's not us. What Groom would leave his bride to suffer the wrath of His own hand? That would be spousal abuse and domestic violence."

Those words brought with them a knowing of the heart of Jesus that Paige had never embraced. Until this moment, His love for her had been more head knowledge than heart awareness. But now, the Lord Jesus was using the most unusual love of this remarkable man to speak into the hidden places of her spirit. His whispers of love reassured her: Love comes for the beloved.

Wyatt's eyes danced as he said, "When He comes to take us home, imagine what He'll have in store for us, what the place is like that He's gone to prepare." His eyes fluttered and he glanced away. "If I get even the dust from a gem in my crown and a hut to live in, I'll be thankful. I just know the worst of there is infinitely better than the best of here.

"I believe heaven is so beyond our understanding, that what we perceive as the streets of gold being so spectacular is more symbolic than we now know. Earthly gold, what we hold as the ultimate standard of worth here, is of so little value there that we will trample it beneath our feet.

"You're a writer, Paige, of colors and scenery. If you used pure gold as a picture of the lesser, how might you explain the better? Close your eyes and consider that." Wyatt closed his.

Paige tried to imagine gold beneath her feet, not as significant, but as worthless. "In that case," she said with no other image forming, "all that surrounds us in our field of vision will be so truly magnificent and indescribable that human eyes can't possibly envision it." She had to stop there.

"Exactly," he said with eyes wide. "We just can't process it. How can we know what to expect when words like spectacular and extravagant and even magnificent fail to prepare us?" With a slight pause, he then added, "I just know this: It's something to be excited over and never dread."

She sighed a little sigh. "If you'll explain it to me every day just like that until the Groom comes, how can I not be excited?"

Greater Love

Day 6, 3:22 p.m.

Wyatt was fidgety as they sat and waited. Paige watched him, how his eyes darted toward the door on occasion as they waited for Mac to arrive. On their way to the café for the meet, he hadn't once suggested Paige not come. That was progress for him.

The team was scattered and on high alert: Cade and Bash sat at neighboring tables, looking rather large and ridiculous in the hipster coffee shop. Hank waited just outside the front door in a running SUV in case, as Wyatt said, things went south. Gunny's dark, Latin eyes glanced at them over his book from a table by the front windows.

Paige felt safe with this band of warriors gathered nearby.

Much of their time waiting, Paige had been more intent on watching the little girl just to Wyatt's left. Her curly brown pigtails bounced when she moved as she babbled to a mother who didn't often look at her child when she spoke. After her conversation about children with Wyatt, Paige's heart was raw still, and she envied this inattentive mother's sweet blessing.

The girl once kicked Wyatt's chair, and her shoe dropped onto the floor, prompting him to turn and say to her, "Hey there, barefoot little lady." He reached for the rubber sandal and placed it back on her chubby foot.

The girl giggled and turned back to her muffin. On occasion after that, she would turn to peek at Wyatt.

This man, Paige thought to herself, would be a tremendous dad.

His words and the way he had spoken them so tenderly in the room that morning came to mind. She leaned in and said, "Because of what you said this morning, I see Him, Jesus, differently. All those years of me fearing the rapture, it was because I didn't really know Him, not like I should have. I knew His Word backwards and forwards but not Him, *the* Word. And just as important, I didn't know who I am to Him. Only now," her cheeks grew warm, "because of you, can I see Him as the Groom who loves me like a bride. It's all different now, seeing what's to come through the lens of His love for me."

Wyatt leaned in and was about to reach for her when Mac walked through the door. He sat back in his seat, his expression turning from one of tenderness back to the on-alert soldier.

Mac sat in the empty seat next to Paige's. She didn't look at Wyatt, something Paige noticed since she was watching for how they might interact at this last meeting.

"Thanks for setting this up," Paige said.

Mac nodded and only glanced in Wyatt's direction when she said, "He just called and said he had a trial run a little late, but he'll be along soon."

"Why here?" Wyatt said, his tone suspicious, more abrupt than she had heard him use with Mac in the past.

"He's not so sure who can be trusted in his office. Groves' reach is extensive."

Paige's phone on the table began to vibrate, so she glanced at Wyatt before reaching for it. He gave her a curious look as she answered the unfamiliar number.

"Hello."

"You'll notice the red dot pointed at the heart of your bodyguard. Smile and nod as if this is a familiar caller."

Paige smiled and nodded. "Yeah, I'm on a road trip with friends."

"Unless you do exactly as I say, a round will pierce your bodyguard and then strike the little girl behind him."

The girl was now propped on her knees drinking chocolate milk through a straw while her mother scanned her phone.

"I understand," Paige said with another smile and nod.

"Leave your belongings behind and excuse yourself to the restroom with Ms. Shelton."

Paige's voice remained steady. "I'll let you know as soon as I'm back in town. We'll get together." She hung up and placed her phone back on the table.

Much whirled through Paige's mind over the next few seconds. Again, she looked at the steady red dot trained on the heart of the man she intended to marry someday. His words from the plane just two days before surfaced, how he would die rather than allow her to be taken. She didn't doubt his dedication to that promise or that he would react to protect her if only she would give him the cue.

Greater love has no one than this, that one lay down his life for his friends. The words came as nearly a song in her mind as she scooted back in her seat knowing her next words would likely mean certain death. "Since we have a few minutes," she said, "I'll go to the restroom."

When Wyatt moved as if about to stand, Mac held out her hand. "I'll go with her."

Wyatt never looked at Mac. Instead, his eyes were fixed on Paige's as he moved to stand anyway. "I'll go."

"Don't be silly," Paige said as she stood. That dot now danced and steadied again. "Mac and I will do the girl thing." For only a second she stood looking at Wyatt, wondering if she would ever see him again. While she wanted to reach for his hand or touch his cheek, she wouldn't dare since the caller assumed him no more than a bodyguard. Her affection toward him would only further endanger him.

"I'll see you," she said with her heart plummeting.

Paige walked at a fast pace with Mac so close behind her that she could nearly feel them touching.

"Just keep moving," Mac said with a quiver in her voice.

The minute they stepped around the corner into the small hallway, Mac nudged her past the women's room and toward the kitchen door.

Their presence as they passed through the kitchen garnered a few curious looks, but most went back to work after no more than a glance their way. Mac was now so close, the kitchen staff didn't likely see the gun Paige felt pressing against her lower back.

"Why are you doing this after all you did to keep my dad alive?"

"Just shut up and keep walking." They exited into a narrow alleyway where Mac nodded ahead toward a bakery van. "There."

The last alley she had entered with Wyatt, he had looked up and around for cameras. Paige did that now and found a camera located just above the café door. Her hope was that Echo would see them get into the van when he looked back at the video footage.

Once they were inside, Mac reached for a ball cap and slid into the driver's seat. "Get down on the floorboard so no one sees you."

Paige stood still for a second until Mac raised the gun. "Do what I say, or I'll shoot you in the face."

With tears filling her eyes, Paige knelt on the floor next to Mac's seat.

"Lower, or Hank will see you when we pass by."

With Paige lying on her side in the van, Mac fired up the engine and they pulled down the alley and onto the street. A few seconds passed when Paige knew they must be out of sight of the coffee shop, so she moved to sit up.

Mac glanced at her. "I have no choice. It was you or my kid sister."

"They have her?"

"Yes. I called my friend Brock this morning and told him you have something on Groves. I really thought I could trust him. It seemed like a sound plan until I got a video half an hour later with my sister crying and begging me to help her." Mac's voice broke. "She's due in just a few weeks. She's not a part of this."

"You know they'll never let you live," Paige said. "You know who Groves is."

Mac took a wide left turn that nearly sent Paige tumbling over. "I do know that," Mac said, "but my sister doesn't know about Groves. I at least have to give her a chance to get away."

"I agree." Paige reached for the dash to try and hold on for yet another sharp turn.

Mac only glanced at Paige. "I guess Groves has gotten to everyone in the DA's office since your dad escaped with Tia. My friend was likely threatened himself or maybe his family. I told him Tia was dead."

"Is she?"

"I don't know where she is now. I looked for her last night. She took off yesterday and scored from her old dealer, but I lost her trail after that."

"You think Groves has her?"

"Maybe. He might just be trying to flush out your dad to get rid of any loose ends." Mac reached for her phone and dialed. "You'll let my sister go in a public place, or I'll kill Donovan's kid right here and now, and you'll never know what she knows." Another turn and Mac said, "When I see my sister walk away, I'll give Paige to you."

Mac hung up and soon slowed the van to a stop. "I didn't tell them you care about Wyatt. They would've used him against you."

"Leveraged," Paige said, "that's the word Wyatt would use. And I'm glad you didn't."

"I didn't tell them your dad was dead either. If they think he's still out there, they will keep you alive to leverage you against him."

Paige tried to swallow the lump in her throat. The thought of what it might mean to be leveraged stole her breath for a second as the image of her ransacked home came to mind. Finally, she said, "That was smart of you."

"I wanted to give you time for Wyatt to come." Mac didn't look at Paige when she said, "I saw how he looks at you. He'll come."

"He will. You just take care of your sister." Even as she spoke the words, Paige knew better. Mac would never make it out of this van.

The phone rang. Mac said, "Yeah, I see her."

Paige watched a barefooted, pregnant girl her own age stumble from the side door of a cargo van nearby and stand for a second looking around in sheer panic. Finally, she bolted toward the door of a busy storefront and entered.

Mac let out a soft sigh as she saw what Paige was now seeing. Three suited men were already closing in, all carrying weapons.

The van door slung open, and the auburn-haired man extended his arm past Paige. A loud pop sounded near her ear, leaving Paige's head ringing. Mac slumped over in her seat as blood formed a ring on the chest pocket of her faded-blue scrubs shirt.

Paige started to scream when a hand covered her mouth and dragged her from the van. The grip of the obese man who had his arm around her waist was vice like, and her efforts to protest were in vain.

Passersby gawked as Paige was being dragged across the street and to the white van. Even as the door was opened and she was thrown in headfirst, no one moved to intervene.

The shooter who climbed in next to her began to strip off her shirt. Paige screamed again and began to kick at him until he doubled up his fist and punched her in the face. "Shut up!"

Disoriented from the blow, Paige didn't have the strength to fight back as the man peeled off her jeans and handed her clothes and shoes to the fat man in the front seat who soon rolled down the window and tossed them out of the van as it lurched into motion.

She wasn't sure what more disoriented her, the ringing in her head from the gun shot or the solid blow to her left eye. That she was on the floor of the van undressed next to the man who had just killed Mac without a second's hesitation was surreal, like she was watching some scene in a terrifying movie.

He grabbed her by the hair and lifted her head from the floor. "That's just in case anyone's tracking you." His next words came with a repulsive sneer. "And it'll save me some time when I show you how I'll make you talk."

A voice came from the driver's seat; the bald man driving said, "Hands off until we hear from the boss."

Paige dropped back onto the floorboard when he released her. Tears streamed down her cheeks as the three men were now discussing the Orioles like water-cooler talk on any ordinary workday.

The van hit a bump that lifted Paige and sent her crashing back down onto her head and bruised hip. She wrapped her arms around her legs, formed herself into a tight ball, and didn't make a sound. With bare skin pressed against the cold metal of the cargo van, she shivered and shook, her act of greater love delivering her to what would be certain death. All she could do was close her eyes tight and begin to pray that Wyatt would come. *Please send him to save me.*

An unexpected kick in the back by the man next to her sent Paige careening into the back door.

"Settle in for the ride, pretty thing. I have big plans for you once we get there."

The van swerved and straightened again. "You heard me, Curtis. Keep your hands off the girl. Touch her again, and I'll put a bullet in you."

Paige didn't look up. Instead, she tucked her head down only tighter to her chest. Even with eyes shut, tears still escaped. *What if Wyatt didn't come?*

Breaking

Day 6, 4:13 p.m.

The least ruthless of the three men so far was the still-nameless, sweaty, fat man. His pale eyes held what Paige hoped to be an ounce of empathy when he dragged her from the van toward an abandoned warehouse. When she stepped barefooted onto broken glass and winced in pain, he lifted her over the remaining shards. If at all possible, she would work on the sympathies of this man who huffed and puffed and bulged out of his cheap suit.

Ahead of them was a red brick building, dirty and crumbling, with a rusted door hanging crooked on bent hinges. Paige looked up at the roof, hoping to find cameras, but the area in general seemed to be deserted and dilapidated and long predated the use of modern technology.

Once inside, she was led through the vast space where dust danced amid the rays of the afternoon sun streaming through the mostly broken panes of windows. They passed a sagging sofa and small fold-out table and chairs.

These men and this operation didn't at all resemble the clean-cut, CIA-like operatives who had invaded her home. If anything, they seemed like small-time thugs from a crime show.

Different than the big guy, Curtis and the baldheaded Tony had zero compassion. What she had hoped was kindness from Tony when he had warned Curtis not to touch her turned out to be only a deferred directive. His abusive handling of her when he grabbed her arm and pulled her toward an adjacent room was the initial indication. Then, while zip-tying her hands behind her back in a chair, he chuckled behind her and reached around to lick her face, his thick mustache prickling her cheek. Rough and dirty fingers trailed along her collarbone to snap her bra strap. "Not long now, sweetie. Once we get the answers we need, how 'bout you and me have a little fun before I hand you over to Curtis?"

Paige turned her face away and drew in a sharp breath. *Lord, send Wyatt. Please let him save me from these men.*

Behind her still, Tony slipped a hand around her waist and allowed it to rest on her belly, then buried his face in her hair. "You smell good. I can't wait to dirty you up."

The phone in his pocket rang, so he stepped back and answered. Paige heard part of his conversation on his way out the door as he gave directions to someone on where to find them. They were miles away from Light Street where they had been at the café, in an area that seemed to have little car or pedestrian traffic. The team might never find her.

She sat staring ahead at the closed door, just waiting for it to open again. Beyond defeated, Paige was demoralized. That was their intention in stripping her of her clothes. The way the two nearly salivated while looking at her had served its intended purpose. Left tied up and so physically vulnerable, they knew what they were doing, how to psych her out while she waited. All she could do was sit and contemplate how they would take turns with her.

She blinked, and an image came to mind, one of Jesus on the cross. In nothing but a narrow cloth wrapped around him, He had suffered their intentional humiliation.

"I can't do this," she whispered. "I'm not strong enough. I'm not a Daybreaker."

Her dad's voice was there in soft response to her fear: *Be strong and courageous! Do not tremble or be dismayed, for the Lord your God is with you wherever you go.*

Footsteps approaching set Paige's heart to racing, and what was once trembling was now outright uncontrollable shaking. Curtis opened the door and stepped inside. When he closed it behind him, she dropped her head and fought back tears. *Make me strong and courageous. Lord, I'm not.*

"By the looks of you, it seems someone's already had a go at you." He poked her bruised hip, but Paige refused to cry out.

With one hand wound through her hair, Curtis lifted her face to look at him. "Let's have a little fun." He turned loose of her hair and backhanded her across the face.

He took a step back. "Where is your father?"

If they knew her dad was dead, would that eliminate their need of her? "I don't know," she said. She didn't. Echo had made the arrangements for her father's body.

Another backhand left her ears ringing and a metallic taste in her mouth. Blood drops fell onto her bare leg and trailed along her hip.

"He has something that doesn't belong to him." With arm drawn back again and a smile that revealed his thrill of the moment, he landed the next blow.

She cried out this time as his fist landed on her cheek and rattled her teeth.

Curtis leaned forward, his face now closer to hers. "Where's the girl?"

His image was mostly hazy, especially through her left eye already so swollen. When his question sank in, Paige now knew that Tia must be safe for the time being. "I really don't know," she whispered.

Another blow left the words ringing over and over in her mind: *The Lord is my strength and my shield. The Lord is my strength and my shield.*

The door opened and Tony said, "Boss said to leave her for now. There's someone on the way, a specialist."

"We don't need help," Curtis said with a snarl. "Another few whacks is all it'll take."

Tony reached for Curtis's drawn-back fist. "We've got orders to keep her intact to bargain with her old man. He'll give up the girl for his kid. That won't happen if you keep this up."

The two men left the room, and Paige dropped her head again and began to cry. What might a specialist do to her?

Her voice was barely a whisper. "Give me the Word, Lord, something to keep my mind filled and my heart on solid ground."

A verse didn't come. Instead, she heard, *The Word fills the Paige.* She shook her head knowing those weren't the words Wyatt had spoken. He had said the Word settles onto a Paige–yeah, that was it. She kept trying to hear his voice and remember the tender expression in his eyes when he had said it.

The words came again exactly the same: *The Word fills the Paige.*

For a second she replayed them, listening closer. It wasn't Wyatt's voice. It wasn't her dad's. It wasn't even her own. Her heart raced at the awareness: It was Jesus.

"You are the Word within me," she said in a soft whisper as bloody spit dripped onto her leg again.

Paige listened closely, longing to hear His voice again, fearing her mind was playing tricks on her. Verses came now, so Paige tapped the air behind her back with her fingers as if typing them onto paper: memory verses from childhood, ones her mother had often quoted, Bertie's soft voice quoting the Psalm that she called the Shepherd's Song, anything that would come, she typed them out as her reminder that the Word filled the Paige.

She whispered, "This book of the law shall not depart from your mouth, but you shall meditate on it day and night." With a slight pause, she closed her eyes tight. "I'm trying, Daddy."

When she heard a car door slam, then muffled voices on the other side of the door, her mind stalled and her fingers stilled. The turning of the doorknob only made her tremble more in the cold and drafty room.

A man stepped inside, tall and dark and lean, a well-dressed man, closer to her father's age as the sprinkling of white hair would indicate.

His kind smile faded when he looked at her. "Those men are barbarians," he said in a soft Southern drawl. "I apologize for their lack of professionalism. They just so happened to be in the area to pick up some collateral this morning and handle your transfer until the security team arrives. I'm here to prepare the way for them."

"Collateral?" Paige's ability to speak at all surprised her, but her anger beckoned her beyond fear. "You mean the pregnant girl?"

He blinked long as if affected. "Unpleasant part of the business, I'll agree."

He drew closer and removed his sport coat, then draped it over Paige's shoulders. "There," he said as he dragged a chair in front of her. He rolled up the sleeves of his crisp-white button-down shirt and made a show of wiping dust from the seat before he moved to sit. "A conversation goes smoother when everyone is more comfortable."

For a long moment he sat looking her in the eye as if trying to look within. Finally, he said, "Hello, Paige."

The tender expression in his eyes was unexpected. The more she looked into those dark pools, the more she saw pain trapped there, floating amidst the smile on his pock-marked face. Something happened within her, like fingers lightly tapping on her heart.

"How does one become a specialist in pain?" she said.

He seemed to study her question, then nodded. "On the job training, I s'pose. I've been on both ends of the conversation we're about to have."

A deep and jagged scar that spanned from his eye socket to his chin bore witness to his words.

"I'm Moses. Today, we'll get to know one another quite well."

"Moses is a fine name," Paige said, "one that set you on a course to be a great man for the Lord."

His eyes seemed nearly amused. "I'm not so sure the Lord would agree."

Seconds passed as they sat looking at one another. Eventually, she said, "You see Jesus in me, don't you, that flicker of Light in the darkness where you live?"

"I do see Him in you." With a slight grimace and a shake of his head, he said, "Which is what will make today all the more unfortunate for me. This will go much easier on you if you'll tell me where I can find your father."

"You won't let me live either way."

"Now that's not up to me, Paige, but if you'll cooperate, I'll make sure my part is as painless as possible." He turned and looked at the door. "And I won't let them harm you like this anymore." He blinked long and glanced away.

"You know what they'll do to me. I know who Groves is and what he's done." Paige was surprised to hear her own voice say with confidence, "A friend reminded me just the other day: I'm immortal until my work here is done." Even as she spoke the words, she realized that maybe this man's soul was her final work. Maybe Moses was her sole Daybreak purpose.

Wyatt's face emerged, and she couldn't help but wish for more time with him. She could scarcely imagine the anguish he was experiencing at this very moment, his frantic search for her and the guilt he likely carried over her capture.

Moses dragged his chair a little closer, his soft sigh giving the impression of regret. "Your immortality aside, I'll have to break your fingers. It'll be painful, so I'm hoping it'll only take one."

When Paige blinked, a tear trickled down her cheek. "You're an unborn-again sheep, Moses. He's calling you to come home to your Shepherd."

"Stop it, Paige," he said with a tone more pleading than irritated. "This isn't what your dad wants for you." Moses' eyes became misty. "He would want you to tell me. I once had a daughter, a church girl like you, so I know that to be true."

"My daddy went home to be with Jesus just this morning." She huffed and tried to keep from breaking down. "I watched him go and sang by his bedside. But I know he's waiting for me there. Your daughter won't be able to say the same of you unless you call upon the name of the Lord. That's all it takes, Moses. Just call."

Moses stood, picked up his chair, and moved it behind her. Paige began to cry harder when she felt him lift the fabric of his jacket and reach for her pinky finger.

Her words were barely a whisper. "Some believe after the rapture that people like you won't get a second chance."

"Where is your father, Paige?" The snapping of her finger made her cry out, and tears streamed down her cheeks. Her finger throbbed and her stomach now churned as if she might throw up.

The voice was soft and distinctive in her head. *I am the Word you speak.*

Even amidst the pain she felt, letters and words from the Daybreak passage about exposing the darkness to light began to settle onto the page of her mind.

Her next words came with a power not her own: "You can step out of your pain-filled darkness, Moses. The Word says, 'Awake, sleeper, and arise from the dead, and Christ will shine on you.'" After a second's pause, she whispered, "He's here now, casting light upon you. He loves you no matter what you've done."

Moses was closer now, his words matching the quiet tone of her own. "I need you to listen to me, Paige –"

"When all the believers disappear," she said amid open sobs, "you'll have to call out and ask for forgiveness. I believe you'll get a second chance. Then you have to lead the rebellion against the Antichrist and guide others to Jesus."

His massive hand applied increasing pressure as he gripped her ring finger, the one where she had hoped to see Wyatt someday place a gold band. Moses' hesitation was evident as he said, "Your dad has taken something that doesn't belong to him. I've been hired to recover it."

"It was a someone, not a something, Moses, a beautiful, young biracial girl; I'm sure much like your daughter. Groves preys on young girls from an inner-city program. That's who he's looking for, the girl he brutalized."

"That's not my concern." His words sounded less calculated than before. "I'm paid to do a job. Today, Paige, you are my job."

"I swear to you; my dad is dead and the girl took off. No one knows where she is. I never met her. All I know is that her name is Tia."

The snapping of the bone came quick, and Paige wailed aloud. Her head was now too heavy to lift, so it hung limp as tears fell onto her lap and bloody spittle dribbled onto his jacket.

Moses reached for her middle finger and stroked it with a gentle touch.

I am the Song you sing, were the words that were now whispered into her heart as a pleasing melody.

Her voice came first as a whimper, then little squeaks of noise as she sang, "Then sings my soul, my Savior God to Thee..."

She felt him release her hand, and for a few seconds he sat close behind her still. Her words were barely audible, and her voice was breaking. "How great Thou art," she huffed and tried to catch her fleeting breath, "how great Thou art."

When Moses jumped to his feet, Paige never even lifted her head to watch him go. Her hand was in excruciating pain, throbbing with every beat of her heart. She tried to sing again for comfort, but when her mouth opened, nothing came but a soft moan. A gentle voice spoke now, reminding her, *The Lord is your strength and your shield.*

Gunfire erupted on the other side of the door. One, two, three shots. Then a second of silence. A fourth rang out, then one more. Her heart erupted in hope. It could only be the team blasting their way to get to her. Paige lifted her head and watched the door, expecting Wyatt to come bursting through to save her.

Call

Day 6, 4:54 p.m.

The door swung open wide and Moses was there, his expression as calm as before. Blood was speckled on his shirt and face, and a gunshot wound was dispersing crimson along his waist. A pistol was in his right hand and a knife in his left. Paige sucked in little pockets of air, pain and terror keeping her from drawing a full breath. Unable to tell his intention, her head dropped in resignation over what was to come next. "The Lord is my strength and my shield," she said. "The Lord is my strength and my shield."

Moses moved behind her and cut the zip ties from her wrists. He pulled her to her feet and dragged her behind him. "We've got to get you out of here."

The fat man was sprawled on the couch with a single shot to the forehead, and Tony and Curtis were both face down on the floor, blood still pooling on the cement.

Her adrenaline was pumping so high now that she barely felt the pain in her fingers or even Moses' hand on her arm pulling her along behind him. He was first through the door and didn't slow as he dragged her along to the waiting sedan.

With the back passenger door open, he placed his hand behind her neck and tucked her inside. "Get on the floorboard and cover yourself with my jacket."

Paige did exactly as he told her and never said a word. Within seconds the car lurched into backward motion, came to a screeching halt, then moved forward. Bumps and ruts in the parking lot had the car rocking, so Paige braced herself by propping her good hand and her knees against the seat above her.

"Stay still and stay quiet," Moses said as the car began to slow.

She heard his window roll down when they came to a stop.

"Donovan is dead, and the package is in the wind," Moses said. "The daughter didn't know any more than that."

"I hardly need to ask with the blood on your shirt, but did you take her out?"

"I did," Moses said. "Those guys will clean up the mess. Nothing left for you to handle."

"Yeah, we'll go check things out anyway and report in."

Moses' tone was casual. "Suit yourself. I'm calling it a day." He rolled up the window and shifted into gear. The car moved forward slowly at first.

"Stay put," he said. A few seconds and one turn later, they began to gain speed. "You can get up now."

Paige moved onto the seat and wrapped Moses' enormous sport coat around her. With only two buttons as a closure, she still felt exposed and tried to hold the jacket together with trembling hands. She looked down at her two fingers, broken tips tilted in an unnatural position. In the moment she could hardly feel them. Actually, she felt very little, not the chilly air on her bare legs or the pain in her face. All she felt were bumps and turns as the car sped along.

"There's a bag there," he said. "You can get a shirt out and then put the coat back over you."

Moving in what felt like a dream state, Paige unzipped the brown leather bag and dug through it with her good hand. When she came across a white t-shirt, she unfolded it, removed the jacket, then slipped the shirt over her head using her good hand and the undamaged fingers on her left hand. With the jacket back around her and a pair of black socks on her feet, she finally stopped shivering.

"Where can I take you?"

Paige looked at Moses' reflection in the rearview mirror for the first time. Her mind was blank in response to his question. Without her phone she had no way to contact Wyatt or the team. They had checked out of the hotel that morning before the café, so she wasn't sure where to find them.

"I don't know how to contact my dad's team."

"We need to dump this car and get you off the street."

Paige climbed over the console and into the passenger seat. "No, that's what I need, a street cam. They'll find me that way."

"So will the guys who by now know you're not dead."

"I'll have to take that chance."

"Paige, I'm trying to keep you alive here."

"I told you, I'm immortal."

"Yeah, so you said." He didn't look at her. "No cams that I can see." They were still in an industrial area, and now Moses was driving slowly through a parking lot, scanning cars. "That one," he said.

"You can't steal a car."

"Sure I can. I haven't made that call yet."

She studied his words, but he parked and was out the door before she could ask.

"Stay put 'til I get it started," he said when she opened her door.

Paige watched with interest as the still-bleeding man opened the unlocked, older model Mustang. She rolled down the window to get a better view of his body hanging partially in and partially out of the floorboard of the driver's side. "You're bleeding so much."

He kept working and said, "I've had worse."

Against his instructions Paige opened the car door and stepped out, the cool night air causing goose bumps to form on her stubbly legs. Just then, the Mustang's engine roared to life.

"Get in," Moses said as he powered down his phone. "I'll grab my bag."

He tossed the bag in then went behind the car and disappeared for a few seconds. She had to guess he was swapping the license plate with the next car.

Before long they were backing out of the space. As if this were any ordinary road trip, Moses said, "I had one of these when I was a younger man. Feels good to be back behind the wheel."

"Someone will be crushed when they discover it's gone."

"Think of it this way," he said with a quick smile, "we're just borrowing it. We will drop it off and the police will get it back to the owner."

Paige looked in her side mirror to see if anyone was following them. Even though the coast was clear, the memory of the SUV crashing into her side of the car just two days ago gave her reason to doubt. She had seen the aftermath of the three vehicles when they had stopped at the airfield. "As long as they don't find us, you mean. If they do, there's no hope for this car."

The memory of the car chase gave Paige an idea. "Take me downtown to Light Street."

"What's on Light Street?"

"It's the one place the team knows I'm familiar with."

"I'll get you there, but I can't promise I'll keep you alive."

"You won't have to," Paige said.

Moses mumbled something under his breath.

"What was that?"

"I know," he said, "the Lord is your strength and your shield."

"He is." Paige hesitated. "Well, for today He seems to be using you as my shield."

While idling at a four-way stop, Moses shrugged and looked at her with what seemed to be resignation. "I don't know that I had a choice. And after taking out mob guys, I sure hope I'm immortal too, at least until my work is done."

It came to her when he drove on, what he had meant before stealing the car. He was referring to her telling him that those who called on the name of the Lord would be saved. "You can make that call any time, you know."

Her heart grew tighter in her chest at the realization that this may possibly be the only opportunity Moses had to hear the Gospel. Other than kids at Vacation Bible School, Paige didn't have much experience in leading people to the Lord, especially adults. Uncertainty held her tongue for a few seconds until she remembered the songs she had sung with the kids each year.

"I used to work with kids at Bible school. We would tell them that becoming a child of God is as easy as the ABCs. You admit you're a sinner, which," she said with a raised hand displaying broken fingers, "you totally are. You agree to turn away from your sin. Then you believe that Jesus is God's Son, lived a perfect life, and died for your sins on the cross."

Moses nodded. "I agree to all that."

"That leaves the C: You confess Jesus as Lord. That's not as easy as it seems. That means you're giving Him your life. You can't live this life, Moses." She paused a quick beat and looked at his blood-stained shirt. "I can't imagine this life is too much to hold onto."

He didn't look at her when he said, "This isn't living at all, but I can't imagine the Lord would pick up if it was me calling."

"I promise on my current immortal life that He will. He brought you into my life for such a time as this. The enemy meant my capture for evil, but God is using it for good."

His expression held a mixture of skepticism and guilt. "What good will come of your battered face and fingers this sinner broke?"

"You, Moses. You're the good."

"Just because the Lord used me to help you, that doesn't mean I can make it to heaven. God used Pharaoh for His plan, then still drowned him in the Red Sea."

"Only because Pharoah wouldn't bow his knee and call Him Lord. Every man has a chance." Paige's eyes filled with tears. "I would take this battered face and two more broken fingers if I knew it would make a difference in your life. I want to know you'll go with me to heaven."

Moses looked straight ahead, his jaw clenching and loosening and clenching again.

The next moments were quiet. Paige allowed her words to settle in with Moses, to give God time to work on his heart. Her own mind and heart were held captive by a God who would save her in such an extraordinary way. She had asked Him over and over to send Wyatt to save her. Instead, God Himself saved her. He did for her what He had done many times for His people, turned their enemies against themselves. She knew it happened in more than one passage, but at the moment, she could only remember one such instance, how the Lord had set ambushes against Israel's enemies. That's exactly what had happened with the Lord using Moses against the mob guys.

After a long silence, Moses said, "You good? It won't be too long before shock sets in."

She looked down at her fingers, for sure feeling the pain again now. Amazed at how calm she felt under the current circumstances, she had to wonder if maybe this was shock. How could she remain so steady after the day she'd had? It was shock or Spirit. A stirring within assured her it was Spirit.

With her good hand, she began to roll up the way-too-long-for-her sleeve on her left arm. "Better than you might think."

Moses pulled the car over and parked. "Before we get into our next firefight, let's get you fixed up." He reached in the back seat and pulled his bag over onto the console, then dug around until he pulled out a pair of boxers.

When he began tearing them into strips, Paige said, "So you're going to doctor my hand with your underwear?"

He chuckled. "You're half dressed, you've got one heck of a shiner, a busted lip, and two broken fingers. If that weren't bad enough, you've got a hit-squad after you. I would think strips of underwear on your hand would be the least of your concerns right now."

"They're clean, right?"

Moses sat back in his seat and actually laughed out loud. "I'm glad I saved you, Paige. This world needs a mouth like yours."

His statement meant more to her than he could understand. If she had ever known anything in her life, it was that God had brought her together with this man for a reason. The Lord had given her the words to speak, to call His sheep-to-be home. Maybe she would be a Daybreaker after all if the Lord got her back to her team.

In barely a whisper, maybe not even for Paige's sake, he said, "You remind me of her."

"What was her name?"

"Nicole."

"How did she die?"

"Home invasion."

"I'm so sorry. That's what I saw in your eyes, the pain of her loss."

He blinked a long few seconds, then gave a little shake of his head as if to chase away her memory. "This won't hurt as much as before." Without any warning he straightened her ring finger. Before she was through yelping aloud, he straightened her pinky. "We'll wrap them together with your middle finger to stabilize them."

Paige broke out into a cold sweat as she watched him look around the car and rummage through the glove box. When he found an ice scraper, he broke off the handle and used it to immobilize her screaming-at-her fingers.

"This'll do until you can get them set properly."

Now, with the strips of fabric tied around her hand, Moses sat with her hand resting on his for a few seconds. Tears glistened in his eyes, prompting Paige to say, "I forgive you."

"You shouldn't," he said and reached for her right arm. He then rolled up her sleeve so that the loose fabric wouldn't remain hanging nearly a foot below her hand. "Can you handle a gun?"

Her eyes grew wide. "If I have to."

"Unless the Lord Himself steps down from heaven as a shield, you'll have to." With one more inspection of his bag, he drew out a smaller pistol than the one tucked into his waistband and handed it to her. Paige dropped it into her right coat pocket.

"What about you?" she said. "You need help."

"It's only a flesh wound." Moses leaned up over the steering wheel and looked out the window. "Let's get something to eat. We need to kill some time and wait until closer to nightfall."

The word nightfall was like a punch in Paige's gut. Wyatt had used it more than once, how the idea of nightfall stole sleep from him. Today, the terror he must be feeling in his search for her was something she could nearly feel inside. "I'm not sure I should wait. The team is out there. I know they are."

"More than your team will be coming for you. We have a better chance of eluding them under the cover of darkness. Your team would tell you to wait. Listen to me, Paige."

She nodded, his warning making sense. Wyatt would want her to wait. With a long blink she wondered what he was doing with an emotion he had no experience processing. *Calm his fear, Lord.*

Without another word Moses put the car into gear and sped away.

Paige closed her eyes. *I pray this man makes that call.*

Light Street

Day 6, 5:35 p.m.

Paige watched Moses eat his burger as if he wasn't shot and they weren't both about to be under attack. They sat in the busy parking lot of a grocery store on the outskirts of downtown Baltimore.

She held the chicken tender she had only taken one bite of. No way, with her stomach in knots, could she eat this greasy mess of food sitting in her lap, but the warmth of it felt good on her legs, so she left it there and watched him.

"Do you see what we see, Moses, the darkness rising?"

With mouth full and taking a sip of soda, he nodded, then set his drink back in the holder. "I've been telling people something's not right. I was special forces. I knew a bioweapon when I saw one. Something bad is coming and fast."

"Did you go to church as a kid?"

"Until I was twelve. I lived with my grandmother until she died."

"That makes sense," she said. "That's how you knew about Pharaoh."

"You can't have a name like Moses and not know the whole story." He hesitated. "You know, it used to really tick me off that God would use Pharaoh for His glory then kill him. It seemed so unfair and always made me wonder why anyone would let God use them. But I think I see what you meant before. Pharaoh remained stubborn even after he saw all the miracles God had performed on behalf of the Israelites."

"I think that's easy for any man to do, to remain stubborn."

He took a smaller bite this time and chewed as he seemed to be considering her words. Finally, he said, "You think that's me, that I'm being stubborn?"

"Yeah, I do. I think you think you're feeling undeserving or ashamed because of your past. Or maybe you're still blaming God for what men did to your daughter. But ultimately, you're just being stubborn. When someone offers you a free gift and you refuse it, that's on you." She paused, then said, "I know stubborn from personal experience."

Moses turned and watched a woman next to them load groceries into her car. After she was loaded and gone, he turned to look straight ahead rather than at Paige. "I have a lot to think through."

"You do. But I think you know what Nicole would want for you."

"I do know." He turned to her with a soft smile. "That girl was singing Jesus Loves Me before she could form complete sentences. She sang in church, even from a young age." His next words were quiet. "None of that was due to me. Her mama was a good woman."

"Did they both die that night?"

Moses nodded, crumpled his burger wrapper, and stuffed it into the bag. "I had the life that dreams are made of until I got that call. The Navy got me home. I retired and spent the next months tracking down those men. There wasn't much you could call good in me for a long time after that. It set a new course for my life, one my girls would weep over if the Lord let them see the man I've become."

"Not today, Moses. They wouldn't be weeping at all. They'd be rejoicing over your change of heart, making you the same promise: Jesus isn't just waiting on your call; He died in order to keep the line open until you do."

"That's pretty stuff, Miss Paige."

A soft sigh escaped her. "The Word fills the Paige."

"You sure got some words all right," he said as he started the car and backed out of the space.

Hours later, now dark enough for Moses' comfort, he came to a stop and put the Mustang into park. "Are you sure you want to do this?" he said as he looked out the side window at a camera mounted high above them. "All hell's going to break loose when you do."

Paige glanced across the street at the Hyatt, the hotel where the team had stayed both times in Baltimore. "I'm sure. They'll come for me." Under her breath, she said, "He'll come."

"I hope you're right. This place will be crawling with Groves' guys in minutes."

"You don't have to stay." She looked down at his wound. What he called a flesh wound was bleeding still, and he seemed paler now. "You should go get treated."

"I'm not leaving you to face this alone."

"I'm not alone."

"No, Paige." He touched her hand just above her splint. "You have me." Moses opened his door and walked around to her side of the car, his hand dragging on the hood as if holding himself steady. When he opened her door, he squatted down and looked at her. "Whatever happens next, I need to tell you this: We sang 'How Great Thou Art' at my wife and daughter's graveside."

Tears sprang to Paige's eyes. "It wasn't me, Moses."

"It was that mouth of yours. That's all I know."

She reached for his hand. "I sang it for both my mom and my dad, so I understand how it is special for you."

Moses blinked long, flipped his hand over to grasp hers, and said, "So he really did die this morning?"

"Yes."

"And the girl?"

"I don't know where she is. I wish I could help her."

"Let's just get you back with your dad's team. I'll see what I can do about the girl."

Paige stepped from the car with head raised high. She moved onto the sidewalk and began looking up and spinning slowly so that every camera close by would capture her image. "Echo," she said in barely a whisper, "send Wyatt."

Clearly, she was quite the spectacle in her t-shirt dress and man's sport coat, not to mention her black eye and busted lip. Onlookers openly gawked, one woman even reached for her phone when a bloody Moses grabbed Paige's arm and began pulling her along the sidewalk.

The last thing she wanted was for someone to call the police since Groves had so many officials paid off. "I'm okay," Paige said to the woman. "I'm with him."

People stepped far around the beaten and bloody pair as they made their way to the small waterfront park just down from the hotel. Paige's heart pounded as she waited for the emergence of vehicles to swarm them. They were likely on the way already. Her only hope was that her team, her family of Daybreakers, would arrive first.

"Sit here," Moses said when they reached a row of benches overlooking the harbor. "I like water nearby. If worse comes to worse, we'll jump for it."

Paige sat and pulled her legs up to her chest, then pulled her shirt over them. "He'll come."

Moses sat next to her and draped his arm over her shoulders. "I'm so sorry."

"Just make the call, Moses. Do that one thing for me. The Lord's coming to get His church soon." A tear tumbled over her lashes. "No man left behind, especially you, Moses."

Horns blew on the nearby street and tires screeched as a caravan of SUVs drove off the road and onto the green space and walkways of the park. Moses jumped to his feet and lifted Paige to hers. He moved her to the rail behind them and covered her with his body. "When I give the word, you jump."

"What about you?" Paige said.

"Just do what I say. Stay under water as long as you can, and swim to the other side of that boat if you can make it with one breath."

With head propped against Moses' back, she nodded and waited for the sound of gunfire to erupt. He had one arm behind him holding her in place, using his body as a shield before her.

The command was sound and steady. "Drop the gun and move away from her."

Paige let out her held breath at the sound of Wyatt's voice. She tried to step from behind Moses, but his arm held her firm.

Louder now, Wyatt said, "Lower your weapon and move away!"

Paige shook loose from Moses' grasp and moved to stand in front of him. "Don't shoot, Wyatt! I'm okay!"

Wyatt approached with gun held steady, pointed over her head at Moses. The team all swarmed them with weapons drawn.

"Come to me, Paige." He was taking steps their way.

"Please, Wyatt, lower your gun. Moses saved me."

The look in his eyes was the relief of a groom, but the gravity in his expression was the intent of a soldier.

When Wyatt tucked his gun behind his back, Paige ran and jumped into his waiting arms. The embrace was only seconds long before he stepped back, as sirens blared in the background. "Can you run?"

She nodded but then turned back to look at Moses who had now dropped onto one knee. In his weakened state, he wouldn't make it back to the car. "Moses!" she screamed and tried to go to him.

"We have to get you out of here now!" Wyatt lifted Paige into his arms and turned, hesitating only a second to say to Cade, "Take care of him."

Paige watched behind Wyatt's shoulder as Cade and Bash approached Moses, lifted him onto his feet, and then supported him as the three made their way to a nearby SUV arm in arm.

That was it. Paige had nothing left. The adrenaline was gone now, and all she could do was rest her cheek on Wyatt's shoulder.

Wyatt's words were soft. "I've got you, babe. You're safe." Seconds later, he set her in the back seat and closed her door. When he got in the other side, Hank jumped in at the wheel, and they sped away.

Paige reached with her right hand to pull the seatbelt across her lap, but Wyatt stopped her as she tried to snap it into place. His breath came in rapid bursts as he slid onto the floorboard between the two seats, scooped her into his arms, and dragged her onto his lap. With face buried in her hair, for the longest time he rode like that, holding her to him in silence.

Cradled in his arms, all the fear from the day now slipping away the farther they drove from Light Street, she felt herself dissolving into a puddle. This was exactly where she belonged, with this man.

She raised her head to look at Wyatt, placed her fingertips on his wet cheek, and whispered, "Marry me."

He let out a soft sigh and nodded. Like hers, his words were quiet. "I will when you love me."

"Only the love of a bride could see the red dot on your chest and stand and walk away from that table on Light Street."

"Well then," his smile was soft and his expression tender, "the love of a groom says yes." He smiled a little brighter and moved in to kiss her forehead like he had done on his dad's front porch. "When that lip of yours heals, I'm coming for that real kiss."

Healed or not, Paige leaned in and planted a soft kiss on his lips. "That was a little down payment."

Stronger

Day 6, 8:23 p.m.

The SUV came to an abrupt halt, and within seconds, the door opened and Hank reached out a hand to Paige. She took it, and Wyatt helped to hoist her out of his lap. The moment Wyatt stepped out behind her, he scooped her up again and was soon jogging up the steps of the plane.

Once inside and with the door closed, Wyatt knelt before her and reached to snap her seatbelt. "I don't want to be on the ground even a minute more than we have to be. When we get in the air, you can get changed. I have your bag."

Paige nodded.

He seemed to be held captive there looking at her. She hadn't gotten a good look at her face yet but suspected it was more painful for Wyatt than for her.

"I'm okay," she said.

"I'm not okay." He didn't move. The plane was taxiing toward the runway, but he stayed there, looking at her rather than moving to his seat. He slid his hand behind her neck and pulled her closer. "I've prayed all day; it's all I could do. I'm so sorry I failed you," he said with eyes closed tight. "I failed the Apex."

"You didn't fail either one of us."

He looked back at her and reached to touch her bruised left cheek. "You should've never walked away," his eyes took on a tender expression, "no matter the bride's reason."

"I couldn't let them shoot you."

"Paige, I'm trained to analyze a situation and react. I would have come up with a plan. The team was in place."

"I didn't want to risk you getting hurt. And they threatened the little girl next to you. It all happened so fast." Tears stung her eyes, and though she struggled to hold it back, one fell.

"Don't." He wiped her cheek with his thumb. "It's okay. I just need you to promise me you'll never do something like that again. We will always be stronger together than apart. You have to trust me, that I'll come up with a plan."

"I want to promise that." If given the same situation again, she was sure she would protect this man rather than watch a bullet pierce his heart.

He leaned in and rested his head on hers. "I'm not sure I'll let you out of my sight again after a day like today. You'll be tired of me."

Paige let out a soft sigh. "I'm not so sure I could ever be tired of you."

He moved back, the look in his eyes uncertain. "I should've said after tomorrow I won't let you out of my sight."

"Why after tomorrow?"

"I'm taking you to my dad's."

"You're going after Groves, aren't you?" Her stomach twisted into fresh knots.

With a firm nod, he said, "I plan to end this. We'll either capture or kill him. It'll be his call. I won't risk him coming after you again. I won't let him hurt anyone the way he's hurt Tia and the others." He blinked long and looked back at her. "You can't imagine what was on that drive. That man isn't human. No human would do what he's done to those girls."

Paige sat looking at him, at the determined expression in his eyes, part of her wanting to beg him not to go. She knew better. This soldier of hers would always run into the fight and never away from it. In the days to come, she would have to get accustomed to letting him go when the darkness needed an arrow of incorruptible light.

She said the words her heart didn't want to hear. "You're the team leader now, not my watcher. Be who the Apex raised you up to be. My dad is proud of you, Wyatt."

"I'm not sure he would want me to leave your side. As long as Groves is still out there –"

"If anyone comes for me, then Waylon will rain down fire on them. Trust your dad. Trust me to be okay with you gone." She paused and pointed up. "I trust Him with you."

"I'll try to get better at that."

They began their takeoff, so Wyatt stood and reached for a blanket, then draped it over her legs. "There," he said as he took his seat. "That'll help until you can get changed."

Wyatt reached out and with a gentle stroke touched the back of her hand. "We'll get you fixed up soon."

She only nodded and took a deep breath, trying to push away the memory of Moses' strong hands breaking her fingers. With heart beating faster, she blinked long and whispered under her breath, "I pray Moses calls You."

Moments passed. Wyatt was quiet, and Paige sat looking out the window more than at him. The pained expression in his eyes, the blame he carried, was all that kept her from falling to pieces. That's what she needed. Now, with the dust settled and the danger passed, she needed to cry. She needed to pray. She needed her mind to stop playing the reel of Curtis standing before her with a depraved smile and Tony promising to dirty her up. Then the images soon shifted, and she had to wonder if the sight of those bleeding dead bodies would ever leave her?

A little flutter came and rested in her heart. It wasn't a feeling of being unsettled; it was more of a burst of excitement when the words she had spoken began to ring in her head like music: *You are my strength and my shield. You are my strength and my shield.*

Her head snapped around to look at Wyatt. "I see it now; I needed what happened today to happen."

"How could you say that?"

"It made my faith stronger. I encountered Jesus today in a way I imagine few people ever will." She thought of her words to Moses. "I would take another black eye and two more broken fingers to know the God I now know."

Wyatt dropped his head and moved his hands to his eyes. The way he drew in a sharp breath and huffed a few times, it was evident he was fighting back tears.

Finally, he whispered, "I won't fail you again."

"You didn't fail me, Wyatt. God didn't fail me. I'm safe. I'm His." A smile tugged at her lips. "I'm yours. I think we can call today a win for the Daybreakers."

Without a word he rested his head on her shoulder, so she leaned her head on his. A couple of times he reached to wipe his eyes.

His words were soft. "I love you, Paige."

"I love you, Wyatt." That was the strangest sensation, to now love a man she had considered a stranger less than a week ago.

They were both quiet for a few seconds. Finally Wyatt said, "This has to be a record. Here you are in love and engaged in six days."

Paige nodded and smiled and placed a soft kiss on his head. "And I even did the proposing."

He looked up at her and grinned. "I beat you to that by three days."

"Was that just three days ago?" She blinked and blinked again, hardly believing so much had transpired in so few days.

"Feels like weeks now, huh?"

"It does." She hesitated as she remembered that first day when Wyatt had held up two fingers as a countdown. A lifetime was lived each day since then. "I meant what I said before. I needed today. I've needed every one of these days to get me where I'm supposed to be, to make me who I'm supposed to be. I don't have months or years to get on board with my call. There's a countdown. I have a job to do."

"I'm here to help you do that."

"You were right before: We are stronger together. But I needed to become stronger in Him first."

Paige tried to rest her eyes but found it only brought images she would rather not face. Now, she sat upright in her seat and reached for the bag next to her feet. She looked down at her splint and wondered how she would get undressed and redressed with her lame hand. Even using the good fingers on her bad hand sent excruciating pain radiating up her arm.

"I'll help you," Wyatt said. "I'll only open my eyes when I need to."

She nodded and handed him the bag. "I have a clean t-shirt, and I can wear my jeans from yesterday."

The process was slow going with a lame woman and blinded man. They laughed often as Paige guided him. "Turn the shirt around," she said.

She was glad Wyatt couldn't see what she was seeing. Blood dribbles and splatters were on her chest and legs, and her bruised hip was now deep purple. The sight of her would only intensify his sense of guilt.

Finally, dressed and seated again, she waited while Wyatt took her t-shirt dress and sport coat to the back of the plane. When he rejoined her, he said, "Are you going to tell me about today? You need to debrief. It's an offloading of what you've been through."

She drew in a sharp breath and held it for a few seconds, then said, "There were these horrible men who took me. That's who killed Mac."

Wyatt looked away. "I'm sorry I trusted her."

"I did too," Paige said. "We had every reason to trust her. She hadn't planned this before this morning. It wasn't until they took her sister that the setup began."

"Still..." He leaned forward and propped his elbows on his knees. "If I would've done this your way, none of this would've happened."

"What, you mean me getting in touch with Bryce?"

He only nodded.

Paige leaned up, too, and placed her hand on his back. "The possibility only crossed my mind. I don't know that it would have worked out any better."

"I do. What happened today wouldn't have if I hadn't been jealous."

"So that's why you're blaming yourself?"

"I didn't even discuss the possibility with you. I should have." He rubbed his face and nodded. His words were quiet when he finally spoke. "Did they hurt you besides what I see?"

"Look at me," she said as she pulled his hand away from his face. "What you see, that's all that happened. If not for Moses, I have no doubt it would have gone there."

"Did he work with them?"

"No, I think he was just brought in to find my dad. I'm not really sure."

"Why did he help you?"

She hesitated, then said, "All I can say is that God turned him on those men. He killed them." She closed her eyes. "I saw them dead."

When she remained quiet, he pulled her to him. "You don't have to tell me any more, not until you're ready."

"I'm not ready."

He whispered near her ear, "I thought I lost you today."

She whispered back, "I'm immortal until my work here is done. And stronger."

Weaker

Day 6, 9:35 p.m.

Paige stood behind Wyatt and peered out the open doorway of the plane in time to see Waylon's green truck barreling toward them at rapid speed. Another truck was right behind his; both came to a screeching halt side by side. Two men jumped out of the truck with Waylon, then four exited the other truck.

With evident hesitation Wyatt moved down the steps in front of her with his gun drawn, holding her behind him with his free hand as the group of men approached and escorted them to Waylon's truck.

Once they were near the truck, Waylon reached for Paige's shoulders. "Look what they've done to that pretty face." He pulled her to him. "I've got you, sweetheart. I'll watch over you now."

His tender words brought tears to her eyes. With her dad gone, Waylon was now as close as she would have again. "I think I'm better than I look."

Waylon stepped back and looked at Wyatt. "I'm not letting you go in without support."

"Thank you, Dad."

"Don't thank me, son. Just put a stop to the men who would do this to our girl."

"Yes, sir, I will."

Wyatt opened the passenger door for Paige. "Here," he said as he leaned the seat back, "you can rest on the way to my dad's. I know you're spent."

She didn't argue. Paige fell back onto the seat and rested her cheek on a rolled-up towel. Wyatt draped his dad's windbreaker over her. "I'll be back tomorrow." Even as she opened her mouth to speak, he said, "You know I'll be back. I will always come back for you."

"I know you will. And I know the God who sends you into the darkness will bring you back into the light."

His kiss was gentle, lips pressed more on her cheek than her busted lip. "I'll be back for that kiss you still owe me."

Once Wyatt shut her door, Paige overheard voices outside the truck, decisions being made as far as how many men would go with them as an escort back to Waylon's and how many with Wyatt.

Waylon climbed in and started the engine. "We'll stop off and get that hand looked at. You can't waste time setting a bone properly."

After that he drove in silence, and soon Paige drifted off.

The exam room was so cold that Paige wasn't sure if she shivered more from the temperature or the pain of her now professionally set fingers. She had never been to a vet for x-rays and medical care before, but now she could say she had.

Currently, she sat on the exam table watching Dr. Liz give Waylon instructions for the patient as if she wasn't there. She smiled as it became clear that the two were either involved or wanted to be. Neither had spoken to her much since they had arrived for her after-hours visit.

When Dr. Liz was talked out, Waylon led Paige back through the waiting area where two heavily armed men followed them out to the truck and then got into the escort vehicle. This time, Paige raised the back of the seat for the drive to Waylon's place.

"Dr. Liz was really nice."

"She's a good lady," he said without taking his eyes off the road. "I met her last year when I had a sick dog."

Waylon drove the next few minutes without speaking. Paige's mind was with Wyatt and the team. The look on his face when he had said he was going after Groves had been unsettling. In truth, Paige didn't want to imagine what would become of the man who had harmed the woman that soldier loved.

She glanced in the rearview mirror wishing those men had gone with Wyatt. There was no telling how many men Groves had to stand against the team. With eyes now closed she whispered, "You have him. I know You have him. You are his strength and his shield."

Finally, Waylon said, "Wyatt told me about your dad. I'm so sorry, hun."

"I'm not sure it's even sunk in yet. After a day like today, that all seems like weeks ago instead of just this morning."

"He called me after you were taken." Waylon shook his head and made a tsking noise. "I could tell he was trying to stay calm, to keep his head about him, but I heard the fear in his voice. I was bringing reinforcements to come find you."

"Is that why those men were with you?"

"Yes, I thought we were meeting that plane to go to Baltimore. Wyatt only called me just before you landed." He gripped the steering wheel tighter. "I want to be with him."

"I wish you were with him too." Her eyes filled with tears. "He'll need all the help he can get."

"The men with him are some of the best soldiers you'll find. There's a community of us here in Greensboro. They didn't hesitate to volunteer to go with him." He reached over and touched Paige's forearm. "And I guess you know that boy would've never left you with anyone he doesn't know. So I'm your guy." With a slight pause, he glanced at her and said, "He's in love with you."

"When he told you we were only friends the other day, we had just agreed to that. He said I was in too vulnerable of a place for anything else."

"And now?"

She smiled and her heart grew warmer. "Two friends just got engaged."

"Smart boy."

"Maybe it was a smart girl who did the asking," she said.

"I don't dislike you at all, Paige."

"I don't dislike you either, Waylon."

A moment passed when she said, "Your son loves you."

"I love my son." He let out a soft sigh. "Nothing better than having him back."

"He's so filled with regret."

"No time for regrets now. We just start where we are."

"I hope you've told him that?"

"I will."

The remainder of the drive was mostly quiet, especially as Waylon navigated along the explosive-laden drive. The escort had stopped at the gate and sat with headlights shining on the path. Once out of sight of them, the pitch-dark woods weren't to be crossed without Waylon's full attention.

When they pulled in front of the house, it was just after eleven. Paige said, "I sure could go for a bowl of oatmeal. I've only had a bite or two to eat since this morning."

"I'll get you fixed right up on that."

He did. They ate together with Paige finishing the entire bowl and scraping the sides.

"I'll make you more if you'd like."

"No, I just need to wash up a little and get some sleep."

"I understand."

Paige followed Waylon to the bathroom where he wrapped her hand with a plastic bag, got her a towel and washcloth out, then brought her a t-shirt and athletic shorts. When he left her there, she inspected her face in the mirror. On the plane she had hardly allowed herself to look. Even at the vet's office, she hadn't looked closely with her hand in so much pain.

Now, she leaned in and inspected her black eye and swollen cheek and lip. When Curtis's face surfaced in her mind, the sight of him biting his own lip as he drew his arm back, she blinked and blinked again trying to chase away his memory. She swallowed hard, drew in a deep breath, and made a quick turn away from the mirror.

A shower wasn't easy one handed, but the warm water was soothing. She scrubbed the blood off her legs and chest, images coming again of Curtis. This time she saw his dead body with blood pooling around his head. Her stomach lurched, and she had to reach for the shower wall to steady herself.

Stronger spiritually may have been the outcome of her day, but emotionally she was weaker. She knew it. No matter how she had tried to convince Wyatt, she knew she wasn't okay just yet.

When she stepped from the bathroom, she found Waylon turning down his bed in the next room.

"I've got you all set up here," he said. "I'm going to do some reading and praying since I'm all keyed up."

"I'll sleep on the couch while you read if you don't mind."

"No way. You'll sleep better..." When he turned to look at her, his expression fell.

Even her voice sounded weaker. "Is it okay if we stay in the same room together?"

Waylon grabbed the pillow and blanket and came to stand before her. "Of course it is. I'll kick that recliner back when I do get tired and stay right there with you."

Paige swallowed hard. "I see them. Sometimes when I blink, they just appear."

He draped an arm around her shoulder. "I imagine you will for a while."

"It'll fade, right?" she said.

"It will. You just need some good to take its place."

"When Wyatt comes back, that'll be all the good I need."

Debrief

Day 7, 8:09 a.m.

The sun was shining overhead as Paige sat with her Bible in hand and her unused fishing pole next to her, prepared to debrief with the Lord. Wyatt had called it an offloading of what she had been through. It was vital that she offload onto the Lord so as not to weigh Wyatt down with undue guilt. Her weaker would only become stronger when her experience was filtered through the heart of the Father. That was her exact intention, to offload her troubling memories onto the Lord as she sat with legs swinging back and forth on Waylon's wooden bridge.

She smiled at what had been Waylon's reluctance to let her sit alone with her thoughts. No question about it, she had a new dad in her life, one she had come to love already. Something about waking together that morning and sharing another bowl of oatmeal seemed to seal the deal for them both. His parting words when he had deposited her on the bridge had been, "I'll give you a little time, then I'll be back to teach my new kid how to fish. Love does that."

The loss she had suffered just the morning before would be a never-ending heartbreak. She knew that from the experience of having lost her mother. Yet here she was with new love growing for the father of the man she also newly loved. The Lord gives and the Lord takes away, were the words that surfaced to remind her that she may never understand His ways even when she trusted His heart. After the day before, how could she not trust Him?

With Bible propped on her left wrist, Paige turned with her good hand to the passage that had come to mind the day before from 2 Chronicles 20. She scanned the familiar verses, how Jehoshaphat had turned his eyes to the Lord when he hadn't known what to do.

Paige closed her eyes, able to hear Wyatt's words whispered to her wounded soul that day on the roadside, to keep her eyes fixed on Jesus. She had been doing that again these past days, a fact that had helped her with the words she had spoken to Moses the day before.

Even without trying, the memory of those early moments with Moses surfaced in her mind, how the words she had spoken had come without any thought of her own. From the very second she had looked into his eyes and encountered such unmistakable pain, it was like something else–Someone else–had taken over. Her spirit had known exactly what he needed to hear.

It hadn't been like that with the other men. Their memory caused her to shudder and to intentionally offload onto her Lord the fear they evoked within her. Evil was so evident in their presence that speaking to their hearts had never occurred to her. But with Moses it was entirely different. The Word had literally flowed through her like living water.

Her first day at Overwatch came to mind, how the verse from John had resonated then. It began with, "If anyone is thirsty..." While he didn't know it, what Moses thirsted for was Jesus. That was why the Word, the Living Water, had so easily poured from her lips. It had come in response to Moses' greatest need.

Still, she could hardly make sense of what had happened next, how Moses had bolted from the room. Even his later explanation of how the song had been played at his family's funeral was a stunning revelation. Those lyrics had just come tumbling from her lips, the ones she had sung for both her mother, and her father that very morning.

Paige glanced down at her open Bible at Jehoshaphat's story, then back up and across the pond. She blinked and did a bit of a double take when she looked again at the one word that had caught her eye: singing.

"When they began singing and praising, the Lord set ambushes against the sons of Ammon, Moab and Mount Seir, who had come against Judah; so they were routed."

Those two words kept resounding in her head: singing and praising. Mostly, she noticed how the people's singing and praising came first, before His miraculous deliverance. The text suggested that God had been moved by their worship, prompting Him to set ambushes against their enemies.

Her own pitiful, barely audible song the day before, expressed out of utter desperation and sung in response to His internal whisper, had moved the heart of God. Just as He had done for the Israelites, for Paige, God set Moses as an ambush against the men who would have done unspeakable things to her if given the opportunity.

God had intervened in two lives in that moment: saving her life and offering new life to Moses. Jesus was not only her strength and her shield, but He also proved Himself to be her strength and her song.

Awestruck in a way she had never known, Paige could only burst into tears at the mighty hand and tender heart of God. More than just the realization of God showing up on her behalf, the weight of the past days came flooding over her. All she had given up and gained now mingled into an onslaught of emotion that brought tears filled with grief and glory, thanks and praise.

Only seconds passed when a concerned Waylon approached and moved to sit next to her. Clearly he hadn't gone far from the pond for him to arrive so quickly. His expression was kind when he reached for her hand. "I'm here if you need to talk."

"I'm not upset," Paige said. "I'm just so..." She sat looking at him. "God did something so phenomenal yesterday that I can hardly wrap my mind around it."

Misty eyed, Waylon said, "He's done something pretty phenomenal in my life this week too. If I were the type, I might just have a good cry with you."

Waylon had received his son back after all those years, and Wyatt had his dad again. Both realizations made her cry even harder.

A moment passed, and Paige finally pulled herself together. She sniffled and wiped her nose. "Please don't tell Wyatt you found me like this."

Waylon's words were soft. "It's okay to cry."

A smile came. "Your son has said those exact words to me before. I know him, though, that he's carrying the weight of what happened to me."

"It's understandable," he said, "after what you went through yesterday." Waylon reached out and rested his hand on Paige's back. "You were his responsibility. I know he feels he's failed you."

"That's exactly what he feels."

"Then you have to allow him to feel what he feels. Let him work through it. A soldier with an assignment who sees a face like yours is bound to feel the burden of your capture."

"You're right," she said. "I know how much he loves me. I know watching over me has been his mission. Even when I gave him no opportunity to help, he regrets allowing me to walk away from that table without him." With eyes closed tight for a second, she said, "I'm so thankful he allowed me to go. If not, they would've killed him.

"It's not just yesterday that's weighing on me," she said. "In the past six days..." She hesitated until a phrase came to mind, one that had dropped into her spirit that first day at Overwatch. "Training ground," she said. "That's where I've been these past days. I've learned this world isn't at all what I thought it was, that the darkness is rising, and the light is running out of time.

"I now know that I have a place where I belong with people who've been waiting for me to join them. I've lost my home and father, but even in light of that fact, I know I'm not homeless or orphaned.

"I've found love and family and *my* God." She grew quiet a moment. "Like Jacob, God is no longer the God of my father; He's my God.

"He's raising me up." Her next words were quiet. "What was an uncomfortable thought just six days ago now has me so stirred up inside that I'm ablaze with longing. The Lord has something for me to do, some way of reaching people to share what's coming. The words keep echoing in my mind." She paused and said, "Actually, they started when I was here before: I have to warn the lost and wake the found.

"It all feels so overwhelming, though, that I don't know where to begin. Words and thoughts are all jumbled in my head."

Waylon scratched his chin and gave a little shake of his head. "I've been on a different journey, but the place I've landed is the same as you. I feel that fire burning. I keep asking what I can do, how I can make people see what I see. And like you," he shrugged, "I get so overwhelmed that I kind of do nothing. I know what it feels like to tell the truth and have people look at you like you've lost your mind. I know what it feels like to wonder if maybe I did lose my mind."

"Maybe," Paige said with a smile, "we can figure it out together. I just know that I'm done sleeping." Her heart stung at the thought. "Don't you know how it hurt Jesus when He kept finding his disciples sleeping rather than praying? How about you promise to keep me awake, and I promise to keep you awake?"

"It's a deal." His eyes smiled even before his lips did. "For now, how about we get to some fishing?"

With her debrief behind her, Paige felt strong again, free to spend her morning praying for Wyatt and casting a line with his dad. "How about I show you how it's done this time?"

Good Father

Day 7, 9:33 a.m.

Rest, that was the word that came as Paige cast again. For six days she had toiled; now, today, was a time of rest.

Her fishing couldn't have gone any better. Paige had caught three so far and Waylon none. With each fish Waylon had placed in the ice chest, Paige had gloated just a little bit more.

"And here I was hoping your kids would have to come here to learn how to fish from their granddad," Waylon said.

Her own smile faded and her stomach sank. "We won't have kids."

Waylon stopped mid cast and turned to look at her. "You can't or won't?"

"Won't," she said.

"Why in the world not?"

"We don't want to bring a child into a world like this."

He looked at her as if he already knew the answer to his next question. "Do you both feel that way?"

She sat for a second pondering that question. "I've barely had time to think it through since I didn't even know I would be loving that son of yours."

"So it's Wyatt who feels this way?"

"He's been seeing the impending darkness for a lot longer than I have. Yeah, it's what he's felt for several years now."

"You can't allow fear to stop you from living. That's what you'd be doing. The devil wins then. If you want a kid, have a kid. It'll be a small part of each of you shining a little more light into this dark world." He paused. "You think it over. Maybe I'm just being selfish. There's nothing I'd like more than to teach my grandson to fish."

"You think I would let you bring my son to a booby-trapped land?"

Waylon shrugged. "Well, yeah."

She smiled. "I sure would. There's no safer place than here." After a second's pause and new light dawning on her, she said, "It's not lost on me how Wyatt tucked me safely away here at his father's house before all hell broke loose."

He seemed to study her words. "You see it as a picture of the rapture?"

"I do. I've struggled these past days believing in that. I don't struggle anymore."

"I don't struggle with that either. It took me some time to wrap my mind around it and the timing of it all, but now I find it easier to believe than that God would leave His kids on earth when He intends to punish those who aren't His. I sure wouldn't do that to Wyatt. No good father would."

"Thank you for that," Paige said. "Wyatt keeps giving me reassurance from the groom's perspective. It's nice to have a father's take on it too. My dad wouldn't either. He proved that by sending Wyatt."

His words seemed to be less directed at her and more to himself. "Wyatt would be a good dad."

Waylon grew quiet, and after a long moment Paige said, "It makes me sad too."

"I was just thinking of when he was a kid. That boy would get himself in the darndest situations." He smiled a faraway smile. "He was the absolute light of my life. I guess that's why I was so affected last year when a friend started telling me how many kids go missing, how many fall victim to child trafficking."

"I can't think of anything more horrific," she said. "I'm proud that my dad did what he did to save a girl from harm. He would argue that his life was well spent in her rescue."

"I'm guessing that's how many Christians get drawn into the movement."

"Movement?"

"Q," Waylon said. "When you were talking about staying awake, I thought that was what you meant."

"What is Q? Wyatt said something about it but never told me what it meant."

"They're a group of people, millions of people, who connect online and watch current events. It's actually called QAnon. There are information leaks called drops, supposedly from government officials, updates on what's going on behind the scenes geopolitically. It's way more than politics. It's said to be a good versus evil movement.

"Many believers are involved in it since Q often focuses on efforts to protect children from trafficking." He stopped and shook his head. "It's some graphic stuff they share.

"Scriptures are used in the forums, so for some it's a faith-based movement. That was a draw for me. I read some stuff early on and connected with true believers who wanted to do good, but then I encountered many people who were more like darkness trying to veil themselves as light. It got hard to tell who was who."

He held out one hand. "I'm not saying all the people involved are bad. My buddy said he knows of some who have actually gotten saved in the community.

"But what gave me reason for pause was that they kept predicting, promising even, that things would happen, and bad guys would come to justice. Then nothing ever happened. All the misinformation didn't sit right with me, so I went back to looking at the world through the lens of Scripture.

"Some of the Q followers believe a utopian society will form out of this good guys versus bad guys plot they're developing. That's not what I read in the Word. My Bible says only bad and worse are on the way until the very end when Jesus reigns on earth. There's no other way to read the book of Revelation without seeing that."

Paige said, "I've never heard anything about them before this week."

"Now that I have stepped back and looked at it more objectively, I see that some of what happens in the Q movement may be used by the enemy as a form of deception. If believers are convinced that good is coming to save the day, then it keeps people sitting on the sidelines. Sure, they may be telling of the darkness that's happening, calling people to wake up, but they aren't warning of what's really coming: the rapture and tribulation. They are expecting the best outcome to happen here on earth and often through political or military figures."

"I'm with you," she said. "I don't see good coming, and I sure don't see a utopian society on the horizon except what the World Economic Forum says will come when 'we will own nothing and be happy.'" She hesitated, a little shiver running along her spine at how sinister their secret motives truly were. "Kind of odd that both groups are saying the same thing, huh, that utopia is coming?"

Waylon let out a soft sigh. "Now you've just given me a whole bunch more to ponder."

"It seems to me," Paige said with a heavy heart, "that they all stay one step ahead of us. No matter where we turn, we just can't figure out their next move."

"That's not true at all." Waylon seemed to think for a second, then said, "We're already a step ahead of them just in knowing the truth. They're not fooling us. We have a good Father who tells us in writing what they'll do even before they do it."

"That's one of the wisest things I've heard all week," she said. "The truth does keep us a step ahead."

Waylon grinned and sat staring at Paige. "Want to know a little secret?" When she nodded, he said, "I've got this little sensor in my pocket that says that man we love is about to walk through the clearing."

Unshakable

Day 7, 10:10 a.m.

Paige scrambled to her feet, not an easy task with only one hand. Just as she had done when Wyatt returned from Arlington, she broke into a run and reached the edge of the clearing just as he stepped around a cluster of trees. And just as before, they collided and clung to one another in a tight embrace.

"Tell me it's over," she said.

"It is over."

She took a step back, only then noticing the blood on his leg where a bullet had left a hole in his pants.

Even before she could ask, he said, "I promise it's okay. I've had it looked at and bandaged."

Paige closed her eyes and rested her head on his chest. "Is everyone else okay?"

"Yes." He gave her a little squeeze and stood for a while without speaking. Finally, he said, "This is what I fought for, to be back here with you." When he moved her back to look at her, he reached out to touch her cheek. "How are you feeling? I've thought of little else but this battered face. And I know you're grieving over your dad. I should've been here for you."

"You were exactly where my dad would've sent you. I really am doing okay." She turned to look behind her at an approaching Waylon and took a step back. "I've had some good company."

"Son," Waylon said when he drew near. He never stopped until he reached Wyatt and wrapped his arms around him. "Your dad's glad to have you back."

Wyatt stood motionless, looking over his dad's shoulder at Paige, his eyes conveying emotion she had yet to witness with regard to his father. Finally, he wrapped his arms around his dad, and they stood in that embrace for a few seconds.

When Waylon stepped back, he said, "I've kept an eye on your girl."

"I appreciate that. I knew you would."

"Did you keep your mind on the mission?"

"As best I could, yes, sir."

"That's not the answer that keeps a soldier alive." Waylon nodded at Paige. "You can always trust me with this girl." After that he left them without saying any more.

"Let's sit a while," Wyatt said and took Paige's hand to lead her back to the bridge. When she moved to his left, he said, "Sit on the other side. I want to hold your hand."

She stood looking at him, wondering if he had his sides mixed up until she realized he meant he wanted to hold her injured hand. When they were both seated, he lifted it and placed it on his open palm. "I've been wondering about this hand much of the night."

"You heard your dad. You can't have your mind on me when you're in the field. Not ever."

"I couldn't do much else but wonder how you were. I kept seeing your face when I blinked."

"This will all heal. No real harm done."

His words were quiet. "It could've gone so much worse."

"Because of Moses, it didn't. Let's just be thankful for that."

"I'm more thankful for Moses than you could possibly know." He hesitated a second, then said, "Moses was there last night. He took out the head of security, his old buddy who brought him in to find your dad. Then he went after Groves."

"Did he kill him?"

"He did, after getting Tia's last name."

"He's going to look for her?"

Wyatt nodded. "He said he won't rest until he knows she's safe. And he wanted me to tell you his girls would be proud of a man who would fight for that girl, too."

Tears welled up in Paige's eyes. Even now, she could see the look in his dark eyes, the unexpected compassion when he had stepped into the room where she had been bound.

"He said to tell you something else: He made that call."

Tears streamed down her cheeks now as Paige nodded and wiped her face.

"I'm guessing he means the Romans 10:9 call?"

"Yeah," she said in a soft whisper.

"You did a good job, Daybreaker. I couldn't even sleep on the plane. I just kept thinking what a soldier you were yesterday. A man converted and a new brother now on the team. I'm sorry I ever doubted you." He lifted her fingers to his lips. "And here you came out with only a black eye and a couple of broken fingers." He grimaced. "And that busted lip of yours."

"This busted lip doesn't hurt like you would think if you have any ideas."

Wyatt leaned over and kissed her. Like the night before, it was soft and more cautious than necessary.

Paige sat back and looked at him. "Someday, I'm expecting that real kiss I've been promised."

"You'll get that kiss soon." He moved in and lightly brushed his lips along her cheek. Close still, he said, "I'm sorry I doubted your decision in the café. I would've done the same as you if your life had been on the line. I won't doubt you again."

"I never doubted my decision. I was terrified, but I knew I had done what I had to do. I knew you would come for me. Mac did too." She hesitated, the memory of Mac slumping over into her seat flashing like lightning through her mind. Then Curtis's face appeared as he had begun stripping her of her clothes in the van.

"I wasn't afraid of dying," her words were soft, "not of going to be with Jesus. That's the first time I've ever been able to say that. That's such progress for me." She blinked long. "I was more afraid of leaving you, of what it would do to you."

With a slight nod, Wyatt said, "I kept thinking the same thing about you last night, how much I wanted to come back to you."

"Your mind really wasn't on the mission, then?"

He shook his head. "Barricade took a round because of me." Before she could speak, he said, "He's okay. But he shouldn't have had to step in the way he did. It was more than me thinking of you. I was acting out of emotion. I kept thinking of what Groves had done to you and to your dad. My mind—or my heart rather—wasn't in the right place. I'm called to serve justice. But there, in that man's presence, my heart was set on vengeance."

Paige whispered, "Vengeance is mine, says the Lord."

"That's right. Barricade was wounded because I was after revenge. I had my eyes on Groves and didn't see a man approaching." For a moment he fell silent. Finally, he said, "I was more of a liability than an asset last night. Until I get my mind and these feelings sorted out, I'll stay at Overwatch."

"I can't say that I'm upset about that." She rested her head on his shoulder. "You'll be home with me."

"So," he lifted her chin to look at him. "Emotions were running pretty high last night."

The way he had pulled her onto his lap on the floorboard had stayed with Paige much of the night. All the while, as Dr. Liz had examined and reset her fingers, that was the memory she had clung to in an effort to escape the pain.

"They were running high."

Wyatt said, "Did you maybe ask something last night that you regret this morning?"

She broke into a smile. "Not one thing. I would marry you standing right here on this bridge if your dad was a preacher." With her eyes fixed on his, she said, "Did you maybe say yes to anything last night that you regret this morning?"

"Not one thing." He lifted her hand and kissed her palm. "I can't put a ring on this swollen finger for a while."

"We'll wait, then, if that matters to you."

Wyatt chuckled. "No way. We're doing this before you change your mind."

"I'm a whole week into this thing. I'm invested now."

His eyes grew wider. "It's mind-boggling that it's only been a week. One week ago, the night you came, the reason I was up all night was that I was getting your room ready for you. It all happened so unexpectedly. I washed your sheets and cleaned your room. The one thing I had wanted for months, to know you in person, was happening. It was surreal. I literally didn't sleep a wink.

"Paige," his eyes grew heavy with sadness, "your dad had wanted you there all along too. He knew you would rise to the challenge. If the Lord will let him have a little peek down here at you, he sure would be proud of his Daybreaker."

Her heart was flooded with warmth at that thought. "My dad's Joshua verse and the verse about God being my strength and my shield followed me along that awful journey yesterday. The Word carried me through."

For a few seconds she considered all that had happened to bring her to where she was this day, this brand-new woman who would go on to live a brand-new life.

"Unshakable, that's what I'm becoming," she said. "I'm not there yet, but I've figured out what it takes. You said something my first day at Overwatch, that I have to stand on solid ground as the world begins to shift beneath my feet, or I'll live constantly shaken."

He smiled and nodded his remembrance.

"There's a passage at the end of Hebrews twelve. I scanned it this morning while your dad made our oatmeal. It talks about us receiving a kingdom which cannot be shaken. What most caught my attention was that it was in the same chapter that tells us to fix our eyes on Jesus.

"Early this morning I was thinking about the day we were on the way to Aunt Bertie's, how on the roadside you whispered in my ear to fix my eyes on Jesus. That's what's changed in me since I've been with you, what's helping me to become unshakable. You said you would, and you did help me get my vision back. My eyes are fixed on Him. I can't thank you enough for that."

"We'll do that in the time we have together," he said, "remind each other to keep our eyes on Him more than anything here, even the ones we love." He raised his eyebrows and gave a sheepish look. "I could see me focusing on my bride more than Him if I'm not watchful."

"You're a faithful watcher," she said. "You'll keep us straight."

Wyatt said, "How about we spend a few days here? There's no threat, but I sure wouldn't mind some time alone with you here off the grid with no noise."

"Sounds like a plan to me." A moment passed when she said, "When I can, I've got to call Aunt Bertie and let her know about my dad."

"I've talked to her already. Echo got her number, and I got in touch with her."

"How did she take it?"

"Like the strong woman you know."

"I'll call when we get back to Savannah."

Paige sighed and looked out over the still water. The only sounds were the buzzing of insects and the occasional chirping of a bird. "I'm not sure what it is, but I sure like sitting on this bridge. We can stay here as long as you'd like and just love each other."

Wyatt planted a soft kiss on her head. "I'm not sure there's anything else in the world I'd rather do."

Bridge

Day 7, 11:30 a.m.

When they returned to the house, Wyatt dropped her fish off with his dad while Paige went inside to wash up. Even before she left the bathroom, Wyatt came to stand in the doorway.

"You look exhausted," she said. "You haven't slept since the hotel, have you?"

"No." His lips curved into a slow smile. "I'm hoping you need a little sleep too."

"I can always sleep."

"Let's take a nap, then we'll fry up the fish when we wake."

Wyatt led Paige into his dad's bedroom, then went to the closet and dug out a sleeping bag.

"I can take the couch," she said. "You take the bed; you need decent sleep."

"You'll climb into that bed," Wyatt said, "and I'll sleep just fine right here on the floor." He unrolled the sleeping bag and reached for a pillow from the bed.

Paige knew the drill, that she wouldn't likely talk him out of it, so she climbed into bed.

Wyatt sat on the bedside and kissed her cheek. "I'm right here if you need me."

"I'm right here if you need me too," she said back.

His eyes seemed suddenly sad. "My dad said you had several nightmares last night."

She only nodded.

"It's normal. Your mind is trying to sort out all you've been through. I want you to be able to talk to me about it. Don't try and shield me because you think I'll feel guilty. I'm here for you."

The word shield stung her heart. He was right. She had intended to do just that, to hold back and not share. If anyone could be trusted with how she was feeling, it was him. And like his dad had said, Wyatt had a right to feel what he felt. They would work through it together. It wasn't her place to shield him. The Lord would be his strength and his shield.

"I see them and hear them," she said. "I think that's what kept waking me up in the night."

"When you wake like that, with their faces or voices in your head, whisper a verse into your heart. We'll find you one this afternoon."

Paige sat up and wrapped her arms around his neck. "They were the most evil men I've ever seen."

Wyatt held her a little tighter. "I've never felt the presence of evil the way I did at Groves' place." He held her back to look at her. "What that man did to those girls was beyond perversion. It was satanic, I believe. Carlos was the first to say it, but I sensed it too."

"He'll never hurt anyone else again," she said.

"That's right. What he did can't be swept under the rug either. Echo tapped into his security cams and loaded video from the flash drive. When the police arrive, they will see it all. And he sent videos to news outlets and to the justice department. It's everywhere now. So the people on Groves' payroll will see and know the twisted man they've enabled.

"Now," he said, "with one less man of darkness in this world, we can sleep in peace." A smile came. "That's your verse when you need to chase away bad images at bedtime. It's from the end of Psalm 4. We will look it up later, but it says something like, I will sleep in perfect peace because the Lord makes me dwell in safety."

"I like that."

He kissed the tip of her nose and stood. "Use it. If you need anything, the weird guy who loves you will be just down here." He dropped onto his sleeping bag.

"You really can sleep in this bed with me. I trust you."

"No way I'm climbing into that bed. In case your dad does get a peek, that would be a throw-a-chair-out-the-window-of-heaven offense."

Paige grinned at the thought and scooted over close to the edge of the bed and laid there looking at Wyatt's muscular arms propped behind his head. He blinked long, struggled to open his eyes, then blinked so long they didn't open again. For as long as she was able, she watched him, the sound of his breathing now truly familiar from their nights spent sleeping in the same room, instead of just remembered from her dream of him.

She glanced down at her hand, wishing she were seeing a gold band rather than splinted fingers, and thought of Moses. Because of him, the men whose images continually came to mind and sometimes whispered the nasty things they would do to her, would never hurt anyone else again. Even the one with compassion in his eyes died for his refusal to intervene.

They were lost. But no matter how wicked they were, Paige would never rejoice over their eternal destination. Soon, many like them would face a world that would likely make them darker and angrier and more violent.

Then there were those like Moses, who, even unknowingly, thirsted for streams of Living Water. Those were the people Paige longed to reach.

She blinked, then gave up the struggle to open her eyes again.

"Are you going to sleep all day?" Wyatt said.

Paige rolled over and found him standing in the doorway. "Prolly, if you'll let me."

He grinned. "I'm as hungry now as I was sleepy then."

"How long did we sleep?"

"Me, two hours. You, nearly three."

Paige sat up, sore now in her back from where Curtis had kicked her. "I'm ready when you are."

"It's ready now. Dad has a mess of fish in there waiting for us."

Paige found she had to drag herself out of bed. After a night of interrupted sleep and praying for Wyatt during her waking moments, she was spent.

She followed Wyatt to the kitchen expecting to find Waylon there. "Where's your dad?"

"He took off a few minutes ago. He has some work to do." Wyatt smiled. "I'm not complaining. I like being in this isolated place with my girl."

"Your girl likes it too." She sat a few seconds looking at him then stifled a yawn. "I find myself hiding things from you, to shield you."

His eyes were trained on hers as he sat across from her. "Don't do that."

"I'm not anymore." With a shake of her head, she said, "Truth is, I'm worn out. I hurt. I need to sleep." She hesitated. "This Daybreaker thing has me baffled. I know I'm supposed to be one." She stopped and blinked. "I am one, but that's only in name for now. I need to become one in word and deed. This time will be good for me. I need to sit on that bridge and read and talk to Jesus about it."

"That's exactly what we'll do, then," he said, "give you time to rest and talk to Him. If you want my opinion, though, these past days have already proven you to be a Daybreaker in word and deed." Wyatt smiled and reached for her hand. "After we eat, we can rest more or sit on that bridge."

"I think I'd like to sit."

Paige ate as best she could with a busted lip, tucking little bites in so as not to open her mouth too far. She slowed soon. The more she ate the sleepier she grew. It wasn't sleep she needed now.

When they were finished, Wyatt said, "This mess will be here when we get back. Let's head on out while it's still daylight."

Paige stood, followed Wyatt from the kitchen, and reached for her Bible on the way out the door.

They walked hand in hand along the worn path around the side of the house and through the adjacent field.

"Marry me soon," Wyatt said.

"That's an easy yes."

"Good." Still in motion, he leaned down and kissed her head. "For as long as we have here, I want to be married to you."

"I want the same thing."

They walked a minute more when Wyatt said, "I promise this will be the last time I wonder. Are you sure it's not all the emotions of these past days that have led you to feel this way? You've lost a lot. It would be easy to cling to what feels safe."

"It's totally all the emotions of these past days that make me feel this way. I've gained more than I've lost. That sounds crazy considering how much I loved my dad, but it's true. This, what I feel, is real emotion, real love, a real desire to marry you. Because you burst into my life, I'm close again with Jesus. I know truth." She chuckled. "And for the record, from what I've seen so far, you are the least safe man on the planet."

"You are safe with me. I'll protect you better from now on."

"I do know that."

He gave her hand a squeeze. "That's it then; I'm holding you to this engagement."

"I think I'll hyphenate."

"I'd be disappointed if you didn't carry on his name. He's an awfully great man–is, not was."

"I couldn't agree more."

When they stepped onto the bridge, Paige went ahead of Wyatt until she reached the middle. "Right or left of me?"

"Good hand to hold," he said and stepped around to her right side. "I may doze a few minutes while you read." Once seated, he laid back and closed his eyes and kept his hand resting on her arm.

For nearly an hour she read, flipping around in Scripture, looking at verses that only intensified the stirring she already felt within.

Wyatt sat up behind her and rested his chin on her shoulder. "Whatcha reading?"

"The passage that most reminds me of you, the 'fix your eyes on Jesus' verse. I was just noticing something. I'm to remember He is the author and perfecter of my faith. He has written me into this final chapter of the Church Age for a reason. All I've experienced has given me insight to help people. I can use what was once my own doubt to get into the heads of others, to craft a message that'll stem from empathy."

"That makes a lot of sense," he said. "This past week has changed me too. I've learned about empathizing with others. I needed to know what fear felt like before I could do that. For me, it's not fear of death–never has been–but I sure fear losing you to death. I see it now, that it's not just their lives they're worried about when it comes to the virus. They fear for the ones they love. It alters my perspective entirely and gives me great compassion."

His eyes flashed with irritation. "That may make me even angrier at what a lie it is, how they've terrorized people with false numbers and allowed people to die without treatment. I can't imagine how helpless so many husbands and wives have felt." He hesitated. "Like your dad."

"Her death really did change him," she said.

"It would me too, Paige. I was faced with that possibility for only a handful of hours yesterday. It did something to me."

"I'm here and safe. I have a brand-new life ahead of me." She patted the weather-worn wood. "I see something, maybe why I'm so fascinated with this bridge. This week has been a bridge to my new life, a bridge to my calling." She shook her head. "It's like I'm driving along on a foggy morning. Up ahead, I see my call emerging, but it's still surrounded by the mist. I have no clue what it will look like, but I'm saying yes even before it comes into view.

"I told your dad this morning that I feel ablaze with longing to reach people, to warn them. When I say ablaze, I don't think it's passion I'm feeling. It actually hurts my heart to think of them being left behind, living in such terror.

"Whatever it does look like," she said, "I know you'll fight the darkness with your arrows. I'll fight it with my pen."

His hand was warm when it rested on her fingers. "I should've known you were going to say something so beautiful when I saw your fingers tapping the wood."

"Okay, mine will be a keyboard, but a pen sounds more poetic."

"See what I mean?" He sat looking at her. "Words settle onto the Paige," he pointed at her, "in a way they don't with others. You're able to express images in a way that brings them to life. All we see around us, the darkness rising, you'll shine light on it with the power of the pen."

"You're not so bad yourself, soldier, with bringing words to life."

"I read every word you post. I guess your ink is rubbing off on me."

She sat for a second looking at him. "I'll have to step away from that, the tourism and travel writing. This needs to be where I focus. I feel like that's what I heard the Lord whisper to me earlier, that I need to get it on paper."

"Well then, we'll make a way for you to do that, for you to cross the bridge to your calling."

Safe Haven

Day 10, 3:01 p.m.

The flight was smooth but irritating. Wyatt wouldn't tell Paige where they were going. Since that morning over breakfast–eating the last bowl of oatmeal she could handle for a while–Wyatt had refused to even give her clues. All she knew was that they weren't going to Overwatch or to her house or even to Savannah for that matter.

A pick-up was waiting for them at a private airfield, a location which gave her no indication of a city or state so far.

"What if I don't like your surprise?" she said.

"Then I'll take you somewhere else. Anywhere you want."

Paige slid into the passenger seat of the Chevy, then Wyatt closed her door. She genuinely wasn't amused. "I need clothes," she said when he climbed in. "I've been alternating between wearing your dad's baggy shorts and this same pair of jeans for the past three days.

"You wear them well."

"Wyatt!"

He turned to her. "I've got this covered. You have every reason to sit back and trust me."

Paige giggled, remembering her first encounter with him in the taco-scented van. "Did you just politely tell me to sit back and shut up?"

He let out a soft chuckle, just like that day. "Not intentionally. I just meant there's not much more for you to know than I've got this. You're my mission. I don't fail."

She let out an easy breath and sat back in her seat. "No, you don't fail."

It wasn't long before she noticed landmarks: restaurants and local hotels on the way to Landry. Her heart raced. "We're going to Aunt Bertie's!"

"Where else would we catch fireflies and eat watermelon on the porch?"

"Why didn't you just tell me?"

"I wanted it to be a surprise as long as possible."

"No better surprise." She leaned her head back on the seat and placed her splinted hand on Wyatt's. "Nothing could make me happier than this. We're safe. I know my dad's okay. This will be a better visit."

"That's what I was hoping for."

"I'll call her and let her know to expect us for dinner."

"No need," Wyatt said with a smile. "I've got that covered too."

She knew his words were meant to make her wonder what he might be up to. She did, but she wasn't going to let on that it bothered her. With Wyatt, she had discovered that the more something drove her crazy, the more he tormented her with it. This life with him would be a fabulous and frustrating adventure.

"Hungry?" he said. "We can stop off for a bite."

"No way. I've got cookies in my future." Paige grinned. "You know she's got them made already. I'm hoping for snickerdoodles this time."

"I love snickerdoodles," he said in a soft sigh. "Maybe you'll sneak a few for your husband-to-be?"

"No way to that either. You'll have to learn the art of Robin Hoodery like me."

"Will you give me a few pointers?"

His sad brown eyes stirred her enough to give in. "I'll share mine with you. You're too straight of an arrow to use the five-finger discount."

"I'm glad I've got a wife-to-be with no moral compass."

"You're welcome."

The remainder of the drive was spent with Paige watching the sights, remembering the many years of traveling along this route. This drive gave an already peace-filled heart even greater reason to smile.

The final miles blew by, so by the time they neared Aunt Bertie's mailbox, Paige's hands were fidgety, and she already had her seatbelt removed.

"What's this?" She said when they approached a tall gate at the entrance. At the top of the ironwork was a plaque with an engraving: *Safe Haven.*

Wyatt slowed to a stop at the gate. "Looks like someone has added some security measures."

"You did this?"

"I know you'll be safe here."

Her eyes grew even wider. "Why will I be here?"

With a soft smile, he said, "I want to do life here together."

"You mean you've bought it already?"

"I did. Hank has been making it a fortress, a safe place for you. It'll be our home."

"Where's Aunt Bertie?"

He wrinkled his eyebrows at what was clearly a ridiculous question. "Well, here. You don't think I would get rid of the woman who bakes the cookies, do you?"

Paige let out a little sigh. "We'll live here, really?"

"Until we go home," he pointed up, "yes." The car began to roll.

"Go faster," she said once they cleared the gate. "I need to get home."

"We had a crew go in and get your things at your house, what was salvageable anyway, and bring them here. I hope that's okay. If you want to go –"

"No, there's nothing left there for me." Tears came, and she allowed them their freedom to fall. "You could give me no better home than this."

Aunt Bertie was waiting on the porch for them and made her way down the steps when they came to a stop.

"I'm so sorry about your dad, sweetie." She drew Paige into her arms. "I'm here."

"I know you are."

Bertie stepped back and rested her hands, light as a feather, on Paige's cheeks. Tears floated in her blue eyes. "Look at you, my pretty girl."

"I'm okay. It's getting better every day."

"You're more than okay, darlin'." Her words gained in power. "You're strong and bold and brave. You are your mama's daughter."

Tears fell again, so Bertie wiped Paige's swollen cheek with the back of her hand. Paige said, "So you don't mind that we're here?"

"Mind?" she said with a wave of her arm, "I'm having the time of my life." Bertie paused and her eyes grew wider. "For the first time in a very long time, I feel I have purpose again."

Paige only then looked around and saw Waylon heading their way. He called out, "I came to build you a little something." He pointed toward the pond. "Your very own bridge." With a shake of his head, he said, "That was a labor of love. Y'all have those blasted gators down here. I built it high enough over the water where you can still dangle your legs over the sides and keep your feet." He grinned and looked at Wyatt. "And wider than mine since it's a resting place for two."

Paige stepped into Waylon's arms. "Thank you for my bridge. It means more to me than you can know."

"I hear you might be getting married on that bridge."

She turned to look at Wyatt.

With a quick shrug, he said, "A guy can hope."

"A girl can't say no to that."

Inside her bedroom Paige stopped by the bed and looked across the room at her white sundress with black and yellow flowers hanging on the door of the closet. Her yellow ribbon was draped around the hanger, cascading down the dress. An air vent nearby blew just enough that the ribbon flapped back and forth in the breeze, just as Wyatt said it had done the day he had watched her eat bread with honey.

Wyatt stepped into the room behind her. "Marry me," he wrapped his arms around her waist, "in that dress?"

"Yes. Every day is another yes to that question." She spun around in his arms. "Is this real? Can we really live here and love here and steal cookies here?"

"We can."

"And you'll run Overwatch from here?" she said.

"Close, but not exactly. Hank has been busy. Mr. Cox has sold us his place. Did you know he has nearly forty acres? Between the two locations, we can have everything we need for the team. Halo is scouting out ground to build a landing strip. Echo is already next door running wire for his coms center."

"What did you do with poor old Mr. Cox?"

"He's right there in the thick of things, bossing people around, so I hear. He's not likely going anywhere soon. He gave the money from the sale of the farm to his daughter." Wyatt's lips formed into a gentle smile. "But he plans to be a Daybreaker with us."

"This is wildly insane and impressive." She was quiet a few seconds, then said, "My dad would be so proud of what you're doing here. It was my mom's favorite place." A smile tugged at her lips. "And his."

"Your dad was a visionary, but I don't think even he could've seen this all coming together." He pointed up. "That's someone else's genius."

Tears welled in her eyes again. "That phone call, those shots in the background, there was no way he could have known the firestorm they would create in my life." She hesitated, feeling the burn within. "Or the fire he would stoke in my heart to carry on his work as a Daybreaker."

"Your dad would be so proud of you, Paige. I know I sure am. You've withstood a storm this week that few could endure and be found standing. I'm proud to serve alongside you, not just as your husband, but as a brother in Christ. You'll make an impact and shine like a burst of starlight against the black canvas of this world."

She cut her eyes at him. "You stole that line from Aunt Bertie."

"I like to call it a little Robin Hoodery." He took a step back, his expression now one of tenderness. "You look tired. Rest if you need to. Most of your clothes were fine. They're clean and put away. You can get showered and changed out of your three-day-old jeans, then meet me downstairs when you're ready."

Before he could walk away, she slid her hand behind his neck and moved in for that real kiss.

His grin when they parted made her grin.

"It's about time," he said. "I've wanted to, but that poor fat lip of yours begged me to wait."

"This poor fat lip can handle a little sugar now."

Wyatt kissed her once more then stepped into the hall and closed the door behind him. Once alone, Paige scanned the room, only now noticing the hodgepodge of things sitting on the dresser and side tables. Her things from her house and her room at Overwatch were here, including her mom's writing desk and jewelry box.

Paige opened the box and removed her mom's gold band to look at it. She knew it fit since she had slid it on the afternoon of her mom's funeral.

"I think I'll do a little Robin Hoodery of your ring, Mom. I can't imagine anything would make you happier than me wearing this ring."

She smiled and placed the ring onto the dresser, then removed her dad's ring from her chain. Until her finger was ready for her mother's ring, she would allow both rings to nestle together where she could see them. Nothing was more fitting than that, the wedding bands of two forever-connected hearts resting together at their Safe Haven.

Bride

Day 14, 4 p.m.

Paige sat at her mother's desk reading,

> *"If I go and prepare a place for you, I will come again and receive you to Myself, that where I am, there you may be also."* (John 14:3)

She read the words once more, the bride in her catching a glimpse of her own groom in the passage. Wyatt had done just that, prepared a place for her and brought her to be with him.

Over the past week since arriving at Safe Haven, Paige had watched the synchronous movements at their new home as Hank had led the team in building a safe room into the existing structure and beginning an outbuilding to house vehicles. They also installed cameras throughout the now fence-secured and booby-trapped compound, thanks to Waylon. The result was a fortress where Paige felt safe again, a place where nightmares were fading and life was even better than what she had once known as normal.

What a beautiful image of the day her Groom would come. She could only imagine what the Lord Jesus was doing up in heaven as He prepared a place so much grander, so much safer, than this.

Days after being there, the words from the psalmist had reminded her how the Lord had guided those who called out in the midst of a storm to their desired haven. That was her now, at her Safe Haven, a place where she knew her call would eventually settle into her heart and understanding.

Since her arrival, Paige had prayed over her role as a Daybreaker. So far, rather than an answer as to how she would reach the masses, all that had come was that she was to provide for her family, her large, extended family filled with men who sure liked to eat.

The day of her dad's small graveside service in Savannah, the men had stood with her and Aunt Bertie as his remains were placed next to his beloved wife's. Something happened within her that day, a surprising sense of new purpose when she looked at those men. They were truly family, not just a team.

The loss of their leader had brought the team together, a time for them to regroup and determine their next steps, and a time to rebuild what would become their new base of operations.

All but Aunt Bertie, Wyatt, and herself were housed at Overwatch with bossy old Mr. Cox, a man nowhere as fragile as his dwindling appearance made him out to be.

At Aunt Bertie's insistence, the group came together for breakfast and dinner at Safe Haven. Lunch was Paige's assignment from Aunt Bertie, to make sure the Overwatch kitchen was stocked with plenty to make sandwiches and quick meals during the day.

A few days into her new position, a word had come floating from the sky like dew: *prepare.* She wasn't sure what it meant, but she did know it partnered with what she had been reading in Proverbs about the wisdom of a wife Paige had never identified with as a single woman.

A smile tugged at her lips as she glanced at the clock and reached for her ribbon. That would only be the case a few minutes more. Soon, she thought as she looked around her room, she would share this space with her watchful soldier and groom. With eyes closed and heart beating faster, she whispered, "Thank you, Daddy, for raising that man up to be like you."

A tap sounded at Paige's door. "You about ready?" Bertie said when she cracked open the door.

"I'm just about done." Paige continued with her work of tying her yellow ribbon with one and a half hands.

"You're breathtaking." Bertie's eyes sparkled with joy. "A dress filled with eye-popping flowers is the perfect wedding dress for a girl so bright and sunny and especially fitting for a garden wedding."

Paige grinned. "Wyatt has made this wedding awfully easy."

"On the bride maybe." Bertie moved to help Paige tie her bow. "I've been cake baking for two days now. Our army has an appetite, so even making cake is an extended chore."

"We suggested ordering a cake."

"You're not ordering a wedding cake when I make better cakes than any bakery in town." Bertie went for Paige's black pumps and set them before her.

Paige stood and held onto Aunt Bertie's shoulder while she slipped into them. "You do make better cakes. And I also knew you would say no to a bakery cake when I offered to buy one. I know what I'm doing." With a quick grin she kissed Aunt Bertie's cheek.

"You know I don't mind–ever–cooking for our new family, don't you?"

"I know you love every minute of it. And those of us on the rotation who help you cook know you're as bossy as old Mr. Cox."

"There's no one that bossy." Bertie paused and looked at her as if suddenly far away. She reached out to touch Paige's now yellowish bruised cheek. "Your mom and dad would sure be proud of you, Paigie."

Paige glanced over at her parents' photo on the desk. "My mom met Wyatt. Maybe even she suspected he was the man for me. And I know for certain this is exactly what my dad wanted for me, to love Wyatt and to be a Daybreaker."

"Whether or not your dad wanted it for me," Bertie said, "I love Wyatt and am a Daybreaker too. I can't believe the end of my life is such an adventure."

"I feel the same," Paige said. A final glance at the clock got her moving. "Speaking of adventures, I have the Arrow waiting for me."

"We better not keep that man waiting, then."

Paige stood at the bottom of the steps watching through the glass panes of the front door. Wyatt, dressed in his new black suit, walked Aunt Bertie down the steps where Waylon took her arm and led her to her seat.

It broke Paige's heart that Wyatt's mom had refused to come because of his dad. While Wyatt tried to play it off as if it were no big deal, it was. She felt it. Aunt Bertie felt it, too, and had made as much of a fuss over Wyatt in advance of the wedding as she had Paige.

Paige's heart beat a little faster as Wyatt came back up the stairs and pounded on the door.

"What's the password?" Paige said.

Wyatt's voice was loud and determined like the first time she had heard it. "Lemonade!"

She swung open the door and smiled. He smiled in return and held up two fingers. "You have two minutes."

"I should fix this." She reached out to straighten his black tie speckled with bright lemons.

"A minute and three quarters," he said with outstretched hand.

With her hand in his, he guided her over the threshold to stand on the porch. There, he held his arm out for her to take. In her father's absence, Paige had known the only man he would trust to walk her down the aisle would be Wyatt, this man after his own heart.

"I've hoped for this day for a long time," Wyatt said.

Her grip on his arm tightened. "I'm sorry it took me so long to catch up with you."

"You were right on time–not one day too early or too late."

Paige looked ahead of them. Household chairs of various kinds, threadbare and worn and well-used, were placed close by and facing Paige's bridge. It was very likely that her parents had both sat in each of those chairs at one time or another. That imagery brought the people she loved there to witness her joy-filled day.

They walked along the path framed by flowers from Aunt Bertie's gardens. No elaborate or expensive wedding could ever rival this setting, these people, or this day. The team sat watching. Aunt Bertie and Waylon sat next to one another on a small settee. The pastor from Aunt Bertie's church waited on the bridge. Crystal vases brimming full of cut flowers and tied with various shades of yellow ribbons were scattered along the bridge.

Once they stood before the pastor, they turned to face one another. Paige found Wyatt's expression to be exactly what she had expected when envisioning this moment, one of absolute devotion. He smiled a nervous smile, a man who very well may have been fighting back tears in front of his assembly of onlooking soldiers.

Pastor Reynolds said, "Wyatt and Paige, I want to remind you of words penned in Ecclesiastes, a book of wisdom found in God's faithful Word.

"'Two are better than one because they have a good return for their labor. For if either of them falls, the one will lift up his companion. But woe to the one who falls when there is not another to lift him up. Furthermore, if two lie down together they keep warm, but how can one be warm alone? And if one can overpower him who is alone, two can resist him. A cord of three strands is not quickly torn apart.'

"Here, before your family and friends, you are committing to join your lives together today. You have both assured me that you will daily invite our Lord Jesus to walk with you, to be with Him a cord of three strands.

"Wyatt, is that your commitment today?"

Wyatt said, "It is." He took Paige's left hand, stared at it a few seconds, then said, "A wife of noble character who can find? She is worth far more than rubies." Next, he removed Paige's chain from her neck, then took her mother's gold band from his pinky and slid it onto the chain. "That's what you are, Paige, noble and strong and brave, a precious gem and rare treasure." His words were soft, "I recently told you if I received even the dust of a jewel in my crown in heaven, then I'd be content. Now, I wouldn't even dare hope for that, not after having you as the crowning jewel of my life here." He placed the chain back around her neck and said, "With this ring I commit my life to you as one in our cord of three."

Tears filled Paige's eyes at the beauty of his praise for her. When Wyatt had suggested they each share a verse that reminded them of the other, she had known her verse for him immediately. The past days spent wondering what verse he would choose for her had her suspecting it would be something about her love of the Word. She should have known he would choose a passage that ushered her into her new role as the bride he had once come to rescue.

To her, Pastor Reynolds said, "Paige, is it your commitment today to join with Wyatt and invite Jesus to walk with you as your third strand?"

"It is." Paige took Wyatt's left hand into her right one. For a few seconds, she stood looking at him, her heart now ablaze with more than ordinary love for this soldier of hers. She said, "'Grace be with all those who love our Lord Jesus Christ with incorruptible love.'" She smiled at him, and her eyes fluttered closed and open again. "That's you, Wyatt, an incorruptible man, a straight arrow who loves with unchanging, honorable love. All you do, in word and in deed, you do in the name of Jesus."

Wyatt's eyes became misty at her words, so he blinked long before looking back at her.

"I admire your incorruptible love for the Lord, and I melt inside when I see the evidence of your staggering, incorruptible love for me. In you I see not only my groom, but *the* Groom who cherishes me and will someday come for me. She slipped the ring on his outstretched finger. "With this ring I commit my life to you as one in our cord of three."

"Wyatt and Paige, it is my great honor to pronounce you man and wife before the Lord."

Wyatt lowered his head and whispered, "Two weeks, that's really got to be a record."

"Hush and kiss me."

Cheers erupted. Wyatt led Paige along the bridge that now joined their lives together. They shook hands and hugged necks with friends and family all the way over to the table where Aunt Bertie was already cutting a cake the newlyweds had decided to eat later. On a bench nearby were a loaf of bread and jar of honey. They sat, and Wyatt tore off a hunk of bread for his wife and handed it to her.

Paige opened the jar and drizzled a stream of golden honey onto her bread and then his.

Wyatt took a bite and wiped the dribble of honey from his lip. "I really never saw this coming, getting married on our second date."

"And I never really saw our first date."

"True enough." He took another bite and pointed at her bread. "You aren't eating."

Her plate sat in her lap, but Paige had something else on her mind. "Your verse from before," a soft sigh escaped her lips, "I was just thinking about that exact chapter before I came out here. I've been reading it the past two days. How did you do that?"

"It could only be Jesus," he said. "I struggled for a few days over what verse to use. Of course I thought it would be more obvious, one about the Word settling onto the Paige. But as I was searching, I just kept thinking what a treasure you are. The verse about us storing up treasures in heaven wouldn't let me rest. You are certainly a treasure I will take with me there." He leaned his head to touch hers. "Then it just came, about you being more precious than rubies." Now it was he who sighed a little as he moved in to kiss her.

Paige moved back from that kiss, lifted her bread, and licked the dripping honey from her finger. "You've set the bar pretty high with that Proverbs 31 passage. I had a pretty good gig going with you cooking my meals and cleaning up after me."

Wyatt nodded toward Aunt Bertie. They both watched her flitter around like the vibrant, hospitable butterfly that she was, checking on the men, making sure their glasses of lemonade stayed full.

"For the most part, I've made sure you keep that pretty good gig going," he said. "You just be my precious, sparkling little gem."

With a soft giggle and a nibble on her bread, Paige shrugged. "This bride can't help but sparkle."

Nook

Day 21, 10:07 a.m.

With Bible open and notepads scattered across her metal table-turned-desk, Paige sat in her small nook at what was now called Overwatch. The tiny second-floor bedroom in Mr. Cox's farmhouse was where she had spent much of the past week since her wedding as she tried to figure out and carry out her role at Daybreak.

When she had run across this old table in a donation pile one evening after Aunt Bertie's garage purge, Paige insisted they keep it and bring it to the main compound building, where she could feel more a part of the team. Cleaned up but not yet painted, it was a treasured memory from childhood, the table where her dad had given her lemonade as a password. For sure a coat of lemon yellow was in its near future.

For now, she had more on her mind than decorating. The call was getting louder, as if the Lord was bending near to say, "This is the way, walk in it." The Word was like that when ingested and applied over time. Still, so far, her role as a Daybreaker was more in title than in deed.

One notepad was labeled: Warn the Lost. The other: Wake the Found. A phrase often came to mind: Get it on paper. She was working toward that. New thoughts and ideas and verses were splattered across the pages in no certain order. She kept her pads with her Bible so that when a verse jumped out at her, she would make note of it to later watch and see where the Lord might plug the puzzle piece into the bigger picture. From those ideas, her narrow vision was beginning to expand.

Great adventure, that's what this was.

"How's it going?" Wyatt said when he dropped into the nearby paisley chair.

Duct taped, for now, to keep the torn stuffing in place, the chair served its purpose: It never failed to remind her that Jesus sat with her in her cozy little nook each day and guided her efforts.

In moments like this, when her groom would plop down and check on her progress, it also served to remind her this soldier of hers had saved her from her own stuffing being plucked that day when he had arrived to rescue her.

"Some days I'm crushing it," she said. "Some days it's crushing me."

"You have to trust the process. You're seeking the Lord. You're staying in the Word. He will define what you need to do."

"I know He will, but for now I have this boss who keeps checking in." She winked at Wyatt. "I want to give him something to show him I'm making progress."

Wyatt scooted up in his seat and rested his elbows on his knees. "Because your boss loves you, he wants to say there's no pressure. That's not true, though. We both know every daybreak only brings us closer to nightfall. So give me something."

"A few things are coming together already," she said. "Echo has been helping me with the website. I'm pulling together links for videos and documents. Much of what Echo showed me at the beginning I'll share on the site. I have some content written and saved as a draft until I better know the direction I'm supposed to take.

"All kinds of verses are pointing me in the right direction, like us being sons of light and sons of day and encouraging one another while it's still called today."

She tapped her Bible on the table. "We know it won't be called today much longer. Until believers see the urgency, they won't tell or encourage others.

"Waking the found is huge; it's where I'm supposed to focus for now. I'm trying to figure out how to tell my own story. The way you taught me that this world isn't what I thought it was, I want to do that for others, to help them see what we see. Only when they sense the urgency we do will they help to open the eyes of people around them. The awakened found will reach more lost than my efforts alone.

"And preachers..." She paused and her eyes grew wider. "I don't know how or if they will listen to me, but I have to try to convince them to start telling their people.

"I'm watching a sampling of sermons online. You're exactly right; most pastors are silent about what's going on around us, what's coming. I want to believe they just don't see it. I can't imagine they would see and not prepare the people. You called them silent shepherds at my dad's house the night you took me there. Even then I knew what a powerful statement that was. I hope their silence isn't fear based. They can't fear man more than God."

Her voice grew softer. "I just know I'll be no better than a silent shepherd if I don't sound the wake-up call to pastors too."

His face lit up. "You are blowing me away with all this. As your boss, I'm so proud I hired you. That's major progress for a week on the job." He leaned in closer. "And as your husband, the truth is, I was here for a little kiss more than a progress report."

She rolled her chair close enough to give him a smooch. "As a boss, you're lucky I do this for free. As a husband, you can stop by for a kiss anytime." After a pause and with a slight grimace, she said, "It's not easy being married to the boss. I never know which man is dropping into that chair, the one here to grill me or the one here to kiss me."

"Mostly to kiss you." Wyatt sat back. "But now, as the boss, I do have an update for you. Dollar just called to set up a meeting with the team later this afternoon. I wanted to make sure you'll come back here if you plan to go home for lunch." His expression changed. "Based on his concerns, I already have some things in mind I'd like you to think about even before he talks to the team."

"Sure." Paige grabbed a fresh notepad.

"He's looking down the line–not too far down the line–watching for what will certainly become hyperinflation and a down-turned economy. Gas prices are already skyrocketing, and food and building materials are going through the roof and becoming scarce in some cases. It wouldn't hurt to do some stocking up. I'm not saying we become preppers, but I do want to get ahead of the curve so we are ready no matter what comes our way. Whether it's storms and we lose power or hyperinflation devalues the dollar, we will be prepared."

She watched him, how his jaw tensed and his eyes clouded with unease. "There's something else that has you troubled."

"It's like the walls are closing in on us. Dollar is watching a subtle shift toward a digital currency and fears it'll happen without the public ever really seeing it coming. We already know that paper currency is targeted for elimination since they say it can spread the virus. That very well may be their next play. In that case, they will be able to track how and where we spend our money. Them knowing how much we have and how we spend it would be debilitating for us."

He shook his head and blew out a long, steady breath. "It can only go one way, Paige. A digital currency coupled with vaccine passports will allow them to eventually lock the unvaxxed out of the mainstream economy. We have to plan for that eventuality."

Just as he had, she let out a long, steady breath. This wouldn't actually be the mark, but it was certainly the framework that would someday prepare the world to take the mark.

He sat and blinked long. "Part of me hates how fatalistic and cynical I've become. I watch every little happening and try to guess how they will use it against us. Most days I feel like they're ten steps ahead of us, that we can't seem to do enough."

Paige said, "Your dad said something so wise while I was still at his place waiting on you. Because we know the truth, that puts us a step ahead of them. He's right in that. The Lord knows the plan even before they do, and He's told us their end game. Even when we don't know the details of how they will pull it off, just knowing their goal gives us the advantage. That will always help us see through the next lie, the next big deception."

"My dad's exactly right," Wyatt said. "All we can do is observe and then trust God to show us our next step. He's already in every tomorrow, so we can absolutely depend on Him to guide us."

She grinned and nodded. "A good Father takes care of his kids and helps them prepare for what's to come. I know that from personal experience."

"I've got a pretty wise dad and a pretty wise wife." He stood and gave her a peck on the cheek. "I better get back to the coms center to help Echo with some wiring on a new piece of equipment."

Paige just nodded and watched him leave. Their conversation left her feeling... something; she wasn't sure exactly what. It wasn't fear about money or preparing. From the moment he had reminded her how every daybreak only brought them closer to nightfall, a tightness had gripped her chest.

It was true, some days she was crushing it, trusting the process and trusting that God would give her what she needed, but some days she felt crushed by something she didn't comprehend, a hesitance in her own heart that kept her thoughts clouded and her fingers still.

How could she convince believers to act with a sense of urgency when she still experienced such hesitation? In moments like these, tucked away in her little nook and surrounded by men going about their call, wearing the title of Daybreaker made her feel like an imposter.

Storehouse

Day 21, 2:50

The team had all converged in the conference room, what was once the dining room, hypothesizing over possibilities and scenarios that may be coming their way. Some were wildly unlikely, Paige thought only a second or two, before the realization came that most anything and everything seemed possible in a world so tilted.

The one word that was used most often that day was prepare, the word that had come to mind in such a distinct way when she had first begun stocking the Overwatch kitchen. The last time she had really considered it was just before marrying the man now leading the conversation. The Lord was clearly directing them, not to scare them but to prepare them; Paige felt it in her spirit.

A week ago, her thoughts had been merely a primer for this moment. Whatever the decisions and outcome of this meeting, she knew her role was to prepare for her family and to urge others to prepare. No way would she take that lightly.

She watched Wyatt and his interaction with the soldiers; he was very evidently in charge as they all looked to him, not only for guidance but for orders. He seemed comfortable in his new role as leader, likely due to occasionally taking on the position when her father had worked in the field.

One thing she did know: Whatever may come, with Wyatt in charge they had a solid and wise leader. Even the older men showed unmistakable respect for him.

Wyatt ticked off a list as Paige took notes. "So Paige will oversee the procurement of food, water, household necessities, and supplements." He paused and looked at her. "That's not a comprehensive list. We'll work together on subcategories."

To Cade, he said, "You and Bash will work with her on the pick up of items that can't be shipped, and then you're responsible for storage and rotation. Work with Hank on his timeline of the storehouses being completed. I want to store away supplies in any and all other areas available here and at Safe Haven."

She wrote as fast as her hand would move and stayed tuned in as best she could. Old Mr. Cox, with not a tooth in his head, was sleeping next to her, mouth gaping open and snoring. Any other day she would think him the cutest thing ever, but today his doddling head with its ten or so hairs distracted her as she kept reaching to move it back against his headrest so he wouldn't topple over as he had done the day before.

Wyatt wasn't amused either, though the rest of the men hid grins and sometimes chuckled. Paige herself would find it humorous if not for Wyatt's change in mood since their lighthearted time together at lunch.

He nodded at Paige. "For now you're in charge of inventory. We'll make a permanent decision on that later."

"I'm fine with handling inventory," she said. "I can take it long term."

Wyatt continued, "Hank is on exterior: fuel, generators, vehicle replacement parts..." He looked at Hank. "We'll get together and work out some essentials. In the meantime, you need to talk to Aunt Bertie about her plans for a garden next spring. We need to expand it. Help her get that mapped out."

Hank nodded without looking up from his notepad.

Dylan spoke from on screen, "As far as the economy goes, let's just say I remain cautiously unoptimistic. It's difficult to see anything but increasing prices ahead, so any purchases now will save money compared to even a month down the road." Dylan turned to her. "I'll keep you posted as I hear anything relevant, Paige."

"Thanks," she said.

"I want to define my position on the dollar." Dylan grinned at his own pun. "I don't see anything other than its continued devaluation. There's already bipartisan support on transitioning to the Fedcoin, so a shift to a digital currency here in the U.S. is imminent. My suspicion is that it will be something that happens under the radar, a sudden shift, maybe even due to the collapse of the dollar as inflation skyrockets. I may be unduly apprehensive. We may be a year or more out on that, years even, but something inside just feels off, unsettled."

"That's understandable, Dollar," Wyatt said. "We're all on heightened alert these days. I would rather plan for what doesn't happen than not plan for what does."

When he glanced at her, Paige saw something familiar, something she had only seen once in Wyatt's expression.

Discussions went on only a moment more before the meeting broke. Gunny helped Mr. Cox, an ex-munitions expert himself, from the room and led him to his main-floor bedroom for the next in his daily series of naps. Wyatt was engaged in a conversation with Hank, so Paige went back up to her nook to begin more comprehensive lists of what they would need to purchase.

For some reason Paige couldn't get Wyatt off her mind, his unusual expression when Dylan had spoken to her directly. Nothing about it had seemed like jealousy. It was only a quick flash of something, but she had picked up on it.

Paige returned to her notepad filled with categories she would need to expand upon. She stopped and reached for her Bible. At the end of Proverbs, she found the phrase that had been resonating with her: "She looks well to the ways of her household." Several earlier verses spoke of providing food and goods for her home. This was why the wise woman had been whispering to Paige from the Book. Paige was to take her role seriously.

Even if her home and family had all they needed, if hard financial times came and others around them were in need, the Daybreak team would be a source of help. To offer a can of soup to a neighbor in need and share the love of Jesus would address a spiritual need while also meeting the physical.

Storehouses, the word Wyatt had used, swept down like a massive wind and carried her over to Joseph's story. Paige flipped over to Genesis and read the familiar and favored account: Joseph saw the famine that was to come. In the years of plenty, he filled the storehouses with grain, preparing for the seven years of lean.

That's exactly what God was calling her to do. A quick trip back to the wise woman in Proverbs reminded Paige, "She smiles at the future." While Paige wasn't sure how much reason she would have to smile at an ever-darkening future, she would do her best not to live in anxiety over her family's provision. Like Joseph, she would prepare.

Lost in thoughts and lists, Paige only realized Wyatt had entered after he spoke. "Want to wrap things up here and head back home with me?"

"If you're ready." She began stacking her notepads and then stopped to look at Wyatt. She said, "May I ask you a question before we go?"

"Anything," he said and moved to sit.

Her voice was low. "Do you trust Dylan? I saw something when he was there in my father's hospital room and then again today."

Wyatt said, "You saw something off about Dollar?"

"No," she leaned up in her seat, "off about you."

For a second he sat looking at her thoughtfully, his cheeks flushing. Finally he said, "I watched him with you that day at the clinic, how he seemed to want to impress you. He's successful and at the top of his game. I guess I wondered if you would be better off with someone like him. He doesn't live like me, looking over his shoulder, fearing retaliation for the things he does."

Paige laughed out loud. "I sure hope you don't feel that way now. My life is a ginormous adventure, filled with intrigue and soldiers and family and preparing for the whatever-may-come."

For a second she grew quiet as the weight of her next words settled onto her in advance of speaking them. "God has written me into the final chapter of this part of human history. He's penned my life story and prepared me for such a time as this." Her heart did that little pitter-pat it often did when looking into her husband's tender brown eyes. "He's placed me here next to the leading man of my dreams." She looked down at her hand, at her still-too-swollen-for-a-ring finger. "My literal dreams."

Wyatt grinned. "I saw those fingers tapping when you first started talking and knew that it would be good." He paused. "I'm not jealous, just so you know. I want the very best for you. I'm glad you think that's me."

"I know it's you."

"Good. Come on, leading lady. Let's go home and talk about filling some storehouses."

Stray

Day 22, 7:02 a.m.

The early morning was quiet as Paige sat on the front porch trying to make notes. More often than working, she found herself thinking back to the night before, catching fireflies and eating fresh watermelon with Wyatt and Aunt Bertie. Paige had placed leaves and grass in her jar of fireflies and kept it on her bedside table overnight. Her jar now sat next to her on the porch step with the last little winged creature teetering on the edge of it, about to take flight.

Joy also teetered on the side of that jar, pointing at Paige, whispering a reminder that she was there in the everyday moments. No dark was dark enough to extinguish joy. Joy was never lost, only overlooked when the eye was fixed on anything other than Jesus.

Paige grinned and looked down at her tapping fingers. Even her splinted duo tried its best to join in her motion of praise.

A soft sigh came and with it whispered thanks to the One who would be so kind as to give her a home and family and brand-new love.

Wyatt was off with Hank working on the landing strip, taking advantage of the cooler morning air. He would show up soon for breakfast, and her heart would do that little thing when she saw him. Each morning she woke to find him sleeping next to her, she whispered another thanks.

Along with Wyatt, the rest of the team would be arriving in caravans of utility vehicles. The boy in them seemed to love their dune buggy-like vehicles and their trodden-down path between the two sites. In some ways their compound reminded Paige of summer camp. Aunt Bertie's kitchen was like the mess hall, where the men rarely skipped meals. That woman was a big hit with her soldiers. For some who had no mothers living, she became a stand-in mom. And for all, she became a spiritual mom. Not only was she that to Paige, Aunt Bertie was a living, breathing example of the spiritual mom that Paige wanted to be.

Even Mr. Cox showed up most days, providing Gunny could drag him out of bed. The two had become fast friends over the past weeks, always plotting and strategizing over how best to fend off a tactical assault of various areas of the compound.

It warmed Paige's heart to see Gunny with a notepad of his own writing down Mr. Cox's suggestions. With age came wisdom, and that old man was full of opinions on how to do most everything. In truth, he was often on point. Wyatt had made notes of his recommendations more than once. This was such a meaningful place to live and serve and grow. Wisdom was regarded as valuable, and two out-to-pasture saints were back in the battle.

Paige looked down at her notepad, at something she had written on her Wake the Found pad, then placed a little star next to the entry:

> Hebrews 5 tells how the mature believer, because of their practice in the Word, has their senses trained to see good and evil.

Paige considered the words and could look back at her early walk with God with an honest assessment and know that she had been mature in her faith and had gained deep revelation. The pain of her loss of both mother and father had caused her to... not stumble exactly. For a season she had simply chosen to close her eyes and not see anything at all. She had lived in darkness of her own making, a spiritual stress sleep, blinded by her refusal to see or awaken.

Others, for various reasons, were doing the same thing, sleeping through the biggest happening to have occurred since Jesus' first coming. This verse in Hebrews would be one she would use to wake the found, to encourage them to invest in and ingest the Word. The wisdom and discernment they needed for the challenging times ahead would only be found through the study of the Word.

Something about her morning on the porch had simplified her task ahead. A visit with fireflies, a burst of sunshine, and a walk through the Word had given her clarity: Besides the busy work of preparing for her family, for now Paige knew her call to wake the found would be her primary focus.

The website and its content would house what she would use to get started doing just that, providing evidence of what was going on around them. Still, there was something more she needed to do to reach out to the masses. Her own audience alone wouldn't make much of a difference. She needed to make a big move, but what that looked like, she wasn't at all certain.

A sound drew Paige's eyes up and to the left to find one of the outdoor utility vehicles traveling through the brush trail from the direction of Overwatch. It wasn't Wyatt. It was Bash and Cade, and they had a familiar passenger in the back seat.

Paige stood and made her way down the steps, then waited as the three big men unfurled themselves from the vehicle.

"We found a stray you might know," Bash said as he made his way toward the steps. "He showed up last night. Can we keep him?"

"Nothing I love more than a stray," Paige said. "I think we can set another place at the table."

Moses stood looking at her long after Bash and Cade went into the house. Finally, he approached as if with hesitation, so Paige took the next few steps his way and wrapped her arms around his waist.

His arms encircled her, and his head rested on hers. "It's good to see you, Ms. Paige."

"It's even better to see you." For a long moment they stood in that quiet embrace. Both lives had been irreversibly changed that night, both saved by the intrusion into each other's lives–a bond created.

She stepped back. "How is your side? I've wondered and prayed."

"It's healing up just fine." He reached for her hand and swallowed hard. "How about you?"

"They're healing up just fine."

"Words will never express how sorry I am. I looked into those sweet eyes of yours and saw Jesus, then went and did that anyway."

A trace of nausea accompanied the resurrection of memories she would rather let rest. "You've been forgiven all this time. How about we just let it die with all the other old monsters."

"I can do that."

"Wyatt said you found Tia?"

"I did." He stood looking down at her, his next words broken. "She's a wrecked girl."

Tears swam in Paige's eyes. "Where is she now?"

"With an aunt in Toledo. I made sure it's a place she will be safe. She'll get her the care she needs. A man named Dollar is handling her medical bills."

The pained expression in Moses' eyes kept her quiet.

His eyes were watery now too. "You had no way of knowing," he said, "but my wife was a porcelain-skinned woman, so my daughter was fair-skinned like Tia, with dark eyes that could make her daddy give in to most anything." His eyes narrowed and his words hardened. "That monster would've done to my girl what he did to Tia. He'll never again have the chance to take another man's daughter."

Moses wiped his eyes. "When she died, Nicole wasn't much older than Tia is now. It felt right to step into that girl's life and let her see that someone cared."

"It was a mission specifically for you, then, Moses. I'm so glad you were there for her. She's safe. Now," she said with a little song, "we celebrate this stray finding a home."

She looped her arm through his. "Come on, let's get you some breakfast." They took a step when Paige said, "We do have one rule here you need to know about."

"I think I can handle one rule."

"We all have to mind Aunt Bertie."

"If there's a woman here who can make you mind, then I'm scared enough to obey her too."

Paige chuckled at that. "And I guess you met Mr. Cox already?"

"I did. He told me I needed a shave and that my slacks needed pressing."

"I bet he did. Oh, he's just getting started."

"He reminds me of my dad, iron-fisted and heart of gold."

By the time they reached the porch steps, Aunt Bertie was standing there with a dish towel over her shoulder and a smile on her face. "I heard we have a new member of the family. Welcome, Moses."

Moses smiled a broad smile and looked down at his feet. "Thank you, Ms. Bertie."

Paige waited for Moses to be told to call her Aunt Bertie, but that never happened.

Bertie took a step down, which brought her eye level with the tall man. Her words were soft. "Thank you for saving my sweet Paige."

"I think maybe it was her who did the saving. Kind of hard to keep a heart of stone with so much talk of Jesus."

Bertie nodded, then blinked a long while as if to chase tears away. "Welcome to God's family, Moses."

Bertie turned and went in ahead of them, but before Paige and Moses reached the top of the steps, Wyatt and Hank pulled in.

"Congratulations on your marriage," Moses said to her. "I meant to say that right off."

"Thank you." She watched her husband climb out of the truck, her heart smiling before her lips could.

Moses gave a slight chuckle. "I hope you've memorized his phone number by now."

That made Paige giggle, too, and she tapped her head. "Committed right here."

Wyatt climbed the steps with outstretched hand. "Glad to have you aboard, Moses. I'm sorry I didn't make it over to greet you this morning."

To Paige, Wyatt's expression conveyed he didn't fully mean those words.

"Glad to be on the right side again, sir."

Wyatt held the door open for Paige and Moses to enter, and they all filed into the kitchen.

Echo was next to enter, followed by Halo, Gunny, and Mr. Cox. Landon was back in D.C. on a family matter.

They were all seated and took hands. Wyatt prayed, "We thank You, Lord, for this meal and for the hands who prepared it. Thank you for our safe haven and for this growing family. I thank you for Moses," his voice cracked, "that he stood against evil and saved my wife." Amens were whispered around the table. "We thank you for love, and we thank you for Jesus. In His mighty name we pray and serve."

All said a louder, "Amen."

Paige looked at Moses who wouldn't make eye contact with her. Conversation broke out and carried her mind beyond Moses' shame.

"When's the last time you went to church, Moses?" Bertie said.

"Been a lot of years."

"Sunday will change that. We go as a family." She gave a bright smile. "Then during the week, I'll be helping you know more about your new life of faith."

"It'll be my pleasure to learn from you, ma'am."

Wyatt cut his eyes at Paige and grinned. Both expected Bertie to throw something at Moses for calling her ma'am since she couldn't reach him to slap his arm.

Instead, she grinned and said, "Ma'am makes me feel awfully old."

"Nothing further from the truth. Just respected, Ms. Bertie."

Was there a spark between this stray and Aunt Bertie? Paige wouldn't blame Moses. Aunt Bertie was a beam of sunlight with her platinum hair and touch of pink lipstick.

Paige glanced at Wyatt, hoping he was picking up on the same thing. Now shoveling food in his face, he was clearly clueless. Not Paige, though. She smiled and her fingers tapped the table: *A sweet gaze and a sprinkle of joy. Oh, what a beautiful new morning.*

Shield

Day 22, 7:50 a.m.

Wyatt kissed Paige goodbye after breakfast. "You'll come over in a while?" he said.

"I'll help Aunt Bertie and get some things done, then I'll be over."

"Let me know when you're ready, and I'll come get you."

"I can drive your boy toys too. Y'all don't get all the fun."

"Maybe I just wanted a chance to be alone with you."

"I'll agree if I get to do the driving."

He shrugged as he backed through the screen door. "We'll see about that."

Paige went back into the kitchen and found Aunt Bertie and Moses washing dishes already. "I'm here to help."

Moses turned, face beaming. "I figured I owed a little labor for the finest meal I've had in years," he patted his belly, "maybe even decades."

Bertie grinned and cut her eyes at Moses. "Flattery will get you everywhere."

He chuckled and she giggled.

Paige just stood looking at the pair who seemed to have already forgotten she was there. "Don't mind me. I'll just get a little work done."

"Okay, Paigie. I'll see you for lunch if you're eating here."

Paige went to the cake keeper and removed the dome. Right there in broad daylight, Paige removed two lemon cookies unnoticed and with no repercussions. That wasn't much fun, she thought as she went back to the front porch.

With one cookie in hand and the other resting on her notepad, Paige reached for her laptop and scanned what she had written so far to address "the found." It was a good start, plenty of content to help people see what Wyatt, Echo, and Aunt Bertie had shown her over the past few weeks. Truly, the world was ever-changing, and the material would have to be updated frequently. New players would emerge. Old tactics would change. For now, though, she was working toward her goal of going live with her site within a week or two.

Her chest tightened at the thought of all the conflict that would likely come in the wake of her friends viewing the site.

Trust the process. The words were quiet and leading but didn't seem to be a re-sounding of Wyatt's words from the day before.

Paige reached for her other cookie and looked out at her bridge. Something about it was beckoning her to come, to dangle her feet too high for a gator to chomp.

With her Bible and notepads in a messy stack, she made her way to the pond and crossed to the midpoint of the bridge. It was only in the early mornings she could sit this way, before the day heated up and drove her indoors. But there was no better place to meet with Jesus. There was a topic of conversation ahead between herself and her Strength and her Shield.

The busywork of studying and researching and writing the site's content had been the easy part. That was her lane, her place of ease, hidden behind a screen and allowing words to trickle from her fingers onto a page, words to inform and rouse the sleeping believer.

The steps that were ahead of her? Not so much. She swallowed hard and looked up at a passing cloud. "As in the days of Noah," she said aloud. A question she already knew the answer to followed: "What was going on?" The answer ordered her next steps, ones she was hesitant to take. Paige flipped to the story in Genesis and said, "Noah was preaching to a people who thought he was crazy."

The first night she had visited Waylon, those had been her exact thoughts. If she started warning people, her friends and coworkers, they would think she was nuts. Then on her next visit, Waylon had said much the same thing. They both knew what people's reactions would be and discussed it on occasion.

This was where Paige continually felt a sense of angst, remembering how she had spoken to her dad, how she had thought he was part of some religious fringe. People would think that of her.

Like Noah, she would have to love her friends enough to keep telling, even when they didn't believe her. It would be a laying down of her life, her reputation, and her sense of comfort. Just as she had loved Wyatt that day in the café and risked her life to save his, now, she would have to do the same for others. "Greater love speaks truth," she said to the Lord.

This was why she felt like an imposter some days. A real Daybreaker would speak no matter what people thought of her.

"It doesn't surprise me one bit that you would sit and talk to yourself," Moses said. "A girl so filled with words probably just bubbles over from time to time."

She smiled at the truth of his statement. "I didn't hear you walk up."

"Do you mind if I share your wedding bridge with you?"

"Not at all."

Moses moved to sit and, like her, dangled his legs over the edge. "I hear you had a fine wedding here."

Paige rubbed her hand along the wood, the words wedding bridge settling into her heart as its fitting new name. "Best day of my life."

"Your Aunt Bertie sure brags on you."

With a little shrug and a grin, she said, "Can you blame her?"

"Not a bit. I'd be bragging on you too if you were my girl." He peeked over the side.

"Too high for the gators if that's what you're wondering."

"I'm a Mississippi Delta boy," Moses said. "You better believe I know to keep my eye out around murky waters like these." He looked ahead of them, at the row of azaleas that surrounded the far edge of the pond. "She's done a fine job here. Prettiest place I've ever seen."

"Maybe you can be a Georgia man for a while."

"I'd like to stick around."

"It's my home now," Paige said with a soft sigh. "You're part of the reason I'm here to enjoy all this. You'll always be welcome where I am."

They sat a long moment. He started to speak once then sat again quietly. Eventually, he said, "I've done a lot of good and a lot of bad in this life."

Paige rested her splinted hand on his. "There was no good enough to make you clean or bad enough to make you beyond God's reach. All bad is washed away now that you made that call. It's a clean slate."

"I want to learn to live a clean slate, to go back to that young man my grandmama raised me to be." He hesitated. "I've been a Marine and a mercenary. I've worked for the right side and the wrong side. But one thing I've never been is a soldier in the army of God." He smiled. "I thank you for enlisting me."

"It's my honor to serve alongside you."

His expression turned thoughtful. "I didn't see it until the dust settled and you were safe with your people. I'm not sure I saw it clearly until just before I found the girl. But that day with you," he slid his hand from beneath hers and touched her fingers, "my life truly changed."

She blinked time and again to keep from crying. "Not much has made me happier in life than hearing you had made that call. Honestly, I've never had

God speak through me the way he did that night. It changed everything for me too."

"When I joined you here," Moses said, "your expression was on the gloomy side, certainly not one I would expect on a newly married woman."

"This newly married woman is happier than she deserves to be with that handsome soldier of hers." She crinkled her nose. "It's me learning how to be a fearless soldier that had me," she paused and thought, "not gloomy. Maybe apprehensive is a better word.

"I have this call, this mission that I'm supposed to tackle as a soldier in the army of God. Yet walking it out has me a little hesitant." Her eyes widened. "Don't get me wrong, I'm doing it–nothing's stopping me from doing it–it's just something scary, something that makes me want to drag my feet."

"What's the worst that can happen if you take those first steps?" he said.

"Did your grandmother or your wife talk to you much about the rapture or the last days?"

With a definite nod, he said, "More than I ever wanted to hear about it."

"That's what I'm supposed to be doing, sharing my story, telling people about what's coming with all these words of mine." She hesitated, blinked once then again. "When I do, I know they will think of me what I thought of my dad, that I'm crazy. Anytime he tried to talk about the rapture coming soon, I shut him down. I pushed him away."

"And you think people will do that to you?"

"I know they will, and I can't figure out why I care. All the people who matter most are right here in this compound. They see what's coming. They've believed for a long time what I now believe. All the others are outside of my circle."

She nodded, affirming the admission. "As much as I can figure, it's pride. I've always been known for being bright and pulled together. I know my group of intellectual friends will think I'm backwards or stupid when I sign my name to all of this. That makes me squirm inside, knowing they will see me so differently." Paige tapped her Bible. "Paul said God chose the foolish things of the world to shame the wise and the weak things of the world to shame the strong."

"You, Ms. Paige, are anything but foolish or weak."

"Moses, you're a few minutes older than me. Why have you started calling me Ms. Paige? You didn't do that before."

A broad smile lit up his face. "I'm well beyond a few minutes older. I'll be sixty-eight next month."

"Sixty-eight? No way!"

"I will be. I've earned every one of those years. And as for me calling you that, I guess that's my grandmama in me. She had me calling all the church ladies Miss This or Ms. That when I was a kid. Feels fitting for you and Ms. Bertie."

"Fitting or not, I really want you to drop the Ms. It makes us seem too far apart. A big brother doesn't call a little sister that."

"I like that, having a mouthy little sister."

Paige smiled. Time for a little fishing. "As for Aunt Bertie, you two seemed to hit it off."

"That's a good woman there," he grinned, "taking in a stray like me."

"Yeah, she's the best. She's taken in all of us strays."

"Bash and Cade have told me what you all do, how you fight the darkness and help people. I'm in for that, if you'll have me."

"Correction," she said. "It's what they do. I'm still trying to pull the trigger to fight the darkness."

"You're a bright and pulled-together girl," he said with a little chuckle. "It won't take you long."

"They all have a background in war. Until the day I met you, I've never had anyone come against me. I've never had a reason to fear. I'll be attacked when I start calling out the darkness. People will say hurtful things. The devil will launch more fiery darts than I can dodge. I was never a threat to him before. I will be once I step into the arena and call out his evil agenda."

"Sounds like what you need is a shield to ward off those fiery darts."

"I know," she said, "the Lord is my strength and my shield. But it's still scary."

"I meant something a little more concrete." He thumped his chest. "Maybe that's my call, to be your shield." When she tried to speak, he held up one hand. "It's not maybe; that is my call. That's why I'm here."

Paige sat looking at him, not knowing what to say.

"I don't know what God sounds like when He's talking to a man, but I know what He did the day I met you.

"I'm retired now and live a quiet life. I fish and do a lot of reading," he patted his belly, "and a little more eating than I should. So when a friend called me to come find your dad, I guess I said yes more out of boredom than anything. I was known for finding people no one else could and hiding the ones who didn't want to be found.

"Maybe it was a case of pride for me as well. I wanted to prove I still had what it takes. I jumped at the opportunity to prove I'm not nearly sixty-eight."

He sat for a second looking straight ahead. "Just that morning before my flight, I was sorting through some junk mail when I came across an insurance ad. It had a shield as its logo. Reminded me of a guy I served with when I was young, a young man infatuated with Captain America. He even had his shield tattooed on his arm one night when we were out hitting the tequila pretty hard.

"Then sitting in traffic on the way to the airport, there was a van nearby with the word 'shield' in big, bold letters. The truck next to it moved, and the whole word said 'windshield'."

He sighed and shook his head. "It was the strangest thing. When I turned the knob to enter that room where you sat waiting, I blinked and the comic book shield came to mind; I could actually see it. I just shook it off and opened the door to find a half-dressed, skinny little white girl. Your face looked so bad, and your eyes were filled with the kind of fear I could feel all the way down to my bones.

"As if seeing the shield wasn't enough to get my attention, you sang that song. Not only did I sing it for my girls, I sang it at my Grandmama Naomi's funeral when I was a boy. You did break me with that song, with your heart willing to praise even in the worst of circumstances. If I could think of a word beyond broken, that would be the word that made me rise up and become your shield that day." He sighed. "Then when I came back into that room, there you were saying the Lord was your strength and your shield. I just know it's my call now."

They sat for the longest time. Still, Paige couldn't understand how it all came about, especially now with this new layer added to an already unbelievable story.

"It wasn't me who did the breaking, Moses."

"No, I know that, but you were the one willing to speak. Why would you do that for a man who would do what I did to you?"

"I guess the Lord showed me, not who you were, but who you were supposed to be."

"You saw me as a sheep," he grinned and nodded, "which I s'pose I am now. But He sees me as a shield, which I s'pose I am now. Or at least that's what I want to be. A shield isn't just an object. It's an action. I want to stand in the way of you and those fiery darts that are sure to come against a mouth like yours. I can watch over you and Ms. Bertie, so Wyatt can do his job without fear."

Paige watched with curiosity as Moses began to tug at the sleeve of his short-sleeve shirt.

"I don't see you as a drinker, Paige, but I'll warn you to stay out of the tequila if you ever start." He grinned. "You can't see it so well this many years later and on this dark skin."

Sure enough, he had a Captain America tattoo right there on his right bicep. She burst into laughter that nearly turned into tears. "Only God could do that. He knew all those years ago you would become this man."

"Yeah, only God could know that."

A sting of conviction came. She had intentionally never told Wyatt that Moses was the one who had broken her fingers. Especially now, in order to shield her shield, she didn't plan to. "You'll have to talk to Wyatt about being my shield. He's the boss."

"I can't quite bring myself to ask, not yet anyway, considering I'm the one who broke his sweet little bride's fingers so that he couldn't place a ring on her hand."

Paige looked down at her hand. "I haven't told him."

"The fact that he shook my hand this morning, the fact that I'm here at all, told me he doesn't know."

"I don't see why he needs to. That's between you and me and Jesus."

"I'm not so sure I agree."

Moses didn't say much after that and left soon. Paige watched him go. His presence at Safe Haven felt right. Him sitting next to her on her wedding bridge had brought unexpected joy. Oddly enough, even watching him in the kitchen with Bertie had seemed like the most natural thing in the world.

He was her people. With a tug at her lips, she flipped over to a passage she had been trying to ingest, to draw deeply enough into her belief system that she would be able to act on it.

"And the Lord said to Paul in the night by a vision, 'Do not be afraid any longer, but go on speaking and do not be silent; for I am with you, and no man will attack you in order to harm you, for I have many people in this city.'"

(Acts 18:9-10)

Paige could see what Moses could see: God had made him her shield. In that case even Wyatt, the team leader, the boss, the husband who seemed to have suspicions about this newcomer, wouldn't be able to stand in the way of that.

So Be It

Day 27, 11:17 a.m.

Blaze. That was the word Paige wrote on her notepad and circled. She looked out at her bridge and drew her legs up in her rocker, hearing that word sound again and again, just as when she had woken that morning.

For nearly half an hour she had lain there trying to make sense of the word. It wasn't ablaze, the word she often used to describe how her heart was bursting with fire to reach people. Images and words had come about sunlight overtaking the darkness, but still the concept never fully formed. She had eventually sat up and done some reading until her need for coffee outweighed the comfort of bed.

Paige had found, in her newly-married life, that her sleeping soldier wasn't stirred by lights turned on or Bible pages being flipped next to him. His sleep remained so sound that she could even move about their room with no issue. But let her open that door, and he was immediately awake. He said that was his internal alarm no matter what time it was, her heading down to get coffee.

A butterfly landed on the railing of the porch and flapped her yellow wings. Paige smiled and said, "Good morning. Do you happen to know what blaze means?" When no answer came, she then looked back at her notepad and decided to tuck the word away with all the other imagery that traveled through her mind as she waited for what she felt would be her go-ahead from God.

It was indeed a good morning, something she had once thought would never come again. But each new daybreak brought with it joy in her life, joy and peace even amidst the darkness of the world that each sunrise scattered. That thought made her smile. Whatever may come, her cord of three strands kept her feet planted firmly on unshakable ground. Those little moments of angst over her call visited her less and less frequently lately. Deep inside, she no longer felt like an imposter, just a human.

John the Baptist's call to "prepare the way for the Lord" had helped to ease her greatest fears. People thought him crazy, yet he called from the wilderness anyway. His end looked nothing like he thought it would, yet he was told, "Blessed is he who does not take offense at Me." John's message from the Lord assured him that no matter what people thought of him, no matter the death he was destined to die for the name of the Lord, he had answered his call just as directed. Paige had to do the same.

She tapped her pencil against her chin and sighed a little. Her warnings and wakings wouldn't likely be taken well by most. That had to be okay with her. She just had to be a willing messenger, to speak forth what she knew, to expose what was coming. Like He had done with her since her dad's phone call, the Lord would have to be the one to shed light into the hearts of believers and unbelievers. Ultimately, it was His work. All she had to do was tell, to sound the wake-up call that Jesus was coming and the world was living on borrowed time.

The phrase in Jesus' tribute to John the Baptist reminded her that "wisdom is vindicated by her deeds." She circled that phrase written on the page and tucked the pad back between her chest and legs.

Through a spectacular series of events and adventures, Paige had been given eyes to see and the wisdom of God's prophetic Word to comprehend what was on the horizon. That wisdom would be proven by what she did with it. She would type and tell, a Daybreaker in word and deed.

Because she wasn't alone in this mission, she was becoming more and more emboldened. What sustained her went beyond her union with Wyatt. It was her Daybreaker team, her intense, silly, amusing group of believers, the ones the Lord used to keep her lifted up and determined.

That was one thing she was including on the Daybreak site, how vital it was to join forces with others who believe and who see. The found had to find other found and link arms, becoming their own cord of many strands to support and encourage one another.

With the rapidly changing world in which they lived, it was difficult to predict or fully prepare for what was to come. Believers would need greater strength and courage to stand strong. It was time to get back to the basics of local community, following the example of the early church. That was a major new theme that rambled in her head since finding her family of Daybreakers.

"Here you are." Wyatt stepped onto the back porch with a sandwich in one hand and a glass of lemonade in the other. "I've missed you today."

She grinned. "I've missed you, too, even though I just saw you two hours ago."

"Has it only been two hours?" He sat in the rocker next to her. "Feels like at least three."

"It's been a good morning," she said. "I helped Aunt Bertie get her donation pile sorted. I figured I would work from here until you came for lunch."

"Making progress?" he said.

"Some new ideas for the site." She hesitated and sat thinking. "The Lord gives me imagery that sparks new ideas. I just try to follow along the lighted path."

"When do you plan to go live?"

Her stomach tightened into a knot, not due to nerves but because her boss had shown up rather than her husband. "Not sure yet. I'm getting there. It doesn't feel right yet, like I'm still waiting on some elusive image to come into focus."

"Echo gave me a preview. I like what you have so far. It's all you can do: point people to Jesus and direct them to the truth of what's going on."

Paige knew his words were true, but still there was something beyond what she was seeing. As she had told him on the bridge at Waylon's, it was like driving along on a foggy morning, knowing something else was still ahead of her surrounded by the mist.

Wyatt finished his sandwich and sat for a moment. He looked at her with an unusual expression, a troubled one.

"Something wrong?" she said.

"Not wrong. I guess I just need to get some things out. I haven't done it yet, but I need to debrief."

Why was that such an unexpected admission to her? With what she viewed as Wyatt's strength and bravado, it hadn't even dawned on her that he had such needs.

"I'm not okay," he said. "I've got to figure out how to get my mind back on mission and less on you. Cade and Bash just headed out for the U.K. to accompany a doctor to Washington. He's in danger; attempts have been made on his life. I'll be running the op from Overwatch. I need to be a leader.

"This isn't about me being a googly-eyed newlywed; it's about me being a watchful soldier who has you as my primary mission. When you're here and I'm there, I keep wondering if you're okay. I keep switching on the video feed, making sure no one has breached the perimeter."

"I didn't know you were going through that," she said. "I'll stay at Overwatch when you're there if that'll help."

"That's not fair to you. Aunt Bertie needs you here too. And it's often louder at Overwatch with people coming and going. I know you work well here where you can be outdoors and have peace and quiet. I see the serenity in your face when you're here. Nature sparks your creativity much more than a little nook facing a white wall."

"So do it," she said, "debrief. Tell me what happened that day. I can't even imagine what you went through when I never came back to the table."

Dead space filled the air for some time. Paige could see his mind was whirling, her strong man trying to admit his weakness.

"I didn't stay seated for any more than a minute. It's like I just knew. Mac hadn't made eye contact with me when she sat. I thought it was because she saw how I felt about you. I should've known something was off.

"Next thing I knew I was pounding on the door of what ended up being an empty bathroom. When I saw you weren't in there, I exploded and started grabbing workers in the kitchen, asking where you were. The team surged in behind me and filed into the alleyway looking for you." Wyatt rubbed his chin. "Echo was en route back to Overwatch, so we were blind for that first half hour. All I can say is that I was out of my mind and out of control.

"When Echo finally tapped into the city cams and we located the bakery truck, the police were swarming. I saw an officer across the street bagging your clothes for evidence. I swear I died a little inside. I knew one thing: Wherever you were, you were waiting for me to come for you. I promised you I always would."

Her words were soft. "I was. That's exactly what I was praying."

"I'm sorry I didn't find you in time, before they could hurt you."

"You weren't supposed to find me then. It's like I said on the plane, Wyatt. I needed to see God show up and save me. It had to be Him. That will always remind me that He rescues."

He sat a minute as if trying to absorb and accept her words. Still, it was evident he carried her capture on his own shoulders.

"Echo sent me the video. He didn't want to, but I lost it with him too." Wyatt grew quiet. His next words were brimming with pain. "I saw you screaming and fighting when they threw you into the van." His voice broke. "People were nearby and did nothing to help you. I couldn't imagine in my wildest dreams how anyone could stand idly by while something so horrific was happening."

With head bowed and hands clasped, for a few seconds he sat as if in prayer. He didn't open his eyes when he said, "That day, I prayed just like this, with hands together like when I was a little kid saying bedtime prayers with my granddad. He told me when we fold our hands in prayer and lace our fingers, it reminds us how powerless we are and that our hands are tied."

Wyatt opened his eyes and turned to look at her. "That was me that day, babe, totally helpless to help you. I've never felt that feeling before, so powerless. I knew only He had the power to save."

Paige exhaled a soft breath. "That's one of the most–no–that's *the* most powerful imagery on prayer I've ever heard: a helpless child praying to his Father."

He rubbed his face hard as if to chase away unwelcome emotion. "We tracked the van until you got near the old industrial park. After that, all we could do was drive from building to building. By the time we got to where you had been held, you were gone."

"So you saw them, those dead men?"

"I did. I couldn't figure out what had happened. I didn't know if there were other players on the field. I knew it was a pro who took them out.

"I was lost at that point. I kept praying you had escaped somehow and maybe that was why those men had been killed, for letting it happen. So I did the only thing I knew to do, I went to the one place I knew you had been."

Paige whispered, "Light Street."

"Yeah."

"Those were my exact thoughts," she said. "I knew if I could get there, you would come for me."

"When Echo saw you on camera, he said you were pretty beaten up but seemed to be okay. Then a man grabbed your arm and started pulling you along down the street with him." Wyatt leaned up and rested his elbows on his knees. "I didn't know whether to be relieved or terrified. I just knew when I found you, I would have taken down an army to get to you or died trying."

"I saw that in your eyes." Paige slid to the end of her chair and reached for his arm. "Until I heard your voice and stepped around Moses, I swear, I mean it when I say this: God Himself carried me until you scooped me up into your arms. I had nothing left. I don't know how I knew to go to Light Street. I don't know how I ran or how I was sustained or how I told Moses about Jesus."

She touched his cheek with her wounded hand. "Will you please allow this to sink in, to become your personal possession, that your God had to become my God? He did that day. If the cost of that is what you've seen on my battered face and fingers, then so be it."

A slight smile tugged at his lips. "I think I can say: My God became more mine that day too." He rested his head on hers. "If the cost of that was the sheer terror and helplessness I experienced, then so be it."

"Then it's time to let go of it now," she said. "I'm safe." She hesitated. "And you have to settle this: If danger comes for me, your God–and mine–will carry me again, back to you or up to Him. He rescues." Her heart felt a surge of warmth. "He doesn't just rescue then, in the rapture; He rescues each and every day."

Wyatt gave her a little squeeze. "Now that's a thought that brings peace. I'm not sure I've ever considered it that way. He does rescue every day."

Fight

Day 27, 11:55 a.m.

Bertie stepped out onto the porch and said to Wyatt, "Moses is waiting for you out front. I guess you two have a meeting scheduled."

"Will you tell him I'll be right there?" Wyatt sat for a second after Aunt Bertie went back inside, looking at Paige. Finally, he said, "Thanks for letting me debrief. I needed this."

"I'm glad you talked to me about it."

"I should've long before now."

Paige sat looking at him, swallowing hard when she could swallow at all. "You're meeting with Moses?"

"Yeah, he caught me after breakfast this morning and asked if we could talk when I came home for lunch. I guess he wants to nail down his role here." He grinned. "We all know his role is to make Aunt Bertie happy. All the guys see it."

With a quick peck on her lips, he stood. "Don't feel like you have to come to Overwatch after lunch. Work here. I'm in the process of getting better. I can't practice being okay without you if I keep you cooped up over there all day."

She stood and followed him into the house. Aunt Bertie gave him a baggie full of cookies and sent him on his way. For a few seconds Paige looked at Aunt Bertie, at the rare unease in her expression. She didn't have to ask. Moses was planning on telling Wyatt what he had done.

Over the past days Aunt Bertie and Moses had been inseparable. The shepherdess and her new little lamb, that's what Paige often thought when she would find them in the living room, Aunt Bertie pouring over Scripture with Moses.

They cooked and cleaned together, gardened together, and went on walks together. Laughter rang out nonstop with those two. The spark Paige had noted at first seemed to be more of an appreciation at having a companion of similar age. Both had been widowed for many years and had lived solitary lives.

Aunt Bertie had turned her never-used sewing room downstairs into Moses' bedroom since Overwatch was full enough without adding another body. From the first day he had arrived, Moses had only left long enough to go get his car at Overwatch.

Paige moved through the house to the front porch where she could see Wyatt standing off in the distance with Moses.

Aunt Bertie came to stand next to her and slipped her arm around Paige's waist. "He needs this to move forward."

"What if Wyatt won't let him stay after this?"

Bertie said, "I'm praying the word forgiveness over that man of yours."

Paige watched. Moses talked a while, then Wyatt said something. Moses spoke again and Wyatt took a step back, covered his mouth, and bowed his head.

Moses stood waiting quietly, then held out his hands before Wyatt.

A few seconds passed before Wyatt raised his head to look at Moses. He just stood there.

Paige let out a held breath and drew in another. Wyatt was deciding Moses' fate. "Please, Lord," she whispered, "don't let him send Moses away."

Wyatt took a step forward and wrapped his arms around Moses. The embrace lasted for several seconds. Even from this distance Paige could see the glisten of tears on Moses' face where that jagged scar traced from eye to jawbone, depicting the violent world from which God's call had offered Moses an exodus.

When Wyatt did step back, he seemed to hesitate, then he drew back and punched Moses in the gut, a hard hit that doubled him over, leaving him coughing and sputtering.

Tears tumbled onto Paige's cheeks. When she moved down the first step, Aunt Bertie grabbed her arm. "You let them settle this."

Moses stood again and waited. Wyatt punched him a second time. This time when Moses doubled over, Wyatt placed one hand on Moses' shoulder and the other on his arm as if to help keep him on his feet.

After a long moment to recover, Moses stood and walked to his car. Wyatt watched him go before he turned and began walking toward the house. When he reached the top step where Paige stood, he didn't slow but only cut his eyes to look at her and kept moving.

Paige tore down the stairs and ran along the driveway. Tears flowed only harder seeing Moses round the final curve behind a row of dense pines.

When Paige got back to the porch, Aunt Bertie was crying just as hard, but she didn't say a word.

Paige hugged her. "Give us a minute if you don't mind."

Inside the house Paige found Wyatt in the kitchen, standing bent before the sink with hands gripping the counter. When she drew near, she reached for his arm and traced her fingers along his tense muscles.

"Why didn't you tell me?" he said with a steady but firm tone.

"Because I knew you would feel this way about him."

"It's because of him that I still can't place a ring on my wife's finger."

"It's because of him that you have a wife at all."

Wyatt stood straight and reached to pinch the bridge of his nose.

Her words were quiet as she used the same reference as before. "If the Lord used these two fingers to save that man's soul, I would offer them up again. I hope you'll be able to say the same thing when you've had time to think about it, to pray about it."

He turned and leaned against the counter with folded arms. "You can't keep secrets from me."

"I don't know that it was a secret. I just didn't fully debrief."

"Don't word-nerd me, Paige. I had a right to know."

"You did have a right to know. I want to say I'm sorry, but honestly, I think I would do it again to have kept Moses here for even a few days. He needed this time to be wanted, to have a family again."

"So you're saying if it fits your agenda, you can keep things from me?"

"I don't know, Wyatt. I'm new at this. I didn't even have a boyfriend a month ago. I don't know what I'm supposed to do and say."

His expression showed his frustration more than his even tone. "Don't keep secrets and tell the whole truth. That seems pretty simple." He let out a loud burst of air. "I think this is our first fight," he said with not a trace of a smile. With that, he kissed her cheek and moved toward the doorway. "I'll see you later tonight. Love you."

"Love you too," she said with a soft sigh. Even fighting with that incorruptible man only made her love him more.

Bertie came into the kitchen, then busied herself as if she wasn't upset.

"Don't be angry with him," Paige said.

"I'm not angry. Just praying for them both." Bertie went to the oven and pressed buttons to preheat it.

"Do you think I did the wrong thing in not telling him?"

"I can't answer that since I wouldn't have told either." Bertie started taking out the makings for cornbread. "I think this was how it had to be. Moses needed to confess what he did. It needed to come from him."

"We're officially in a fight over it."

"I think an official fight has to have some fighting going on, maybe a raised voice or two."

"I know. I just don't want him to be upset with me–or upset at all. He's got an op in the works. I want his mind on the team."

"It's good that it's all out in the open. Moses will feel better. You will too."

Paige's heart sank at the thought: "What if we never see Moses again?"

"Oh, we will."

"How do you know that?"

"Paige," Wyatt said from the kitchen doorway, his expression tender, "will you come out and talk a minute?"

When she reached the hallway, he took her hand and led her out onto the porch. "I'm new at this too," he said with sad eyes. "I think I'm done fighting already. How long before we can make up?"

With a soft smile, she stepped into his open arms. "I'm done fighting too. That was dreadful." She moved back to look at him. "I'm sorry I upset you. I should've told you."

"I understand why you didn't, but next time someone breaks your fingers, you have to tell me."

"That's a deal. I promise."

When she just stood looking up at him, he said, "What?"

"Why did you have to go and punch him?" Tears welled in her eyes and fell when she blinked. "He's nearly seventy years old."

"I tried to walk away." Wyatt blinked long. "I hugged him and told him I forgave him, but he said he wouldn't sleep a full night until I gave him his due."

The sight would forever be burned into her memory. "He wanted you to break his fingers, didn't he?"

"Yeah, two on each hand. When he held out his hands that way, I saw more remorse and humility in that man's eyes than I've ever seen in anyone."

"Did he ask you to punch him?"

"He did." Wyatt paused a second. "Hitting an old guy who cares so much about you wasn't easy."

Paige wiped her face and looked down the driveway where she had tried to catch up with Moses. "If you saw how remorseful he is, why did you make him leave?"

"I didn't," Wyatt said, "Aunt Bertie did."

Her head snapped around to look at him. "She did what?"

"She sent him out for buttermilk for their cornbread-making contest." He grinned at her and pulled her back to him. "Enough about Moses. Let's get back to the making-up part of our first big fight."

Blaze

Day 33, 5:02 a.m.

Her advance toward the opposition this morning was intentional, her strategy different than the day before. Paige reached what were now two squeaky steps on the staircase rather than what used to be one. After Wyatt's debrief, Paige found she could leave the bedroom early without waking him, but these steps were an altogether different story. Yesterday morning the squeak had woken both him and Aunt Bertie too early. Both of them had heightened senses when it came to house noises.

Paige stopped on the last quiet step, grabbed the railing with her one-and-a-half hands, and all but slid down the banister.

"Impressive," Moses said from the hallway below.

She stifled a giggle and tiptoed the rest of the way down the stairs.

"Careful with them fingers." He handed her a cup of coffee. "They've come far from the poor old, crooked things I wrapped in my underwear."

"They have come far." She stopped just before him and whispered, "I'm glad that guy and his underwear are gone now."

He whispered back, "Me too."

Once in the kitchen, she pulled out a chair and sat. "You're up early."

"How can a man sleep when the world is literally ending?"

Paige's laptop sat open on the table next to Moses' cup of coffee. She had loaded the draft to her Daybreak website for him to view after dinner the night before.

"It's a lot to take in, huh?" She smiled, those words reminding her of Wyatt's when he first began to read her in.

"I didn't sleep a wink all night. I knew this world was wicked since I've encountered plenty of evil in my line of work." He sat for a few seconds looking into his cup. "That man in Baltimore was about as wicked as they come. Seems as if men like him are only multiplying."

"Thank you for going, for helping the team." Her heart beat a little faster. "Wyatt wasn't himself because of what had happened to me. Even if he didn't know it, he needed a shield."

"I had more to draw me there than the team. I didn't want to believe my buddy could work for such a man and know just how evil he was, but I've worked private security plenty over the years. You know what a man is capable of when you're part of the inner circle. It's your job to see that he can do what he wants and get away with it."

When Moses became quiet, Paige said, "That's who called you in to find my dad, Groves' head of security?"

Moses nodded. "I guess tequila and tattoos didn't bond us for life after all."

With a slight gasp, Paige drew her hand to her mouth.

"I don't know how he fell into such darkness. I guess neither one of us wore that shield well in our later years."

When she reached for his hand, he wrapped his around hers. "You're wearing yours well now, Moses."

"I'll have to." He pointed to the computer screen. "This is beyond your everyday criminals and mobsters and cartels."

"It really is," Paige said. "It's like the plot of a blockbuster movie." She blinked hard. "Then you find out you're in that movie, with a leading role if you're willing."

"I see you're willing." He looked back at the screen. "So this group, they really are trying to take over the world?"

"The World Economic Forum, yes, they will eventually. The Bible says a one-world order and economy are coming. The U.N. is a part of it with their Agenda 2030. Many wicked men and organizations are doing their individual parts. This has all been decades in the making, slow and methodical, waiting for the opportune time. As you see, the World Economic Forum says with their own words that they are using Covid as an opportunity to bring about the Great Reset."

Paige nodded toward her laptop. "Did you watch the 'We will own nothing' video?"

"I did." He paused. "It's creepy, like some kind of cult indoctrination. And beef? They plan for us to cut down on meat for the good of the planet?" He grumbled under his breath. "Cows aren't doing no harm to this planet."

"I agree. But now, from their viewpoint, everything we've always known as good is suddenly bad."

"And people are buying this stuff," he said. "I see it now in advertising and the way they're trying to change how we live our lives."

He clicked on another link. "Now I see the Pope's gone off the rails, leading the way toward a one-world religion like Ms. Bertie showed me in Revelation."

Paige nodded. "If he's not the false prophet, then the Pope sure is paving the way for the man who will be. He's lost touch with conservative Catholics. You can't believe how many are screaming online that he isn't representing their long-held beliefs in many areas."

"It's all too much." Moses began to read aloud, "Crashing the dollar and moving toward a digital currency. Bioweapons and marking people with tattoos. Requiring vaccine passports to fly and buy and work. Censorship and cover ups and greed." He let out a long sigh. "I'm glad my girls aren't here to see all this."

"I didn't want to see it," she said. "Now it's all I can see some days. That's what Wyatt and the team have done this past month, expanded my vision beyond what the media has spoon-fed me these past years. That's what I plan to do with the website, help others to see."

He paused a few seconds. "I see from the site that you think what Ms. Bertie does, that the vaccine passport will eventually become the mark of the beast."

"In some form, I do. Once it's used to combine medical records and financial information. It's as clear as day to people who study prophecy.

"Already workers are losing jobs if they refuse to get the vaccine. What other thing are 'they' insisting all the world–every person on the planet–get? What other thing do you see some businesses, stores, and restaurants requiring that determines if a person can buy or sell or use their services?" Her voice grew a little louder. "Being unable to buy or sell just happens to be the phrase used in Revelation for people who refuse the mark.

"Current paper and phone-app passports are merely an open door to what will become implantable devices for vaccine status, digital currency, and tracking people worldwide. For all the believers who fail to see it, this is one of the most telling and terrifying turns our world has ever taken.

"For those of us who refuse the shot, the world will change. We'll have to build a network of people who can trade with one another once we're locked out of the vaxxed world, unable to buy or sell."

She paused, noticing the look of uncertainty in his eyes and knew where his mind was going. "Remember, Moses, we can't take the mark, but we can sure feel the pressure of the vehicle they will eventually use to mark the entire world."

He sat looking as if studying her. "No wonder the Lord gave you a shield. You're coming against global elites and governments, Big Tech and Big

Pharma. I'm not sure who'll show up looking for you first, a hit squad or the FBI."

"That should scare me, huh?"

"No, little sis. That'll just allow me to do my job."

Paige smiled. "Funny that I was worried about something as silly as my friends calling me crazy."

"Oh, you're crazy alright for jumping into a fight like this. But I'm just crazy enough to jump in with you."

He sat for a few seconds in silence, the look on his face reminding her of what it had felt like to first learn all this.

"Grieve first," she said. "This world isn't what you thought it was. You have to grieve and prepare to let go."

"I've got nothing left here to grieve or hold on to but you and this new family of mine." He pointed up. "My old life, my girls, are already above."

Paige said, "Aunt Bertie helped me see that we have to intentionally find joy in the world around us, even with all that's going on outside that door. There's still so much to live for and to fight for."

"I do know that." Moses fell silent. "I've been given that second chance you talked about the day we met. I'm just glad I made that call on this side of the rapture. I won't waste a minute of it in sadness."

"I'm glad to hear that," she said. "We've got to get to shining some light if we're going to make an impact." She went for her notepad on the sideboard.

He tapped her pad when she sat. "All your doodles and scribbles, I've been wondering about those."

"The guys fight the darkness in their way: keeping people safe and stopping bad guys. My job is there," she pointed to the computer screen, "to shine light on what's hidden in the darkness." With a pause, she considered that something about that didn't ring true, that her job was more than showing the evidence.

"So when will you make this thing public?"

"I'm not sure. I don't know what I'm waiting for."

"Remember," he said, his tone reassuring, "I'm your shield when they start firing back at you."

"It's not that. I'm not afraid. There's something I'm missing. Whatever it is, I feel like it's close."

His expression turned solemn. "I'm not kidding when I say: Maybe this should be anonymous. You really are setting yourself up as a target."

"No way. I'll sign my name to it: Paige Donovan-Fletcher." That made her smile as Echo's words came to mind, how even her initials, PDF, had to do with words and paper.

"If you're set on making yourself a target, then I've got job security." He chuckled. "And I guess that makes me immortal until my job is finished."

"We both are," she said.

"Tell me, Paige, what can I do to help? How can I shine light while being your shield?"

"Be a Daybreaker by my side. Laugh with me. Cry with me. Shine light here in our home. I'll need that, especially when I find myself looking at the darkness too long. Wyatt has to remind me that we have to keep our eyes fixed on Jesus, the Light, more than the darkness. I forget that too easily when I'm researching and watching videos. I start falling down a hole and all seems lost. Remind me," she said, "to look at the Light when I get overwhelmed. Those are ways you can help."

"I can do that."

"Banding as believers strengthens me. Together we shine brighter. God's people are His strength for one another. I'm finally getting what may be a glimmer of good, of victories and triumphs of the believers on this side of the rapture. Maybe I really have given too much power to the darkness. That only serves to diminish the light."

Her words were quiet. "I've been praying for a while now, trying to figure out how to help people see their place in this last-days world where we live. When believers actually discover this world isn't what they think it is, it'll be easy for them to bury their heads or shrink back in fear. Either way, they'll choose to do nothing.

"It's more than telling and helping them to see the evidence of what those people are up to and how last-days prophecy is coming to life. That's all the rising darkness is, evidence that points to one thing: Jesus is coming soon. We, as Daybreakers, need to invite others to join us and encourage them to do something with what they learn." Her voice rose, her heart now ablaze with passion. "Once we see this world for what it is, all that's coming, love has to speak, no matter the consequences, no matter what others think or how crazy we seem. No matter how it alters the world where we live by taking a stand."

She came to an abrupt stop, the word only now making sense to her. Blaze!! Brilliant light dawned, giving her a broader understanding. Paige wrote notes as she spoke. "The sun comes bursting forth each morning, each daybreak in a blaze of glory, and scatters the shadows. I want to be that: a blaze of glory for Jesus. It has to be more than us telling and warning about the darkness and shadows. We have to help believers see the urgency, that it's their time to rise and shine, to blaze in a way that people lost in darkness will see the Light. Ephesians says, 'Walk as children of Light.' That's what a Daybreaker does: sees the darkness but focuses on casting the Light.

"When I know the Lord gives me the go ahead, I'm going to take this shot at the darkness and be a blazing ray of sunlight. We can't know how many daybreaks remain before the sun sets that final time and leaves the world in perpetual nightfall. Until then," she said, "love speaks; love shines." She grinned. "No, love blazes like the Son," she said pointing upward.

"I don't even know what all that means for me yet," Moses said, "but I'm going to blaze with you rather than fizzle here at the end of my life." He slid his chair back and said with a broad grin, "I'll get started right after I take a little nap before breakfast." With an exaggerated shake of his head, he said, "You and these words of yours are going to do me in, li'l blaze."

Once alone, Paige sat scribbling notes and pondering new ways she might blaze her way through this ever-darkening world. As she had done many times before, she sketched out how the team and Aunt Bertie had slowly and methodically helped her to see the world for what it truly was.

"What are you scribbling now?" Bertie said as she poured herself a cup of coffee.

"Besides the website, I'm trying to figure out how to share my story."

Paige looked up from her notepad. "I just know if anyone, my dad or you or a friend, had given me what I have listed on the website, I wouldn't have kept reading once I saw the first entry."

"I know, sweetie," Bertie said and moved to sit in the chair next to her.

"It took me living this out, through all the twists and turns, for me to believe it over time."

"Then write your story. I remember you as a little girl, filled with great imagination and fantastic tales."

Paige sat staring at her for a few seconds, imagery and words already swirling around in her head. She whispered, "How better to tell the tale than as Jesus did, as a storyteller."

"I would read it," Bertie said. "I could share it since my words get so tangled and my friends get so baffled when I try and explain the vastness of what's going on now and all that's ahead."

It was getting closer; Paige could feel it in her blazing heart. Go-day was fast approaching.

Go-Day

Day 33, 7:08 a.m.

The return trip up the stairs had been no easier, especially with coffee in hand, as Paige had to skip the two noisy steps with one large leap. She would much rather wake Wyatt herself just to see his sleepy smile when his eyes fluttered open and he saw her sitting there.

At their bedside, her chest did that little thing again when she stood looking at him, that feeling of heaviness and lightness. Loving him filled her and took everything all at the same time.

"Are you going to sleep all day?" she said as she sat on the side of the bed.

"Maybe," he said with eyes still closed. "It's Saturday. I can."

"You can if you want."

He peeked one eye open and smiled. "I smell coffee."

"With tons of sugar."

That made him sit up in bed and reach for it. "I've got to start getting up early and running again."

Paige placed her hand on the blanket and rubbed his leg. "Do you think you're healed enough for that?"

"It's fine now." He took a sip of the steaming coffee, then patted his belly. "I'll be looking like Moses before long if I don't get back in training."

That brought a smile to her lips. Moses did that after most meals, patted his belly and complained that Aunt Bertie was ruining his girlish figure.

"Thank you for my shield, for letting him stay," she said. "My time with him this morning was better than a cup of creamy coffee."

"Thank you for your shield," he said back. "You brought him into this family. Now I can sleep late and not worry about you. I saw him in action that night at the harbor. I'd hate to be the one to try and go through that man to get to you." He chuckled. "And as an added bonus, Moses gets a third of your words every day. That's a load off a quieter-than-you soldier."

"I guess you and Aunt Bertie are glad not to have to split listening to me down the middle anymore."

He grabbed her hand. "You can talk all you want to me. Nothing is better than having you and all your words in my life."

"Well, me and all my words are going down to help Aunt Bertie get breakfast on the table."

"Stay a minute more." He placed his hand on her stomach and sat looking at it for a few seconds, his expression now one of sadness. "My dad says he thinks maybe I've made a decision for both of us, and that you may not feel the way I do about having a baby."

She rested her hand on his. "I don't know what I feel these days."

He looked up at her. "I'm not firm on that decision. Not at all. What if my dad is right, and our spark someday creates a little light of its own?"

"I like the sound of that," she said, "our spark creating a little light."

His words were soft. "We still have to live the life we're given here and not fear tomorrow. I can't imagine not seeing you as a mom. We've carved out a safe place for our family." With a little sigh, he said, "If we decide it's what we want, let's do it. I won't give the enemy that kind of power over us, to make that decision for us."

"I've always wanted to be a mom. It's still what I want. I see the joy it would bring. But I don't know if it's what I need right now. I'm just getting my bearings with this call of mine." Paige paused then said, "And I'm seeing how maybe writing my story for others to read may help. A baby would consume me and get me off mission."

"I can see that," Wyatt said. "It would me too. We don't have to decide now. I just wanted you to know it's totally okay with me if or when you want to."

"For now, I want to focus on spiritual children." Then, she said with a soft smile, "But someday, I sure wouldn't mind a little Catherine Joy in my life."

"Or Evan..." He wrinkled his face. "I'm not sure what goes with that. We're not using Waylon."

"We've got time to consider boy names," Paige shrugged, "but I'm a pretty big fan of Moses."

"We're not naming a kid Moses either."

Paige kissed his cheek and stood. "That just might be our next big fight."

"You don't really want that do you?"

With a chuckle and a smile, she stood. "I'll see you downstairs for breakfast."

Amused as she left the bedroom, she had to admit, she wasn't kidding at all with the name Moses.

The steps weren't an issue for Paige this trip since she could make some noise and not wake Wyatt. The first board squeaked beneath her foot, and she stopped. Words came trickling from heaven: *Enter Mission*. She stood still, thinking of her mission, her fingers tapping her legs: Warn the lost and wake the found. A smile formed as she tapped again: Blaze like the Son, so bright the found will wake and the lost will see.

Notepad, she thought, I need a fresh notepad.

Once in the kitchen, she found a flurry of activity. Moses was there doing the breakfast dance with Aunt Bertie. The guys were already parading in one after another through the back door.

"Did you get a little rest?" she said to Moses when he passed by her with a plate of buttered toast to place among the food on the table.

"Who can sleep when the world is ending?" He glanced behind him. "Or when Ms. Bertie is clanging around in this kitchen?"

Wyatt came in and sat. The others sat as well, and the room was filled with the usual morning chaos: chairs scooted, men chatted, and Aunt Bertie fussed over the final details of the meal.

Paige eyed her notepad now sitting on the sideboard. She had work to do, a story to write. Who had time to eat when the world was ending? Then she caught sight of a plate of cinnamon rolls next to her usual seat and remembered she had life to live too. Enter Mission could wait one meal.

There, it was finally inscribed with pen onto paper: Enter Mission. Well, it was pencil actually, but pen was sure more poetic. She grinned and let out a soft sigh. This was her missing element: Writing her story was her mission and what had her on hold and waiting on go-day, when she would fire her first shot into the darkness. Though she would have to leave out any mention of the team and their mission, she could at least tell her part of the story on the Daybreak site, how the truth of what is happening in the world was revealed to her piece by piece.

This mission of hers was more than telling her story and exposing the darkness. Hers would be a Daybreak invitation to believers, a call to blaze like the Son and wake and warn their own circles of family and friends.

She underlined the verses again in her Bible, making the lines so dark that the passage would always jump out at her:

"...for you were formerly darkness, but now you are Light in the Lord; walk as children of Light (for the fruit of the Light consists in all goodness and righteousness and truth), trying to learn what is pleasing to the Lord."
(Ephesians 5:8-10)

Wyatt's early words came to mind: Seeking truth requires action, accepting truth requires open eyes, living truth is a product of finding it. Each believer would now get to choose.

Daybreaks were dwindling and time was of the essence. Paige could feel it in her own spirit: sunset was coming. For her, go-day had finally arrived.

"Let's try again," Wyatt said as he stepped out onto the back porch. "We were close yesterday."

Paige looked at her notepad and blinked long and hard. Her mind was jumbled, filled with letters and words and phrases that needed to land on that page.

"Sure thing," she said. "Let's try." She set her notebook aside and took Wyatt's extended hand. How could she not put her mission on hold for yet another wedding?

They walked without speaking around the house to their wedding bridge, moving to the exact spot where they had joined their lives together. Wyatt removed her necklace and allowed her ring, her mother's wedding ring, to slide off onto his palm.

Since she had stopped wearing her splint the past few days, Wyatt had tried each day to fit her ring onto her finger.

"I think it's less swollen today," he said, "almost normal."

"I think so too." Her eyes followed his movements, and on occasion she would glance up at the tenderness of his expression. This was better by far than notepads and doodles.

"With this ring," he said, his voice soft and low, "I..."

Wyatt slid the ring as far as the knuckle and stopped. His face fell. "Not today."

"Give it a little push," she said.

"I don't want to hurt you."

Paige peeked over his hand at her finger. "Only the knuckle is swollen now. Once you get it past that, I'll be fine."

"I can't do it."

"You have to do it. I can't put my own wedding band on."

His expression held uncertainty. "If it hurts even a smidge, you say so."

"Even a smidge." She grinned up at him. "I'm pretty tough, though."

"You're very tough." Wyatt drew in a deep breath and pushed.

In more discomfort than pain, Paige said nothing as she watched him.

When the ring slid over her knuckle, he broke into a broad smile and said, "With this ring I commit my life to you as one in our cord of three."

"It's about time," Paige said, stood on tiptoes, and kissed her soldier.

Wyatt held her back to look at her. "I've wanted to wait until this moment to tell you: The verse you used and the things you said that day moved me in a way I couldn't even voice without crying. You were so happy. I didn't want to make you sad." He was quiet a second and stood looking at her. "Your dad called me that, incorruptible."

"I know. Echo told me."

"Your dad may have said it to him, but Echo couldn't have known that your dad used that word to describe me the day he gave me watch over you. He said he was giving his greatest treasure to his incorruptible son." With a shake of his head, he whispered, "When you said that word here, it meant everything to me–still does. I won't let him down."

"He knew what he was doing," Paige said. "I see why he gave me to you. I see why you were a man after his own heart. You are a man after mine too."

Wyatt traced his fingers along her cheek. "It's not much of a honeymoon, but maybe when I get back, we can sit a while on our wedding bridge. I'm going now with Gunny and Mr. Cox to pick up an order."

"An order?"

"You don't want to know."

"How much munitions can one team need?"

"They're concerned about shortages. This was Mr. Cox's idea. You know we just do what he says at this point, don't you?"

"I do know that." Paige looped her arm through Wyatt's and admired her ring. "Exactly like I thought it would look."

"It's been a long time coming." He shrugged. "At least for me."

"Time has really flown for me," Paige said with a quick smile at the husband she had only known a month.

When they neared the house, she said, "Let's at least get you some coffee to go. I may have a little surprise for you in the kitchen."

His face lit up. "You're going to swipe a few of those snickerdoodles for me to dunk in my coffee?"

"No need for that. I made those snickerdoodles."

He cocked one eyebrow. "You did not."

"I did too. I'm going legit, giving up my cookie-thieving ways." She smiled and batted her lashes at him. "So I'm saying you can have all you want–up to three. I don't want to spoil you."

Wyatt followed her into the kitchen. While Paige poured his coffee, he removed the glass dome of the cake keeper and reached for three cookies.

As if sensing a burglary was in progress, Aunt Bertie came into the kitchen and stood with hands on her hips. "What are you doing? You just had breakfast." She took the cover from him. "And nobody said you could have these cookies."

Wyatt glared at Paige with her prank now dawning on him. "My wife said she made them."

"She did no such thing! When have you ever seen Paige bake something on her own?"

Paige burst out laughing and tore out of the kitchen and through the back door with Wyatt on her heels. The second she reached the top step, Wyatt grabbed her around the waist and lifted her off the ground.

"You totally set me up!"

"Moses!" she called to the man who sat in a nearby rocking chair.

"I've got no part in this," Moses said, more amused than concerned as he closed his Bible.

"You're supposed to be my shield."

He stood and walked toward the door. "You're on your own, li'l blaze. I won't get in the way of the Apex."

When Wyatt set her down, Paige turned in his arms to face him. Before she could speak, he said, "I've told them not to call me that."

"But they should," she said in nearly a whisper. "That was his plan, for you to become the tip of the spear."

"Those are some pretty big shoes to fill." His smile was warm and maybe even a little sad. "Maybe that's why he drew you to Light Street; he knew it would take two of us to fill them."

"Maybe so." She shrugged. "The Apex will likely need to do a little Robin Hoodery from time to time. My straight-shooting arrow is a little too incorruptible for that part of the gig."

He gave her a quick kiss. "I'll pray for you, Paige Donovan-Fletcher. You really need to adjust your moral compass."

"Go get your guns," she said. "I have work to do, a story to write. It's go-day for me." She swallowed hard. "I'll soon get to do a little Ephesians five of my own and shine Light into the darkness."

His eyes lit up. "You found what you've been waiting for?"

"It came this morning; my mission just floated down from heaven onto the Paige." She paused and drew in a long, steady breath. "Today I enter my mission. I'll be a Daybreaker, not just in word, but in deed."

Enter Mission

Day 0, Now

An intermission is a time between two parts, an interruption in the flow of something. In this case our "enter mission" is the time between life as we once knew it and that twinkling-of-an-eye moment when the Groom will come to rescue His bride. Rest assured, He will come for you. Love comes for the beloved.

Enter mission means there is a choice set before you: to make an impact or to remain in the sameness of the life you've known–to blaze or to fizzle. You either shine the Light or enable the darkness. You speak out in faith or sleep on in silence.

Chapter by chapter you, along with Paige, have watched light be cast upon the darkness, exposing the last-days world in which we live. Through the pages of this story, truth has been revealed and puzzle pieces have been put into place. Now you see it: Life isn't what you think it is. The extent of the evil agendas and deceptions revealed in this book are merely tiny fragments of what is actually going on around you.

Yes, I know how crazy I sound. But look for yourself. Research. Investigate like Paige chose to do. It's all out there for you to see.

- The World Economic Forum, a sponsor of Event 201, actually exists. Their goal, as stated on their website, is to use the Covid pandemic as an opportunity to move toward what they call the Great Reset, to bring all nations together economically.

- We've truly been lied to about safe and effective medications that would have saved hundreds of thousands of lives from the Covid virus. This deception is rooted in a last-days agenda: for all the people in all the world to take the shots and boosters.

- The use of a vaccine passport is now required in some nations and is being adopted by states in the U.S. Those without the shots are losing jobs and being denied access to goods and services.

- A digital currency is inevitable; the days of cash will soon be gone. This not-so-subtle shift will move the world toward an implantable device (Revelation 13:17) to house medical and financial records–the ultimate control of the masses.

- Censorship is now so blatant that differing opinions or debates are no longer allowed. Doctors and scientists and pastors who speak the truth are "canceled" from social media platforms.

- The mainstream media is hiding truth from you, feeding you lies and half-truths that fit "the narrative."

- There is genuinely a push toward a one-world religion. Chrislam isn't a fictitious name I created for this book. It's real and happening today.

- From the moment of the regathering of the nation of Israel in 1948, the clock has been counting down the last days to these final hours.

The rapture of the church is soon. The devil knows his time is near and has been using the greedy and the wicked to prepare the way for the Antichrist. What we see now is frightening yet merely a shadow of the horror that will befall those who are left behind to endure the tribulation. A heart can scarcely peer into such a bitter future for those we love and not be crushed. A heart can scarcely wake up to the real world in which we live and not be filled with fear and panic and sadness.

Take time to grieve. Fix your eyes on Jesus, *the* Light. Study and process the information you've learned. Read God's Word for yourself. I'm providing you with several key rapture verses at the end of this epilogue. Read the book of Revelation; it is the only book of the Bible that promises a blessing to its reader and hearer. Seek out reputable prophecy teachers, those who teach what God says about prophecy in the Bible, not ministers who are calling themselves prophets and making predictions.

I've tried to shake you gently, to help you rise and shine, ready to step into your Daybreak call. The word has now been whispered into your spirit: *awake.* Will you?

While reading, you have been treading upon your own training ground. No matter how small you feel in this world or how limited you see your reach, God has penned you into these final chapters of His kingdom story and has a plan to use you for such a time as this. You matter. Your voice matters. Your willingness matters. You are being raised up in preparation to warn the lost and wake the found. At risk of your reputation, do you dare speak forth?

Greater love has no man than to lay down his life for his friend. If you and I have to lay down our lives, reputations, and what others think of us, then so be it. If the breaking of our hearts over their reactions is the cost of them hearing truth, then so be it.

We as believers are all Paige, the place where the Word settles and the Spirit dwells. None are more uniquely qualified than others. We all just have a distinctive place to shine–to blaze our way through this ever-darkening world. You are surrounded by sleeping loved ones and unborn-again sheep. Shine so brightly for them that the found will wake and the lost will have light cast upon their path to guide them to the Shepherd.

Daybreak will dawn only so much longer, then soon the sun will set and nightfall will come, casting the world into seven years of darkness. Time is of the essence.

What can I do? That's what you're asking. That was Paige's question. That was my own question. For months after seeing the imminence of the rapture and approaching tribulation, that question pounded in my head. Then finally, the answer settled upon me like a guiding light from heaven: I'm a fiction writer. I write. What better way for me to wake the found than by tucking truth within the pages of a story?

I pray your heart is set ablaze with truth—with *veritas*—so much so that you can do nothing but be a voice for truth in the world where you live. Use this story to do that, to wake others. You can share the free ebook or PDF from the Daybreak.Team website with any and all of your friends. Give it away. Help your friends and family to see the unveiling of truth as they follow along with Paige and Wyatt's adventures.

Also at Daybreak.Team I've provided links to a few videos, articles, and sermons to get you started in your research. In such a fluid world, you will need to continually read and investigate beyond what I provide. Even as I've written *Daybreak*, so much has happened that I've had to go back and update the storyline. Share the information that you find helpful with others.

Find your team of Daybreakers, in person and online, believers who see what you see. Join with them so that you can stand together with God's people, as this world will only get more dangerous to traverse.

"And the Lord said to Paul in the night by a vision, 'Do not be afraid any longer, but go on speaking and do not be silent; for I am with you, and no man will attack you in order to harm you, for I have many people in this city.'"
(Acts 18:9-10)

Today is day zero of your Daybreak story. Seek the Lord regarding your role. Find your voice; tell your story. You can't only wake up; you must speak up. Keep in mind that this is more about blazing the Son's light than screaming about the darkness. Our goal should always be to prepare the way for the Lord, to attract unbelievers to His light and not alienate with crazy posts and conversations. Speak kindly. Teach tenderly. That's how Jesus operates, and He is our model to follow.

Remember, all the pieces that are now falling into place, those things that will eventually become tribulation realities, warn us that the rapture is coming soon. They are the evidence we use to generate urgency, to help others see, but they should never be our main focus. My favorite pastor and prophecy teacher, JD Farag, says, "We need to get Jesus to people and people to Jesus." That's really it–the main thing. Blaze for His glory in such a way that those held in bondage to this darkened world will see Jesus. Don't give up on the people you love even when they think you're crazy. They will.

Take heart as we wait, knowing that our suffering until He arrives will be used to reach those who would otherwise be left behind. They are worth our extended time here. In those moments when the heaviness of what you're seeing and experiencing comes crashing down on you, fix your eyes on Jesus, knowing He has fixed His eyes on you. He adores you and is coming to your rescue. You are not alone, beloved. You. Are. Loved.

Coming Soon!

If the Lord tarries and gives me a continuation of the story, I hope to release the sequel to *Daybreak* in 2022. The working title is *Sunset.* I will continue to offer a free e-version of this series.

Rapture Verses

Watch for your coming Groom, your rescue. Here are a few rapture verses to get you started:

"Because you have kept the word of My perseverance, I also will keep you from the hour of testing, that hour which is about to come upon the whole world, to test those who dwell on the earth" (Revelation 3:10).

"... and to wait for His Son from heaven, whom He raised from the dead, that is Jesus, who rescues us from the wrath to come" (1 Thessalonians 1:10).

"For the Lord Himself will descend from heaven with a shout, with the voice of the archangel and with the trumpet of God, and the dead in Christ will rise first. Then we who are alive and remain will be caught up together with them in the clouds to meet the Lord in the air, and so we shall always be with the Lord. Therefore comfort one another with these words" (1 Thessalonians 4:16-18).

"For God has not destined us for wrath, but for obtaining salvation through our Lord Jesus Christ, who died for us, so that whether we are awake or asleep, we will live together with Him" (1 Thessalonians 5:9-10).

"... looking for the blessed hope and the appearing of the glory of our great God and Savior, Christ Jesus" (Titus 2:13).

Note from Lisa

I can't express how humbled I am to have been a part of writing Paige's story. Never in all my years of writing have I encountered God on such a powerful and personal level. I now see how this work is a culmination of my many years of interest in Biblical prophecy coupled with my passion for writing about the tender love Jesus has for His people. Only His guiding light and leading hand could have taken a topic so vast and frightening and narrowed it down to this: Fix your eyes on Jesus. Look more at the Light and for the coming Groom than at the darkness.

Connect with Lisa
Please visit Daybreak.Team or LisaHeatonBooks.com for additional resources.

During the writing of this book, my Facebook account was hijacked and stolen. The Lisa Heaton Books page you may encounter there is an inactive account. With the current climate of censorship on social media, I have left all other mainstream platforms. Any future social media activity will be provided on my website.

Special Thanks

To all the pastors and teachers out there who are bold enough to proclaim God's prophetic Word without fear or compromise: Thank you for helping me to see truth and challenging me to live it out.

To Kimmie: This book wouldn't be a reality without your editorial help, enthusiasm, and encouragement along the way. You are truly my sister and fellow Daybreaker. If I have to live out an end-of-the-world scenario, I'm glad it is with you.

Other Titles by Lisa

Blue Skies

Rising Waters, sequel (Spring 2022)

Deceiver

Unmending the Veil

Under the Gun, sequel

On 4/19

Beyond 4/20, sequel

A Thousand Blessings

Room to Grow

Women's Nonfiction:

You. Are. Loved. Live the Love Song

Made in USA - Kendallville, IN
21981_9781734018271
12.07.2021 1232